WEREGIRL

everyone has an animal inside

A Novel
C. D. Bell

CHOOSECO™

WAITSFIELD, VERMONT

Book design: Stacey Boyd, Big Eyedea Visual Design
Cover design: Dot Greene, Greene Dot Design

For information regarding permission, write to:
P.O. Box 46
Waitsfield, Vermont 05673
www.weregirl.com

ISBN 10 1-937133-55-9
ISBN 13 978-1-937133-55-9

Published simultaneously in the United States and Canada
Printed in the United States

10 9 8 7 6 5 4 3 2 1

Publisher's Cataloging-In-Publication Data
Names: Bell, C. D. (Cathleen Davitt).
Title: Weregirl : a novel / C. D. Bell.
Description: Waitsfield, Vermont: Chooseco, [2016] | Series: [Weregirl series]; [1] | Interest age level: 12 and up. | Summary: On a nighttime run, high school junior and cross-country runner Nessa Kurland is badly bitten by a trapped wolf that she tries to free. Nessa's quick recovery is followed by improved running times and all her senses are heightened. She has transformed into a werewolf.
Identifiers: ISBN 978-1-937133-55-9 | ISBN 978-1-937133-56-6 (ebook) | ISBN 1-937133-56-7 (ebook)
Subjects: LCSH: Teenage girls—Juvenile fiction. | Werewolves—Juvenile fiction. | Cross-country running—Juvenile fiction. | CYAC: Teenage girls—Fiction. | Werewolves—Fiction. | Running—Fiction. | LCGFT: Thrillers (Fiction)
Classification: LCC PZ7.B38891526 We 2016 (print) | LCC PZ7.B38891526 (ebook) | DDC [Fic]—dc23

To RK and RM

All stories are about wolves. All worth repeating, that is. Anything else is sentimental drivel.

— Margaret Atwood,
The Blind Assassin

CHAPTER ONE

"Well, well," Mr. Porter said. "It's not often that I meet with a junior so early in the school year. I have seniors who wait until October before I pull them in here kicking and screaming."

The guidance counselor held up his hands in mock surrender, as if Nessa were pointing a gun at him. "I tell them, 'Hello! People! There is *life* after high school.'" He laughed. Nessa did not. He cleared his throat. "What can I do for you, Nessa Kurland?"

Nessa pulled at her straight, dark blonde hair. She tried crossing her legs, but her foot banged against Mr. Porter's desk. She'd grown three inches in the past year, and she'd lost her gauge of distance from industrial furniture.

Mr. Porter's office had the counterintuitive look of the place where dreams came to die, not be born. It had few if any signs of life—just a faded University of Michigan pennant and a matching *Go Blue* Wolverines poster. Everything on his desk seemed like he'd gotten it for free: a mug from Sandy O's Window-Washers was filled with pens from local banks and insurance offices. Even his travel coffee mug was emblazoned with the spare but recognizable three-triangle logo of the research monolith Paravida. Their newest facility had sprung up in the town of Tether this time last year, taking over the old Dutch Chemical plant along with a bunch of the company's patents.

"I need a full scholarship to go to college," Nessa blurted. While Nessa's sister, Delphine, was something of a poet, and her brother, Nate, could talk for hours, emitting streams of words over and over, Nessa was the ambitious and responsible one. She had the "gift" of being clear and direct.

She pulled out a crumpled sheet of notebook paper she'd had tacked to the wall above her bed all summer. She had planned to type the whole thing up to look very pro, but she ran out of time. Last night, someone had brought a dog in for Nessa's mom, Vivian, to look at. This happened from time to time when the vet's office where Vivian worked was closed, or a friend couldn't afford to pay. After twenty years as a vet technician, Vivian could do pretty much anything the vet could. Dr. Morgan even looked the other way, offering her supplies and extra medicines because he knew she needed the money.

It was a dog last night who'd gone wandering and been attacked by a coyote or maybe even a bear.

"He managed to drag himself home only to collapse in the driveway," the owner had said tearfully. "Do you think he can be saved?"

While Vivian patched him up in the garage, Nessa had finished cooking up the pasta. She'd called Delphine and Nate in to eat. Then, because her mom had looked so spent afterward, Nessa had volunteered to wash the dishes and get Nate to bed.

Now, Nessa pushed the paper toward the guidance counselor. "You can see I've got my 5K time down over the end of last season." Mr. Porter shifted in his seat and glanced down at her paper. He pressed the space bar on his keyboard to wake up his computer and began clicking around with the mouse.

"I'm pulling up your grades," he said, and then, sipping his coffee, he scanned what was up on his screen, making a few more clicks. "I see. Hmm, yes." He clicked one more time. "Too bad about Bio, huh?"

Bio. Ironically, biology was one of Nessa's favorite subjects. She'd loved the natural world from when she was little. Nessa had caught and raised tadpoles until they were frogs, collected snakeskins and rare wildflowers. She had even tried to crossbreed two kinds of pole beans using Mendel's laws. But freshman year Nessa had had to miss school because Nate had got it into his head that coats were evil, and he wouldn't wear one no matter if you begged him or forced him, and he kept getting sick, all winter long. Vivian had missed so much work that eventually it was Nessa who had to stay home with Nate when he had a fever.

"But aside from that, you're a solid student, Nessa. I know you work weekends at the vet's and help your mom out with your brother. He's got Asperger's?"

Nessa shrugged. Her brother was autistic, and the name of the condition didn't much matter anyway. Nate was just Nate. He was different but so was each one of the Kurlands, really. In a town like Tether, being different was probably a good thing.

"Well, your mom doesn't have it easy, with the three of you, and one like your brother. I know you're a big help to her, and all told, I'm impressed." Mr. Porter folded his hands. "But yes, a sports commitment will help."

"But, do you think it might lead to a scholarship? I really don't know how else I'll be able to go to college. I was training all summer. I kept track of everything."

Mr. Porter politely stifled a yawn and pulled the paper closer, put down his coffee cup, and scanned the scrawled lists of dates and times and split times and notes about weather and course conditions. "I was following a program," Nessa explained. "I found it online. I was working too, so I ran in the mornings and cross-trained with free weights after work. My friend Bree helped by—" Nessa stopped.

Okay, Bree hadn't *really* helped unless you call "helping" lying on a picnic blanket, giving herself a mani-pedi, and shouting motivational phrases like, "My grandma could run faster than you!"

"I'm running a 5K at a sub-18-minute pace," Nessa said, swallowing a laugh as she thought of Bree.

"That's good," Mr. Porter said.

"Not every time," Nessa rushed to explain. "But I know I can keep improving this fall. If I get below a 17:30, I can make a good showing at Regionals and maybe get to States."

Mr. Porter pushed the paper back in her direction. "I like your ambition, Nessa," he said. "I really do. But scholarships aren't given for what you think you can do. And a lot of high school athletes are running sub-18s. *Consistently* running them."

Nessa knew that. She'd been trolling the internet all summer, following write-ups on individual kids. She wondered if she'd ever get good enough to feel comfortable creating a professional athletic profile like some of the ones she'd found.

"I can get there," she said. "I'm not there yet, but I'm still growing. Tell me what I should do. How can I get in front of recruiters?"

Mr. Porter sighed. "I'll tell you what," he said. "You know Cynthia Sinise is in contention for a track scholarship this year. Why don't you see if she can give you some tips? You're friends with her, right?"

"Friends with Cynthia?" Nessa said, hearing how hollow her voice sounded, but trying to be positive.

Cynthia was the quiet and intense captain of the girls' team, but she rarely spoke to Nessa. Or anyone else on the team. She came to practice, ran what Coach Hoffman told her to, and went home. People in school respected her, but Cynthia wasn't exactly warm and fuzzy. Nessa wondered whether Cynthia had ever even noticed Nessa was there.

"That's settled then," Mr. Porter said. "You get together with Cynthia. See if training with her can help you. See how the fall goes. Then let's talk again in December." He made a note in his calendar program.

Nessa picked up the paper and slid it back into its folder. She knew she could do this. She had to. But how was she going to get Cynthia Sinise to take her under her wing?

CHAPTER TWO

finally figured out a clinic plan," Bree announced. It still felt like summer. She and Nessa were unpacking brown bag lunches at the poured concrete tables and benches on the patio outside the cafeteria of Tether High. As reigning three-year student council member, Bree had campaigned all last year for juniors and seniors to be allowed to eat lunch outside. Now, on the first day of this glorious new privilege, it felt like they'd all cut school to go to the beach. The juniors and seniors were out in force, checking out who was tan, who was taller, who had gotten a haircut and become, suddenly, hot.

The school security guard, "Pasty Pete" Packer, had stationed himself in clear view and was glaring at everyone, daring them to misbehave. He was sharp-eyed but robotic and mean, and he never made exceptions for anyone. He'd fought pretty hard against Bree's outdoor lunches, saying it would double his workload, but she'd prevailed. Nessa had been surprised to see Pete Packer out and about—the rumor was he'd been so mad at Bree's win that he'd taken a job somewhere else.

Bree was enjoying the moment, waving to friends, her dark glasses allowing her to scope out groups of kids with impunity, especially as Cassian Thomas selected his table and sat, creating the gravitational center of the lunchtime orbit.

Bree had a crush on Cassian. So did Nessa. So did at least thirty-five more members of the sophomore and junior classes. Tall, broad-shouldered, with loose blond hair, tawny skin, gray-blue eyes, Cassian was gorgeous, funny, popular, and the star of the soccer team. Captain Obvious.

That was the external Cassian.

Nessa thought she saw things in him other people missed. She could see how smart he was. How he was so clearly bent on getting out of Tether, like her. How he didn't follow the straight and narrow path of popularity stardom.

Sometimes Cassian spent lunch with the gamers, strategizing RuneScape, their eyes never leaving their touch screens. Those guys liked him because he wasn't a poser. He really knew the game. An occasional evening checking in to a gaming party wasn't beneath him.

Cassian rocked it on the debate team, traveling all over the state during the winter, charming judges and getting write-ups in the *Tether Journal*. He was polite to everyone and got perfect grades. Nessa had once overheard him saying he wanted to be in the film business. On looks alone, he could easily be a star.

Nessa was staring at Cassian now. Even from a distance, he could make her feel that anything was possible. "Are you listening to me?" Bree asked. Nessa jerked her attention away from the vision of Golden Cassian in the sunlight.

"I was like a spy!" Bree confided, her curls bobbing a little and her glasses dropping down her nose. "At the clinic. I totally pretended I knew what I was doing. I said your mom had sent me."

"What? Wait," Nessa said, swallowing a bite of tuna on wheat. "You went to the clinic, like, physically? Without me?"

Bree shrugged, looking innocent and unbothered, slipping her glasses back over her eyes and returning her gaze to the guys. "I didn't do anything wrong. I just asked if I could change Nate's appointment." Nate had been visiting the clinic weekly since he was eight. He was part of the study connected to the Dutch Chem cleanup—all the kids his age in Tether were. Initially it had been the whole kid population, but over the years the numbers had dropped to those truly impacted: kids who had developed problems from the contamination or were considered at risk.

Nessa was a little hazy on the details of the study, but it was her job to take Nate to his appointments because her mom worked during the hours the health clinic was open.

"It was brilliant," Bree said. "They have the schedule on the computer, and I kept pretending none of the times they were offering worked, until finally the woman turned the screen around so I could look for myself. It was easy. From there all I had to do was find Cassian's little sister's name and then say that was the only time we were free."

Nessa's gaze flitted to Cassian's table. She recognized Cynthia's ponytail among the crowd of beautiful seniors.

"I can't believe you did that," Nessa said. "Sometimes, you know, Bree, you make me feel like…like I'm so boring."

"You, boring?" Bree said. "Save boring for people who aren't assisting with animal surgery in their garage."

"No, that's definitely not boring," Nessa agreed. "Maybe it's more like I'm missing out on the entire teenage experience."

Bree pulled her glasses down again, her gaze meeting Nessa's.

"You know," Nessa shrugged. "Boys. Fun…"

"Tell me about it! I have been single for like, what, six weeks?"

"Four," said Nessa.

"It feels longer. Okay, let's just define teenage life. First: boys," Bree said, holding out an upturned index finger, like she was about to count off a list. "We can make that happen. What else? Lip gloss? Crop tops? Your own beauty tutorial video channel?" Bree fake-smiled and finished her sarcastic finale. "ACTUAL TEEN MAKEOVER!"

"Get real," Nessa groaned.

"No, seriously, just stop trying to break the four-minute mile or whatever, and we'll get you a boyfriend." Bree adopted a mischievous tone. "Maybe, if my plan works out, we'll get you Cassian."

"Oh, please," said Nessa. "You know and I know, Cassian doesn't know I'm alive. How do you know he'll be the one taking his sister? What if we go to all this trouble and we're sitting there all dressed up and it's only Cassian's mom?"

Bree took a sip from her thermos of ginseng tea. She smiled, showing off her dimple. Bree was like a soda bottle all shook up and ready to explode. "Do you think I haven't thought of that?" she said. "The mom would be even better."

"Better?" asked Nessa.

"Better because once we meet the mom and she sees how nicely we're playing with Sierra, who do you think she's going to turn to next time she needs babysitting help?" Bree replied.

"Are you kidding me?" Nessa said, laughing.

Nessa noticed that across the lawn, Cynthia Sinise was standing and looking for someone. She rarely smiled, but she was smiling now. Nessa followed its direction and it landed on Cassian. He smiled back and moved toward her. Nessa was too far away to hear, but it looked like Cassian was making some kind of joke and Cynthia was laughing.

Right. Of course. Cassian's girlfriend from the year before had graduated and gone to college. Everyone was waiting to see who would be next. Maybe they wouldn't have to wait much longer.

"Look," Nessa said. "Look at the way he and Cynthia are talking."

Bree whipped her head around. "Cassian and Cynthia?" she said. "Hardly. They're like cousins or something. They grew up on the same street!" Bree knew what was going on in everyone's high school love life with the same degree of accuracy she knew the lives of celebrities she followed online. "Have patience, young Padawan. You have to—" Bree's voice faded. She put a hand on Nessa's arm. "Who," she said, in a different tone, "is *that*?"

"Who, where?"

Bree lifted her chin in the direction of…

"Oh. Luc Restouille?" Nessa said, following her friend's gaze. "He's on cross-country."

"He's new?" said Bree.

"Yeah," Nessa said. "I guess so. He doesn't really talk much."

"With those cheekbones, he doesn't need to."

"Hormones, much?" Nessa said. "Bree, seriously, that guy's kind of odd. He never talks. He's *really* intense about running. Like a machine."

Bree rolled her eyes. Nessa swung a leg over the bench, heading for the trash. "One of these days, Nessa," she said, "you're going to stop running for no reason and start *chasing* after something more fun."

CHAPTER THREE

Twenty minutes after her last class ended, Nessa checked in with Coach Hoffman, who sent her off on a one-mile jog to start practice. Nessa felt the tension of the first day of school leaving her muscles as they warmed up and stretched out. With each footfall, her stride loosened into the natural and assured pace that was as familiar as her own reflection in a mirror.

The course took her behind the football and soccer fields—she had a glimpse of Cassian heading the ball. Even from this distance she could see that his jaw was set and his attention fully focused. He was playing with his shirt off, the contours of the muscles running from his shoulders down to the waistline of his shorts.

After passing the soccer fields, the course turned left and ran through a gap in the chain-link fence. The athletic fields at school backed up against a coniferous forest, and Nessa pushed through a terrarium of brambles that gave way to the orderly rows of stately pines. Nessa loved this part of the trail. The trees were like columns in a naturally occurring temple, the thickness of the growth creating an evening effect even on a bright afternoon. Nessa could see dust motes rising on the few slanting beams of light. She remembered why she started running cross-country in the first place.

And then she remembered to speed up.

Nessa came in from the warm-up lap with Cynthia in her sights. She noticed that a freshman had come up behind her—Hannah Gilroy, the fast freshman from pre-season.

Nessa hadn't realized how fast. She had to sprint to maintain her lead. Even as she began to hear the fear tracks playing in her mind—*you can't keep this pace going much longer; you're going to puke; you're going to end up leaning over your knees, breathing hard*—she lengthened her stride, picked up her tempo, pushed her chest forward, and sprinted through the end of the course.

Walking off the wave of nausea that almost always greeted Nessa when she ran her fastest—which she took as a sign she hadn't been slacking off—Nessa made a decision. *I'm going to always beat Hannah,* she vowed to herself. *If I make it a rule to never, ever let Hannah break out in front of me, it will keep me focused. Keep me on pace.*

For a second, Nessa flashed on another thought: *What if I beat Cynthia, too?*

Coach Hoffman called the team over from the lowest bench of the football bleachers, where he was sitting with the first aid kit and his clipboard. Nessa loped over, crossing one foot over the other and dropping from the waist to stretch her IT band. She watched Cynthia, who was stretching sitting down, her legs wide, her fingertips resting on the toes of her brand-new running shoes. Cynthia bent her head to the ground, her pony-tail fanning out on the grass.

Luc arrived from his warm-up and stood near Cynthia. Because Nessa was behind them, she could hear Cynthia say to Luc, without looking up, "I've been running at night."

Luc didn't look at Cynthia either, but kept his chin pointed at the sky, his hands on his hips. It was like they were spies exchanging information without looking like they knew each other. "And how's that going for you?" he said.

"Well," Cynthia said, switching poses. "I don't make excuses. I drive myself over to the trailhead on Route 18, I park my car, and I put in the miles."

Nessa realized she wasn't the only one listening to their conversation when Tim Miller piped up. "You run in the woods?" he asked. "Is that safe for you? Shouldn't you have company?"

"I think I'm fine, Tim," she replied coolly. And she was right. Very few people could keep up.

Cynthia turned to Luc directly now, making it clear she was speaking only to him. "You wouldn't be afraid of night running, would you?"

Luc smiled, but not in a way that was necessarily friendly. More like he was accepting Cynthia's challenge.

Nessa lifted herself up onto her toes, working on strengthening her calves. Cynthia was never going to help her. Nessa would have to find a way to unlock her speed on her own.

But then, walking to the locker room after practice, Nessa felt a hand on her arm and looked back to see Cynthia, falling into step next to her as if it were normal for the two of them.

"You pumped for the season?" Cynthia asked.

Nessa knew she should come up with an interesting way to answer that question, something that might be impressive, but she had nothing. "Yeah, pretty psyched," she said.

"You've been training hard," Cynthia went on. "You scared?"

"Of what?" Nessa said.

"I don't know. Maybe not measuring up? 'Cause you know when you commit to trying, to really going for something, that's when you have the most to lose."

Nessa cocked her head and looked at Cynthia. Was this a trap? Was Cynthia trying to psych her out? Why would she do that?

"If you don't commit, you don't stand a chance at all," Nessa said, playing it safe.

"Yeah, duh," Cynthia laughed, walking past her, leaving Nessa with the feeling that she'd just been offered an opportunity.

Nessa waited a second and revved up her courage. She could turn this around. Jogging forward, Nessa blurted out, "I want to run with you." She didn't care how awkward it came out, how direct. She needed to say it. "At night. I need to get faster."

Cynthia looked at Nessa for a full beat, and Nessa looked back. She knew she couldn't look away first. She had to appear strong.

"Okay," Cynthia agreed. "Meet me at eight. At the trailhead at Route 18, by mile marker 12. I won't wait for you if you're late."

"I'll be there," Nessa said.

CHAPTER FOUR

Nessa arrived home from practice just in time to help her mother pull groceries out of the trunk of her car. She took a bag and followed Vivian through the garage. Last night's injured dog, Tucker, was resting in a crate. He looked up hopefully when he saw them approach, his tail thumping.

"Aren't you cute," Nessa said to him. She slipped into the high voice she knew would make his tail wag faster. "How are you feeling, big guy?"

As if he could understand her, the dog batted the plastic cone wrapped around his head against the crate door. "I know," Vivian said, pushing her frizzed-out hair away from her face. "It's not fair you have to wear the cone of shame."

Nessa laughed. Her mom talked to animals the way she talked to kids—like they were all in on the same joke. Animals trusted her immediately. Nessa had seen feral cats and snarling dogs settle under Vivian's competent touch many times. Vivian had that effect on people too. When Nate was panicking, Vivian could reach him in ways no one else could.

"Help me with him, will you?" Vivian said to Nessa. She put her groceries on the step by the door to the kitchen, and Nessa followed suit. Without having to be asked, Nessa spread one of the old, clean towels on top of the folding table while Vivian opened the crate and then, reaching her arms inside, gathered up the dog's full weight and lifted him gently out. Nessa helped, and together they placed Tucker on the table. Keeping one hand on the dog's shoulder, Vivian reached behind to turn on the utility light.

Nessa gasped. She was used to seeing wounds on animals who'd been bitten or gotten into fights, but she'd never seen anything like this before. While her mom looked at the wound, checking for signs of infection, Nessa silently counted the black-threaded stitches across the eight-inch gash. Twenty-two total.

"What happened?" Nessa asked.

Tucker raised his head, and Vivian reached her hand into the cone to calm him down with a nose rub. "Sue Little said she didn't know. He ran off into the woods chasing squirrels and must have run into something bigger than he was. Poor guy managed to limp home on three legs. He had some torn muscle and a nearly severed ligament, which I stitched up. If it had been much worse, I would've had to bring him into the office for a transfusion."

Vivian rubbed the dog's chest between his two front paws.

"I'll tell you what, Tucker," she said. "I'm gonna call your mom and tell her she can come pick you up, that's what. You're healing nicely, and if you keep this cone on and don't pick off all my nice stitches, you'll be just fine." Giving the dog one last pat, she nodded to Nessa, and they carefully put Tucker back in the cage.

"So what do you think it was that got him?" Nessa asked. "A coyote?"

"Bigger than that," Vivian said. Closing the crate door, she moved toward the kitchen, picking up the groceries on her way. "And if it were a bear, we'd have seen gashes. They tend to maul, not bite."

"So what, then?" Nessa asked.

Vivian shook her head. "Wolf, if you can believe it." With her thumb and first finger pretty much fully extended, she replicated the expanse of the deepest punctures in the dog's hind leg where the wolf must have locked on. "The jaw span's pretty big, even for a wolf."

Nessa shivered. Vivian leveled her with a look that Nessa recognized. She nodded at her mother. It went unsaid that she wouldn't repeat this to Delphine or Nate.

It wasn't just that Nessa was the eldest; she also knew about animals the way her mom did. Vivian had spoken to her about the wolves passing through Tether for years, as part of their slow repopulation of the more remote areas of Michigan. Nessa knew wolves weren't like bears, who found the smell of garbage irresistible. Wolves liked fresh meat, and they knew about maintaining territory. They'd eat squirrels and hedgehogs if they got hungry enough. But attacking people's dogs? This was something she hadn't heard before.

Inside, Nessa set the groceries on the counter and cruised straight for the living room of the small, split-level ranch. Delphine was on the computer and Nate was watching *Nova*—his favorite show. It was a good thing he liked educational TV, Vivian always joked. He was likely learning nothing at school because he got really mad when teachers told him to do something he didn't want to do.

Nessa flopped down on the sofa. She wasn't thinking about the homework that lay ahead. Instead, she was dreading that she'd told Cynthia she'd meet her.

Nessa slid up close to Nate, something she'd picked up from her mom. Her brother liked the feeling of another person pushing up against him—he even said he liked the feel of the blood pressure cuff tightening on his arm. But Nate was so absorbed in watching the show it was like Nessa wasn't even there.

Delphine looked up from the computer, taking in Nessa's sprawled position, the grass stains on her legs, the sweat drying in her hair. "Rough practice?" she asked. Delphine made no secret of the fact that she thought voluntary exercise was crazy.

"I need new running shoes," Nessa said. "And spikes."

Delphine rolled her eyes. "You always need new shoes." Then she went back to the screen. "Except they're nothing I can ever borrow."

Pretty and popular, Delphine was also really into programming and had started writing code in seventh grade. She'd been sure that her outfit-selecting app would make her millions, but so far it just occupied the majority of the family computer's hard drive space.

Nessa let her head drop back and her eyes close, relaxing to the music of pots and pans rattling in the kitchen, the tapping of computer keys under Delphine's fingers, the mellow voice of the narrator describing the latest techniques for archaeological digs. Nate startled when a locomotive whistle sounded in his show and then settled back in against Nessa's side. "Hey Nessie," he said, like he used to do when he was just starting to talk and she was in second grade. He put his head on her shoulder.

And for the next ten minutes, Nessa slept.

After dinner, Nessa fished Vivian's headlamp out of the catchall basket in the kitchen and headed toward the door. "You're going for a run *now*?" Vivian asked from the table where she was sitting with Nate while he struggled to finish his homework. Considering how much Nate knew—about trains, birdcalls, the presidents, and the periodic table—it was amazing how hard it was for him to do something as simple as basic fractions. His homework could take hours.

"A girl on my team swears by it," Nessa said. "I'm meeting her."

"Well, I hope you'll be careful," Vivian said, and Nessa was about to let the door swing shut behind her when her mom added, "Do you think you could check on Tucker?"

"Quickly," said Nessa, going to the garage door. She had just enough time to look in on him and still meet Cynthia. But when she saw that the papers in the cage were dirty and Tucker wasn't lying down, she changed them. This was one of her tasks at her weekend job at the vet's, so she moved quickly. But still, by the time she'd finished, she was running a few minutes behind.

She'd been planning on a slow, easy jog to the trailhead, but she had to sprint. Even so, she was late. Nessa saw Cynthia's car, but no Cynthia. She put her hand on the car's hood—still warm—and peered up and out into the woods, where she saw the flash of Cynthia's pale arms and legs disappearing into the trees. She must have missed her by only a minute.

"Hey!" Nessa called out. "Cynthia!"

Cynthia didn't stop.

Nessa took off after her, switching on her headlamp, sprinting even harder to try to catch up. She knew she couldn't catch Cynthia if Cynthia was running her race pace, but maybe Cynthia ran at a relaxed pace when she was just setting out.

Then she saw Cynthia again, another flash of white. Or was it something else? The flash had disappeared. Thinking she might see farther out in front of her if she relied only on the moonlight, Nessa turned off her headlamp and increased her pace. She almost laughed when she realized that between the sprint to the trailhead and the burn she was putting on trying to catch up to Cynthia now, she was probably getting the speed workout of her life.

Nessa ran farther. This was a trail she'd hiked many times— she knew the five-mile loop well. She wasn't worried about getting lost, but Tim Miller was right. It didn't feel totally okay to be out in the woods alone after dark. She almost tripped twice on roots growing across the trail, and the darkness was getting to her. She tried not to think about what could be lurking in the shadows, but it was hard not to imagine that someone could be waiting, unseen, to jump out for her at the last minute. And what could she do if that happened?

Fear powered her adrenaline production, and Nessa moved

at a faster pace than usual. The woods opened up into a meadow that Nessa hadn't expected to reach yet—she was really cooking. She realized she was almost back on the road, and the run almost over. Nessa was hit with relief just as she broke through the thickest stand of trees and into the full moonlight. After the long run through darkness, it was suddenly so bright Nessa nearly had to squint.

The meadow stretched behind the house of a farmer whose land butted right up against the trail, and Nessa scanned across the field for movement. Straining for a glimpse of Cynthia, Nessa saw something at the end of the meadow, a dark shape against the light grass. She could not judge how tall the figure was or whether it was Cynthia or maybe a spooked deer, and then it was gone. With a renewed burst of energy, Nessa shot forward after it.

She could hear the voice in her head telling her to slow down, telling her she didn't want to gas out. But for once, she didn't listen. As the tips of the grasses brushed her elbows, she heard the wind making a rushing sound, saw a gust dip into the grass on her left, like it was a hand making a print in wet sand. She lifted her knees higher, pushed out her chest, and sped up even more. Running out here—running totally alone—running in the dark where nothing looked quite like itself—maybe this was how you released what you had to release to go fast.

At the end of the meadow, Nessa plunged back into the woods, still going full tilt, hearing her own breathing in her ears, straining to see down the path for another glimpse of Cynthia, holding out the hope that maybe the spurt of fast feeling she'd had in the meadow would translate into a gain on her rival.

But Cynthia wasn't there.

Then who was? Nessa saw another flash of something out up ahead. The trail twisted. It was definitely something.

She heard a sound—a small cry—and for a second it all came together. Cynthia must have hurt herself. She must be lying on the ground. A sprain? Something worse? By now Nessa was close to the spot where she'd seen the dark shape move. Cynthia gave a plaintive whine that ended with a shrill yip. And then a warning bark.

Cynthia was barking?

Trying to stop herself, Nessa almost passed by a skinny but large German shepherd standing at attention on the side of the trail.

Except it wasn't a German shepherd. This animal's fur was lighter—a tawny brown touched with gray, with white markings along the ears and the oversized snout. The highlights caught the light and appeared almost blue. The animal looked at Nessa but she knew enough from working with dogs to avoid looking directly in its eyes. Instead, she focused on the erect ears, how skinny the animal was at the hips, the length of the legs.

It was the tallest husky Nessa had ever seen. The skinniest too. The most wild looking. With the longest snout.

This was not a husky.

This was not a dog.

Nessa felt her insides burning hot, as though her lungs had been transformed into molten lead, formless but also on fire. The animal barked and she jumped back, her mind desperately scanning her options. Stand still? Run? Call for help?

It was a wolf.

Where was Cynthia and why hadn't she stopped? Was the

wolf there when Cynthia ran by?

Why was the wolf so still?

The wolf barked again, as if in frustration, then took a step back, turning. Nessa saw that his front left paw was caught in a trap.

"Oh!" she said out loud, a hand coming to her mouth. Maybe the farmer had set it? Would he come check the trap soon? A wolf could starve to death in a trap this way.

"You poor thing," Nessa said, kneeling a bit, but then the wolf lunged at her, and Nessa cried out and reeled back. She knew that if the trap had not pulled back on his foot, he would have jumped her. At the thought, her insides turned over. The wolf looked to weigh at least 200 pounds.

She knew what Vivian would say. *He's more scared of you than you are of him.* But the wolf did not look scared of Nessa. The wolf looked angry. He started to moan and then deepened the moan into a growl. His eyes were red, his fur dirty and matted on the side. His very large teeth, which he was showing her—a bad sign—were yellowed near the gum line, saliva dripping from his jet-black lips. His teeth looked so sharp that for a second Nessa wondered whether they might have been filed into points.

But then the wolf stepped backward, whined, lay down, and started to gnaw on his foot. "No," Nessa said. She had heard stories of animals biting off their own paws in order to escape a farmer's trap. "No," she said to the wolf in her firmest voice. He stood up again, lunged for her, got pulled back by the chain, growled. When he moved, for a split second Nessa thought she saw an incision on his belly. She must be seeing things.

"Cynthia!" Nessa cried, hoping that the other girl might

hear her and come back. She listened. There was nothing. "Come back, Cynthia. I need your help!" she called.

Still nothing.

Maybe Nessa should run after Cynthia? Or maybe Nessa should run *like* Cynthia. Cynthia had run past the wolf in the trap and ignored him. Hadn't she? Had she just split-second decided it wasn't her problem and run on?

Maybe this was the line between human beings that Nessa could draw in the sand: some people would stay and help an animal and others would only help themselves.

The wolf was agitated now, growling, tugging on its foot, so it was hard to get a look at the trap, but she saw something. "Hold on, buddy, I'm working on it," Nessa said. She used the voice that usually brought comfort to animals, but was doing nothing for this wolf, who only glanced in her direction. There was something so wild, so cut off about this wolf. Nessa shuddered. From what she knew about wolves, she'd be safe as soon as she sprung the wolf from the trap. The wolf would probably run for its life. It was probably desperate to get back to its pack.

Nessa looked around for a sturdy stick and found one just off the trail. She moved slowly and carefully toward the wolf, talking in a low voice.

She knew wolves were smart. Maybe this one could pick up on nonthreatening cues in her voice if she tried to express them.

"Good wolf," she said. "I know how you feel. You just want to run free. Me too." She pushed the stick gently toward the trap. "I'm just out here for a little jog through the woods, like you. I don't want to hurt you." She pushed the stick further. "See this stick? I'm just going to pop open the trap with it and get you out of here." She looked at the spring coil of the trap. It seemed that if she hit it just right, it would release.

The wolf regarded Nessa suspiciously, growling, turning his head to view her out of the corner of one eye. "Oh, boy," Nessa said.

And then she couldn't believe it but she actually managed to make contact with the trap. She could feel it through the tip of the stick for a brief second before the wolf moved and the stick dislodged. Nessa was so startled that she jumped back. Nessa took a deep breath and tried again. The wolf took small steps forward and back, whining, giving little tugs at his foot as if he knew. Nessa felt proud of herself. They were on the same page now. This was all going to be fine.

But just as she managed to make contact with the trap again, she heard a noise in the brush behind her. Thinking it had to be Cynthia, she turned. But it wasn't Cynthia. It was another wolf, this one white with yellow markings and black eyes. All Nessa could really see were the animal's teeth because this new wolf was coming at her with a wide-open mouth, seemingly frozen in mid-leap—or at least that's how Nessa would remember it.

It all happened so fast, Nessa didn't have a second to feel scared. She just hit the ground, feeling the full force of the impact on her back even as she felt a sharper sensation in her hip that registered more as heat than pain. Within seconds, the heat grew to a burn so excruciating she could hear herself calling out, but the noises she was making were separated from her own body, like someone else was screaming. Nessa didn't know why she was screaming, but she had a terrible feeling that she was begging for her life.

After that, she blacked out.

CHAPTER FIVE

When Nessa woke up, she found herself looking straight up into the eyes of Dr. Kalish, her old pediatrician. They were in an exam room at the local clinic, the far end of the building she came to with Nate for his appointments.

She moved her head slightly to the left, and there was her mom, looking grim and pale. Nessa wondered what was wrong.

"Is Nate okay?" she said. "You look worried."

Nessa was surprised at how faint her voice sounded. She was still trying to puzzle out what she and Dr. Kalish and her mom were doing down here at the health clinic. It was like one of those weird dreams when you're back in first grade but your dog's in the classroom with you and everyone is riding bikes and Bree is the teacher and she's annoyed because no one is listening…and…

This wasn't a dream. She was awake. Her mom was saying, "Nate's fine, sweetheart, but you had a close call," and that was weird because Nessa felt fine, except maybe a little fuzzy. The last thing she could remember was saying goodbye to her mom in the kitchen and heading out for a run, and then…Cynthia… and then the woods…and then suddenly Nessa felt the pain again. Her hip.

She must have stiffened, because Dr. Kalish had a hand on her shoulder and was saying, "Easy now," and "Sorry if that pinched." Vivian leaned forward, her expression serious. "It's really important for you to lie still right now, Ness; the doctor's just finishing up with a stitch or two."

"Stitches?" Nessa said. "What…what happened?"

"That's the question we were about to ask you," Dr. Kalish said in his raspy tone. Nessa smiled. She'd forgotten how much she liked Dr. Kalish and his curly white hair and strong, tanned hands. When she was little, he had a private practice in the front rooms of the house where he lived with his family, and she always felt like he was a dad from a show on TV.

Dr. Kalish had retired when the clinic opened. As part of the Dutch Chem settlement with the town, everyone in Tether had free health care there for ten years. The children most at risk from chemical exposure were monitored as a preemptive measure, including Nate. Dr. Kalish now worked at the clinic on alternate weekends and was sometimes the doctor on call.

Nessa sat up a bit, trying to get her bearings. She noticed she was wearing a cotton robe and terry cloth slippers on her feet. Where were her clothes? Scanning the room, she saw her running shoes on the floor near the wall, placed on top of a couple of sheets of newspaper. There was something wrong with them. Were they muddy? That wasn't quite the right color. Nessa sat back as she recognized that they were stained with blood. A lot of blood. She looked at her leg and saw there was caked mud and blood all down her calves, stopping in a line where her socks would be, like the farmer's tan she got from running in the summer.

She searched out her mom's eyes. "How…?" she said. She wasn't even sure what question she should be asking.

"Joe Bent found you in the woods near his house."

Nessa nodded. The running trail cut into his farmland near where she'd seen the wolf.

"His dogs were going crazy behind his field and he found you there, just off the trail, bleeding," Vivian added.

Suddenly Nessa remembered. The wolf frozen in midair, bearing down on her.

"Nessa, were you…?" Vivian began. "Do you remember an animal?"

Nessa let her head fall back on the pillow. It suddenly felt heavy. She was glad to be lying down. "There were two," she said. "Wolves."

Dr. Kalish caught his breath.

"Did they bite you?" Vivian asked.

Nessa nodded. "One of them did. The other was trapped." She thought for a minute. "I was trying to free it. Didn't Mr. Bent see him?"

"No," Vivian said. "You were talking about them when they found you. Maybe you don't remember. Joe looked around but couldn't find a thing. And then after the ambulance came, he went back to make sure. He just called to say he searched all over, and let his dogs out to see if they could find an injured animal somewhere. There was nothing."

"That's nice of him," Nessa said.

"Nice has nothing to do with it," said Dr. Kalish. "We have to find out if the wolf is rabid. Most cases of wolf bite are accounted for that way. Not that you see much of it—or any wolf bite these days. I mostly remember it from my residency."

"What would a rabid wolf have looked like? Would it have been foaming at the mouth?" Nessa asked. She felt sure that the white wolf hadn't been. She shuddered at the instant image of the wolf coming for her, teeth bared, all four paws in the air, how he had knocked her down. Her hip began to throb.

"The fact that he didn't go for your head and neck area is lucky," said Dr. Kalish. "I've given you the medication regardless. And then there's this."

Reaching around to a small steel table on wheels, Dr. Kalish soaked some surgical gauze in rubbing alcohol—the smell stung Nessa's nose. He pinched something up in a piece of gauze from a stainless steel dish. The object was white and shiny.

"Is that a tooth?" Vivian said, leaning over.

"Yes. It was embedded in the wound, which is unusual," Dr. Kalish replied. "It's also unusual that you didn't sustain more damage than this. A full-grown wolf can bite through bone, and certainly tear muscle fiber. You seem pretty intact—this is mostly surface and the muscle damage is largely bruising. You'll feel it. But you don't need surgery."

Nessa could not take her eyes off the tooth in Dr. Kalish's palm. "That tooth sure is big," she said.

"You want to keep it?" Dr. Kalish asked.

Nessa nodded and held out her palm. She looked at the tooth, then over at her mom.

Vivian folded Nessa's hand around the wolf tooth into a fist. And then she wrapped her own weathered, larger hand around Nessa's. "Please," she said. "Worry about yourself, not the wolf. No more running in the woods after dark, okay?"

Nessa nodded. She could see how worried her mom was. She herself wasn't much looking forward to standing and putting weight on her sutured hip.

Then Dr. Kalish sat down on a stool, looked at her mom, and looked at Nessa. "No more running, period," he said. "Not 'til you're fully healed."

"What?" Nessa said. "That's impossible. I have a meet in two weeks. I can't *not* run. I'll lose my conditioning."

"You'll lose a lot more than that if you tear out these stitches or run on torn muscles."

"For how long?" Nessa said. She could feel a pit of panic form in her stomach.

"A month at a minimum."

"But that's almost the full season!"

Dr. Kalish shook his head. "I'm sorry, Nessa. A month," he repeated firmly.

It was tricky getting home from the clinic. It hurt like a mother to bend at the waist to sit in the front seat of Vivian's car, and then stand up again and take the few steps into the house. But the pain was nothing compared to the inner bleakness that descended on her the second Dr. Kalish had finished delivering the terrible news.

It didn't seem real. Running, to Nessa, came as naturally as breathing or eating. She thought about it when she was falling asleep at night, when she was in the shower, when her attention was wandering during class. How could she go on without it, without something she wanted so badly?

For two nights Nessa slept on the couch because it hurt too much to climb the stairs. She also stayed home from school. It hurt just to get up and go to the bathroom. It hurt to roll over in her sleep. She kept forgetting what Dr. Kalish had said and then remembering and then feeling the weight descend on her all over again.

It felt like a guilty verdict without the benefit of a defense. No cross-country meant no cross-country scholarship. Her mom kept telling her that one month was not the end of the world, that she could recover quickly. But Vivian didn't understand. Nessa had been working for six months to get to where she was now. In a month, all of it would be gone.

On top of that, she was having nightmares. Three nights in a row, she woke in a sweat and had to remember that she was safe. She might be shaking, alone, and miserable. But she wasn't out in the woods. There were no wolves here.

Bree got everyone in school to sign a get-well card. She came by every day with candy and gum and homework so Nessa could keep up with her classes.

Coach Hoffman called and told her he was sorry. Afterward, Nessa hung up the phone and cried, but she never cried in front of anyone.

Her mom had enough on her mind.

Three days after the bite, Nessa woke up early from pain. Sometimes it helped to put a clean dressing on the wound, so she hobbled into the bathroom to change it.

She carefully assembled the materials she'd need—gauze, alcohol pads, tape. To reach the site of the stitches, she had to twist at the waist, moving the skin on her hip with her hands to try to make it come into view. The movement hurt, and feeling the pain again, her stomach swelled with nausea.

Nessa felt sick and light-headed every time she looked at the wound. There was seepage, discharge. Suddenly she saw the white wolf coming toward her. The image was so real that she actually gasped. She remembered the wolf's open jaws and its dark eyes. Nessa put her hands on the sink to steady herself and looked at her face in the mirror. She remembered the wolf in the trap too, the black lips over red, rotten-looking gums, the teeth that were so sharp they could have been filed.

Why hadn't the wolves been there when Joe Bent came upon her with his dogs?

Where had they gone?

CHAPTER SIX

Spending days alone in the house was the worst. Nessa kept seeing the wolf in her dreams. So when it was time for Nate's clinic visit the following Monday, Nessa insisted that she and Bree could still bring him, even though Vivian offered to take off work.

Bree picked up Nessa and Nate after the school bus dropped Nate at home. As Nessa got into the passenger seat and stowed her crutches, Bree said, "You're wearing that?" looking pointedly at Nessa's track pants, slides, and bright blue hoodie.

"Cassian will have to deal," Nessa said, rolling down her window of the enormous clunker of an old Buick that Bree called the Monster.

"The crutches are good," Bree said. "Conversation starter?"

Nessa laughed. It felt good to be back riding in the Monster. Bree hit the gas, and the car's ancient V8 engine sent them flying out of the lot. Nessa loved this car.

The familiar (if loud) churn of the engine made it hard to talk, especially with the windows open (the air-conditioning didn't work), but the day was warm and they blasted the music and sang along. Nessa loved singing at full volume. She couldn't carry a tune, but with Bree it didn't matter. For a few moments she forgot all about the bite and running and scholarships and Cassian.

The health clinic was on the edge of downtown, its boxy industrial design disguised by yellow siding, blue shutters, and a gabled roof that made it look like a house. In the parking lot, Nessa felt her heart skip a beat. Cassian was right there by Bree's car. He was getting out of his pickup with his sister, Sierra, sliding out next to him. Nessa felt a rush of happiness.

Sierra had blonde pigtails and little purple moccasins. Cassian was wearing shorts that hung down low on his narrow hips and indoor soccer shoes without socks. His hair was tousled and Nessa could see the many different shades of blond. He looked up and over at Bree and Nessa and Nate. And then the most amazing thing in the world happened. He smiled.

At them.

Nessa could feel Bree pretty much melting into the earth next to her. Nessa felt pretty melty herself. She got even meltier when Cassian took a step closer to them. And then another. Just the way he walked was amazing. He rocked on his feet with the rhythm and confidence of a cat, his gray eyes crinkling into a smile, his jaw tightening as he held up a hand in recognition. Bree actually did collapse at that point, landing on the Monster's rear bumper, then quickly masking the movement by pretending she had to check the straps on her lace-up sandals. Nessa reached a hand back to signal Bree to stop being so obvious. She couldn't look back because her eyes were glued on Cassian's face. She could feel herself smiling at him hesitantly. Was he coming to talk to her? To Bree? He was definitely headed their way.

Then Nate stepped out in front of Nessa, with his own hand in the air and it turned out Cassian wasn't waving. He was holding out a hand for a high five. To Nate.

Nate?!

Was Nessa missing something? Nessa gave Bree a "what-the-heck-is-going-on-here?" look, which Bree returned with an "I-have-absolutely-no-idea" shrug.

"Hey soccer buddy," she heard Cassian say to Nate. "You gonna play with me today?"

"Yeah, C-man," said Nate. "If you can handle how hard I kick the ball to you."

"Oh, dude!" said Cassian. He turned away from Nate and put an arm over Sierra's shoulders. "You guys are going to slay me."

Nessa swung up onto her crutches. She was getting better at moving on them but she still made a lot of clomping noise. Cassian didn't even turn his head.

In the waiting room, Cassian didn't lose any time setting up the "soccer" game, using a plush ball from the bucket out in the little kids' play zone and making a goal out of upholstered cubes meant for climbing. Nessa noticed it wasn't so much a game as it was scoring practice, which was perfect for Nate, who had a hard time with cooperation, but who loved glory.

Sierra didn't shoot the ball, but, clearly worshipful of her older brother, she fetched it when Nate and another boy, Billy Lark, kicked it hard at the wall and made it ricochet all over the waiting room. No one minded because the room had only Dutch Chemical study kids. The study encompassed every child in the town born within about five years of Nate, so the waiting room was always full and the kids all knew each other pretty well by this time. Nate once described the feeling of waiting for his appointment with Dr. Raab as a very boring birthday party.

When the study began, all the kids in Tether had been included in it, but over the years the numbers had dropped to those really affected: kids who showed signs of exposure or were otherwise at risk. Nessa assumed Billy was there because he had juvenile rheumatoid arthritis, but she had no idea why kids like Nate and Sierra were on the "watch" list. It had something to do with markers in their blood. Three kids had developed unusual cancers, and others suffered autoimmune problems like lupus or Crohn's disease. Paravida was paying for their treatment, too.

Nate had trouble interacting with kids his age. So having Cassian organize the game and having Billy Lark join in was good for him. Billy was a cute kid too, small for his age and an only child. He had a scar from cleft palate surgery that Nessa could remember from when he was born. Because his family didn't have health insurance at the time, his mom had made coffee can coin collectors for every store counter in town with homemade labels decorated with the slogan "Help Billy Smile."

Billy's mom was here now. Mrs. Lark looked like Billy— red-haired, small-boned, pretty, and quick to smile. She was always passing Billy homemade snacks: slices of pesticide-free fruit and her own granola bars. Now she was writing down numbers in a notebook.

"Does your mom do this?" she asked, showing the page to Nessa.

"Do what?" Nessa asked. She looked over Mrs. Lark's shoulder at a notebook filled with columns of dates and notes.

"Track Nate's vitals after each of these study visits? I check Billy's temperature, weight, blood pressure before and after. I suppose I'm paranoid, but knowing what our kids were exposed to because of those Dutch Chem hoodlums, I just think you can't be too careful."

Since the lawsuit, everyone in the United States knew what had happened to the water and soil and citizens of Tether. Dutch Chem had dumped more than 9,000 tons of PFOA sludge into "digestive" ponds around the town, knowing full well that it would slowly poison and ultimately kill first the wildlife, then the livestock, and finally the people who lived nearby. Their own internal studies going back 40 years showed as much. All sorts of virulent autoimmune diseases appeared in the human population, followed by a range of rare cancers. Dutch Chemical had been gone for almost ten years, but they said it could take 1,000 years to clean the water table of Tether. The kids in the current study had tested highly positive for various blood markers that could precede all kinds of conditions. Their monitoring and ongoing health care had been part of the settlement struck as the Dutch Chem lawsuit went to trial.

"I don't know why, but he always comes out of these appointments with—" Mrs. Lark lowered her voice. Everyone in the town was so grateful to have the kids finally safe and being monitored, they would never complain that the visits were so frequent. Or that sometimes the kids in the study seemed oddly worn out after they'd come in. "Billy comes out of these appointments with a fever," Mrs. Lark whispered. "And low blood pressure."

Bree leaned across Nessa's lap to ask, "Are you worried these visits aren't good for him?"

Mrs. Lark shook her head. "I trust the clinic," she said but sounded as though she needed convincing. "And Dr. Raab. They're *doctors*. Still, it's just so hard to feel that your child might be at risk and you can't do anything."

Nessa nodded. She didn't have to imagine. Because of Nate, she knew.

The receptionist, Gina, called Mrs. Lark to the desk. Nessa liked Gina. She had gone to high school with Vivian.

Bree's attention was glued to her phone. She had a nice one from her dad, a long-haul truck driver who came back from every trip with a present to make up for his absence. He had given Bree the Monster after almost a whole summer without him.

Nessa stood up and hobbled over to the water cooler on her crutches. She wasn't thirsty but she thought she might catch Cassian's attention. However, it only resulted in Nate's saying, "Ness, hurry up. I'm gonna shoot and you're in the way."

"Sorry!" Nessa said, shaking her head. "I'm not as fast as usual!" She leaned out of Nate's way and her gaze crossed the reception desk, where Mrs. Lark was bent over a form. Nessa noticed Gina had the same travel coffee mug that the guidance counselor Mr. Porter had, with three interlocking triangles forming the Paravida logo. Sheesh. Adults in this town loved freebies from *anywhere*.

"Well, this is interesting," Bree said when Nessa got back. "I just googled Dr. Raab. You won't believe it. He's not even from Michigan. I mean he doesn't live here. Right now. Look." She held out her phone. "He works out at the University of California at Davis."

Bree held the phone so Nessa could see. There was Dr. Raab, complete with his neat, dark brown hair, long chin, heavy eyebrows. He was staring out from behind a very large desk, wearing a lab coat and surrounded by about 40 other adults, also in lab coats. Behind them were tall windows showing only sky.

"I wonder if all those people work for him?"

Nessa used her index finger to open a link. "It says here he's a world leader in human genetics," she said. "He's a Nobel laureate!"

Bree started opening other tabs.

"His coworkers don't leave him very good reviews!" she whispered with an evil glint in her eye. Bree was a sucker for gossip, even about an adult they hardly knew. "Look, this nurse calls him Dr. Crab!"

Just then, Sierra was called in for her appointment. For a brief moment, "Dr. Crab" himself appeared in the doorway before ducking back inside.

Cassian watched Sierra go, holding the ball at his chest between two outstretched hands like he was about to make a push pass, his eyebrows drawn together in a look of worry. Nessa noticed that Sierra looked a little frightened, too.

"Hey, Cassian," Bree said, her voice jumping up an octave. She cleared her throat, stood. "Excuse me," she said politely. Cassian blinked at her, like he was wondering where she had come from. Was it possible he hadn't even realized Nessa and Bree were in the room? "If you want, since Sierra's not here, I can field the ball for you."

Nessa had a hard time not smiling at Bree's offer. Bree hated sports, not to mention her sandals were a little complicated for soccer footwork.

"That's okay," Cassian said. Gone was the welcoming tone he'd been using with Nate and Billy when they kicked the ball with Sierra. He was being polite to Bree, nothing more.

"Oh," said Bree, smoothing her skirt. "Of course. Just—you know—call if you need me."

"Call if you *need me*?" Nessa said in the car. She was laughing—hard—and Bree, after a few outraged *What?!* looks, started laughing too. They were laughing so hard that Nate looked up from Bree's phone to tell them he couldn't hear the Ninja screams in the game he was playing.

Nessa and Bree ignored him.

"Like, 'here, let me give you my number'?" Nessa shrieked. "Just in case you need help? With the…Nerf ball?" Nessa was not being less loud. "Call *anytime*. Day *or night*."

"At least I'm putting myself out there!" Bree protested. "I'm not sulking in the corner like some people. You should thank me, actually. I'm getting us noticed. He's going to look up one day and say, 'Nessa, Bree, I never noticed how beautiful you two are.'"

Giving up on his game, Nate reached between the front seats to help himself to one of the sesame candies Bree carried in a little plastic sandwich bag. "But you are beautiful, Bree," he said, without the slightest sense of embarrassment or irony.

"Aw, Na-ate!" Bree said shaking her head. "I love you!"

Nessa turned to see how that went over. Nate was blushing

to the roots of his hair, sucking on his candy, looking like the cat who had just swallowed the canary.

It was so good to get out of the house that Nessa felt better for the rest of the day. It felt like the bite wasn't even hurting anymore, like she could do things that would have been painful only hours before. That was impossible—she knew the pain would probably come back worse than ever—but then, that night, changing the dressing on the wound, Nessa noticed that it was starting to close up. Dr. Kalish hadn't told her that would happen. He'd said she could expect it to be oozing for a week. Just as she was thinking of calling her mom in to check it, she heard a knock on the door. "Just a sec!" Nessa called, quickly dabbing on ointment and taping up the new bandage, covering it over again with the waistband of her pajamas.

When she opened the door, it was Delphine. "Sorry," Nessa said. When a family of four shares a single bathroom, spacing out, obsessing over your wound—even if you'd been bitten by a wolf—was not cool.

"No, I'm not waiting," said Delphine. She stepped back into the hall, leaned back against the wall. "I was looking for you, actually. I have something for you." She led Nessa into the room they shared, and plucked a small manila envelope about the size of a business card from the top of the bureau and handed it to Nessa.

Nessa opened the envelope's flap and slid a hard object on to her opened palm. It was the wolf tooth—the one that had been embedded in her wound. But it wasn't just the tooth. Delphine had turned it into a necklace, running a tiny ring through a hole drilled in the top of the tooth, then attaching a silver chain to the ring.

"I made it in shop," she explained. "I had to use the smallest drill bit they have. Mr. Russo said I was lucky it didn't crack."

Nessa held the tooth in her palm, closed her fist over it, saw the white wolf, felt the rush of her blood pumping in her own ears all over again.

"I don't know if you know, but you've been talking in your sleep," Delphine said.

"Oh, yeah?" Nessa was trying not to sound worried. Or surprised.

"Nothing that sounds like words," Delphine said. She looked embarrassed, like now that she'd brought it up she couldn't take it back, but she didn't want to explain either. "It's more like you make this gasp, like you're surprised. And then you kind of—I don't know."

"What?" said Nessa.

"Okay," said Delphine. "You make this noise. It's kind of like a whining sound."

"Whining?" Nessa said.

"Yeah," said Delphine. "Like a dog who's afraid." She moved her curly dark hair off her face. She looked like their father, wherever he was. Nessa looked like their mom. "Like a whimper. Like you're scared."

"Oh," said Nessa. She didn't say anything else because, what are you supposed to say when your sister tells you that you're dog-whimpering in your sleep?

Delphine rushed to cover up Nessa's discomfort. "So I thought the necklace, I thought it might help. I don't know. It could be like a talisman. You know, keep away whatever it is that's freaking you out."

Nessa looked at the tooth. It was larger than any dog's tooth she'd ever seen, about the size of a house key. She pinched open the clasp on the chain and, moving aside her ponytail, connected the two ends of the chain behind her neck, allowing the clasp to close. The tooth lay against her skin and she shivered, thinking how this tooth was part of what had cut open her own skin, had dug into her flesh.

"I hope I'm not waking you up too much," she said to Delphine.

"No," Delphine said. "That's not it. I just, Nessa—you got attacked. That's scary. You might be, I don't know, you might have trauma. Like a veteran." Veteran trauma was something they learned about in health class. There were vets in Tether, guys eight or ten years older than Nessa who had gone off to fight and come home broken.

"Yeah, you might be right," said Nessa. She smiled at her little sister's concern. "Thanks, D."

CHAPTER SEVEN

D r. Kalish was surprised Nessa's wounds were healing so fast but still said she should stay off the leg for one more week. By Thursday, Nessa began to think she could handle walking on it. Or at least not stay alone inside all day long. She decided she needed to get back to school.

After hobbling around the house pretty effectively when her mom wasn't home, Nessa also decided to leave the crutches in Bree's car when Bree dropped her off at the main entrance.

Nessa was glad to be back. School was distracting. Practice was not. She sat next to Coach Hoffman on the bench, sitting on her hands, squinting out into the sky, waiting for the runners to come back, trying not to see the wolf, the teeth, the black lips, the drip of saliva, trying not to think about how winning races—and her one chance at getting out of Tether—would be all but impossible now.

"You can read if you like," Coach Hoffman said. "If you have homework."

"That's okay," Nessa said. "I'll just watch."

No one on the team talked about what had happened to her. Especially not Cynthia, who had yet to mention to Nessa or anyone else that she had been running on the same path on the same night at the same time. Maybe she hadn't known Nessa was running behind her, but still, Nessa thought: *She knows now*.

Nessa stayed out on the bleachers with Coach Hoffman until the end of practice. When it was over, she found herself walking next to Luc, heading toward the locker-room doors. He had his little black duffel bag slung over his shoulder—his sneakers hanging from his fingers, his feet already stretching out in flip-flops. "So, wolf bite," he said, in totally the wrong tone of voice. Almost like he was about to make a joke about it.

"Yep," said Nessa, turning her head to look at him, then facing forward again. She had never really spoken to him before.

"Cynthia was there?" he said. "But she didn't stop to help you?"

"She didn't see me," Nessa said. "She didn't know."

"But she saw the wolf, right? She ran right past it?"

Nessa nodded. "I think so."

She wasn't going to make a big deal out of it, but she wasn't going to lie either.

Luc shook his head slightly, blew air out through parted lips. "Wow," he said. "That's cold."

And then, without saying anything else, he walked away.

"See ya?" Nessa said to his back, under her breath.

Weird guy. Definitely.

After her first day back, Nessa's hip was so sore she had to spend the rest of the night on the couch. Vivian was sure she'd overdone it, and Nessa hadn't even told her about going crutches free. "Do you want to stay home tomorrow?" Vivian asked. "If you're not ready, you're not ready."

"I'm ready," Nessa said, her jaw set. And truthfully, she was. She made it through the next day much more easily and didn't feel as wiped out that night.

On Saturday, Bree offered to take over Nessa's shift cleaning cages at the vet. Nessa accepted the help but felt well enough to tag along. Bree picked her up a little before eight.

Bree launched into a fairly epic story involving her ex-boyfriend, Sad Matt, who had flooded Instagram with sappy photos of them together (again) the night before. "I reported every single photo and they took them all down. I want someone new, someone more mature. A senior maybe?"

Suddenly Bree broke off. "Nessa, are you even listening to me?"

"Sorry," Nessa said. "Yeah, I'm listening."

"No, you're not," Bree said. "You're thinking about something else."

Nessa didn't want to admit she was thinking about the wolf.

"Okay," Bree took a deep breath. "I get it. You're not running and you're really stressed about that, and you're Nessa, which means you don't want to admit that anything is hard."

Nessa laughed wryly. "Something like that, yeah."

Bree smiled. "Here's what I think you need to do. I think you need to do some positive imaging."

Nessa groaned. "You sound like your mom." Bree's mom was into all that hippie New Age woo-woo stuff.

"I'm serious! I think you need to savor and value the moment in which you got that bite."

"What good could it possibly do, if I went back in time?"

Unruffled, Bree just laughed. "You could own the fact that you are the type of person who does their best to save a trapped animal, regardless. You could own that. Because you're Nessa."

"Because I'm stupid," Nessa grumbled.

"No, bonehead, because you're big-hearted," Bree looked over at Nessa and smiled a big, goofy smile.

"Um...watch the road, please?" Nessa said.

"Fine. But listen. Seriously. The thing with the wolf. You were trying to do the right thing. That's got to help you in some balance-of-the-universe, good-karma kind of way."

"Karma," said Nessa, rolling her eyes, looking out the Monster's window. Suddenly, she felt a confession bubbling up. She'd been so determined not to complain, but here it was. "I just can't believe I'm out for the season," she said, in a low voice. "I don't know what's going to happen to me if I don't get a scholarship."

She rubbed a worn spot on the knee of her jeans. This was the first time she'd said any of this out loud.

"I know," said Bree. "And I would feel the same way. But I'm just saying that at some point you're going to let that go and you'll find that something else is there."

Fourteen days after Nessa had been bitten, Dr. Kalish looked at the scar forming and scratched his head. "Have you been seeing the shamanic faith healer?" he said, chuckling. Nessa loved Dr. Kalish but the man would repeat the same joke for years. She'd forgotten that about him.

"No," Nessa said. "No wolf bite magic for me." She paused. "Can I run again?"

Dr. Kalish lifted her leg at the knee and rotated it into a few positions meant to test the strength of the muscle.

"Nessa," he said. "The healing you see here is the healing on the skin. But a wolf's jaws—the healing I'm most concerned about is what's going on under the skin."

"I want to run," she insisted.

The doctor moved her knee up in a way that caused her hip to twist. For a second, Nessa felt a pain so sharp she had to bite down to keep from gasping.

"That's still hurting?" Kalish said.

"No," Nessa said.

Dr. Kalish patted her on the shoulder. "Athletes," he said, shaking his head. Then he got serious. "Okay, you can run. But if it does hurt, even in the smallest way, you stop whatever you're doing. As you know, I thought this was going to keep you out of commission for a month, so as far as I'm concerned you're getting a bonus here. Don't push it."

Nessa nodded, doing her best to look responsible and trustworthy. "I won't. I swear. I understand."

"Good girl," said Dr. Kalish, patting her on the shoulder again.

Coach Hoffman didn't believe that Nessa was cleared for practice until he spoke to Dr. Kalish personally on the phone. Then, Coach told her that he wanted her moving slowly and staying close to school. It was the day the team did a long run all together, but he kept Nessa running one-mile loops, checking in with him every time, stretching and resting. Halfway through practice he had her stop entirely so she could ice.

She knew this was the only way they would let her run at all, so she followed Coach's instructions and kept her speed down. Except when no one was watching.

In the woods, alone, she found herself sprinting, running harder and faster than she had ever been able to before.

CHAPTER EIGHT

*O*n the morning of the first cross-country meet of the season, Nessa woke early. Careful not to disturb Delphine, she eased open the sticky door to their room and got dressed in the bathroom—she'd laid her clothes out on a corner of the sink the night before. She wore flip-flops with her team shorts, and appreciated the softness of the lining of her new team sweat-shirt, though she still would have traded it in a heartbeat for the softness of her comforter and pillow.

Brushing her teeth and splashing water on her face helped. She started to remember that she cared about the day. The race. She forced herself to take a deep breath—she knew part of her challenge was to remain calm leading into it.

In the kitchen, Vivian was already awake and making oatmeal. She'd laid out a protein bar on the counter and a plastic bag packed with moleskin, nail scissors, Band-Aids, a tube of Neosporin. "Thanks Mom," Nessa said, letting herself fall into the worn wooden chair by the window. "You didn't have to do all this."

Vivian smiled, frowning as she checked the thickness of the oatmeal. "Are you kidding me?" she said. "I'm proud of you. You've been through something scary, and you're working so hard."

Her mom put the oatmeal on the table and Nessa topped it with chia seeds.

"Good Lord, put some sugar on that or something," Vivian said. "It makes me sad just to look at it."

Nessa wanted to eat. She knew what an effort her mom had made to get up extra early to cook for her. She knew the food would translate directly into the energy she needed to win today. But the first bite seemed to stick somewhere in her throat and would never make it down to her stomach. "This is really nice, Mom," she said.

"Ha!" Vivian waved a hand in the air to show she knew that Nessa was lying. "Nice try." She reached into a cabinet—the low one she'd set up when Nessa and Delphine were little and needed to be able to get snacks when Vivian wasn't home. "Here. Have a Pop-Tart."

At school, the sun was up, but just barely, as Nessa found Coach Hoffman waiting with the cross-country bus in the parking lot. It was a crisp enough morning that he had the heat on, and the windows were steamy. The bus was a bright spot in the dark. Inside, Nessa could identify the hunched forms of her teammates, heads bowed, earbuds in, everyone keeping in their own head space, still half asleep. Coach Hoffman was leaning against the driver's side door, checking names off a list on a clipboard, his hair sticking out from under his baseball cap at funny angles.

Traverse City was on a bay off Lake Michigan—almost two hours from Tether—and when the road ran along the top of the bluffs on the lakeshore, everyone crammed into one side of the bus to catch a view of the water. It was pale blue, with rippling sand bars visible under the surface.

Nessa noticed that Cynthia barely turned her head to look, as if a glimpse of Lake Michigan wasn't a big deal. Luc stayed in his seat also, in the third row from the back, his chin in the air, looking out the window like he didn't know what everyone else was so excited about. Nessa wondered if maybe he had lived near Lake Michigan at some point, if that's why it did so little to impress him.

After the sight of water, everyone was awake and chatting, like they were here on vacation. Nessa heard Tim Miller talking about his night of cruising, which meant driving around aimlessly up and down Main Street in Tether, meeting up in parking lots, drinking warm beer out of the back of a pickup until the cops came to send everyone home.

The freshmen were squawking over a cell phone, tunelessly belting out lyrics to hip-hop songs. Nessa kept stealing looks at Cynthia, who wasn't talking. She rode the bus with her head down, her knees pulled up to her chest, strong but compact. As the bus got closer to the school, Cynthia started to brush and braid her long black hair.

By the time they reached Traverse City, where the invitational tournament was being held, the day was bright and warm, and it felt like the cold morning in the Tether High parking lot had existed in another dimension. The team straggled after Coach Hoffman, dropping their pillows and sleeping bags in the area he had staked out, like they were setting up towels on a crowded beach. The freshmen started warming up, drinking water, running laps to the bathrooms, while kids in the varsity and junior varsity races sprawled out on top of their sleeping bags and pulled out homework, checked their phones, or pinned on their race bibs.

Finally, Coach called them into a circle, and as he began his pep talk, Nessa tried to focus on what she remembered about the course. It started on a football field, and looped around the school, into a nearby park and up a hill, on to school grounds again, along a suburban street, and then back down around, finishing in a chute to the side of the playing fields.

Cynthia was tightening the red ribbon she always wore in her hair. It matched the team's red tanks and running shorts. Nessa retied her shoes, stretched her bum quad muscle one more time. She tried to shrug off the pain she felt and the tightness in her hip.

They lined up by team with Cynthia and Nessa in the number one and two spots and Hannah Gilroy, the fast freshman who had made varsity, just behind. The whistle blew and the girls shot off. As always, the first thought Nessa had as she was running was, *Not fast enough*. And then she thought, *Too slow*. No matter how well you knew your own pace, it was almost impossible to gauge what you were running in the first thirty seconds of pack movement at the opening.

Coach Hoffman told them to find a runner they recognized from another school and to set a pace to match theirs. Nessa saw Dawn David. She'd seen her at races last year, and Nessa knew they ran at about the same pace.

"Let her be your pacer," Coach had said, meaning that Nessa would be conserving energy, letting someone else set the pace.

She settled in behind Dawn, following her as runners jockeyed for position before the course narrowed into a trail in the woods. Dawn took tiny movements to the left and the right, careful not to sacrifice too much in an effort to pass, but knowing that getting stuck behind a slower runner meant you wouldn't be running your own best time, but someone else's.

Nessa focused on a spot dead center between Dawn's shoulder blades. She watched the swaying of Dawn's tank top. Nessa's chest was already hurting and she felt that she was lifting her legs too high to compensate for the uneven ground.

The course left the woods and ran about a half mile along the park path and then turned right. That was the two-thirds marker, and Nessa was pretty sure it was time for her to make her move.

But still, when the course started up the one big hill, before swinging past the school again, Nessa held back, waiting for the downhill to let herself fly, stretching out her stride, letting gravity do the work.

Heading down the hill, she was up at Dawn's shoulder, then she was past her, and the next runner in her sights was Karen Lund. Nessa passed her as well, just before the hill bottomed out. She didn't know where the power in her legs was coming from, but around the next bend, she spotted Cynthia's black ponytail and red hair ribbon disappearing around the back of the gym. Seeing her was exhilarating and Nessa hoped she could catch her. She lifted her knees higher and passed Amanda DuChamp by stepping around her, and then hopping back in a step ahead.

Nessa felt good. Amazing, actually. As if an invisible hand were pushing the back of each leg from a spot just above the knee, the muscles linked up to her abdomen, working like the thick rubber bands they were. She passed Rosemary Kolvig, Katie Samuels, Juliana Ortiz, and two girls she didn't know. By now, there was only a half mile left in the course, and it traveled back around the school, behind the parking lot, across the driveway in front of the school, then looping back around to enter the chute, a strip marked by cones leading to the finish line. She could see Cynthia finish only a few hundred feet in front of her. Nessa would be in Tether's number two spot for sure.

Or not for sure.

Just then, she saw a flash of red on her left as she entered the chute. Before she could even register that it was Hannah, she was staring at the girl's back, the tiny elbows pumping, the head straight, Hannah's feet striking at an impossible tempo. Nessa heaved her body forward, but it felt heavy and sluggish now. She could feel her arms swinging to the side, her head lowering as if she could summon strength that way, like a bull. She told her legs to move faster, and they did, but not nearly as fast as she wanted them to. It felt to Nessa suddenly that she was running in slow motion, as if underwater.

She had no memory of crossing the line, only walking with her hands on her hips, her face hot and flushed, looking down at the ground, thinking, *How did that just happen?* It was all she could do not to cry.

Embarrassingly enough, Coach Hoffman came over to comfort her. "Good work, Nessa," he said. "Welcome back."

Nessa didn't say anything. She swallowed.

"Hey," he said. "You okay?"

"What was my time?" she choked out.

"17:48," Coach said.

Nessa wiped the tears away with the back of her hand. That was a strong time for someone who wasn't looking for what she was looking for.

CHAPTER NINE

Nessa spent the day fretting about the race. Had she held back? Maybe this was the problem. Maybe she'd been holding on too tight. Maybe Bree was right. What she needed to do was let go.

Just to see how that would feel, Nessa increased her pace, running after dinner. It was getting dark out—the moon was waxing, just a sliver. Kind of weird that two weeks ago, her whole run had been lit up by the giant full moon.

Don't think about that, Nessa told herself. She slowed for a second but pushed past the fear this time, keeping her stride long and her tempo rapid, trying to let go of her fear of both the wolf and failing to finish, of falling apart before she got to the end of her run.

Her lungs burning, her muscles screaming in pain, Nessa kept up her sprinting pace. She was surprised at how long she was able to go. She changed her plan and decided to make this a short sprint instead of a long jog. And then, as it became a long sprint, Nessa could feel complaints coming from parts of her body that she didn't often hear from. The hip where she'd been bitten was aching, her temples were pounding, and the inside of her mouth felt both salty and rough, like she'd bitten her own tongue. The backs of her hands were itching, too. She started to scratch them, but that slowed her down so she just let them itch, telling herself the feeling would go away if she got herself up past a certain speed.

The days passed. Nessa ran.

Even as the teachers started piling on homework, talking about how important grades were junior year, Nessa ran.

Even as Nessa increased her hours cleaning cages weekends at the vet's to pay for her new racing spikes, she ran.

She ran before the sun came up so she could be back in time to get Nate to the bus when Vivian took the early shift at the vet's.

She ran as it was setting, on weekends after work, following a road behind the old Dutch Chem plant, noting the glow of the new Paravida complex through the trees.

She ran as the first maples started to change color, then the oak.

She jumped over roots, she sidestepped brambles, her footfalls echoing off plank bridges traversing streams.

She was the first person at practice. The last to go home. She ran for speed. She ran for distance. She stretched carefully first thing in the morning and last thing before bed.

There were nights when her calf muscles seized up in bed and she had to bite down on her finger while Delphine rushed her a banana. There were times where the bottoms of her feet felt like they'd been brushed with sandpaper. The itching on her hands came back.

The bite on her hip wasn't bothering her so much anymore, but other injuries presented themselves. A toe swelled. A knee twinged. When Nessa limped across the living room on the way to bed one night, Vivian put new running shoes on the credit card. Bree drove Nessa and Delphine to school in the Monster, and sometimes Nessa stretched out in the back looking up at the tears and stains on the ceiling, blissfully thinking of nothing as she felt the rhythm of her own footsteps echoing in the regular bumps in the road.

"Wow," said Coach Hoffman one day at practice when Nessa ran a 5K in 17:27. "Nessa, you just shaved more than twenty seconds off your race time."

"Are you sure?" Nessa said. She was breathing hard, hands on her knees, recovering. Coach showed her the watch. There were the numbers, the chubby clean digital lines, the collection of dashes arranged in a 1 and a 7 and a 2 and a 7, each one a miracle. She could feel the smile stretching out her cheeks.

The strange thing was? The next day, timing herself in the morning, she ran a 17:17.

CHAPTER TEN

By late September, Nessa felt like she was trapped in Mr. Porter's giant motivational poster where junior year is a mountain, but she was still at the bottom. The number of tests and quizzes seemed to have doubled from the year before, and every teacher mentioned grade point averages and SAT prep at least once a week. Bree's locker, once decorated with a single raw crystal on a piece of pink yarn, was now papered with vocab flash cards defining words like "Machiavellian" and "gregarious."

Nessa and Bree were in the same chemistry class, and in an effort to counteract her biology disappointment and battle with the "Z score" or weighted averages on all exams, they started a weekly study group. At least that's the reason Nessa joined the group. Bree's latest crush, a certain Gabe Trudeau, was the reason Bree hosted it.

Nessa was a little bit *less* enthusiastic than Bree about the study group, particularly on nights like tonight when it was just the three of them. Third wheel, anyone? She tried not to give Gabe dagger eyes as he reached for the second-to-last brownie on the plate. And then the last! The jerk!

With a sigh, she heaved herself up from the kitchen table and upstairs to the bathroom. Washing her hands (twice) with Bree's mom's not-very-sudsy health food store soap, Nessa screwed her face into a happier expression for Bree's benefit.

"She hates me," Gabe said, clear as a bell. Nessa rolled her eyes and turned off the tap. She could *hear* him chowing down on that final brownie.

"You didn't need to glare at him all night," said Bree after Gabe had gone home. "When you were in the bathroom, he told me he thought you hated him."

"Yeah, I actually heard that," Nessa said, half-smiling.

"Wait?! How could you hear that?" Bree said. "He was whispering. And you were upstairs."

"I don't know," Nessa shrugged. "But don't change the subject. He took the last two brownies without asking if anyone else wanted one. He's not good enough for you. And Cassian will be jealous."

"I told you. You can have Cassian," Bree said. "Gabe is into me, and Cassian doesn't know who I am."

"I can *have Cassian*? Thanks. But he doesn't know who I am either," said Nessa.

Later, it occurred to Nessa that it *was* a little odd that she'd heard Gabe whispering in the kitchen when she was upstairs at Bree's. She was lying in her bed with the lights out, waiting to fall asleep, listening to her mom speaking over the phone to Aunt Jane—Nessa could often hear the low murmur of Vivian's voice, but now she could make out the words. Maybe her hearing had always been great and she'd just never noticed before?

"She's got so much energy," Vivian was saying. "I don't know where it comes from. I know it's good, I know…Something is going on with her…"

Absentmindedly, Nessa fingered the wolf tooth on its chain. She didn't like that her mother was worried about her. And she didn't like that maybe her mom *should* be worried. Why could she hear her? Her mom wasn't in the next room. She was all the way on the other end of the house.

A few mornings later, Nessa stumbled into the bathroom before an early run and washed her face, then looked clear-eyed in the mirror. *Oh no*, she thought. *I slept in my contacts.*

Nessa's vision was bad enough that she usually couldn't see anything in the mirror but an unidentifiable blur. She groaned and grabbed for her lens case with her right hand, sticking her left hand to her left eye to dig out the forgotten lens. But the little blue discs were swimming in saline, just as they should be. *What?* Nessa blinked at her reflection. She'd been farsighted since she was seven years old!

Now Nessa could see herself quite clearly. She could see *everything*. She burst outside into her run, noticing that colors seemed brighter, shadows more well-defined. Had the Kindells had their house painted turquoise? Their regular blue paint job seemed to vibrate with life. The maple at the corner of Nessa's road was positively, shockingly fluorescent.

And as if her improved vision sharpened everything else, sounds were crisper now, too. She could smell more. The acrid odor of pine from a freshly cut tree on the trail was almost overwhelming. She caught the whiff of rotting leaves and, without thinking about it too much, she knew under which downed branch that particular leaf collection was located.

After her run, Nessa popped a single lens into her eye: blindness. Her vision was perfect without them. Not wanting to scare her mother, Nessa left her contact solution out on the counter so Vivian would assume she was still using it. Normally, she told her mother about most things in her life, especially happy things, but something made her stay quiet on this. An overnight vision correction was magnificent. But *why*?

"Wow, you just can't seem to get enough of those," Vivian commented that evening as Nessa took a third helping of venison sausages a neighbor had given them—he hunted in the Upper Peninsula and brought back a couple of deer every year. Nessa couldn't remember enjoying them this much last year.

The next morning, surveying the breakfast options—cereal, toast, muffins, waffles—Nessa started to feel frustrated until it occurred to her she could eat plain turkey. A pound of it. Delphine—who liked turkey sandwiches for lunch—was pissed.

"Uncool!" Delphine said, holding up the empty turkey wrapper, while Nessa tucked the last piece of sliced meat into her mouth.

"Nessa needs meat," Nate said that night at dinner, with gusto, as Nessa slid two burger patties between her bun, "so she can jump off the deck."

Vivian and Delphine looked at Nate strangely. While he could tell you the names of every bird on the planet, and would talk for hours about the acceleration capacities of various locomotive engines, he was not usually that observant of the people around him. "She jumped off the railing and didn't get hurt," he said.

"But that's over five feet from the ground!" Vivian said, looking at Nessa now. "What were you thinking?"

"It's not *that* far," Nessa said, trying to keep it casual. At the time, the urge to vault the railing had felt natural. All she'd registered was that she was in a hurry to bring in the laundry from where it had been hung out to dry.

"You know very well it is!" Vivian said.

Nate stood up from his chair. "She landed like this." He got into a stance like a surfer would assume on a board, feet apart, knees bent, arms straight and out to the sides.

Vivian was staring at her. Nessa felt her face turning red. Jumping off the deck had been incredibly stupid. What if she'd sprained an ankle with Homecoming time trials only a week away? Her time at trials would place her at Sectionals. They were critical. Lots of scouts would be there. But the truth was, she hadn't even thought about the decision when she was making it. It had seemed obvious. She'd known she could land the jump.

"I was in a hurry?" she tried.

"Wow," Coach Hoffman said when Nessa came in from

running a 5K. She knew she'd been going fast. She could feel it, but she hadn't had the usual fear that came with picking up her pace, doubting that she'd be able to maintain it through the full course. "You just ran a 5K in 17:10."

"I shaved thirty-eight seconds off my best race time?"

Coach was nodding. Nessa felt a smile spreading across her face.

That night, just to see, she went out on her own and did it again.

"I think something strange is happening to me," she told Bree when they were driving to the vet's office that weekend—Bree had decided to come along to get another dose of puppy love and Nessa was happy to get a ride to work.

Parking the Monster in the rutted dirt parking lot behind Dr. Morgan's, they looked into the enclosure off to the side of the building and saw that the puppies were out in the small yard, rolling and playing while their mother watched. They'd gotten bigger in only a week—and were now running and falling and then running some more, hiding behind plastic milk crates. Their mother, Betty, was lying down with her head up, keeping an eye on them.

"Hello, puppies!" said Bree, jogging over to the fence and pushing her fingers in for a little nibble. She'd named her favorite Henry—he was fawn colored with brown markings and white paws. "Henry," she called into the enclosure. "Did you miss me?" She turned back to Nessa. "He *remembers* me!"

But as Nessa jogged over, Betty started barking, a warning, repetitive bark. Nessa looked at Betty with alarm. The mama dog was on her feet now.

Betty's hair raised along her spine and she barked right at Nessa. "It's okay girl, it's just me," Nessa called out to her.

Nessa held the back of her hands forward, so Betty could sniff.

Betty growled. Nessa backed away. "I'm not going to hurt you," she told Betty in the gentlest tone she could muster. Betty lifted her snout and barked a few more times into the air. Bree was looking from Betty to Nessa to Betty again.

Nessa shrugged. "I'm going inside," she said to Bree. Bree waved.

As soon as Nessa entered the kennels, the caged animals began freaking out too. They all acted just like Betty. A cat pushed her rear end up into the air, her hair standing on end, her tail high, and hissed at Nessa. A dog whimpered, cowering in the back of his cage, trying to make himself small enough that Nessa couldn't see him.

Nessa pulled out the cleaning supplies, put on rubber gloves, and began to work through the crates as best as she could. Bree came in and helped out, which was important because some of the animals looked like they were going to bite Nessa.

Nessa was shaking as she signed out at the desk, and Ashley, the receptionist, said, "Nessa, honey, did you get highlights?"

"No," Nessa said.

"It looks really pretty," she said. "But it could be the smell of the hair coloring that's getting to the critters."

"But I didn't do anything to my hair," Nessa insisted.

Bree had her head cocked, looking at Nessa. "It does look lighter."

That night, Nessa stood in front of the bathroom mirror

with all the lights on. Ashley was right. Her hair was lighter—or parts of it were, a few streaks were lighter blonde, almost white.

Nessa slept fitfully and dreamed she was running, but low to the ground, on all fours. Panting.

Snarling.

Her skin felt uncomfortable—itchy. She looked at it and then watched in horror as hairs emerged on her forearm, growing quickly. In a panic, Nessa checked her other arm. There was hair there too. She looked at her legs, her head moving from one to another, thinking that this was impossible. She kept rubbing over the hairs with her hands as if she could rub them away.

But her hands had become large paws, her fingers shrinking, her joints gnarled like a dog's, fur growing out between them, her nails hard and long. In the dream, she ran to a mirror, checked her reflection and there was hair on her face as well, covering her forehead and cheeks, her eyebrows growing, her jawline disappearing under the thickening fur. Her teeth were longer, her nose smaller, and she felt the full horror of the trans-formation, reacting in the dream just as she would react if it were real. Her heart pounded, her mind was saying, *No, this isn't possible*, her eyes filling with tears, her mouth and throat dry.

She woke sitting straight up in bed, and had to turn on the light—Delphine rolled over but did not wake up—to make sure her skin was still skin, her face still a face, her hands her own. But still, she couldn't forget the horror of seeing herself become something she was not. Her skin was tingling and crawling as if fur actually had been sprouting from its pores, her face itching, and she had to resist scratching all over her body.

It was close to dawn, and she never was able to fully get back to sleep, eventually giving up and heading to the bathroom. Before stepping into the shower, Nessa looked again at her newly lightened hair. And then she noticed something on the top of her shoulder that made her gut tighten and her throat close up. It was a light dusting of fine, white hair.

She looked all over her body. Her leg hair was longer too, thicker, and again, that same white color. She squeezed her eyes closed. She turned on the shower. She turned off the light.

And when she got out of the shower, the hair was gone.

"Um, Mom, why is there dog hair in the shower?" Delphine complained at dinner, glaring from Nate to Nessa to Vivian. Nessa looked down. Easy enough to blame her mom for tracking it in from the vet's office. She didn't admit that it might have been hers.

Later that night, Nessa was watching TV on the couch with Nate. Delphine was using the computer. "Can you do some research for me?" Nessa said. Maybe Delphine could make sense of what felt so confusing to Nessa.

Without looking up, Delphine said, "Do it yourself. It's the internet—accessible to all."

"Yeah but I'm tired, and you know you're really great at finding stuff." This was true. Delphine could do something as simple as googling and take it to the next level. "And you're also so nice. And very pretty. And I folded your laundry once last month. Remember that?"

"No," Delphine said. "But fine. What do you need?"

"Wolf stuff," Nessa said. To keep from scaring Delphine,

she added, "I need to understand what happened to me. Are there a lot of wolves coming into our part of the state? Are they causing problems for people or whatever? Is anyone else getting bitten?"

"Okay," Delphine said.

"And also." Nessa cleared her throat. She took a deep breath. "What's with werewolves?"

"Werewolves?" Delphine said, spinning around in the desk chair. "What are you talking about?"

"It's just—" Nessa said. "It's just something I need to know. It's not real or anything. Just, in those dreams…" She let her voice trail off.

Delphine looked at her, clearly wondering if she needed to be worried. "Nessa," she finally said. She didn't sound like she'd been able to reach a decision exactly.

"What?"

Delphine sat very still, staring at her older sister. "Nothing," she replied.

Like the good sister that she was, she gave Nessa a pass. When Delphine turned back to Nessa to make her report, her sister had fallen asleep on the couch.

CHAPTER ELEVEN

During lunch the next day, Nessa went to the library, quickly eating her sandwich on the way. She sat down at a computer terminal and took a deep breath. Would typing the word into the Google search make this real? Would it make her crazy?

She typed anyway. She typed one word, a general word, a word that didn't capture everything that was happening to her, but captured enough.

Wolf

She read things she knew—that wolves mate for life, raise pups in families, hunt in packs, and rarely kill more than they can eat. She read that wolves avoid humans, even though, thanks to humans, there are very few wolves left, where there used to be thousands. She read things she didn't know. Wolves can run for miles without tiring; wolves run on their toes, which gives them a longer stride. An adult wolf weighs in at about 175 pounds, but, working in packs, they hunt mostly moose, which weigh 1,000 pounds or more.

Nessa read that wolves are highly adaptable to different climates and surroundings: forests, grasslands, mountains, swamps, and frozen tundra. She read about wolves using language, the different barks and howls and what they mean. She read about wolves living on the site of the Russian nuclear reactor meltdown at Chernobyl, blocked off to humans for decades. Animals had taken it over, and wolves were thriving again at the top of the food chain.

Nessa opened twelve browser tabs, taking in all of the info. She furrowed her brow. There were wolf-lovers and wolf-haters, blogging opinions to their hearts' content.

But reputable scientific sources were also saying contradictory things. She found out that scientists had been studying wolves on an isolated island in Lake Michigan for five decades. Their reports indicated that wolves never killed for "sport," eating everything they brought down. But then the Oregon Outdoor Council collected news reports going back years showing times when wolves would obliterate farmers' sheep herds, and leave whole carcasses behind.

Do wolves attack humans? The U.S. Fish and Wildlife Service said no, quoting a wildlife ecologist who'd been studying wolves in Yellowstone Park for sixteen years. But then, elsewhere on the same government website, Nessa found a catalog of human-wolf encounters that did not end well for the humans.

Nessa read and read, and took notes, and printed pages. Every question seemed to produce not answers, but more questions. Wolves had poor eyesight. Her eyesight was enhanced, almost perfect. She felt like maybe her research needed to veer into comic books and not these scientific sources.

If wolves had been around for millennia, how was it that science still didn't seem to have a handle on basic facts about them?

And if science was so foggy on wolves, how could she possibly expect to find anything about what was actually happening to her?

Then Nessa felt her blood turn cold. On the fifth page of results following her search for wolves + returning + bite + Michigan, she saw the words "Tether" and "attack."

She clicked through and came to a blog post called "Why I Would Move Away from Tether (If I was stupid enough to live there in the first place)" written by a rancher in Wyoming.

What was someone in Wyoming doing talking about Tether?

Could there possibly be a town called Tether in Wyoming too?

No, Nessa saw, this guy was talking about Tether, Michigan. It was right there in the first sentence of his blog entry.

In the first sentence of his entry was the line: "The best wolf is a dead wolf." He wrote: "The best wolf is a dead wolf, but if you live anywhere near Tether, MI, chances are getting much more likely the wolf is coming to get you."

Nessa read on, all about how wolves coming back into

Wyoming had started attacking his sheep herd, and he had started tracking news reports. He had a link to a website cataloging wolf attacks on animals and humans in the United States and Canada. In the last year, there were eleven attacks on livestock or humans within the Tether town limits, more than any other municipality in the country.

"Not surprising," the rancher went on, "given that the Algonquin word for wolf—'mahigan'—is basically the state name. Don't give me that BS they teach Michigan children in school that it's from the Chippewa 'meicigama,' for great water, after that big lake they've got up there. Which word sounds closer to you?"

Was she living in a state that was basically named after wolves? Was Tether the epicenter of a wolf-demic, as the rancher said?

And if she was, why hadn't she heard anything about it?

Nessa quickly scouted the *Tether Journal*'s website. There wasn't a single report of a wolf attack in the past twelve months. Much less eleven of them. The last mention of any wolf was a sighting at the north end of town four years ago.

Maybe the rancher was just another conspiracy kook. The internet was full of them.

But then she thought of Tucker, the dog her mom had treated the night before school started. And of Dr. Kalish's questions about rabid wolves.

Why Tether? Why wolves?

And why her?

The bell rang, signaling the start of afternoon classes. Nessa carefully erased her browsing history and left.

CHAPTER TWELVE

riday night before October Homecoming weekend, the cross-country team didn't have a regular practice. Instead, they had a stretching session in the gym and then watched *Chariots of Fire*, a movie Coach Hoffman had memorized line for line. Luc slept through it. Hannah looked as nervous as Nessa felt. Cynthia was secretly using her phone.

The boys' soccer team must have been having a light practice as well, because about halfway through the movie, Cassian sneaked in to watch it. He slid into the chair next to Cynthia and poked her in the arm. Then he spun around to face the rest of the cross-country team, as if he were at a party and wanted to see a) who was there, and b) who got how funny it was that he had crashed.

Nessa got how funny it was, and for a second they locked eyes before Cynthia punched him in the arm and said, "What are you doing here?"

"I'm hanging out with you and…uh…" He turned in his seat to face Nessa. "You're a junior, right?" he said.

Nessa swallowed. She laughed. She said, "I'm Nessa," as if she couldn't be both those things at the same time. Cassian didn't say anything else, so she sank back into her seat.

"Cassian Thomas, are you running for me tomorrow?" Coach called out, putting the movie on pause.

"Got it," Cassian said, slowly standing and moving out of the room. "Just trying to bring a little life into this gathering?" Nessa didn't know if she was just imagining it, but he seemed to be looking right at her as he bounced on his heels and out the door.

The movie continued on from there, but Nessa felt less nervous. Cassian had looked at her. He'd *talked* to her.

When Coach turned off the movie again, she realized she had no idea what was going on onscreen. Had it ended?

It must have, because Coach was launching into his pre-race pep talk. "Tomorrow I want all of you to stay loose," he commanded before sending them home to carbo-load and rest. "The weather's going to be unseasonably warm—into the 80s I've heard—so I want you to drink lots of water and stay out of the sun. And most of all, I want you to think about the team, not yourselves. Think of yourself as part of something larger than just one person. You're like a chain, all of you pulling each other along. A team is stronger than any one group of individuals."

He made them stand in a circle with their eyes closed and

call up an image of their best possible race.

Nessa remembered her dream of being a wolf, the feeling of running where running felt more like flying. She remembered what she'd read about wolves running on their toes to extend their stride. She would do that. She wouldn't think about gassing out, about pacing herself. She'd just reach for that feeling of flight.

It had been over a month since the night she'd followed Cynthia. She wouldn't think about the white wolf and the bite, the strange transformations she'd been going through. She'd think about the kernel of speed pulsing just under her sternum. She wanted this more than she'd ever wanted anything in her life, and as far as she could see, she was in a good position to get what she wanted.

"Another full moon, huh?" Luc said, pointing up to the roof of the gym as if it were a stand-in for the sky.

"What's that supposed to mean?" Nessa said, giving him a look.

Luc shrugged. "I don't know. Maybe that we'll have good luck tomorrow?" He offered her a fist bump. Nessa returned it.

But luck, it turned out, was not on Nessa's side.

CHAPTER THIRTEEN

When Nessa woke up the next morning, her body was covered in the same fine, white hair again. Before, it had been a downy covering, a small patch, but this time it was… well, there was no other word for it. It was fur. Her arms, her shoulders, her legs. Horrifying. She ran to the bathroom.

Nessa nearly gagged on panic. Her first thought was that she couldn't race like this, but the panic quickly spiraled. She couldn't leave the bathroom like this. She couldn't *be* like this.

She felt her throat closing off, her heart racing, her breath coming faster. This couldn't be real.

She looked down at the counter, trying to steady herself, but she couldn't. She was breathing too fast. She was going to be sick. She sat down on the closed toilet seat lid. She rubbed her left hand over the hair on her right arm. It was too thick to shave. Too short to cut with scissors. She could still see her skin beneath it, looking like human skin, brown from the summer running, soft like human skin should be, not thick and coarse the way animals' skin often appeared beneath their fur. She tried pulling at the hair—could she pull it out? That only hurt.

Nessa heard a door opening into the hall. Someone was up. Her mom? Delphine? No one could see her like this. She had to hide. She could spend the day in her room. But she'd have to kick Delphine out first. She could move into the garage. She had a sudden image of herself crawling into one of the large dog crates, like the animals who had been afraid of her at the vet's last week.

She looked at her arm again. She rubbed her skin and felt a searing pain when she pushed the hair back. A pressure was building behind her eyes, in her throat. She pressed her hands into her face to try to get some relief.

She had to do something.

Nessa slipped her pajama pants back on and wrapped a towel around her upper body. She opened the bathroom door a crack, stuck her head out into the hall. It was empty. She darted into her bedroom, closed the door behind her. Delphine was still sleeping and the room was dark. Feeling around on her closet shelf, Nessa located a hoodie and, tossing the towel to the floor, pulled the hoodie over her head. There hadn't been any hair on her face, but she kept the hood up anyway, pulling the laces to cinch the opening as tightly closed as she could and still be able to see. Reaching into her sweatshirt, she pulled out the wolf tooth necklace and ran it under her fingers, a soothing gesture that had become a habit.

When Nessa opened the bottom drawer of her dresser, it made a sound, and Delphine rolled over. "Wham op," she murmured.

"Go back to sleep," Nessa said in a voice she was trying to keep low and normal. What she'd really wanted to say was, "OH MY GOD DELPHINE HELP ME OH MY GOD WHAT AM I GOING TO DO OH MY GOD!!!!"

Nessa started pulling clothing out of a drawer. Even though the room was dark, she could see perfectly what each item was. Which only freaked her out more. These were the mixed-up running clothes she didn't wear a lot: the shorts with the stretched-out waistband for laundry emergencies, the long-sleeved tee with one of the cuffs ripped off, some fleece-lined warm-up pants for super cold weather. Finally she found what she was looking for: her running tights, a polypropylene running shirt, and, for good measure, her running gloves. Baggy track pants, too, because she was afraid the tights would show the fur beneath. She was going to roast in these things, but what choice did she have?

She had friggin' white fur all over her body.

Nessa was going to have to go to the doctor. But not yet. Not today. Going to the doctor meant telling her mom and telling her mom meant…well, it just couldn't be done. She was going to run in this race—she just had to. Homecoming weekend was the first meet recruiters would look at. Her score here would help her qualify for States. This was how she was going to get to Regionals, to Nationals, to college. Nessa squeezed her eyes closed and fought back a surge of panic.

What if a doctor couldn't help her? What if no one could? What was happening to Nessa had probably never happened to anyone before.

Darting back through the hall with her hood still pulled up

over her head, Nessa closed the bathroom door, locked it, and leaned against it, almost as if she'd been chased. She kept the lights off and didn't look in the mirror. She wondered if maybe she was in shock. She wondered if maybe this was a hallucination.

She wondered if she was going to sweat to death running in Lycra tights and track pants and a hoodie.

She didn't have a choice.

She called Bree. "I can't bike to school," she said. "Can you give me a ride?"

"Nessa, um, are you okay?" Bree said. The races had already started and Nessa was hiding in Bree's car in the parking lot. She'd texted Coach Hoffman, letting him know she would be late but that she would be there before the race began.

Looking out the window, she could see people moving toward the racecourse from the parking lot—parents, dogs, and siblings. Kids dressed for their own soccer games still in shin guards. Other athletes from the high school starting to assemble for games held later in the day.

At Homecoming in Tether, all sports competed in what was a town-wide event. Almost everybody was a parent or grand-parent or aunt or uncle or cousin of someone competing for the school. The student council was selling coffee and donuts by the football bleachers. Later in the day, they'd switch over to hotdogs and soda, though with the sun already heating up the air as if it were a summer morning and not a week into October, they probably could have made a killing on Popsicles. That night there would be a dance. Bree's slinky pink dress had *barely* passed the Mom Test (Dad being fortunately out of town). She'd figured out something for Nessa too. They were going in the Monster.

But not like this.

"Can you please explain what is going on?" Bree said. "What's with the sudden body image issues?"

Nessa rolled her eyes. Out of nervousness more than anything, she choked out a laugh. Bree straightened up in her seat, pulling on the steering wheel, proud of herself for breaking the tension.

The cross-country meets were held early in the day, with the freshmen races already over and JV girls off and running a few minutes before—Nessa had heard them called to the starting line by the announcer.

Strangely, she'd heard other stuff as well. She'd heard the nervous exhalations of her team members. She'd heard the squeak of leather as a JV runner made one last adjustment to her shoelaces. By now the varsity girls would be stretching and warming up, she knew. It was time to go, but she couldn't get herself to leave Bree's car. She'd even insisted that Bree park it in the back corner of the lot, far away from where anyone would see.

"I just can't go over there yet," Nessa said. "I'm not ready."

Bree gave her a quizzical look. "Are you that nervous? Your race starts soon."

Nessa shrugged.

"And aren't you going to roast in long sleeves and—?" Bree looked at Nessa's outfit as if searching for language to convey her disdain. "Nun garb?"

Nessa just shook her head, turned her phone on to see the time, then turned it off, a gesture she'd repeated about ten times in the last minute.

She wished she could explain to Bree what was happening,

but she was coasting on what felt to her like a thin surface tension of sanity. One tiny wiggle of the glass and everything would collapse. She didn't have a plan besides some half-formed thought that the less time she spent outside the car, the less chance she had of getting noticed.

"Can you do me a favor?" Nessa said. Bree leveled her a look.

"*Another* favor?" Nessa corrected.

Bree nodded.

"Go tell Coach I'm in the bathroom. Tell him I'll meet the team at the starting line. Make it sound like I'm sick but be very clear: I'm going to run."

"But why?" Bree said. "Why not go tell him yourself?"

"Just please?" Nessa could hear how plaintive her voice sounded. "I need you to help me. Get my race bib from him. Tell him I asked you."

"Okay," Bree said skeptically, getting out of the car. Bree rushed to join the little groups of fans heading up from the parking lot—Tether families and parents of runners from other towns. Nessa spotted Cassian, already in his cleats and soccer uniform. It felt like such a long time ago that he'd snuck into the *Chariots of Fire* screening, that he'd been so funny and cool and had looked at her like he finally could tell that she was there.

She lost him in a crowd of his friends, and then she remembered to track Bree's pink Tether High sweatshirt. But Bree had also moved out of sight. Nessa turned her phone on, checked the time, turned it off.

It was getting harder and harder to depress the tiny buttons. Was she just nervous, or had her hands started to swell?

And was there any possible universe where what she was planning to do might work?

CHAPTER FOURTEEN

After delivering her message to Coach Hoffman and picking up Nessa's race bib, Bree meant to go straight back to her car to check on Nessa. But the sophomores who were in charge of the student council stand had run out of water and they waylaid her. She explained how to get more from the side spigot—sophomores could be clueless—and then Bree saw Cassian heading over to the table.

Suddenly she heard the announcer calling over the sound system that all varsity racers should come to the starting line. Had Nessa heard? Where was she? But then Cassian was there, ordering a donut, and Bree stepped in front of the sophomores so she could be the one to take his order. Being an upperclassman had to mean something!

Bree put the change into Cassian's palm.

"Did you join the track team?" he asked, scarfing a huge bite of cinnamon cruller. He pointed to Nessa's race bib.

Nessa! Bree thought.

"Uh, no, it's my friend's," Bree stuttered. "I've got to get it to her."

"I'll say," Cassian replied. "The race is about to start." He turned to his friend, Evan Branchik, and nodded toward the track. "Let's go. I told Cynthia we'd watch her."

As soon as he turned away, Bree was off like a shot.

"Nessa!" she yelled, careening toward her car.

Bree intercepted her friend and handed Nessa the bib as she jogged past across the grass toward the starting line.

Nessa was still dressed all in black, including black gloves and a baseball cap Bree recognized as her dad's—the Peterbilt hat he'd brought back from his last cross-country haul, boxy and not Bree's style, a literal trucker cap. Not wanting to hurt her dad's feelings, Bree had worn it out of the house the day he gave it to her and then left it in the back seat of the Monster.

Bree jogged after Nessa, catching up to her just as Coach Hoffman did. He was waving frantically, shouting an exasperated, "Where have you been?" Before Nessa could begin to explain—and Bree for one was getting curiouser and curiouser about what that explanation might be—the final call for the race sounded and Coach Hoffman shooed Nessa toward the line. He gave her a meaningful we'll-talk-later look for good measure.

Bree followed Nessa at a brisk walk and by the time Bree reached the starting line, weaving among spectators, she had said, "Excuse me," and "Sorry about that," and "Pardon" about a dozen times. Nessa was already standing on the line, looking like a crazy person with her hat pulled down over her eyes and her tiny racing tank top stretched over a black hoodie, her legs hidden by the track pants she'd been wearing in the car. A few of the other runners gave her strange looks. Bree went from feeling exasperated with Nessa to feeling protective in the space of half a breath.

Nessa had barely been on the line thirty seconds when the starting horn sounded and the girls shot off, quickly forming a pack with one racer—not from Tether—out in front. The other runners fell into two clumps behind her.

Bree knew that the girl out in front wasn't going to win. "You never want to be that person," Nessa had told her. It was easier, physically and mentally, to hang out in that early runner's tailwind, and then, depending on how fast you could run and how long you could maintain a sprint, make your move about a mile or a half mile from the end of the course.

Bree spotted Cynthia about halfway back in the first pack, just where you were supposed to be. Nessa was trailing behind her. In her hat and baggy clothing, Nessa looked weighed down and out of place as the group of racers ran a perimeter of the playing fields, and then cut into the woods. "Nessa, get up there," Bree said out loud, but under her breath. Some guys from another school who were standing near her thought she was talking to them.

"Everything okay there?" one said. Bree gave him a little wave, and then hurried to the other end of the field, where she knew she would be able to see the runners emerge from the trail with about a quarter mile to go before the end of the race.

The race photographer was already there.

Bree waited at the end of the woods for ten minutes. Finally, she saw the race photographer crouch down into ready position and put his eye to the camera. Bree looked for the lead racer.

What came next happened so fast that Bree's brain didn't process it until it was over. Suddenly, there was Nessa—incognito Nessa in gloves and a hat and all black—streaking past Bree like a gazelle, her feet almost perfectly quiet on the path, her legs stretching long, her arms held close to her side, as if nothing she was doing required the slightest effort on her part.

Bree couldn't see Nessa's face, but she could see how still every part of her body had become. She knew how intensely Nessa must be concentrating. And then behind Nessa—a good eight seconds behind—came another girl, wearing purple, from who-knew-what school. She was absolutely flying also, her feet touching the ground at a pace Bree could not have reached for even a short sprint. Behind the purple girl was a pack of three runners, including Cynthia. She looked like a pure arrow of intention slicing through the air in front of her. But Nessa led. By a wide margin.

Bree had not so much as closed her mouth when it was all over. She had not had a chance to cheer Nessa's name. "Wow," she said to herself as that freshman Nessa had been so worried about—Hannah—crossed in front of her. "Wow," Bree said again before jogging to the finish line to find Nessa, to jump on top of her. Bree had never been so proud of anyone in her life.

By the time Bree reached the area near the finish line, it was crowded with varsity finishers, not to mention sweaty survivors of the JV and freshman heats, their parents, their dogs on leashes, their colorful sports drinks, their cameras, little kids sitting up on shoulders or chasing each other in and out of everyone's legs. Nessa was tall. She should have been easy to spot wearing the Peterbilt hat, but Bree could not find her and ended up turning around in circles just looking. But Nessa was not to be found.

Suddenly she was face-to-face with Luc Restouille, and no matter what Nessa said about him, Bree thought he was even better looking up close than he was from a distance, with his intense black eyes, olive skin, jet-black hair, and those cheek-bones.

"You're Nessa's friend, right?" he asked.

Bree nodded.

"Have you seen her? She took off after the race."

"She did?" Bree was confused. It was hard to think straight with Luc looking at her. She couldn't tell if he was angry or amused.

"Yeah, she ran so hard she should have been puking on the sidelines, but she just kept going. I don't even think she slowed down."

"I was wondering," Bree said, "where she was."

"If you find her, tell her she broke the course record." He shook his head like he was still digesting the news. "By ten seconds."

"Wow," said Bree. Records were usually broken by half-second differences in time.

Before Bree could think of anything to say, Luc was gone.

Bree had to run to the grocery store for more sodas for the

student council concession and by the time she got worried enough about Nessa to go looking for her, it was already afternoon. She looked at the soccer game and went by football and concluded Nessa was no longer at school. With a sigh, Bree left the shouts and yells of the games she wanted to watch behind, and headed for Nessa's house.

No one was home, which made sense. Everyone in Tether who wasn't working would be at Homecoming right now. Bree knocked a few times anyway. *Nessa was probably watching Cassian take a corner kick*, she thought. Just in case she *was* wrong, Bree tried the door anyway. It was open.

Bree called Nessa's name and made her way through the house. She poked her head in the kitchen and climbed the stairs until she reached the closed door of the room Nessa and Delphine shared. Standing outside, she gave a light knock, and when there was no answer, she tried the handle. It was locked.

"Nessa," she said. "Are you in there? I saw your finish. It was…amazing. Luc was asking about you. Everyone was. Coach Hoffman accepted your trophy. You won a trophy. Isn't that awesome? He said you broke the course record. Did you know that? You broke it by ten seconds!"

Bree thought she heard movement. But still no answer. "Nessa?"

Something Bree liked about Nessa was how undramatic she was. How honest. Nessa was not the type to lock herself in her room to get attention. This had to be something serious.

"Nessa, open the door," Bree said in the firm voice she used when freshmen showed up to the first student council meeting of the year with "ideas" about changing the cafeteria menu or staging a dance *every* weekend. "I'm starting to get worried."

"I'll be okay," Nessa said from inside, her voice muffled like she had her face buried in her pillow.

"You don't seem okay," Bree stated. "I'm your best friend, and I can tell. You know you can trust me. Open up this door, tell me what's going on, and we'll figure out what to do."

From inside the room: nothing.

Bree waited. There was nothing like having a truck driver for a father to teach you that silence can sometimes be the best strategy to win a negotiation. But silence was not Bree's strength, and she was already thinking that she'd been quiet long enough and it was time to start threatening, when there was a squeak of bed springs and a thump from inside the room, like Nessa's feet had just hit the floor. Bree heard steps. She felt the doorknob move as Nessa turned it and yanked the door open. Bree gasped.

"Oh. My. God."

CHAPTER FIFTEEN

$\mathcal{B}$ree was too stunned to scream.

In a flash of movement, Nessa pulled her friend inside and slammed the door shut behind her. As her eyes became accustomed to the dim light, Bree saw that Nessa had changed into a gray tank top and shorts. And suddenly the baggy black race outfit made horrifying sense. Nessa was covered in a beautiful silver-white fur. The long hairs had an opal sheen that seemed to capture and reflect the light. Nessa's arms, her legs, her chest, and the backs of her hands were covered in it.

The two friends locked eyes. Nessa's were filled with tears.

Nessa's face looked the same: her strong jaw, straight nose, and full lips. Her piercing blue eyes rimmed by thick lashes.

But Bree wasn't looking at Nessa's eyes. She was looking at the line of fuzz across Nessa's cheeks. She was looking at her hairline, which seemed to be descending down her forehead in a point of darker silver. Nessa was standing straight-backed, like someone trying to be brave, her eyes focused on a point above Bree's left shoulder.

Nessa held her breath while she waited for Bree to do the obvious—run, screaming.

But Bree stayed.

Yes, she was collapsed against the wall like she had lost the ability to stand. Yes, she wasn't looking Nessa right in the eye. But she was here.

"What…what happened to you?" Bree said. Her voice was shaking, but she sounded pretty sure that Nessa had an explanation.

"Remember the wolf bite?" Nessa asked.

Bree nodded.

"You know how it healed faster than Dr. Kalish expected?" Nessa asked. "*Much* faster?"

Bree nodded again, wide-eyed.

"After the bite healed, everything began to change. I can see without my contacts. I can smell…*everything*. I can hear my mom buttering toast when I'm in the garage. And I'm running faster."

Bree didn't know what to say.

"Gabe! I remember when you heard Gabe from upstairs during our study group!" Bree whispered.

"It all got stronger as the moon grew full," Nessa said quietly. "Day by day. A few days ago the…hair…started to appear. But it washed off. Or I could rub it off, at any rate."

Nessa took a deep breath, and Bree thought it sounded more like an animal than a human.

"And then today I woke up, and, well, you can see for yourself."

"Nessa, I can't believe this," Bree said. She felt many things but number one was sympathy for her friend. "Are you *okay*?"

Nessa let out a barking laugh. "No," she said, sighing again. It was good to have Bree here.

Bree's mind was spinning. "Does anyone else know?"

Nessa shook her head. She wasn't used to putting her problems on other people. And this was more than a problem. This was…what?

"I don't know what to do," Nessa said. She had to stifle a sob. Several long seconds passed.

For once, Bree had nothing to say.

"Have you thought about going to the doctor?"

Nessa shook her head. "I don't think doctors are really going to know what to do with this."

"Yeah," said Bree. "But Selena might."

"Selena? Your mom's friend from work?"

Bree nodded. Nessa took a deep breath and let it out slowly, the way you might if you felt really, really nauseated but were trying not to throw up.

Bree's mom worked in an insurance claims processing office in the industrial park south of the town center. Selena worked there too. She was the one who got Bree's mom into native healing practices. They took it very seriously and even had a study group.

"Is it okay if I try her?" Bree asked in a hushed voice, pointing at her cell phone.

"Listen, I've turned into a wolf. I haven't been in a friggin' car accident," Nessa said. "You can talk in a normal voice."

Bree was already punching numbers into her cell phone. When Selena picked up, Bree described what was happening, and answered a few questions—where the fur was, how long it had lasted, and where they were right that minute, and hung up. "She's on her way. She says she knows a shaman you need to see right away."

"Leave it to Selena to act as if turning into a werewolf was an everyday sort of thing, with a shaman to match," Nessa said glumly. Which made them both laugh.

The next half hour lasted forever. Bree tried to look at one of Delphine's magazines. Nessa tried not to pace like a wolf.

She didn't know what the most frightening part of it all was, that it was happening—that there was *fur all over her body*—or that it kept getting worse. The fur was even thicker now than it had been that morning, and it was forming on her face, on the tops of her feet, on the back of her hands. Her joints ached just like when she'd had her last growth spurt: her elbows and knees especially, but also her shoulders and hips.

Nessa had started to pant like a wolf. She was trying to keep it under control, but sitting on the edge of her bed, her newly misshapen hands hidden between her knees, Nessa found it was getting harder and harder to breathe like a normal human being: through the nose. It took all of Nessa's self-control to keep her lips closed.

"Look," she said, showing Bree her hands. The swelling and puffiness was exaggerated by the thickness of the fur, but still, you could see they were rounder and blockier than they'd been even that morning. Opening the door to let Bree into the room, Nessa had looked at her hand on the knob—seen how it was difficult to grasp. Her knuckles seemed gnarled, like her grandma's had been when she was having arthritis flare-ups.

Bree shook her head, looked away. She didn't know how to help Nessa. "Selena will know what to do," she kept repeating. "This must be a *thing*, it must have happened before."

"God, I hope so," Nessa murmured. She shook her head. Nessa didn't have much faith that a shaman would help. She imagined a man who would be middle-aged like Selena, peaceful, "wise," with shelves of jars and herbal supplements, and a beard and faded jeans—one of those sad, alternative-life-style people who drone on about finding your personal power but seem to have very little themselves.

But when Selena arrived, she looked less middle-aged and frumpy than Nessa remembered—she was wearing tight jeans, a long-sleeved black tee shirt, and sunglasses pushed up into her short salt-and-pepper hair. Her car keys were still in her hand when she stopped short at the sight of Nessa and said, "Oh," then, "Yeah." She looked Nessa in the eye. "You need to see Chay."

"Okay," Nessa agreed.

"First, you should cover up," Selena ordered. She pulled the discarded track pants off the floor, grabbed the Peterbilt hat from the closet doorknob, and threw an oversized plaid shirt around Nessa's shoulders. "Better. Let's get going. I don't know much about this. Shape-shifting is esoteric teaching. But the sooner Chay sees you, the better. I know that."

As they were loading up into her Subaru plastered with

bumper stickers with slogans like "Be the Peace You Want to See in the World," Nessa looked back at her house. On the one hand, she was deeply glad her mom was out of town, visiting Aunt Jane for her fortieth birthday with Nate and Delphine. On the other hand, she also irrationally wished that Vivian were home to save her and make all of this go away.

Nessa climbed into the backseat, and Selena said to Bree, "Get in the back with her."

"Why?" said Bree, her voice high and light. "What could happen?"

"I have no idea," said Selena. "But if I were her, I'd be scared out of my mind, and I am guessing she is too."

Nessa choked back a sob.

Then Selena pulled out of the drive and down the street quickly, like they couldn't get to where they were going fast enough.

CHAPTER SIXTEEN

*I*n In the back seat of Selena's car, Nessa's phone buzzed. Bree picked it up for her and showed her the text. It was from Coach Hoffman.

> What happened? Where are you? Everything okay? I have a trophy for you. You broke the course record! Call me ASAP.

"I can't talk to him!" Nessa said, shout-whispering as if he might be able to hear.

"You have to sooner or later," Bree said.

"Just text back that I'm okay. Tell him I had a stomachache."

Bree typed the message and pressed send. Not ten seconds later, there was a response.

Drink lots of fluids. Call me please.

Using the one finger that she could still move, Nessa powered off her phone.

"If you don't talk to him, he's going to really worry. You've got to, or he's going to think something's wrong with you," hissed Bree.

"Something *is* wrong with me," Nessa answered.

Coach knew her. She couldn't get on the phone with him and not have him know something was going on. He would be able to tell. She looked at the frown lines of worry on Bree's forehead. "I'll call later," Nessa said. "I promise."

Selena's shaman friend lived on the side of town where the railroad station used to be, back when Tether had a railroad station. That was 50 years ago—even Vivian didn't remember when the train lines were in operation. The old depot had become a grain and feed store for farmers, with the surrounding warehouses repurposed as businesses that never lasted very long.

Selena pulled into a small mechanic's repair shop behind the old depot and stopped the car.

"Mike's" was painted over an old Exxon sign, its logo still visible.

"The shaman is Mike?"

"No, Mike's his friend. Mike's a guy who works on cars and rents out rooms in the back to his friends. It's kind of like a clubhouse for guys in their group."

It didn't look like a clubhouse. It didn't even look like a place you'd want to take your car. The asphalt was patched and pocked with holes, the gas pumps had been removed, though you could see the concrete block where they had once stood, and two ancient Buicks with $3,200 written on their windshields in soap were parked off to the side.

The only thing in the place that looked new or well cared for was a single motorcycle—a gleaming Harley with shining chrome and high handlebars and black leather saddlebags that looked like they'd been recently oiled.

Nessa wasn't moving. She didn't like the looks of this at all. She could see Bree didn't either.

"The shaman lives *here*?" Bree said.

"Not permanently. He's been traveling. He's got some personal stuff he's working out," Selena replied. "Follow me."

"Okaaaay," Nessa said, opening the back door of the car and taking a deep breath before standing. She pulled the hat down lower over her face, the shirt closer around her body. She felt like every pair of eyeballs in the universe was focused right on her, even though the parking lot appeared to be deserted.

Through two open garage bays, Nessa could see an antique Porsche of some kind up on a hydraulic lift with a guy working underneath. What was *that* doing here? She heard the clink of tools, the tightening of a ratchet, a radio playing hard rock. Selena made her way toward the guy working on the car. He was heavy, dressed in a filthy jumpsuit and big boots, curly dark hair trailing down his back and dirty hands. "Can I help you?" he said.

Nessa kept her eyes focused on the ground, her hat brim pulled low, her hands hidden behind her back. She hunched her shoulders to provide an extra aura of protection.

"Chayton's in the back," the big man grunted, recognizing Selena.

From the corner of her eye, Nessa saw him toss his wrench

into a wooden box of tools, then take a long draw on a beer that he seemed to have stowed in one of the pockets of his coveralls. Finally, he pulled on a welder's helmet, flipped down the visor, and fired up his torch.

"Nice. Operating heavy machinery while drinking," Bree muttered sarcastically under her breath, as Nessa smelled burning metal. Was the shaman—Chayton?—going to be like Mike?

"Follow me," Selena told the two girls, leading the way through a door in the back of the garage. Nessa followed, checking back quickly to make sure Bree was behind her. Bree gave her an eyebrows-raised, I'm-just-as-clueless-as-you-are-but-I've-got-your-back look of reassurance.

They entered a little apartment behind the garage. Its door opened to a living room, man-cave style. It was dark and carpeted in brown high plush, with wood paneling on the walls, a nasty brown velour sectional sofa, and a bar with stools. A man was standing at the bar with his back to them, a laptop open on the bar. Because he had his shirt off and his arms braced on either side of the computer, Nessa could see two things about him right away. The first was that he was *cut*. Rippling muscles stood out in relief across his broad-shouldered back.

But what caused Nessa to stop was the man's tattoo.

Blue and gray ink stretched across his back and shoulder blades depicting a lake, pine trees, a moon, a wolf. Something about it seemed specific and familiar, like she'd seen it before. She almost felt she could name the lake.

The man straightened, flexing his back muscles, but didn't turn to face them. Nessa got the feeling—she wasn't sure where it came from—that he was waiting for her to make a move. Or to make a mistake.

"Chayton," Selena said in greeting, and finally, the man pushed up off the counter and turned around. His eyes were large and his skin was clear—it seemed almost to glow with health and life. Then he reached down to the bar stool and pulled a shirt on over his head. Even in that gesture, he exuded so much power, Nessa felt herself preparing for danger the way she did in the presence of a Rottweiler at the vet's. Selena walked up to him to kiss him on the cheek. "This is Nessa. The girl I was telling you about on the phone. The one who—" Even Selena sounded a little flustered in his presence.

Suddenly, Nessa felt it was important that she speak for herself.

"I was bitten by a wolf," Nessa said, feeling his eyes move onto hers. He looked at her steadily, and then, like he had all the time in the world, he smiled a slow, in-joke, smile.

"Yeah," he said. "I can see that." Then he looked Nessa up and down like she was for sale and scowled. "You're the white girl who's shifting."

If he'd pushed her, Nessa could not have been more confused by him. What did being a white girl have to do with any of this?

"After the bite," Nessa went on, her eyes traveling to Bree's and Selena's, then back to Chayton, who had not stopped staring at her in a way that was making her blush, "stuff started happening."

Chayton nodded, crossed his arms, listening.

"First it was my hearing," Nessa went on, determined not to let him intimidate her.

"And she can see better," Bree piped in.

"I can see without my contacts. I smell everything."

"I bet you do," Chayton said.

"And I'm running faster," Nessa added.

"She's on the cross-country team," Bree explained.

"Yeah, and there's this," Nessa added. She took off her hat and the plaid flannel shirt. She still wore her gray tank top, but the white fur was everywhere.

Chay took her wrist and pinched the fur sprouting from it.

"Beautiful," he said. Even though he had directed the comment to Selena, as if she were a horse he was examining, when Chayton smoothed the hairs back into place, the gesture did more to calm her than anything she'd felt in a long time.

He bent to examine her wrist more closely, and she noticed Chayton's smoothed-back black hair looked clean and soft and smelled of musk and clean oils. The skin on his collarbone glowed in the dim room, and Nessa had the sudden urge to touch it.

Then Nessa's necklace caught Chayton's eye. "That's quite a talisman you're wearing," he said.

Nessa reached for the wolf tooth, hiding it with her fingertips. "It's just a necklace," she said. "My sister made it."

"Oh, it's *just* a necklace?" he asked. He gestured to her body with an open hand. "And this is just a shape you happened to shift into?"

Nessa felt herself blushing again. She knew it wasn't safe to feel this off balance. Screwing up her courage, she said, "Look. Selena said you can help me. Can you? 'Cause you don't look like a shaman to me. You look too young."

Chayton tucked his chin, looked down at Nessa through half-closed eyes. Then he did something with his shoulders, and somehow, she knew what this movement meant. It meant: So you want to play with the big boys, do you?

He suddenly shifted topic.

"You know that no one can know about this," Chayton said, turning to Selena and then zeroing in on Bree, who looked scared. "Are you someone who can keep a secret?"

Bree raised herself up and nodded vigorously. From the look on her face, Nessa wondered what Chayton might have asked her that she wouldn't have agreed to. He arched his back, and Nessa saw Bree staring at his chest as he strolled lazily across the room. "Selena," he said, "I'd like to speak to...Nessa, is it?" He looked at Nessa. Nessa nodded. "Alone."

Selena pulled Bree away. "We'll be nearby. Just come get us when you're done," she said, before pulling the door shut.

Chayton sat down on the ancient couch. He gestured for Nessa to sit on the opposite end. Nessa sat.

"I'm twenty-three," he said. "That old enough for you?"

Nessa nodded. "I didn't mean—" she began.

"Forget it." He grimaced in a way that made her suddenly wonder if she had actually hurt his feelings.

"Are you really a shaman?" she said.

"I don't say shaman," he said. "I practice Shamanism, but the title shaman—that's not something you call yourself." He reached for her hand and pulled it toward him. He held her forearm and wrist between both of his, and gently turned it over so her hand was palm up. Then he put two fingers from his opposite hand on her wrist, and asked, "Are you really a wolf?"

Nessa felt her throat go dry. Chayton was looking her directly in the eye, and she couldn't keep her eyes locked on his. It was too intense.

"Maybe?" she said.

Chayton shook his head, like he should have known better than to trust her with a question of that magnitude. Keeping his finger on her wrist, he looked at his watch, counting in silence. It took Nessa a few beats to realize he was measuring her pulse. "Hmm," he said, nodding. "May I see your tongue?"

"I'm not sick."

"No," he said. "You're in perfect health. Except you're turning into a wolf. Tongue."

Nessa leaned forward, opened her mouth, and stuck out her tongue, feeling ridiculous as Chayton moved his head from one side to the other, examining it from different angles. Nessa wondered if he was doing this just to punish her. She still had the feeling he was angry.

"Something *is* wrong with me," she said at last, though it came out garbled because her tongue was still extended.

Chayton made a gesture with his first finger, like he was reeling in fishing line. Nessa put her tongue back.

"Nothing is *wrong* with you," Chayton said. "I wanted to see how your body is reacting to the change. Eastern medicine teaches us how much you can tell about a body from a pulse and examination of the tongue. You're in good health, at least. Sometimes, those who are chosen reject the animal, but you are strong." He paused. "Do you have experience with animals?"

Nessa nodded.

"I thought so."

"You practice Eastern medicine, too?" Nessa ventured.

"Every culture learns in its own way, adapts, and discovers. You learn what the people need. Back to you, though. What were you doing out in the woods at night?" He sat back and crossed a foot over a knee, as if he were expecting her to give him the long answer.

"I was running. For cross-country practice. I'd tried to meet up with another girl on my team. One night, about a month ago. But I was late, so I was running alone, trying to catch up to her when I came upon a wolf in a trap. In the woods behind Joe Bent's farm."

Chayton leaned forward, like this was highly interesting. "The wolf who bit you was in a trap?"

"No, that was another wolf," Nessa said.

"There were *two* wolves?" This seemed to strike him. "What did they each look like?"

Nessa took a deep breath. "The wolf in the trap was very big and had matted fur. Brown with white markings. He was frustrated and in obvious pain, but not violent. The wolf who bit me," Nessa paused. "He was white. I didn't get a good look at him but I keep seeing him. All the time. In my dreams."

"You've been dreaming about the white wolf?" Chayton asked, as if this was the detail he found most relevant. "What color eyes does this wolf in your dreams have? Is it also over-sized? And does it snarl at you?"

Nessa answered as best she could.

"The wolf's eyes are dark. It's bigger than other wolves in the pack. It hasn't snarled at me, I don't think," Nessa rushed through the details.

"And you were bitten a month ago, at the last full moon. How long since the changes began?"

"About two weeks ago. The wound healed faster than the doctor expected."

"What doctor?"

"Doctor Kalish," Nessa said. "At the clinic."

Chay looked truly concerned for the first time.

"At the clinic," he repeated. "You got medical treatment there?"

"They took me there," she said, almost apologetically. "I was unconscious after the bite. The last thing I remember is the big white wolf lunging toward me, and I woke up in the clinic. Joe Bent found me. But he didn't see any wolves, not even the wolf in the trap."

"What time of day is your hearing and running best?"

"Night," Nessa said, although she hadn't truly considered it before. She'd been so busy reacting to the incredible changes that she had not noticed some of the patterns he was calling out until now.

"And you dreamed the hair before it appeared?"

Nessa nodded.

"It fell off in the shower," she told him. "The first two times. But now it seems permanent. Do you know? *Is* this permanent?"

"Were you running last night?" he asked instead of answering. "Have you been running at all by the moonlight during this full moon?"

"Um," Nessa said. "I don't really pay attention to the moon that much." Nessa was getting overwhelmed. She could feel it. She was starting to wonder about Selena and Bree—to think maybe she should bring them back into the room. Or better yet, leave.

"The moon matters. You haven't noticed it calling you?"

"I mean, yeah, maybe? I just…I don't know. Do you think all of this could have been some kind of mistake?"

"A mistake?" Chayton said. And then he stopped asking

questions and just looked at Nessa for a minute, a blank but calm expression on his face. "No, it's not a mistake. I'd like to do some drumming. Do you mind?"

Nessa shrugged. She was losing patience. And she did mind. "I just want to get this fixed before my mom comes home."

"Yeah," Chayton said, as if this confirmed what he already suspected. "We're going to have to get out the drum."

But Chayton didn't use an actual drum. He tapped out a rhythm on the table in front of them, instructed Nessa to match it, and then while she kept the main beat, he started to improvise.

Nessa was never the most musical of human beings, and she had to really focus on keeping her part of the beat steady, especially when Chayton was off on his little drumming tangents. As she did this, she wasn't sure if it was something happening inside her head or in some objective space, but it was there, the beat, and she could feel her head nodding and her brain relaxing.

Nessa decided she liked the drumming.

And she didn't feel like leaving anymore. She didn't need to go get Selena. She didn't need to get this wolf problem fixed. She didn't need to worry about when her next training run should be and if she should stretch out her stride or go for interval training. She didn't need to worry about anything. The way Chayton was looking at her, the rhythm that seemed to organize her mind—Nessa felt more relaxed than she had in days. This room wasn't dark and nasty after all. It was a sanctuary.

Chayton stopped the drumming and put his hands over Nessa's to let her know she could stop as well. She took a long, slow, deep breath.

"Do you notice that?" Chayton said. "The way you're feeling now?"

Nessa nodded. "Did the drumming do that?" she asked.

"Yes, and now you're going to be more relaxed, but don't worry. You're still in control. Just feeling content. I had to put you in this state because I'm flying a little blind here. I've never worked with someone like you before, and I need you to leave all your uptight personal material behind for a little bit."

Nessa might have been offended but wasn't.

He continued, "This is the state where you're going to be able to understand the things I need to tell you."

Nessa nodded, feeling happy and relaxed. She scooted closer to Chayton on the couch. "I think you're very handsome," she said. And as she said that, she had to wonder: Why hadn't she said it before?

Chayton nodded indulgently. "We can talk more about that later."

"But let's not forget," Nessa said.

For some reason, Chayton laughed softly.

"Am I being funny?" Nessa said. "I feel kind of funny."

"No, you're being perfect," Chayton said. "Don't worry about anything, just listen to me. You're ready to listen, right?"

"I'm listening," Nessa responded.

"Okay. Because this is important. This could save your life."

Nessa nodded, more because she wanted Chayton to know she was following his instructions than because she felt any of the urgency he was expressing.

"The first thing you need to understand is that you have been chosen," Chayton said simply. "You have been chosen by the wolves. They have called you to help."

"Help with what?"

"That's the question you need to figure out. They know something is not right in their world. In our world."

"A wolf bit me," Nessa said.

"A wolf *chose* you," Chayton corrected her. He put a hand on her hip where the teeth had gone in, even though she hadn't told him which hip had been bitten, or pointed out exactly where. "If the wolf had wanted to harm you, you would not be walking right now."

"That was what Dr. Kalish said," Nessa commented sleepily. "A wolf's jaws could sever muscle and break bone." She shivered lightly at the thought, though generally she couldn't even go near it in her mind. Chayton got closer to her on the couch, fingered the tooth talisman. Nessa loved the feeling of having him this close to her.

"The wolf gave you this tooth," Chay went on. "He gave you a part of himself. He is a part of you now. He has made it so you will run like him. You will smell, see, hear like him. You will assume his shape. But you must be careful. You do not want to disappoint the wolves. You must always bring your best self to them."

"That sounds like a lot of pressure," Nessa said.

"That's why I'm explaining it slowly," Chayton said. "I'm trying to put it into words you can understand. The first few transformations are important. The wolves don't know who you are yet. They're trying to figure out what kind of wolf you are. You won't be able to tell what they're thinking, but if you want to check in on how your wolf-personality is emerging, pay attention to the way people are seeing you when you're in human form. You're going to get attention, and it's going to be different from any attention you've gotten before."

Nessa thought of Cassian paying attention to her suddenly.

"Do you have a girlfriend?" Nessa asked and then before he could answer her question, she spoke exactly what came into her mind. "A guy like you? You probably have a girlfriend."

Chayton shook his head again, smiling. "You're going to remember what I'm telling you, okay? Because I've got a lot of stuff going down in my life, and I don't have time to be babysitting a white girl."

"For the record, I think you're being a little bit racist."

Chayton cocked his head, pulled back. "Me, racist? That's where you want to go right now? Let's get back to the part where I talk and you listen."

Nessa nodded. "Gotcha," she said. "Lay it on me."

"So one, be good. There's a reason the wolves chose you. Be pure of intention. Let the wolves see you. You got that?"

"Yup."

"You need to pay attention to the moon," he said. "Eventually you'll get yourself under control and you will shift when you're ready. You'll learn not to always shift with the moon, though that's harder. For now, you're going to be pretty powerless around the moon. The full moon. And the new moon."

"I thought people—" Even in the state Chayton had brought her to, Nessa had a hard time saying the word "werewolf." "I thought people who changed into wolves had to be locked up at the full moon and stuff. I thought they were…monsters."

"Yeah, maybe in Victorian London. But the Victorians were the ones who brought us the straightjacket as a treatment for depression, and decided eugenics was a science. Here in the United States, they ripped an entire generation of my people's kids away from their families and sent them to boarding schools where they were systematically stripped of all connection to their native culture."

"Wow, the Victorians sucked."

Nessa saw that grimace again—that flash of Chayton looking for one second like he was not completely in control of his feelings. He took a breath, repeated the drumming rhythm on the table. "Keep in mind," he continued, "that at the new moon and the full moon, you're going to have a six-hour window where you can pretty much count on transforming into a wolf at some point. You cannot fight it. Not that you'll be able to, but keep a few things in mind. It's easier to shift shape in the dark. It's easier to change when you're alone. At first, these are probably requirements for you to get anything to happen."

"So no matter what, at the new moon and the full moon, I'm going to look like...this?"

"No," Chayton said. "This is nothing. This was your first full moon, right? Wait until the new moon. Know the date and time it's coming. Don't make plans. Or make plans to be alone."

"So what is this, then?"

"It's the equivalent of peach fuzz. Right now you're half in and half out. When we're done here today, it'll be gone. When you shift, Nessa, you're not going to be half-man—or woman, or whatever—and half-wolf. That's just some crazy way people tell the stories. You're going to be a wolf. You have to be ready. You have to know that it's coming. And you'll have to get yourself out of it."

"How?"

"You'll know, and be sure not to fight it, no matter how great it feels. Because if you stay in wolf form too long, you'll get stuck."

"Stuck?"

"Yes." He paused again, thoughtful. "And something else. You're going to want to tell people about this, but you can't. You have Selena. You can trust her. And your friend, she's fine, she's not going to tell. But no one else. Even your close family must not know."

"Not my mother?"

"Look," Chayton said. "She could tell a friend. Then *she* tells a friend. You'd end up the subject of some medical research project. Trust me. You don't want that. But you knew that already, right? That's why you've kept it to yourself so far?"

Nessa realized she *did* know. She'd already kept it a secret from her mother. She knew she couldn't tell Delphine or Nate.

"You know a lot more than you realize. I want you to pay attention to that feeling of knowing. This is the form of knowing that comes from your heart." He put his hand high up on her chest, over her heart. Nessa could feel it beating into his palm. Then he moved his hand to her forehead, cupping her temple. "You will resist that form of knowing. You will try to know this with your head. But that is not animal thinking. An animal sees first with its heart."

Nessa nodded. But she could feel the fear creeping in at the edges of her thinking.

"I'm scaring you," Chayton went on, his tone matter of fact. "Don't be scared." And suddenly, again, Nessa wasn't. Chayton continued talking, each word out of his mouth pushing the fear farther away from her mind. "What's happened to you is a good thing. It's natural. Everyone has an animal inside. Most people spend their whole lives pretending that animal—pretending their soul, really—isn't there." Chayton waved his hand in the direction of the room's one window, blocked off by a shade, indicating the world outside. "Most people fight the natural process of our bodies seeking wholeness. It is the culture to fight it, but it is unnatural and destructive. Your animal is there. It connects you to the earth. It reminds us that we're part of a system that is larger than our minds can know. Welcome your animal, okay? Make friends with it."

Nessa shook her head. "I didn't ask for this," she said.

"No one does," Chayton confirmed. "But you did decide. There was a moment. A decision you made."

Nessa thought back to that night in the woods. "The wolf in the trap," she said. "I knew I shouldn't try to help him, but I just couldn't leave him there."

Chayton nodded.

"The wolves saw something in you," he explained patiently. "They saw that you have power. So you must find the power within yourself. Then you will come to understand why you were chosen."

"And what if I don't want this? Can't you just make it go away? Is there a powder or a spell or something?"

Chayton shot forward in his seat, grabbing both her wrists, his voice urgent, his grip painful. "It will not go away," he said sternly. "It is part of you. It is in the stars of your future. You must master it. You must find the power I've been describing. If you don't, what the wolves have unleashed will kill you."

CHAPTER SEVENTEEN

"What did he *say*?" Bree asked back in the car.

Nessa shook her head. She couldn't talk about it yet. First, all the embarrassing things she had said. And also, the fear that had gripped her the moment Chay had released her from the trance he'd put her in.

"He said all this stuff about letting go but not letting go. It didn't make a huge amount of sense."

"It's okay," Bree said, seeing how upset Nessa was. "You've been through a lot. Maybe it will start to make sense later."

"I don't think this is ever going to make any sense," Nessa said, gazing out the window. "At least I'm back to normal."

Which was true. Just as Chayton had told her, the moment

he released her from her trance, the fur covering her body was gone.

Nessa remained silent the rest of the drive, as Selena and Bree kept up a running conversation about the insurance claims business. Nessa stared and thought.

Maybe Bree was right. Maybe if she just relaxed, some of the stuff Chayton had told her would return to her. For instance, now she was thinking: *There are wolves in those woods.* She could feel them running along the paths, nosing under rocks and fallen branches, tracking scents, stopping to drink at streams.

As the car sped by the woods that surrounded Tether, Nessa peered through the breaks in the trees. She remembered the rancher's blog post about Tether being the locus for more reporting on wolf attacks than any other spot in the country.

It was impossible. It was all impossible. She would go to school Monday. She would find Coach Hoffman. She would explain that she was sorry about the race on Saturday, that she hadn't been feeling well, and most important, she would explain that it would never happen again.

It couldn't.

CHAPTER EIGHTEEN

Nessa woke up Sunday after a night of dreamless sleep. Her skin was clear, her fingers long and thin again. No fur. She stretched lazily. She felt loose and strong. The sun was out. The air was crisp and clean. She was able to find clean socks *and* clean underwear *and* a shirt—Delphine was in charge of laundry, so this was reason for celebration.

There was even good cereal in the house for breakfast. She breathed a sigh of relief. Maybe everything could just go back to normal?

But when she showed up at school the next day, she realized everything was not normal. In the parking lot, Jake from homeroom gave her an awkward little salute she couldn't interpret and a full-tooth smile.

A group of freshmen girls she could not say she'd ever set eyes on before were falling all over themselves to call out her name from the turnaround where the school buses had dropped them off.

People were looking at her as she walked by, and more than one person who normally didn't speak to her called out, "Hey, Nessa," and "Great job Saturday."

Chayton had said she'd be able to tell what kind of wolf she was from the way people's behavior toward her human form was changing. Was this what was going on?

Nessa turned to ask Bree if she noticed how strange things were becoming, but it was Hannah who was approaching.

"Nessa," she called, breathless from having jogged over to talk to her. "That race on Saturday. Wow."

Nessa didn't quite know how to react to Hannah staring at her like she was a rock star. Hannah had never been rude to Nessa exactly, but she hadn't ever run over to her in parking lots either.

"Thanks," Nessa said. She smiled, but it felt forced. Remembering a beat too late that conversations were not supposed to be one-sided, Nessa said, "How did you do?"

Hannah went red in the face, like she couldn't believe Nessa was actually speaking to her. "Fifteenth overall," she said. She seemed embarrassed. "It wasn't anything like what you did."

"That's amazing," said Nessa. When she was a freshman, she would have been over the moon about a twenty-fifth-place finish. She'd have been over the moon just to be running on varsity.

"Yeah, but what you did," Hannah said. "Nessa, Coach

was going crazy you weren't there for the ceremony. He was shouting, 'Course record! State record!' He said you could probably expect to start hearing from recruiters soon."

"Oh, I don't know," Nessa shrugged. Now she was almost annoyed at Hannah. Exaggerating in this way was like jinxing it.

But once Nessa got into the school building, she realized this was bigger than Saturday's race. Ashley Clark, one of Cassian's beautiful senior friends, was standing by the trophy case flipping through pictures of the Homecoming court she'd been queen of, but when she saw Nessa, she pushed through the crowd. "Nessa," Ashley said. She tucked her chin. "Do you want to see the pictures of our dresses? Why weren't you there?"

Nessa glanced down at Ashley's phone. "Um, you guys look great," she said, passing Ashley back her phone and heading to her locker.

"It'll be you next year!" Ashley called out after her.

"Nessa, what's happening?" Bree said in a low voice. "It's like overnight you got famous. Did you see the way Cassian was just looking at you?"

"Cassian?" Nessa's heart did a small leap in her chest. But then she shook away her own reaction. She didn't want to get too excited. In her experience, this generally led to fall-on-your-face embarrassment, especially with guys. She checked the time on her phone. "Look," she said, "I gotta talk to Coach."

Coach Hoffman taught tenth-grade history—Nessa had had him as a teacher the year before—and she found him in his classroom, carefully setting up the board.

Nessa cleared her throat. Coach looked up and saw that she

was there, his face immediately transforming from a look of distracted concentration to one of extreme joy.

"Hey, hey, hey!" he said, his enthusiasm growing with each successive syllable. "The girl of the hour. Nessa, get over here!" He held out both hands for a high five and then wrapped her in a bear hug.

He released her quickly. "I'm so proud of the way you ran on Saturday I'm not even going to start in on you about what was going on with the lateness and not sticking around and being completely unreachable, though we *will* talk about that later. Nessa, what happened? Where did you find that speed?"

Nessa paused. She didn't want to say something cheesy and not true. She wanted to be real with Coach. But also? It was kind of hard to remember the actual running from Saturday. When she thought about the day, mostly what she remembered was how afraid she'd been. How scary the changes to her body had been. How little she had known about what was going on. How much she'd wanted to run and how frustrated she'd felt that she might not be able to.

She remembered how Chayton had pressed his hand up against her heartbeat and told her to pay attention to the things she knew but didn't know she knew. And she remembered her heart beating during the race, how she'd felt like her stride had gotten about twenty percent longer, how her breathing aligned perfectly with her footfalls. The drumming she'd been doing with Chayton had formed a connection between her heart and the rhythms she heard, the rhythms she felt, the rhythms of her body.

This was all getting totally tangled in her brain.

"I felt…awesome," she said to Coach. She knew she was

saying something true, because he was looking at her intently, his entire face still, the pen he'd been capping and uncapping frozen in place. "I felt really quiet in my head and like I wasn't worried about gassing out. I usually think a lot when I'm running, but I didn't this time."

"What was with the track pants?" Coach said. "And the long sleeves? The hat? You must have been roasting."

"I know," she said. "I wasn't feeling well. My body temperature was all over the place."

"You ran that well when you were sick?"

"Go figure."

"And then please tell me you spent the rest of the weekend sleeping and *that's* why you didn't return my texts and calls?"

"Something like that." Nessa grinned shyly.

The conversation with Coach had gone better than Nessa had thought it would. Everything that day seemed to be going her way. If she raised her hand in class, she'd get called on. Outside at lunch, the coveted spot underneath the hawthorn tree was miraculously empty for Nessa and Bree. Her locker, which almost always jammed, opened easily as if it had just been oiled.

At practice, Hannah was outright staring at Nessa as she slid over to make room. Tim Miller stopped in the middle of a story he was telling about one of the extra science classes he was taking when she joined the stretching circle. He stared at her, star-struck.

"What's up?" Nessa said, giving him a look that signaled, *Please act normal, okay?*

As the team started out for that day's slow and easy 10K—it took them away from school and all throughout Tether—Nessa ran at a pace that felt positively gentle, but passed everyone on the team except Cynthia and Luc.

When she caught up to Cynthia, she fell into step with her.

"Impressive time Saturday," Cynthia said.

"Thanks," Nessa answered, guarded.

"I guess whatever else that wolf bite did to you, it certainly made you faster."

Nessa nearly stopped dead in her tracks.

"What's that supposed to mean?"

"Nothing," Cynthia said, looking studiously sincere. "Just couldn't help but notice the improvement in your times. After an injury, shouldn't it have taken you awhile to build back your speed? But no. You get faster. And…you run in track pants on an 80-degree day. What the heck is going on with you? It's all kind of strange."

Nessa was so surprised in the moment that she couldn't come up with any way to explain herself. Of all the people she'd expected to ask so directly about the connection between the bite and the race—Coach, her mom, Delphine, maybe—she hadn't counted on Cynthia.

After practice, while waiting for Vivian to pick her up on the way home from work, Nessa felt a hand on her shoulder. She turned to find herself face-to-face with Cassian, who had just come out of the locker room, freshly showered after practice, his steely gray eyes locked on Nessa's. She caught her breath. She could smell his soap.

"Hey," he said, and Nessa felt her face warm. How could he make that one simple syllable so sexy?

"Hey," she said back to him, her own voice weirdly breathy and soft.

"Nessa," Cassian said. "Your brother goes to the clinic at the same time as my sis. I've seen you there."

"Yeah, me too. I mean, I've seen you there too," Nessa said, almost stuttering she was so nervous.

"I'll be there this weekend again. Maybe I'll see you there?"

"Yeah, sure, probably," was the best Nessa could come up with in reply.

"Yeah, sure, *probably*?" Bree said on their way to school the next morning.

"At least it was better than, 'Call if you need me,'" Nessa pointed out.

"No it's not!" Bree said. "With a guy like Cassian, if you don't act at least mildly interested, he's not going to waste his time."

"If everyone's falling all over themselves around him, it's better to be the one person who isn't."

"In books maybe," Bree said. "In reality, most guys are incredibly insecure and need all the ego support you can give them."

They were pulling into the parking lot now, and there Cassian was, with Cynthia sitting on the hood of his car. She had a notebook open, resting on her knees. Cassian was lying back next to her, propped up on his elbows, his eyes hidden behind aviator shades. A car pulled up next to his, and one of the girls on the spirit squad brought Cassian a coffee. He sat up to take it, lifted the lid, breathed in, and raised his eyes suggestively at the girl who brought it, which caused her to collapse in giggles and punch him in the shoulder.

"Somehow," Nessa said, "I don't think *that* guy needs help with his ego."

"I don't know what's going on with kids in this school, but if this our-school's-been-turned-into-a-Nessa-fan-club keeps up, you're not going to need any help with your ego either."

"What's your problem?" Nessa joked, flashing Bree her most ridiculous face.

Bree rolled her eyes.

The truth was that all of the attention Nessa was getting *was* kind of fun. And it wasn't just kids. Coach Hoffman called her in for a lunchtime conference to go over her training regimen. Mr. Porter, the guidance counselor, wanted to schedule another meeting to "reinitiate that conversation about college prospects."

It wasn't just her running that improved. Her science teacher, Mr. Bloom, kept her after class Wednesday.

"I've got to say," he said, showing her her lab write-up, "I'm really impressed by your work. Your hypothesis was smart, your data collection rigorous, your analysis thorough and far-reaching. Frankly, this is college-level work. What's going on with you?"

"I don't know," Nessa said. "I think I'm just focusing better?"

"Okaaaaay," Mr. Bloom said, as if he were letting go the fact that this couldn't possibly be the whole story. He tossed her lab notebook to the pile but overshot it. Nessa, without thinking about it, caught the notebook before it fluttered to the floor.

And then she froze in place, notebook in hand, while Mr. Bloom just stared at her, open-mouthed.

Nessa had reached out about eight feet to snag the book, a grab the equivalent of a frog nailing a mosquito with its tongue.

In the awkward silence, Nessa tried very hard not to make a move, not to try to explain away what she'd just done, hoping that if she just stood there, like everything was normal, Mr. Bloom would decide to see things that way himself.

Which he eventually did, letting the episode go with nothing more than a question; as she walked toward the door, he asked, "Have you ever thought about playing on the softball team in the spring?"

Nessa hadn't been lying to Mr. Bloom. She *was* more focused. Wednesday night, she had to write a paper for English—something she generally hated—but instead of getting up seven times to get another Oreo or text Bree something inane or play a round of Wii Bowling with Nate, Nessa stayed at the computer, headphones on, music full volume, somehow able to think about nothing but the words on the page.

She constructed an outline. She wrote, "There are three reasons why…" She wrote, "The first example…" She wrote, "In spite of this…" and "It is, however, true that…"

Using her index finger to nail the final period onto the last sentence in the last paragraph on the last page, Nessa thought, *Yes! Done! Bingo!* Right on cue, the song she was listening to came to an end, and Nessa pressed pause on her phone to keep the next from beginning. She felt almost out of breath, like it had been a physical, not just mental, exertion. She removed her headphones. It was only nine at night and she felt so good, she decided to drop to the floor and knock out twenty-five push-ups.

The bedroom door opened as Nessa reached nineteen, and

Delphine just watched her from the doorway until she was done. Delphine was wearing pretty white lace pajamas, resting against the door frame with her eyebrows raised and her arms crossed.

"You're my sister, and I love you and all, Ness," Delphine said. "But you are seriously turning into a total fitness freak. Are you training to be a Navy SEAL or something?"

Nessa grunted out a single, "Ha." Then: "Twenty-three, twenty-four, TWENTY-FIVE!"

"Seriously!" Delphine said. "I feel lazy just breathing the same air as you. And I'm putting you on notice. If you so much as think about buying a weight bench off an infomercial, we are going to have to have a serious talk."

"Haters gonna hate," Nessa said, laughing.

Delphine pushed herself up off the door frame with exaggerated effort and rolled her eyes.

"Jocks," she said.

Selena had kept her promise about keeping Nessa's secret, but since she knew Bree's and Nessa's mothers, it also meant she'd kept her distance from the girls a bit. She had given Bree one present for Nessa, though: a slim rectangular moon phase calendar for this year, charting every cycle the moon would pass through and the calendar date on which it would happen.

The new moon was scheduled to come at the same time as the next cross-country meet.

And the meet was at another school. She'd be on a bus with the team in close quarters. Sweatpants and Bree's Peterbilt hat weren't going to cut it.

Plus, what had Chayton called her transformation before? Peach fuzz? This next time she would transform more fully. It was too scary to even think about what that meant exactly. To say the word. To think the word. To keep her fingers from googling the word.

She needed to talk to Chayton again, so after Thursday's cross-country practice, Bree picked up Nessa at school, and they drove over to Mike's garage. This time it was open, but when they found Mike, he was sitting on a pile of tires, drinking a double-sized can of beer, his eyes bloodshot.

Only the lingering sense of urgency gave Nessa the courage to ask if he knew where Chayton was.

"Nope," Mike said, over-enunciating. "And I don't expect him."

Bree and Nessa backed out slowly. There was something creepy about this place. Nessa had read that wolves have an instinctive awareness of vulnerability. Someone here was sick or weak or old.

Rather than plan, Nessa relied on hoping…that the transformation wouldn't happen. Or that it wouldn't happen the way Chayton had said it would. That she would be more in control. That the race would get rained out. That the moon would not follow the three different calendars she'd found online. That between now and the next big race weekend, something major would change.

Anything, let it be anything, she prayed in her mind.

But then "anything" came along, and Nessa wished she had been a little bit more specific.

CHAPTER NINETEEN

The Friday after Homecoming, Nessa arrived at school with Bree and wasn't surprised to see a freshman girl from cross-country heading straight for her. Nessa was getting used to being treated as a quasi–school celebrity, so she smiled at the runner, Maryn.

But Maryn didn't look worshipful. She looked worried. "Nessa, you've got to go see Coach right now. He keeps asking us if we've seen you. I think something might be really wrong."

Not caring that the first bell was about to ring, Nessa headed straight for Coach Hoffman's office.

Before she was even close, she heard voices coming through

his open door—Coach Hoffman, Mr. Porter, and Principal Sarakoski. The hallway was filled with sound and people and conversations and slamming lockers, but still, she was able to hear every word, every nuance, as if she were in the room.

"Tell me this isn't raising a red flag for you, Hoffman." This was Principal Sarakoski. Nessa recognized the way her high voice got a little nasal with emotion.

"It *is* a little unusual," Coach was saying.

"Unusual? I had the Commissioner of Youth Sports on the phone last night. I believe the word he used was *unprecedented*."

"She's a highly focused young lady." This was Mr. Porter speaking now. "We shouldn't rush to judge."

"I'll tell you who is going to rush to judge. The state's Commission on Illegal Substance Use in High School Athletics, that's who. In case you don't know, this is a group convened by the legislature *just this past year*. And we thought when we learned about it, 'Great! Not our problem!' Everyone assumed that the districts affected by this kind of pressure are the down-state towns with the big programs. We've got poverty and OxyContin addicts and Lord knows what else, but rich kids gaming the sports system? We thought we were immune. All those metro-area charter schools—how much of a coup is this for them now? It's going to be quite a feather in their caps to have the test case come from up here."

"Andrea," Coach Hoffman began, "we don't know—" but Principal Sarakoski clearly wasn't done.

"It's bad enough an entire generation of children in this town is being studied for cancer, that the only thing anyone knows about us is that we sat by and allowed ourselves to be poisoned. Now we'll be the town where kids are poisoning themselves via the use of performance-enhancing drugs in high school athletics. A dead-end school district where kids will do anything just to get out."

Nessa had reached the door to Coach Hoffman's office by now, and Mr. Porter spotted her. "Nessa!" he called, the fake cheeriness in his voice meant to signal to his boss that she should stop talking in such blatant tones.

Principal Sarakoski managed to rein herself in, but Nessa could see that she was still pretty worked up. Nessa could practically feel the throb in the big vein visible at her temple.

"Coach Hoffman?" Nessa asked. "You wanted to see me?"

"Yes," Coach said. He looked up at Principal Sarakoski, then at the floor. He seemed not to be able to look Nessa in the eye. "Sit down," he said, pointing to a chair. She took it, a little reluctantly. It felt weird to be the only one sitting. Coach Hoffman was standing behind his desk, Mr. Porter was perched on a low bookshelf, and Principal Sarakoski was pacing behind both of them.

"First off, Nessa," Coach Hoffman said, "before we bring up some very serious accusations that have been made, I just want to know if there is anything you'd like to tell us. Sometimes—well—all of us—we do things and they lead to other things, and then we find ourselves going down a path that we never exactly intended, and we turn into versions of ourselves we never could have predicted we'd encounter, and..."

Nessa had no idea where he was going with this. Every word seemed to be causing Coach Hoffman so much pain, Nessa felt almost sorry for him.

On the other hand, she was starting to get the idea that she was in very serious trouble. Was it possible they'd found out about what had been happening to her?

"You see—" Coach Hoffman began again, but this time, Principal Sarakoski cut him off.

"Good Lord, Peter, let's cut to the chase. Nessa, is there anything you have to tell us?"

Nessa slid her hands under her thighs. For a second, she envisioned letting everything that had happened to her during the first month of school spill out. That on top of training and studying and all the things you had to do your first semester of junior year if you wanted to go to college—and especially if you wanted to go to college on a scholarship—she'd been attacked in the woods by a wild animal, been in and out of the doctor's office, had rehabbed her way back onto the team, and then, oh yeah, had *transformed into a wolf? Had been "cured" by a shaman who said it was going to happen again in a week's time? Had no idea how to make it stop so that she could run a race that was also only a week away?*

"No," she said. "I don't know what you want me to say."

"I'm just going to come out and ask you, then," Principal Sarakoski said. "Have you been using any performance-enhancing drugs?"

"You mean doping?" Nessa asked, her brain connecting the dots between the conversation she'd overheard and her presence in this room. Then anger fired up in her. She looked back and forth at the three adults.

"No way!" Nessa responded. "I've been working for this. I've been working so hard. I've never even *seen* drugs like that!"

Coach put a hand on her shoulder. "I know, sweetheart."

"So you won't mind if we inspect your gym locker right now," Principal Sarakoski said in a much less sympathetic tone.

"You want to search my locker?" Nessa knew her anger

made her sound guilty, and she bit her lip and stopped talking.

"There was an anonymous message left on the school's voicemail suggesting that you'd been doping," Coach Hoffman explained further, his tone gentle. "We would have disregarded it if we hadn't found bottles of androstenedione in the trashcan."

"It's school policy to search lockers when a viable threat has been received," Principal Sarakoski said.

"It's actually not school policy, Andrea," Coach Hoffman corrected. "Situations like this are so unheard of we don't exactly have a school policy."

"It's school policy to take action."

"But you can't!" Nessa said. "I mean, it's private property."

Later Nessa would wish she had acted less disturbed by the idea of their opening her gym locker. Or at least explained that it was embarrassing to think about her deodorant and tampons going on display for her principal, guidance counselor, and coach. Her nasty running bra hanging on the center hook where she'd left it to dry.

"Technically, your locker is the property of the school," Principal Sarakoski said. "On loan to you." She nodded to Mr. Porter, who lifted a walkie-talkie to his mouth and said, "Go ahead and open it." That was when Nessa understood that whether she agreed to it or not, the search was happening NOW.

"Shall we?" Principal Sarakoski said, and the three adults escorted Nessa to the locker room where Pasty Pete had already cut open her combination lock with the assistant principal, Mr. Cooper. Pete looked up and met Nessa's eye.

"That's my stuff," Nessa said, noticing right away that the bra was already on the floor. So were the pictures she'd taped up of herself running through the finish line at a race the year before. And the picture of Nate, Delphine, and her mom from last summer, camping with cousins at a lake. Pete was taking no care not to bend or tear the photographs and other objects that were important to her, as he dumped them into a cardboard box on the floor.

Nessa spun around, looking to the crowd of gawking girls to see if any of them would say something. No one did. Even Cynthia, who was there with her friends, said nothing.

"You know me," Nessa said to Cynthia. "You know I'd never do something like this."

"You wouldn't?" Cynthia replied. She shook her head like all of this was making her sad. "Nessa, I've never known anyone who wanted to win as much as you."

"Is this it?" Pete asked, holding up a supplement bottle. It wasn't even scary looking: a regular brown bottle like a vitamin C bottle, with the blue image of a runner and a yin and yang symbol to make it even friendlier. Pete read the label out loud, "'Androstenedione.' Is this what you're looking for?"

Nessa glared at Pete, hating him for his discovery. "I've never seen that before," she said. "I've never even heard of andro...nos...stadon or whatever it's called."

Nessa looked from one face to another, feeling her shame growing with each passing second. The trapped wolf, that's who she had become. All she wanted to do was run.

Nessa was sent back to class for second period—she had English.

As if she could possibly concentrate on English. On anything. She was so angry, she didn't think she could sit down in her seat, let alone talk about nature and nurture and symbolism. She would so much rather be quizzed on math facts or asked to recite formulas for physics than give an opinion about whether people had destinies or what makes a character evil.

She tossed her book bag under her chair and threw herself into her seat with an aggressive thump, sending the angry beam of her gaze toward anyone who had a problem with her being in the room.

She knew news traveled fast in school. Had four minutes of passing time between first and second periods been enough for the lies to circulate? Did everyone in this room now think of her as a confirmed doper? Like she hadn't earned that win? Like it hadn't been her legs, her sneakers, her muscles, her hours and miles and minutes adding up to the way she'd torn up the course at Homecoming?

No one met her eye.

"Nessa, great job," she heard from Ms. Nightingale, who was handing back the papers from the week before. Nessa looked at the top of hers where an A was written in red and circled. Nessa stared at the letter. She remembered the night she wrote it. The feeling of putting the last period on the last sentence of the last line at the very moment that the song on her mix compilation ended. The serendipity of that night was wrecked now. It didn't mean anything to her. How could it?

CHAPTER TWENTY

ivian didn't take off work for much, but when the school called to say evidence had been found suggesting that Nessa had been taking illegal performance-enhancing drugs, she left work and came to school for an emergency meeting with the principal.

Her hair drawn up on top of her head, her chin held high, her legs crossed in a way that brought dignity to her vet tech scrubs and nurse clogs, she listened to Principal Sarakoski describe the anonymous tip, the search, the findings in Nessa's locker.

Vivian swiveled in her seat and faced Nessa. "Did you take these pills or anything else that may have caused your times to improve so dramatically? Tell me the truth now, tell it one time, and we'll deal with this whatever the case may be."

"I didn't do this," Nessa said.

"Thank you," said Vivian. Then she turned to Principal Sarakoski. "You heard her. She didn't do it. Now what?"

Principal Sarakoski's face looked pained but firm. "There's a state initiative to investigate this kind of thing, and it looks very bad for the whole county, our whole half of the state, if rumors are flying that we're being lax on this up here. You'll get all the Detroit people complaining that the funding we get up here for our after-school activities is coming from state dollars while theirs comes from towns…." The principal's speech veered off into charter school politics and tax incentives, Title I funding, and Title IX. Nessa shifted in her chair and stared at the floor, but her mother's gaze remained clear and fixed on the principal.

"That's all well and good for the state," she said. "But what I'm interested in is my daughter. What does any of what you just said mean for her?"

"If it was only up to me, Vivian," Principal Sarakoski said, "I'd take her word for it. But as it is, she's going to have to take a blood test. And…" Principal Sarakoski paused.

"And?" Vivian repeated.

"And she's going to have to be suspended from competition pending the results of the test."

Vivian continued to stare the principal down.

"And her results from the Homecoming time trials will be withheld until her other test results are in."

Principal Sarakoski looked down at her desk with finality.

Vivian looked over at Nessa's face, and Nessa could see that her mom registered what this meant for her.

"And what happens if Nessa doesn't want to submit to a blood test?" Vivian said.

"Then she forfeits her position on the team," Principal Sarakoski replied.

"Oh, is that all—just her chance of attending college?" Vivian snapped, descending to sarcasm when it became evident that Nessa was in pain and there was nothing Vivian could do.

Nessa spent the rest of the morning in a daze, ending up at lunch not being able to eat a mouthful of food.

"Hey," she heard, while debating whether to just trash her turkey sandwich entirely. She turned and saw it was Cassian. "I've been looking for you."

"For me?" Nessa said.

"Yes." Cassian shrugged. Nessa was tall, but he was even taller. His shoulders were broad. He smiled at her. "You changed your nail polish," he said.

"What?" Nessa blinked at him and then looked down at her hands. "Oh. Yes, I did," she said. Then she couldn't help but smile. Delphine had given Nessa a dark gray manicure last night to be "calming." It obviously had other effects. She didn't expect Cassian to keep up with the status of her nail polish. "Thanks for noticing."

"Mind if I sit?" he asked. Nessa was too fatigued to say anything, so she slid over on the webbed metal bench and nodded yes.

"I just thought, you know, with everybody making this big thing about the androstenedione, you should know that not everybody thinks you did it. I don't think you did it."

"You don't?" Nessa said.

"I know what it's like to want to get out of this town, and I know why you'd want to dope to make it happen," he went on. "But I don't know—I just don't think you did."

Nessa smiled. She felt like a window had cracked open in a dark room.

"Well," she said. "Thanks. I appreciate it."

"I'd like to see you someplace other than the health clinic," Cassian added suddenly. "I think we're more alike than you think."

Nessa just nodded and tried to keep her face from wrinkling up, completely overwhelmed. *WHAT?*

"Do you like bowling?" Cassian asked.

Visions of a failed venture when Nate was about six filtered through Nessa's memory. Delphine hated the shoes and Nate… hated the entire time. "Bowling?" Nessa repeated.

He cleared his throat. Did Cassian Thomas look…nervous? "Well, *I* like bowling," he said. "And it's a good thing 'cause Tether doesn't have movies or roller skating or any of the other things that I might want to ask you to do with me this weekend."

Nessa felt like her brain was firing on a single cylinder, and that cylinder was not capable of parsing exactly what was happening. With Cassian looking right at her, it was hard to concentrate.

"So maybe you'll…go bowling with me? Next weekend? After the clinic?"

Nessa was a little charmed by his nervousness. "Sure, I'll go bowling." She laughed. Like an idiot. Nothing here was funny. "I'd—sure."

It wasn't until she was lying in bed that night that she thought how odd it was that Cassian could so easily pronounce the word "androstenedione." It wasn't exactly common vocabulary. And the word had just slid off his tongue.

Nessa's first date with Cassian was oddly not exciting her. Instead, she felt a burning need to see Chayton.

Nessa tried Chayton's number at the shop. She tried his cell. She texted him for the twentieth time, but she didn't have to worry about being a pest—every text she'd sent received a red exclamation point in response: they weren't going through.

Finally, she called Selena.

"This is just Chayton," Selena explained. "He disappears. He's not trying to be cagey. He's devoted to his friends, and he gets really absorbed in what he's doing."

"How long is he usually away?" Nessa asked. She was trying not to sound desperate.

"Days, sometimes," Selena said. "But other times he can be gone for months."

"Months?" Nessa said. It came out like a squeak. She suddenly felt how much she'd been counting on his help.

"I need to talk to him," she said. "I've got to take this blood test, and I don't know if I should, and I'm not sure when this wolf thing is coming, and I just…" How could he have left her to manage this all alone?

"I'm so sorry," Selena said. "I wish there was more I could do. He'll be back, Nessa. Chayton always comes back."

That night Nessa dreamed about the white wolf again. She hadn't seen him since she visited Chayton, but now here he was, coming for her, his jaws dripping, his teeth merging in her mind with the teeth of the wolf in the trap, the ones that were filed to points.

Nessa woke up soaked in sweat. She didn't know if she'd cried out in her dream, but Delphine didn't seem to have woken up, so Nessa hoped she had not. She put a hand on her heart, feeling it pound in her chest. She could hear her blood rushing. She could hear every sound in the house as well. Her mother's even breathing. Nate's snore. The hum of the fridge. She could hear sounds in her neighborhood. Mr. and Mrs. Mullick arguing four houses away. A car engine starting up in the distance. A train whistle, which was strange, considering the closest active freight line was more than five miles away. A skittering of mice in a basement that could have been hers or could have been down the street.

She looked at the clock. It was just after three in the morning. Saturday. The new moon was six days away. She was going to turn into a wolf. She *was* turning into a wolf. She threw off the covers and sat with her legs over the side of the bed, feeling the cold air.

Her stomach grumbled. She needed to eat something. Preferably meat.

Nessa unearthed a pound of frozen hamburger meat and stuck it in the microwave. Vivian could get meat to room temperature without cooking it, but Nessa didn't know how to make this happen and ended up with a cooked, pale gray mess, as tough as if she'd boiled it. Turned out it wasn't bad with enough salt and ketchup, and she switched the internet browser to Private (specifically and forcefully forbidden by her mother) and re-googled the sites she couldn't bookmark. Moon tables. Lycanthropy. Werewolf sightings. Wolf facts.

With enough reading—with enough forkfuls of beef—Nessa developed a theory. Maybe the six-hour before-and-after window Chayton had told her she would transform during, maybe that had to do with the moon's rising. And that was scheduled to happen at 1 a.m. on Friday night. Which meant she could transform anywhere between 7 p.m. the night before and 8 a.m. the morning of.

Or to put it simply: she could turn into a wolf when she was with her family, safely tucked in bed, watching the terror in their eyes when they realized they were (and had been all along) living with a terrifying wild animal. Or she could transform just at the beginning of the bus ride to the cross-country meet on Saturday. Nessa did not like her options.

As the sun was starting to rise, Nessa put on her running clothes and went out for her usual five-mile run. In the days since her suspension, something else had started to bother her. The accusation of doping made her angry, but her wolf transformation was clearly helping to improve her times. Nessa was running faster. Was it the same thing as doping? Giving her an unfair advantage?

It was something she longed to ask Chayton about.

But as usual, her whirling thoughts were soon slowed by the simple rhythm of her footsteps. In the silence, she began to hear a faint singing in the distance. It was enough to make her stop in her tracks. Because not only did she recognize the calling as the sound of a wolf, but she could also visualize which wolf it was.

Nessa listened for a moment, as if it were a song on the radio and this was her only chance to hear it play. Then she started running again. Soon enough, she reminded herself. She could answer their calls soon enough.

The following Wednesday, Nessa ate school breakfast with Bree. All Tether schools provided free lunch and free breakfast to students through a state-funded program, but by high school, most kids weren't willing to eat it. Who wanted greasy sausage and eggs shaped like hockey pucks served on the kind of bargain-brand English muffins that didn't have any nooks or crannies?

Nessa wanted it, that's who, at least this morning. She had eaten hers in about two bites, and was now working her way through Bree's, grateful for the calories, even if she would have traded the muffins and eggs in for four pieces of sausage in a heartbeat.

"I don't want to go," Nessa said to Bree. "I don't want to give any blood."

"Why not?" Bree peeled the foil off the top of her juice container. "You're going to be clean, right? Teach those jerks a lesson. I'd think you would *want* to take the test."

"I'm afraid they might find—" Nessa lowered her voice, "wolf stuff. You know. I think my blood might show something strange in my DNA."

"Oh," said Bree. "Huh. Good point. I hadn't thought of that."

"I wanted to talk to Chayton about it. But he's gone."

"Yeah, what is *wrong* with him?" Bree said. "Don't you think it's weird that he just took off like that? I mean, you might really need him. You have questions. The least he could have done was call Selena and leave a number where you could reach him."

"Yeah, it is weird."

Bree frowned. "Let me think about the blood test. We'll talk more at lunch."

The minute they sat down for second period English, Bree was fast-whispering at their desks while Ms. Nightingale wrote out some poetry quotes on the board for them to "react" to.

"I can't believe I didn't think of this at breakfast," Bree said. "My dad takes blood tests all the time. All truckers do. His company wouldn't be able to afford insurance without them. So I snuck him a call and asked all about it."

"And?" Nessa whispered back.

"The short answer is you don't have to worry. These tests are very specific. It's expensive to test blood, so drug tests are targeted. They don't look for anything that isn't drugs. This guy my dad works with actually sued the company because he had prostate cancer and the test didn't pick it up when they could have. Now, my dad said, you check this box if you want them to screen for certain diseases but you don't have to because that might be a violation of your privacy."

"Okay, wow, that was a lot of information," Nessa said.

"Yeah, I know," said Bree. "Dad hadn't spoken to anyone or slept in eighteen hours, so he was a little chatty. I think I managed to talk him into stopping at a motel for a little rest, too. At least I told him I'd tell Mom if he didn't send me a picture of himself in a motel room in the next hour."

Just then her phone buzzed in her pocket. Bree didn't pull it out. At Tether High, every time you were spotted using your phone during school hours, you lost it for the rest of the day. "That's him now!"

Ms. Nightingale was finishing writing the quotes and starting to speak, so Bree hurried to finish. "All you need to know is that the blood test isn't comprehensive. It's not like they're putting your blood in a centrifuge and analyzing your DNA. They just want to see if there's traces of certain drugs."

"Okay," Nessa said. "Thanks."

That afternoon, Nessa went into the clinic, signed in at the desk, took a seat, read a magazine, got called into the phlebotomist's alcove, counter-signed the form that her mom had faxed over earlier, rolled up her sleeve, felt a stick, and then watched as the technician filled four different test tubes with her blood, each tube coded with a different-colored sticker printed with her name: Kurland, V. (for Vanessa), and the date.

CHAPTER TWENTY-ONE

The rest of that week, Nessa felt like she'd had three diet colas on an empty stomach. She wasn't sleeping and always felt tired. She was jumpy. Smells she normally didn't register were making it impossible to be in certain places—just passing the ninth-grade frog dissection lab, the smell of formaldehyde burned the skin on the inside of her nostrils.

Her elevated hearing was driving her crazy. For once she could actually hear everyone at school talking about her behind her back, calling her a doping maniac. Whispers followed her up and down the halls. Conversations came to abrupt halts the second she approached. Kids turned away from her and talked behind their hands when she so much as got up to get a spoon during lunch. She could hear every word.

Her days were filled with, "So desperate!" and, "Well, if you were so poor you had to get a scholarship..." and, "I can't believe I used to think she was cool," and, "What if all those steroids turn her into a man?" and of course: "Where did she even get them? Do you think I...?"

Cross-country practice was especially awkward. No one knew what to say to her. She was running faster than ever, but her times now made Coach Hoffman look at her suspiciously. Nessa felt he was on the verge of asking her to slow down.

But she couldn't. Running was the only way she got any relief from the stress of counting down the days until the new moon.

Cynthia was acting differently too. Before, she had ignored Nessa as much as possible, stuck in the Universe of Perfection that was Cynthia. Now, every time Nessa glanced at her, Cynthia turned her head abruptly, like she had been watching. Nessa couldn't forget the humiliating moment in the locker room when Cynthia had clucked her teeth and acted like Nessa was the most desperate of cases.

More and more, Nessa began to wonder if Cynthia was the source of the anonymous tip. Nessa began to watch her every chance she got.

She saw nothing but Cynthia's perfect form, disciplined training, her desire to win. She raced well because she didn't get in her own head, she never looked down, she kept her legs flashing high, her chest forward but relaxed. Her high, swaying ponytail was the only part of her body besides her legs that she didn't keep completely still.

The only thing Nessa learned by watching Cynthia was that

the girl was definitely making a play for Luc. She'd plant herself in Luc's line of sight when Coach was giving a talk, then glance his way to be sure he was watching. She'd stretch her shapely leg like she was easing out a muscle cramp, but really, Nessa could tell, she was showing off.

At the end of a set of interval work, when everyone was walking off the sprints, Cynthia casually fell into step with Luc. Her hands on her hips, her chest rising and falling, her head thrown back, she made it look like she hadn't placed herself next to him on purpose, but Nessa had seen that she had. Cynthia caught Luc's eye, then looked away, so he'd be the first to speak.

"Good run?" Luc said.

Cynthia nodded and smiled at him. Nessa almost never saw Cynthia smile. Cynthia was a person who smiled only when she wanted something. "You?" Cynthia said. But she walked away before he could answer. Was she nervous or playing games?

The week dragged on, but then suddenly it was Friday—new moon day—and time for Nessa and Bree to put the transformation plan into action.

Vivian was working late, so after practice, Nessa rushed home, cooked macaroni and cheese for Nate and Delphine, reminded them that she was spending the night at Bree's, then bolted out the door when Bree arrived at 6:30.

In the car, every topic except what they were about to do seemed easier to talk about.

"This will all be behind you in twenty-four hours," Bree said helpfully. "*And* you'll be out on a first date with Cassian."

Nessa rolled her eyes and had to smile.

"I hope so," she reminded her friend. "We don't know if it will work the same as last time." She picked at the buckles of her overnight bag.

"Do you think Cynthia's heard yet that you're going out?" Bree had been monitoring Nessa's mounting fears about what Cynthia was and had been up to.

"I don't think so. She only talks to Luc. Who seems to be walking right into her trap."

"I guarantee you he has no idea," Bree said. "Everyone just wants to be told they're special. If Cynthia's capturing Luc's eternal love by constantly blowing him off, she's good."

"She's not good," Nessa countered. "She's a witch. You know," Nessa shifted toward Bree, "I really think she was the one who turned me in. Which is stupid because getting rid of me doesn't change her overall times. It doesn't make her faster to have me not running, you know? It just makes our team slower overall."

Nessa slumped down, staring at the road ahead. "I'm going to catch her. I'm going to make her pay for this."

"Jeez, Nessa, I've never seen you like this before," Bree said. "You're kind of freaking me out."

"I know!" Nessa replied. She could hear the anger in her own voice, too. She wanted to stop being angry, but she couldn't. She had so much energy. She'd run five miles that afternoon at a sub-eight-minute pace, and still she was jiggling her leg and thinking about asking Bree to pull over so she could just run to the trailhead from there.

"You're really going to spend the night in the woods?" Bree said. "What if you don't transform? It's going down into the forties tonight. Wolf Popsicle."

"I'll deal," said Nessa. "Worst case, I'll climb into my sleeping bag and cinch the top closed."

"Thank goodness for all that Girl Scout training we had."

"All we ever did was sell cookies."

"Which is why," Bree said, a flourish in her voice. "I brought you some!"

"You have Girl Scout cookies? In October?"

"Don't be ridiculous. We finish ours the week they arrive. As do you. It's part of what it means to be an American. I *made* you cookies."

And suddenly Nessa felt the anger and anxiety that had been propelling her through the last stressful week dissipate. "Bree!" Nessa said, feeling a lump in her throat. She thought about her friend, how many times in the past month she had been there for her, how cheerful Bree was, how generous and kind. She thought about how she, Nessa, would never be like that—that she would always be suspicious and prepare for the worst.

"Nessa! My gosh," said Bree. "Are you crying?"

Nessa sniffed. "It's just that," Nessa said, "well, I don't think I appreciate you enough. You're just the greatest...friend, and—" Nessa couldn't finish. She was too choked up.

She looked at Bree, who had stopped the car. They had reached the trailhead. She half expected Bree to be crying too. But Bree was not crying. Bree was laughing. At what? At Nessa?!

"Why is this funny?"

"It's not," said Bree. "I'm sorry."

"Tell me!"

"Okay, it's just that, well, I think it's time for you to go out into the woods."

"Why?"

"You're acting a little crazy."

"No, I'm not."

Bree smiled. She passed Nessa a shoebox. "Here are the cookies. They're meat flavored—people bake them for their dogs."

Nessa stepped out of Bree's car at the trailhead where she'd attempted to meet up with Cynthia a month and a half earlier, her overnight bag slung over her shoulder, a sleeping bag tucked under her arm, dressed in her winter parka and jeans, holding a shoebox filled with meat cookies.

She hiked about twenty feet into the woods, shoveled a few of Bree's surprisingly tasty cookies into her mouth, dropped her stuff in a pile, stripped off her winter jacket, and began to run.

It was the only thing that felt right.

It felt so good that Nessa almost put her head back and sang. She extended her stride, not thinking so much about speed, but rather the sensation of stretching out her legs.

She was running on the pads of her feet, noticing for the first time the softness of the trail, almost dancing over the tree roots and stones in her path. In spite of how dark it was, Nessa seemed to have no problem avoiding them.

She stopped for a second.

Wait.

Pads on her feet? She lifted one leg, then the other. Then the third leg and the fourth.

She couldn't remember what about this should feel strange.

She shook vigorously, her ears pricking at the sound of a squirrel rustling in a tree branch. It was far away. Miles maybe. Of no concern to her. Besides, Nessa wasn't hungry now.

She ran faster and farther than she ever had before. She felt blood pumping into her heart. She was aware of life in the forest in ways she had never been before, though she had always loved it, always found herself happy here. She could see it living and moving all around her. She could hear the running of water, the music of wind in the trees. She could smell the heaviness of leaves turning to soil, the acidity given off by the broken branch of a pine tree.

Her own body was strong and light in a way she had never felt it to be at home or in school. She vaulted over dips in the trail. She leapt up onto fallen trees to get a view of what was ahead.

Everything was glowing and shining, and she herself was flying inside that glow. She could do anything. Be anything.

Nessa had never really felt truly beautiful before, but tonight she not only understood that she *was* beautiful, she understood that everyone was. That for all the competition and fear and knowing that the next runner was coming up behind you, she had been missing out on how beautiful life could be. She should have been watching and appreciating others instead of waiting inside herself for the right time to shine. The time was now.

She ran—danced?—through the loop of the trail and then up into the pastures behind Joe Bent's farm. She didn't like the feeling of being so close to the house—though the barn seemed like an interesting place. She ran over to a rise in the ground and into the woods. She wasn't on a trail. Nessa knew just where she was going, simply by following scents. She spotted a doe and tracked it briefly until she lost it. It didn't matter. She continued to feel blissed out.

She must have run three miles, to the edge of a small lake she'd never seen before. She leapt up onto a rock and she sang.

And then, sensing that she was no longer alone, Nessa looked down, into the woods that encircled her rock, and saw one wolf after another stepping out from behind the trees.

They were singing with her. They were singing the same song, and it was as if Nessa had known the song all her life. She didn't know how long she was there, singing, but the time felt endless and also short. Nessa wasn't thinking about scholarships and homework and helping her mom. She wasn't thinking at all.

It was not like singing with kids at school, where everyone was looking at each other and laughing and not trusting. Being with these wolves was like being with Vivian, Nate, and Delphine. She felt at home.

When the song was done, the wolves wanted to play. One of the smaller ones plowed into her, and for a second Nessa stiffened. Was she under attack? But then the wolf bowed to her, lowering its head, its mouth opened into a smile of sorts. Nessa returned the bow. The small wolf's tail was wagging, and then it rolled on to its back, showing Nessa its belly, and Nessa could not resist. She pounced on it, and the wolf was nipping at the underside of her chin, and then they were rolling over each other. Nessa hadn't played like this in years, not since she was a little girl. She growled. The other wolf nipped. It was amazing to feel so easily understood.

Another wolf joined in the game—Nessa thought of him as the first wolf's brother, and then a third, a playful sister.

They took turns playing with Nessa and she understood their personalities—super goofy. There was another whose style of play was slow and measured. Nessa thought of her as Mama. And a wolf who was so timid Nessa could barely keep the game going. Everything seemed to make him cower.

A big wolf hung around the edges of the group, but did not play. The alpha. He glided around noiselessly in the shadows and Nessa did not get a clear look at him at first.

He stayed aloof, and the others almost always had one ear pricked in case he made a sound of displeasure or gave a signal that it was time to move.

Finally, he met her gaze head-on and she saw his coat shine even in the dark: the white wolf. The wolf who had bitten her. He was the leader of this pack.

She felt an instant jolt of fear. This was the wolf from her dream, the one who had been causing her to wake up sweating. She froze as he padded toward her, his pace deliberate. He sniffed her nose and tail and, though she knew she was unnaturally stiff, she could not move. She could not return the sniffing though she knew she should.

Then the wolf did something Nessa had not been expecting. He lifted his head and showed her his throat. The gesture emerged fluidly mid-face-sniff. Nessa thought she might have only imagined it. Why would the alpha wolf make himself vulnerable to her?

But then he rolled on to his back, exposing not just his throat, but all his soft underside, and there was no mistaking that.

The gesture wasn't impulsive or playful but instead felt ceremonial. Nessa felt her fear slipping away, as it had with Chayton. Opening her jaws—but not biting down—she let the wolf feel her teeth on his throat, on the places where his legs connected to his torso. It was a few touches and then the moment was over, the white wolf back to his feet.

What had changed?

Everything.

They had made a pact. He would be her protector. She would follow his lead. Nessa was not exactly a member of the pack; she would not stay with these wolves forever, but she was a part of them for now.

She understood that the pack had been waiting for her. An alpha, a mother, an omega, two brothers, and a sister. They would be her family now.

Chayton had said she could get stuck in wolf form. Would she want that? To be with this group of wolves forever, learning to hunt, play, rest, sing, take her turn at patrol, speak the language she could tell they were using to communicate?

Could she be like this forever?

And then she remembered, like it was a smell, the cookies Bree had made for her, and suddenly, she knew it was time to go home.

But as she turned to leave, the alpha wolf, Big One, blocked her. He wasn't looking at her but at a point just over her shoulder as if to allow her to look at him, to take in just exactly how much larger he was than the rest of them. She lowered her head to show him that she respected his authority, and he stepped aside, letting her know that she was free to leave.

And then she was running again, covering all the trails she'd been on before, following not what she could see but what she could smell. When she was close to the trailhead, she noticed she was moving slowly, woodenly, without the feeling of dancing. Every step was exhausting and she could hear her labored breathing and feel her heart pounding. She was nearly blind in the pitch-darkness of the woods, and she reached into her pocket—she was wearing clothes again and walking on two legs. She pulled out the flashlight she'd stowed away earlier, and used it to find her way back down the path about fifty feet to the spot where she'd left her things.

She checked her phone. It had been only two hours since Bree had dropped her off. Spreading the cookies out on top of a fallen tree—a thank-you present for the wolves who had welcomed her; she hoped they would find them—she gathered up the rest of her things and texted Bree.

Holy crap, Nessa thought.

I am a wolf.

CHAPTER TWENTY-TWO

When Nessa's alarm went off at six the next morning—she was sleeping at Bree's—Bree woke up only enough to groan, "You have got to be kidding me." They had stayed up really late talking—Nessa describing what it was like to be a wolf, or trying to, and Bree asking a million questions.

Now, Nessa smacked at her phone until the alarm turned off and then got dressed as quietly as she could, sneaking out of Bree's front door to wait at the end of the driveway for Vivian, who was driving Nessa to the cross-country bus.

Nessa's happy mood from the transformation lasted through the drive with her mom, who didn't seem to notice anything different about her daughter.

But when Nessa took her first step onto the cross-country team bus, scanning for an empty seat where she'd be able to unpack her pillow and sleeping bag and get some rest, the mood faded.

She was riding with the team, but because of the doping accusations, she wouldn't be running. She would just have to tough it out.

Everyone on the bus was already curled up and tucked in, but Nessa couldn't get herself to sleep, instead leaning against the window, her forehead cold as the bus bumped along, staring at the farm fields, woods, and one-gas-station-towns they passed through.

Overnight, the orange and red and yellow foliage had dropped from the trees. The bright days of early fall were over, and Nessa had started to dress for winter in the mornings. The sky turned light purple even at four in the afternoon. Nessa should have been getting serious about her grades, her race times, her chances for applying to college next year. Instead, here she was, along for the ride but not dressed to compete.

It was worse when she had to watch Cynthia run, taking second place overall. Hannah was not too far behind. Nessa recognized the look on her face, the look you get when all you are thinking about is passing the one person ahead of you, and when you finish and it's all over, you don't know what to think about anymore.

Rumors of Nessa's doping had spread through the cross-country world. Just as at school, Nessa could hear whispers not meant for her ears. As she cheered for the Tether freshmen, JV, and varsity, standing at the finish line, a hand over her eyes as a shield from the glare, she heard, "That's her." And, "How desperate can you be? So much for the one-race wonder." And, "In high school already? What is wrong with the world?"

At the end of the girls' varsity race, Cynthia stepped up next to Luc and swung her second-place medal on its ribbon. They were almost 80 feet away but Nessa still heard her say, "I could have beat her. I wanted it so bad."

Luc said, "Yeah, I know that feeling," (though Nessa had never seen him lose any race that she could think of).

When Cynthia then whispered, "Maybe I should try taking what Nessa's been taking," Nessa had had enough.

"Hey!" she yelled, fast-walking toward them. "Stop talking about me behind my back. We're supposed to be on a team."

Cynthia seemed surprised and just stared.

Nessa turned away. She missed the wolves, the way she'd felt included and protected when she was with them. They had been accepting of her, no matter what they thought she'd done. With them, she had been more accepting of herself.

To let off some steam, Nessa joined the varsity boys on their warm-up jog, finding herself quickly moving to the front of the pack, next to Luc. Everyone was conserving their energy, but Luc's conserving speed was Nessa's sprint and Nessa was sprinting because she was going to lose her mind if she didn't.

She'd never run next to Luc before, and she found it both calming and terrifying to see how perfect his form was, how strong his body. He was somehow relaxed and intense all at the same time, his shoulders back, his legs flashing at an impossible tempo.

For a while they ran side by side without speaking. Nessa started to feel guilty for disturbing his alone time. She knew what it meant to try to get focused before a race. She was thinking of falling back when he checked her impulse by speaking.

"You okay?" he said, as if he understood what was going on with her—all of it, not just the doping accusations, but the fact that they were unfounded and no one believed her, that she couldn't compete, and that she could hear exactly what people were whispering about her.

"No," she said. She laughed. "I'm really not."

He grunted.

And then Nessa hacked up and spat a loogie. She wasn't like Cynthia. She wasn't cold and calculating, planning her every move to try to get in with some guy. She was done trying to impress everybody. And for the first time—ever?—she heard Luc laugh.

"You're disgusting, you know that?" he said, though she knew he was teasing her. She suspected that he was really thinking that she wasn't afraid to be herself.

Nessa looked at her feet and smiled. "Tell me something I don't know."

CHAPTER TWENTY-THREE

By Saturday afternoon, Nessa was feeling the effects of not sleeping Friday night. She was at the clinic with Bree.

"You're sure Sierra's appointment's at the same time, right?" Nessa said to Bree as they sat in the waiting room with Nate absentmindedly knocking beads together on a toy designed for one-year-olds.

"Obviously!" Bree said, smiling and rolling her eyes. "Maybe Cassian wants to leave a little mystery for the big date tonight. Don't worry so much."

A little bell chimed, signaling someone crossing the threshold to enter the clinic. Bree, Nessa, and Nate sat up straighter, looking at the door, and then studiously looking away from it.

But it was only the Larks: Billy and his mom.

"Hey Nate," Billy said in greeting. Nate didn't look Billy in the eye or move over to make room for him near his seat.

"Nate, remember your manners," Nessa said, which was the code that Nate's occupational therapist had taught Vivian—sometimes kids like Nate had to be trained to do things that came naturally to most people. Smiling to show pleasure. Laughing when someone makes a joke. Making eye contact to establish trust.

Nate looked at Billy and smiled. A little robotically, but, as his therapist had explained, it didn't have to look natural. It just had to happen. At Nate's bit of encouragement, Billy smiled wider and said, "I remember this!" about the toy that Nate was playing with. Nate piled all the beads down at the high point of a wire that looped all around like a roller coaster track, and then pushed them down so they would follow the wire. Billy took a turn next.

Mrs. Lark was checking in with Mary, Dr. Raab's ever-present nurse, and Gina, the receptionist. Nessa and Bree could not help but overhear their conversation.

"I called and left a message for Dr. Raab," Mrs. Lark was saying. "I called three days ago, and no one called me back, so I checked in again this morning. I thought I'd better come down in case he wanted to take a look at Billy? Now, remember, he already had a strep test and it was negative."

Bree gave Nessa a sympathetic look as Mrs. Lark insisted Billy had been running a low fever on and off since the last visit, and she'd been trying to get someone on the phone, wondering if maybe they should skip a treatment until he was better.

"Ann, it's okay," Mary was saying. "Billy's going to be fine. Dr. Raab's been busy. I'll get an answer for you today, though, if I have to force it out of him." She smiled warmly. Mrs. Lark took a second before she politely smiled back.

"Hey, do you think she knows?" Bree whispered. "About Dr. Raab being this major big deal scientist in California?"

"Yeah," Nessa said. "When was the last time he gave a kid a strep test?"

Nessa looked at Billy—he and Nate had stopped playing. Nate found prolonged interactions with other kids exhausting, and Billy looked like five minutes with the baby toy had knocked him out. His eyes were a little glassy and his cheeks were red. He went over to his mom and sat next to her, putting his head on her shoulder.

Just then, the chime dinged again and this time it *was* Cassian and Sierra. Nessa could feel her heart pick up speed and her own cheeks color at the sight of them. Billy seemed reenergized, searching for the soccer ball. Nate was talking a mile a minute about how he was going to use blocks to build the goals and Cassian was saying, "I'll be there in just a minute; you guys get it all set up for me." The reason he wasn't helping them was that he'd taken a seat, the one right next to Nessa, so close their legs and shoulders were touching and she could feel sparks shooting up from every point of contact and her heart was in her throat. Strangely, the feeling reminded her of being with the wolves, and at that thought, she blushed even more.

"Hey," Cassian said. "What are the odds of running into you here?"

"I suspect coincidence," Nessa said, laughing.

"Cassian, come play!" Billy called and Cassian stood up.

Just then, Nurse Mary came out from behind her desk with a file in her arm. "Billy, your turn!" she said brightly and there was a collective groan from Billy, Nate, and Sierra. Leaning forward, Cassian held out a hand for Billy to grasp on his way by, and said, "Next time, man, I want to see everything you've got." Billy ducked his head and mumbled something that Nessa didn't realize was, "I'm going to kick the ball so hard the goal is going to get all knocked over," until he'd already followed the nurse into the exam rooms.

Cassian met Nessa's eyes and they shared a genuine isn't-Billy-Lark-cute moment.

But then Nurse Mary came back for Sierra, and quickly after for Nate, changing the feeling in the room the way it always did when the kids were being examined.

Mary never allowed adults into the exam rooms with the kids, claiming that Dr. Raab needed to move quickly, that the room needed to be kept perfectly sterile, and that kids were by and large better behaved and less afraid of the needle stick when their parents weren't with them.

It was okay now that the kids in the study were older, but back when the study began, when the kids were littler, it had been hard to let them go, especially since some of them really were scared of the needles and cried as they were being led away. If Mary didn't have the disposition of a saint, they probably would have raised more of a concerted objection. All of the kids loved her.

When Mary came back to get something from her desk, Mrs. Lark approached her again. "I really do need to speak to Dr. Raab," she said. "I let Billy go back there because I didn't want to make a stink, but honestly, I don't understand why I'm not getting any answers from him. It's fine if he thinks Billy's fever won't be impacted by the tests, but I need to know that he's made that decision."

"Dr. Raab is planning on seeing you," Mary said. "He told me he thinks Billy is totally well enough for the exam, and he doesn't want to compromise the data by having him skip a visit, but he's going to want to talk to you as soon as he is done."

"I'd been hoping to speak to him before, actually," Mrs. Lark said, and Nessa could see Mary's posture change. Usually Mrs. Lark was pretty timid. Nessa could tell that Mary was surprised by Mrs. Lark's intensity.

The nurse's smile was frozen on her face as Mrs. Lark pushed around the desk and headed for the door to the study room. "I know this isn't your fault, Mary," she said. "But I just can't let this happen."

"Ann," Mary was saying. Then louder: "Mrs. Lark!"

But Ann Lark wasn't stopping.

Exchanging worried looks, Bree, Nessa, and Cassian rose to their feet, moving to the edge of the waiting room where they could see down the hall to the exam rooms. They had a view of Mrs. Lark getting to the door Billy had passed through, and pushing down on the handle with some force, Mary right behind her. Clearly she thought the door would open—she half slammed herself into it and seemed to almost bounce back before she caught herself.

"Can someone please tell me why this door is locked?" Mrs. Lark hissed. It wasn't clear whether she was talking to Mary or straight into the exam room.

She rapped on the door sharply. "Let me in, please. This is Billy's mom, and I absolutely insist on seeing my son."

The door opened from the inside, and Nessa suddenly became aware of noises that she had not heard before. The whirring of a ventilation system, tiny glass pipettes clinking against one another, the sound of papers shuffling, the tapping of keys on a computer keyboard. Later, she realized how weird it was she hadn't heard any of this before. She could hear *everything* usually. For some reason, the doors were made of something that blocked all sound. For Nessa, the question became: why?

"Please come in," Dr. Raab said cheerily, opening the door wide to Mrs. Lark. "Billy's in here. He's just fine!"

Nessa slipped down the hall to look through the door that had been opened for Mrs. Lark. There Mrs. Lark stood, just inside the door, staring into the room.

Nessa could see why. Dr. Raab's cheery welcome belied the fact that Billy wasn't sitting at the exam table, as they'd imagined—the way it would have been if he were at a doctor's appointment. He was lying down on it, his tiny body held in place with heavy leather straps fastened with large brass buckles.

Dr. Raab stepped quickly around the exam table. As if it were the most natural thing in the world, he undid the straps and helped Billy to sit up. "That should be just about it," he said to Billy cheerfully, in the deep and caring voice that Nessa recognized.

"You—you—" Mrs. Lark was sputtering. "You *restrain* them?"

"They're used to it, Ann," Dr. Raab said. Nothing in his voice indicated guilt or even displeasure.

Nessa had always liked Dr. Raab. He had been the one to pull strings to get Nate's occupational therapy funded through the clinic. When Nate was having a really hard time in third grade, he'd taken Vivian's calls after Nate had gone to bed, talking her through treatment options, arranging for a comprehensive evaluation at the University of Michigan medical school that was much less expensive than anything else Vivian had found.

"We had to use these restraints when these big guys were

just pups," Dr. Raab was saying. "And now we stick with them, because, well, as a parent I'm sure I don't have to tell you, routine is your friend. Eh, Billy?" Billy nodded but Nessa thought his nod looked a little nervous and weak.

Taking Mrs. Lark's elbow and escorting her into the hallway, Dr. Raab turned to Billy and said, "Come on, Billy; you're all done for today."

Dr. Raab spoke to Mrs. Lark in the hallway in a low voice, though of course Nessa could hear. "No, I'm not loving that fever," he said, "but to answer your question—and I apologize for not getting back to you earlier—sometimes these clinic study days get a little crazy—there's no possible way that the monitoring we're doing here could impact his overall health in any real way. Have you discussed this with his pediatrician?"

Nessa waited for Mrs. Lark's sigh of relief, but instead Mrs. Lark appeared to be holding her breath.

"We're essentially doing blood work in this study, with an occasional cheek swab or throat culture, blood pressure check. We monitor their vitals, and double what they'd have with an annual exam by listening to their heart and lungs, palpating their bellies, and asking them cognitive questions on a semi-annual basis."

"There's nothing you're doing that could contribute to a fever?" Ann Lark demanded.

"Ann, there's no way. I've watched these kids grow up. Their little systems have been through enough, fighting off whatever contaminants they encountered in the air and water they were born into. I promise you. I wouldn't be more careful if they were my own."

Now, finally, came Mrs. Lark's sigh as she accepted Dr.

Raab's word.

"Let's set Billy up with an appointment here at the clinic. So far—fingers crossed—we've got quite a healthy bunch, and I for one will be sad to see them age out. You know that thirteen's the upper limit for the study?"

"Yes, that's when the funding runs out."

"No, it's not the funding. The funding's good. It's very generous, thanks to the final ruling in the suit. But when a child's body enters puberty, the stuff we're looking for has either happened or it's not going to happen. You're just not going to see those developments impacting them during teenage years and beyond. Which is great news for the kids, for the families. You don't want to be coming in here Billy's whole life, do you?"

"Well, no," Mrs. Lark said. She even laughed. "But Dr. Raab, I want him to get over this fever. Isn't it bothering you that he hasn't been able to shake it over three weeks?"

"Mary?" Dr. Raab said. "May I see Billy's file again?"

Dr. Raab stepped to the side and peered at Mary's laptop with her. They spoke to each other in a low whisper.

Nessa could hear what Dr. Raab and Mary were saying, but most of it made no sense. Dr. Raab wanted to know which number samples they were looking at. Mary read him a list. "Are we doing the 7IRG with him?"

"No, remember you said last week to hold off on that for now."

"Yes, right," Dr. Raab said. "And what about the AVR test?"

Dr. Raab returned to Mrs. Lark. "There is nothing out of the ordinary with Billy," he said. "I understand why you're concerned, but I'm not. Kids get viruses, and sometimes we try this and that, and in the end we don't know if we fixed them or if we just rode the sucker out. I can get him some antibiotics, though, because I don't like it any more than you do. Would that give you some peace of mind?"

Billy was already back in the waiting room, kicking the soccer ball with Cassian.

"Doctor?" Mary interrupted. "I have a quick question."

"Of course," Mrs. Lark said, nodding to indicate that her fears were assuaged and they could leave the conversation there.

Mary and Dr. Raab disappeared into the back, stepping behind the door that Nessa couldn't hear through while Mrs. Lark, looking around the room for a friendly face, caught sight of Nessa. She gave Nessa a relieved smile, her face crumpling a bit at the release of the gesture. For a second, Nessa thought Mrs. Lark might cry, and she braced herself. But Mrs. Lark held it together, taking a deep breath.

"Dr. Raab is very good, isn't he?" she said.

Nessa nodded, but just then either Mary or Dr. Raab must have cracked open the door as their conversation came to an end, and suddenly Nessa could hear the tail end of their conversation.

"That was the AVR-12, not the AVR-10 you're using, right?" Mary asked. Dr. Raab made a grunt in reply.

"Yes, I'll be sure to cross check it," Mary said in reply. "I'd better do it quickly. The university lab truck's picking up at seven, but Paravida needs to make their pickup before five."

Paravida? What on earth are they discussing? Nessa wondered.

Just then, Sierra and Nate were released from their exams. Sierra ran to Cassian, and Nate ambled in, lost in his own thoughts—which gave Nessa a second to remain lost in hers.

The University of California was conducting the study. Or so the various websites said. What did Paravida—the company that had bought Dutch Chemical, the company that was supposed to make jobs happen in Tether—something yet to happen—what did Paravida have to do with any of this?

Sure, everyone in town knew that now that Paravida owned Dutch Chem, they bankrolled their obligations. Paravida funded the cleanup, the health clinic, the study, even if they hadn't produced the kind of job growth the town had been looking for. But why would samples from the study be sent over to Paravida?

Nessa looked at Nate. She couldn't get the image of those thick leather restraints pinning Billy to the table out of her mind. Was Nate tied down on the table every time he came here as well? He must have been.

When they arrived back home, Nessa asked Vivian what she knew about the Dutch Chem study. "Is it connected to Paravida?" Nessa said.

"Paravida?" said Vivian. She was in the middle of paying bills, the checkbook open on the kitchen table in front of her. Vivian hated paying bills, and usually Nessa avoided bothering her when she was doing it, but this was important. "They pay for it, but the clinic is run independently, and Dr. Raab works for some university hospital. I think it's the University of Michigan."

"Actually, Bree googled him. He works for the University of California."

Vivian looked up. "That does seem a little far away."

"And I heard something today that made it sound like they were sending Billy Lark's samples over to Paravida. Like, there was some kind of regular Paravida pickup at the clinic."

"Look, Nessa," Vivian said, glancing down at the checkbook

as if trying not to lose her place, then laying her pen on top of it. "The clinic is one of the best things that has ever happened to Tether. Health care, the doctors there, we are so lucky to have this in our town. And I don't care where Dr. Raab is based. That man has stuck with us through high and low and has been a very good friend to our entire family. Remember what he did for Nate. Mary is great too. If you hear Paravida mentioned, I'm sure there is a reasonable explanation. I've got enough to worry about, and you shouldn't worry either."

"Do you know that they're strapping the kids to the exam tables?"

"What do you mean?" Vivian said, her brow wrinkling in a frown.

"I saw Billy Lark in one of the rooms, just today."

"That's weird," said Vivian. "Did you ask about it?"

"Mrs. Lark did. They told her they had to do it when the kids were little and now they're used to it and they want to keep them feeling like it's all part of the same routine.

"I buy that," Vivian said, drawing out the words like she was still making up her mind as she said them. "I'm not sure I love it, but having worked with dogs and muzzles, I know sometimes helping someone doesn't look that pretty."

"I guess," Nessa said.

Vivian leveled her with a look. "Don't you go worrying about this," she said. "Nate is fine. Dr. Raab is fine. You worry about you. Let me take care of the rest of it, okay?"

Nessa nodded. When her mom laid down the law like this, it was best to listen.

"Okay."

But before she got ready for her date with Cassian, Nessa

sat down at the family computer, in the swivel chair usually occupied by Delphine. Without knowing what she was looking for exactly, she googled "Paravida" and came up with the company's home page.

Nessa scrolled through a slide show of professionally shot images. Kids sleeping in a tent, lit up by flashlights. An oil rig out on an ocean with a clean-cut man in a hard hat in the foreground. A woman in a lab coat holding up a beaker with a city skyline behind her, lit up by signs in Japanese characters melted on to the image.

The company seemed to make everything from light bulbs and nonstick pans to green energy and antibiotics.

Nessa opened a new window. She searched Michigan + Paravida + news + Dutch Chemical and came up with a series of articles from the *Detroit Free Press* website with headlines like "White Knight to Rescue Dutch Chem," "Paravida to Bring Jobs to Central Michigan," and "Paravida Commits Funds to Tether, MI." Nessa read them all, finding the story of Paravida as she remembered it.

Although she was pretty young during the years of Dutch Chem's worst water contamination, she remembered adults discussing the lawsuit. Vivian had explained that the court was forcing Dutch Chem to stop polluting immediately, and after that order, the company, already in bad shape, went into free fall, with layoffs affecting almost every family in Tether either directly or indirectly.

There had been fights in town. People who lost their jobs blamed the families suing Dutch Chem. The families suing were outraged at the outrage. What could be more important than the health of their children?

In the end, it hadn't mattered what people in Tether wanted or didn't want.

Nessa had learned the word "Pyrrhic" then, as in "Pyrrhic victory." It essentially meant empty. It described what happens when you win a lawsuit against a company that's already declared bankruptcy and doesn't have the money to pay the settlement to the affected families or fund the legally mandated health clinic or the long-term study on the Dutch Chem aftereffects.

Nessa had been in eighth grade when the parent company had declared bankruptcy. She remembered the state-funded scientists coming in to run tests in the town. And then, there had been nothing.

There had been no Dutch Chem. And Tether families sank even lower. Dr. Morgan had cut Vivian's hours at the vet's, and they'd gone on food stamps. Some of Nessa's friends had had to move.

Then, just as Nessa was getting ready for her eighth-grade graduation, the news spread through town like wildfire. The bankrupt Dutch Chem had been purchased. At first no one could believe that it was possible—who would take on a company with so many debts to pay? But then Paravida had made an official announcement and, almost overnight, was putting out press releases promising to rebuild Tether.

Of course, the jobs that people in Tether had believed would follow Paravida's takeover had yet to materialize. The plant seemed to be staffed exclusively by scientists and security guards brought in from other Paravida facilities. No one in town ever talked about what they were manufacturing.

So why would Dr. Raab be sending samples from the clinic study over there now?

CHAPTER TWENTY-FOUR

When Cassian came to pick up Nessa for bowling later that evening, she ran out the front door to meet him. No one saw her go: Delphine was at a friend's, and Vivian had brought Nate along to the grocery store. Nessa hadn't told them Cassian was coming to get her—it was too embarrassing. She said she was going bowling and let them assume she was going with Bree. They'd left long before she'd tried seven different tops on over her favorite jeans, finally settling on one the same piercing blue as her eyes.

As Nessa met the car at the curb, she peered in at real live Cassian Thomas, arriving at her house to pick her up for a date.

Cassian opened the door of his car, starting to come around

to her side of the car. Before he could get there, she opened her own door, seated herself, and buckled up.

"You're not going to let me open the door for you?" Cassian said. He sounded amused, and she was surprised by his honesty when he added, "I wanted to make this a real date."

"Sorry," Nessa said. "But isn't that whole open-the-door thing a little out of date?" Now she realized that she sounded a little rude. *Shoot.*

Once they started bowling, the awkwardness of those first moments went away. Nessa had always been a decent but not great bowler, but that night, she was bowling all strikes and spares. Cassian was keeping up with her, and they were trash-talking and drinking root beer. He did a really funny dance along with the animations that appeared on the screen over their lane every time they got a strike, which made Nessa laugh so hard she had to sit down.

Cassian looked at her with wide eyes. "WHAT?!!" he said, pretending he wasn't trying to be funny. Then he collapsed on the bench right next to her so their hips and shoulders were touching. "It's not nice to make fun of people," he said.

Still laughing, Nessa said, "I'm sorry." Then she looked up and saw that a bunch of Cassian's beautiful senior friends had arrived—Cynthia was among them—and Nessa got quiet, bracing for it to be horrible.

But it wasn't horrible. Kelly English pulled Nessa aside to whisper about how she had never noticed how pretty Nessa was until this fall, and what kind of shampoo did she use? Cynthia just nodded at her like they were in a secret club, and Nessa changed the subject so she wouldn't have to answer that her whole family shampooed with diluted health food store soap because it was cheap. When Cassian said to her, "Hey, let's get out of here," Nessa quickly agreed.

"Want to walk around?" he asked when they got outside.

She nodded. They left his car parked at the alley and walked into town.

"I know my friends can be kind of intense sometimes. I hope they weren't too much," Cassian said.

"They were fine," Nessa said to him. She meant it; they really had been.

"People find you…exciting," Cassian said. "You're this amazing athlete, and you're gorgeous, and no one can believe that they hadn't noticed you before."

"Cynthia noticed me," Nessa said.

"Oh, right, you must be friends, being on cross-country together."

"Not exactly…" Nessa said, letting her voice trail off.

"What?" Cassian said. "You and Cynthia don't get along?"

"You could say that," Nessa shrugged. She knew Cynthia and Cassian were friends.

He looked at her intently, so Nessa continued.

"There's something weird about the way she looks at me. Sometimes I even wonder if she was behind the doping accusation. If she was the one who put the stuff in my locker. You know? Who else would know where to even get steroids but the girl who spent the summer at a competitive cross-country camp?"

"No way. She'd never do something like that," Cassian said. "Cynthia's cool. I've been friends with her forever."

"Okay," Nessa shrugged. "I'm probably wrong. There was just something about the way she was there when my locker was broken into. The way she was looking at me, like she was thinking, 'Oh, *that* explains it.'"

"Maybe she was just surprised," Cassian said. "A lot of people were. You did make an enormous amount of improvement in a very short period of time."

A cold feeling seeped into Nessa's gut. She stopped moving. They had gone as far as the tiny health food/sandwich shop with its windows filled with ancient spider plants. The store was closed, but there were lights on in the windows. Cassian's blond hair lit up on one side of his head. He had told her he didn't believe she did it. He'd made a point of saying that to her in the cafeteria the day she'd found out she had to take a blood test. It had meant a lot to her. But now it didn't feel like he'd been sincere.

"Do you think I might actually *be* doping?" she said.

"I know, I know," he said, laughing. "You didn't. All I'm saying is that if you had, I think I could understand. I mean, Nessa, what makes you so cool is that you go after what you want."

"I thought you liked me for my looks," Nessa said, turning it into a joke on the surface. Underneath, she was trying to understand. Was Cassian backpedaling? Or was there more there? After all, he was saying what she'd been thinking all fall. Hadn't their shared ambition been what Nessa had seen in Cassian all along?

Somehow his saying it out loud to her made it sound ugly.

"I guess I shouldn't really say this, but it's true so I will," Cassian went on. "I don't care if you did take whatever illegal substance. I would understand. I would even kind of respect you for it. You see, Nessa, I'm not here because I like you and isn't that sweet and first date and all that crap. I *really* like you. I think this might be serious for me. I think you might be...the most interesting person in Tether. I think you're going to have an amazing future. I think we're both going to have that. And I just…I just want to be around you more."

Cassian suddenly slid his hand into hers as they walked.

Nessa wasn't sure how to interpret what he was saying. "You've dated a lot of people," was all she could come up with. "I've never really dated anyone at all."

"I know," Cassian said. Then, his face turning red, he corrected himself. "I mean, I know I've dated a lot. I didn't mean to say I knew that you hadn't. I don't know what your dating life has been." He held up a hand. "I don't even really want to know. The only part of your dating life I'm really interested in is who you are dating now. And I want that to be me."

He looked worried. Nessa knew she should answer him and say that she felt the same way. But all the air had been sucked out of her throat and she couldn't form words beyond, "All right," and then, "Okay."

"Okay?" Cassian said. "What I said just now is okay?"

Nessa nodded. "Yeah."

"Then I can do this…?" He was smiling as he leaned forward and kissed her. She felt herself smiling back

"Yeah," she said, when he pulled away. "You can do that."

"Oh, really?" Cassian said, looking sheepish and also a little cocky and maybe proud of himself.

"Come here," Nessa said, pulling him back toward her. This time he kissed her for real and she kissed him back. They stumbled toward the wall of the store behind them, and then Cassian moved her into a shadow so they wouldn't be seen— not that anyone was out on the deserted main street of Tether, Michigan, on a Saturday night.

CHAPTER TWENTY-FIVE

Passing the music room on her way to the bathroom during English class on Monday, Nessa stopped just to listen to the song the chorus was learning, some old-fashioned, classical piece with the sopranos singing up in their heads.

A freshman with a bathroom pass gave her a strange look.

"What are you looking at?" Nessa said, because she was tired of everyone talking about her all the time.

"I'm not looking," the freshman said. "I'm listening."

That's sweet, Nessa thought. The kid liked the song just as much as she did. Until he added, "I'm listening to you," and Nessa realized that she herself was singing.

And she wasn't singing, exactly. She was making a high-pitched humming noise that wasn't in tune with the piece so much as it felt like it was an echo of the piece inside Nessa's mind. Nessa clamped a hand over her mouth.

Oh, my god. She was howling. In school.

The freshman turned the corner and Nessa felt her face go red, as she rushed back to class herself.

The whispers had returned. Nessa's name was linked to Cassian's. Everyone was talking about how they had been seen out on a date and the whispers intensified every time Cassian made a point of stopping by Nessa's table at lunch, or offering her rides home, or the one time he led her behind the field house after practice, when it was already dark out, and kissed her where no one could see.

The days turned into a week, and now Nessa was starting to think about the next moon phase: she could see it growing fat in the night sky—and the chart Selena gave her said it would rise sometime during the day on Thursday.

Nessa had been super focused waiting for the new moon— her GPA had never looked this good, and she was hoping her streak would continue as she approached this moon. But instead of becoming super focused, Nessa found it hard to focus at all.

Nessa lost track of the days of the week. She left the books she needed for homework at school. One crazy morning, she simply could not remember her locker combination. And another time, she found herself staring at a pencil in math class, so lost in thought she'd forgotten to fill in the answers on a test.

"Nessa? Nessa!" Delphine said, banging on the bathroom

door when Nessa was touching the bones of her face, thinking about what must happen when she shifted into a wolf—were those her bones still, or did they belong to another creature? Delphine's anger brought her back to reality, in which she was supposed to be brushing and washing and otherwise getting ready for bed.

It wasn't that she'd fallen in love with Cassian, though that's what Bree kept assuming when Nessa spaced out. Nessa was pretty sure the brain-takeover was part of wolf transformation. It was getting worse as the moon grew larger.

"What are you doing *now*?" Bree said when Nessa got up from the lunch table and started walking along the edge of the cafeteria walls. Bree followed her when it became obvious that a lot of kids were staring at Nessa. "Nessa, you look like you think the wall is talking to you or something," Bree said, laughing nervously.

"It is," Nessa said. "Or at least it's squeaking. You can't hear that?"

Bree shook her head, raised her eyebrows, shook her head again. "Should I be able to?"

"There are *mice* back there," Nessa explained. "I can hear them. There are probably about a couple dozen right now, waiting for all of us to go home so they can get at the crumbs. Our school is completely infested."

"Ew," said Bree, covering her mouth with her hand. "That's disgusting."

Nessa shrugged. "They're just animals."

"That carry disease and are probably running all over the cafeteria kitchen at night. I'm putting this on the student council agenda," said Bree.

Nessa's hair was lightening again, and she heard two girls sitting nearby at lunch talking about the exact process they were sure she'd used to color it. Nessa found this so hilarious she sent some chocolate milk out of her nose. "Ew, gross, Nessa, come on!" Bree protested. "It's bad enough you're eating nasty school hamburgers at the same table as me. Do you know how that meat was harvested?"

Nessa didn't care how the meat was harvested. It was Tuesday. The full moon was two days away. If she didn't eat three of these burgers at lunch, she knew her stomach would be rumbling again before practice.

Coach Hoffman found her in the lunchroom on Thursday and asked her to drop into his office before practice. He told her he had good news, but still, she was nervous.

She found Principal Sarakoski, Mr. Porter, and Mr. Cooper all waiting for her in Coach's office. "Nessa," Coach said. "Thanks for coming. Have a seat."

Ceremoniously, he passed Nessa a printed sheet of codes, numbers, percentages, and dates. She looked at it blankly.

"Is this my blood test result?" Nessa said.

Coach Hoffman was smiling. "It is."

"What does it mean?" She handed him back the paper, as though he should read it out loud.

"It means you're racing this Saturday. As I'm sure you know, it's the qualifying tournament for States, so I'm personally very pleased to welcome you back on the team."

"I am?" said Nessa. The cloud she'd been in cleared immediately.

"And I believe Principal Sarakoski has something to say to you also."

"You're back on the team, Nessa," Principal Sarakoski said, "and I hope you realize that the accusations were never personal. It was never about you, you understand. In the face of the evidence that seemed to be pointing in your direction, I just had to be sure our school's name did not get dragged through the mud."

"I understand," Nessa said, wishing Principal Sarakoski would just stop talking and release her.

"I've asked Mr. Porter to reach out to any recruiters he knows and offer to fax them a copy of your clean test, assuming your mother gives her permission. Would that be all right with you?"

"That would be great," Nessa said. Mr. Porter caught her eye, nodded, and gave her a thumb's up, like he'd been on her side all along.

"So we're good here?" Coach asked, looking around the office. Principal Sarakoski nodded, Mr. Porter smiled, and Coach made a sound like an explosion and punched the air with both fists.

"Okay, Nessa, it's time to run!"

Coach's directive gave Nessa an ache, a desire to run. She felt it straight to the bone. She had to take a deep breath and get herself through the next steps: locker room, stretch, warm up.

She was finally back on track, ready to get back on the path she'd laid out for herself. She knew she was going to transform, but she had plenty of time to get back to normal. Friday night she'd carbo-load for the race. Saturday she'd get on the bus with the rest of the team, sleep as much as she could, run as hard as she was able, and hopefully be on her way to qualifying for States.

With the doping issue behind her, Nessa thought she had the next few days all figured out. The Universe had other plans.

CHAPTER TWENTY-SIX

This transformation started out just like the one before. By the time Bree dropped her at the woods, Nessa was riding white-knuckled in the passenger seat, her hand on the door like she was about to be carsick.

Before Bree could pull into the trailhead parking area, Nessa said, "Stop. Stop!" and Bree, looking alarmed, pulled over to the side of the road.

"Nessa, wait," Bree said, but Nessa couldn't wait. Mumbling a rushed, "Gotta go," she had the passenger door open and she was off, running into the woods, finding her way without a trail, her last thought a hope that Bree would remember to leave the phone again.

And then Nessa had to strain to remember what a phone was. She called to mind the image of her phone, but it felt like déjà vu—she could remember remembering it, but that was it. She certainly couldn't imagine picking one up to call or text someone. She couldn't imagine picking one up, period. Her hands were paws already. White fur tufted up from them, glowing in the moonlight. She had a sense of herself as a bright flash of white, a satellite of the moon above.

Nessa had forgotten about how crisply focused everything became when she could smell as a wolf. Smelling was like tasting. It was like feeling. Smells were attached to emotions, even for humans—a smell was one of the few memories of Nessa's dad that lingered: sage, smoke, and soil.

Running, Nessa sensed mice, deer, cats—processing each being's existence. Could they hurt her? Could she eat them? A dog had been through earlier. She could smell the sheep enclosed in their barn at Joe Bent's farm. The wood smoke and charred meat from his dinner table made her hungry and afraid, all at the same time. There were a hundred different acrid burning smells coming from the cars and tractors and ATVs and generators he kept on the property, and another kind of burning smell—leaves?

In the woods, the smells were softer, colder: a decomposing log carried down the current in a stream, sap sprayed from a recently snapped pine bough, an ant hill about a half a mile away, an owl's nest up in a tree a mile beyond that. And, of course, the other wolves.

She caught the trail of the pack led by the white wolf. She recognized each of their scents. She wondered whether she would be welcomed again, and then she plunged forward, remembering how they had run with her and played with her, and wrestled and raced. She heard howling in the distance and picked up speed, knowing that they must have smelled her, too. She sat back on her haunches and called out to them, hoping they could hear her and would know that she meant no harm. For a non-pack member to enter a pack's territory would likely mean death, but somehow she was different. She wasn't one of them, but neither was she a threat.

And then they were running alongside her, surrounding her. She recognized Big One, the white wolf, out in front, the ones who she thought of as the brothers and the sister on either side, flanking her, first one then the other trying to get her attention through an erratic movement, a ducking of the head, a raising of the tail. Nessa wondered if any of these movements might mean something akin to "Psst," or "Hey you."

Mama—Nessa didn't know how she knew this was the wolf's name but she did—was hanging back behind with a lesser adult male as company.

The wolves were running like they had somewhere to be, and Nessa had the feeling they were leading her in a specific direction. Leaving the trail, they headed into some light brush, climbing—Nessa could feel the incline in the way her back legs stretched out so much farther than her front.

One of the brothers made three short yips. Nessa didn't know what they meant, but, given that the big wolf came back to him and gave him a dirty look before returning to the front of the pack, Nessa assumed the wolf had asked an annoying question, "Are we there yet?" in wolf.

Nessa had noticed that within the pack, Big One was constantly establishing dominance over the others. He'd cuff the other wolves or hold his chin and tail high in the air while Mama or the younger wolves, the brothers and the sister, lowered their shoulders in deference and tucked in their tails. The young wolves acted like children most of the time, and the submissive one was worse than that. He acted like he didn't even deserve to be alive except to serve Big One's needs.

They reached an outcropping of rocks, standing above flat farmland, with a single house and barn visible below. Nessa could see the details: the neat, gray, tin-gabled roof, the small barn, the light from the kitchen windows spilling out into the gravel yard.

The white wolf lifted his head. This was definitely a way of "talking" to the others. This one was saying something, and Nessa could understand the gist of it, even if she didn't know exactly which parts meant what.

He was saying, "Look."

Nessa's human self made a tiny stir inside of her, reminding her wolf self who lived in this house.

Billy Lark.

And then the wolves were running again, and Nessa was drawn up into the movement, spooked like she was a deer. Down a slope this time, in the opposite direction, through the underbrush of trees, until at last they emerged from the growth and were passing between the fields, coming up on the farm-house they'd seen from above.

At the corner where the field met the barn, the wolves came to a stop. There were six of them who had been running, including the two brothers, sister, Mama, Big One, and the last one, who Nessa figured was the omega wolf, the one the pack tolerated only because he was completely submissive to everyone in it. He had partially torn ears, a white front leg, and black spots on his gray snout that looked like freckles.

Omega came to Nessa now, nudging her, pulling up a paw and batting at her neck. The movement might have disfigured a human, but in wolf state, his nails did not cut through Nessa's thick fur. Omega never tried to hurt anyone in the pack. His mission in life seemed to be to serve others, to make himself as unobtrusive as possible. His tail was tucked between his legs, his head held low in contrast to Big One, the alpha, who was erect with his tail lifted high.

"Come," Omega seemed to be entreating Nessa. "Please?" He took a step and looked back at her. She moved to follow and he led on.

They were headed to the house, but not toward the light coming from the kitchen windows. Trotting in a wide circle around the light, the submissive wolf led Nessa to a dark window on the house's other side. The sky behind the house was starting to show signs of light, but this side was still in shadow. Except for his one white stocking, Omega had a dark coat and moved without making any noise at all.

Then Omega went up on his hind legs in front of a window and laid his paws on the sill. He alternated looking through it and looking back at Nessa, as if showing her what he meant for her to do, inviting her to partake of a bone he'd been worrying.

Feeling uncomfortable, and definitely worried about the human odors coming at her—they smelled so strong, it was as if they were being blown in her direction by an industrial fan— Nessa sidled up to the wall of the house beneath the window, rose up on her hind legs, and rested her paws against the sill.

She saw a nightlight plugged into one wall, casting a stencil of a moon and stars on to the room's ceiling. Nessa could make out a bed with an indistinct lump in it—it had to be Billy.

Nessa shuddered. Why were they here? She looked at her guide wolf, who was staring fixedly into the room, and she again followed his gaze, even as her front legs were feeling strained.

She knew wolves had an uncanny knack, when hunting, of being able to tell which animals were compromised—old, young, weak, lame, sick—and easiest to bring down in a hunt. Scientists were not aware of how wolves made this calculation, only that they were choosey about what they would expend the energy to hunt, and they were almost never wrong about which animals were the most vulnerable within a herd.

Suddenly, the crack of light along the floor that indicated a door to the hallway grew into a rectangle. The door was opening, and Nessa saw Mrs. Lark's form outlined in the bright light. Billy moved in bed, one bare foot sticking out from under the covers.

Billy pushed off the covers and half sat. Mrs. Lark was holding a glass of water, pills cupped in her other hand. She placed both on the nightstand and leaned over to put a palm on Billy's forehead. Nessa registered the worried expression on her face as she pulled her hand away and turned in the direction of the window. Nessa's wolf guide quickly dropped down, but Nessa didn't think to do the same until she saw the look of first shock and then abject terror on Mrs. Lark's face when her eyes met Nessa's through the glass.

All she could think was that Mrs. Lark *knew* her. So why was she screaming? There must be something else really scary going on, and Nessa wondered, lost in panic, if she herself were safe.

And then submissive Omega did something that could not

be characterized as submissive at all. He plowed into Nessa, the force of the contact indicating he'd taken a running start. Nessa landed on her back, four paws in the air, and then the suddenly not-so-submissive wolf nipped at her haunches to get her back up on her feet and they were both running, quickly joined by the rest of the pack, who had remained hidden behind the barn.

It was a good thing they had moved off when they did, too, because she could still hear Mrs. Lark screaming, and then the sound of the front door opening, and Mr. Lark's voice saying, "Dear sweet lord, get the rifle."

The seven skinny wolf forms were already nothing but marks in the distance, streaking across the open fields, headed for the cover of trees.

Suddenly Big One stopped short. The young wolves, Mama, and Omega pulled up behind him. Nessa stopped too. As soon as she thought to ask the question, "Why are we stopping here?" she recognized that she could smell why.

They'd been running from humans and hadn't been careful. And straight ahead, she could smell a pack of stranger wolves. They were close.

This made no sense. Wolves knew to stay away from one another. Had Big One accidentally led his pack out of their well-defined territory?

No. From the way the big wolf was standing, his front legs locked, his tail straight out behind him—not up but not between his legs either—Nessa knew that was not the case. They were on defense.

Nessa barely had time to think about her own stance, because there was movement in the trees ahead of her. Branches shaking and then a shadow passed between two trees. Another shape emerged to the left from behind a pine, and another on the right. They were wolf shapes, animals stepping silently into the moonlight where the tree cover was thinner.

Big One growled, lowering his jaw, a sound Nessa easily interpreted to mean, "No one needs to get hurt."

And then the wolf facing Big One showed his teeth. They seemed to glint in the light, and Nessa took three steps closer to check whether she was seeing what she thought she was seeing: the wolf's teeth were filed to points, just like the teeth on the wolf she'd tried to free from Joe Bent's trap, back in September, on the night she was bitten. And there was an incision, the length of its torso!

This was *that* wolf? Did he remember her? He wasn't acting like he remembered Nessa. He didn't look like he was paying attention to Nessa at all. This wolf's eyes looked angry. Murderously angry. Nessa had the sudden thought that her pack may have been protecting Billy's house from these wolves.

Just as Big One started to push forward, the new wolf lunged. Big One bent his head down, trying to catch the new wolf under the throat as he charged, but the new wolf managed to jog to the left at the last second, and the two reared up on their hind legs, looking like they were almost hugging, except their front legs were swatting the air madly as they tried to twist themselves into the most strategic position before they fell back down.

Mama went crazy. She spun in a quick circle, whining and whimpering; then she crouched and sprang forward, not joining the fight, but looking like she was acting it out by herself, jogging a few steps to the side, then back again. The siblings were just as agitated as Mama, running back and forth between their parents and the wolf under attack.

Three more wolves emerged from the darkness, kicking everyone's adrenaline up even further. Only Omega was still, his head down, his tail between his legs.

That was probably why the new wolves knew to attack him next. Nessa didn't see the attack begin, only turned to him when she heard him barking and saw that, like Big One, he was facing off with three other wolves, all larger than he was. All larger than Mama and Big One, too.

The two on the outside took turns jumping in to bite Omega on the torso. Each time, he would twist his body and threaten to bite their faces, and they would back off. But Nessa could see fur in their mouths. With each bite, the submissive wolf would move backward, his tail hugged down the back of his body, his shoulders hunched down, as if begging the wolves who were attacking him to notice how insignificant a presence he really was.

He wasn't giving up, though. Omega was barking, growling, trying everything he could to get the other three to back off. His voice was strong and true, but his barking was not nearly as deep as Big One's.

Nessa felt every blow, every nip, every bark and growl in her gut and her heart, the fear both paralyzing her and feeling like it was liquefying her insides. She wanted to make the giant wolves stop, but none of the other wolves in the pack was moving. When Omega went down and the three hostile wolves jumped right on him, she ran toward them, but one of the brothers blocked her. "Somebody help him!" Nessa said, but of course it just came out as useless barking.

The pack would not sacrifice itself for Omega; they would

fight only in defense of their leader. The submissive wolf twisted his body, slid into an upward posture, slithering between the other wolves like a snake, but then they brought him back again.

Nessa knew she couldn't watch a minute longer. She had to get out of there. She turned to the left and the right, looking for an exit, but all she saw were eyes. Many, many sets of glowing, yellow eyes. Aside from the five wolves in the clearing, there must have been another four watching from the woods.

Watching her.

She began to breathe faster as she realized there was no way she could escape, nowhere for her to go, and then she turned and made a break for it anyway, panicking, knowing that there was nothing Big One or Mama could—or would— do to protect her.

Her head was down, her eyes were focused on the ground, and then she felt the first bite. It came from behind; not only did Nessa register the animal's jaws connecting to her ankle, her body felt the pain of the other bite—that *real* first bite—all over again.

CHAPTER TWENTY-SEVEN

essa heard herself cry out in a wolf's whine and then she turned, surprised by the power she was able to summon to push the other animal off her.

Crouching, she faced the other wolf, a low growl escaping her throat, her eyes fixed on the other animal's shoulders—in a guess that she'd see motion there not telegraphed by the animal's eyes. The highly familiar smell of fear and something else she recognized filled her nostrils and, like it was mentholated, it cleared her head. She rolled the smell around on her tongue, tasting it, her breathing almost overwhelmed by the sense that she was meant to kill this wolf.

She was going to do it. Even though it was larger than she

was, there was something reckless about this wolf's aggression. If she let this wolf make the first move, he was likely to make the first mistake as well.

But two other wolves joined the one who had bitten her, and Nessa felt her blood cool. No strategy could save her. It was three against one.

So she thought about Omega and she started to bark, the way he had, barking like she would never stop barking. She saw how the wolf who had first bitten her blinked a bit with each bark. The two who had come in to help him took micro-steps away from her every time she barked. Her barking bothered them. She could start there.

Nessa barked louder, deeper, and as ferociously as she could. She could feel it resonating inside her chest as if it were the pounding hoofbeats of an army of wolves on horseback come to her rescue. It was happening without her intent. Was she really this powerful? Was it just her imagination, or could she hear another wolf barking with her when she barked?

Her attacker must have been wondering the same thing, his eyes darted to one side and then the other, looking to see if she was alone. His eyes rested off to Nessa's side for a moment, and he took a step back. Nessa kept quiet, and distinctly heard barking. Someone was coming to help her.

Nessa wasn't alone.

A gray wolf with black markings came up alongside her. He was long legged, taller even than Big One and about the same height as the wolves with the filed teeth.

The gray wolf lunged at Nessa's challenger, and the wolf cried out in surprise—a whimper—and backed away. The two wolves who had been standing at attention, waiting for the center wolf to make his move, took a step forward and then veered off to either side, as if they had been meaning to head off in those directions anyway. The new, gray wolf then charged the wolf who had been the most aggressive toward Nessa, and he turned tail and also ran.

Disbelieving, relieved, taking a few deep breaths, Nessa finally took a good look at the new wolf.

He was tall. He was thin too, as though he didn't eat much. His smell did not frighten her. It was familiar, but she couldn't place it. She could only say it reminded her of the woods.

The gray wolf looked over his shoulder and, as if saying, "Let's go," he bounded back toward the pack wolves. Nessa followed, noticing as she ran that she wasn't hearing noises anymore. No more barking. No growling. Was the fight over?

For a moment, she was seized with worry. What if Big One, the brothers and their sister, Mama…what if they were dead?

But she found them standing at attention, their faces pointed toward the tall gray wolf, waiting for him.

He strode into the clearing and immediately went to Big One.

Big One greeted the new wolf as if he and this wolf were equals, turning to sniff each other then circling slowly and finally brushing noses. They clearly knew each other but from the way Big One was treating the new wolf, Nessa could tell they weren't pack mates. No one in Big One's pack got away with treating Big One like an equal.

The gray wolf touched noses in turn with Mama and each of the three younger wolves. Nessa wondered if he'd do the same with Omega, or if that wolf was too lowly to count.

But wait a minute, Nessa thought. Where *was* Omega? Had he snuck off?

Her eyes found him lying on the ground. Nessa ran to him.

"He needs a doctor!" Nessa wanted to say, but she knew, looking at him, that even her mom or Dr. Morgan would only be able to end his misery sooner. One eye was closed, bloody. The other stared out as if not knowing what it saw. She could see his back legs splayed at weird angles, like they'd been broken. He was bleeding from his abdomen and from his neck. But his tail thumped at Nessa, and she nosed him in the intact ear. She could hear the wet, gurgling sounds he was making as he struggled to breathe. A rib might have punctured a lung. And then his breath gurgled one last time, and his good eye closed, and Nessa realized that he was dead.

She stayed in a crouch for a while, waiting, not moving, frozen, staring at the spot where the wolf had been alive and was now just a dead body.

She could smell blood, as rich as warm milk—not Omega's. The smell was mixing into her own popcorn-smelling fur. She looked at her ankle. The blood was flowing freely, bright red on the white.

Nessa could feel the adrenaline that had been pumping through her system begin to fail. Her back legs were trembling. She needed to go home.

The tall gray wolf pushed her away from the body of the submissive wolf. He pushed her toward the path heading home.

She ran.

CHAPTER TWENTY-EIGHT

When Nessa finally found her phone in the place where Bree *had* left it, her sock was soaked, and there were streaks of dried blood on her skin beneath her jeans. She could barely put weight on the leg where she'd been bitten, and after Bree texted that she'd be there soon, Nessa sat on the picnic table at the trailhead. She put her hands between her knees, shivering, her teeth chattering.

She couldn't believe the difference in the way she felt now and the way she'd felt when Bree dropped her off two hours ago. She'd been so cocky, so sure of herself, thinking of her transformation to a wolf as one more item on her to-do list, thinking she knew exactly what this was going to be.

"What happened to you?" Bree said, taking a look at Nessa's bloody ankle while the light in the car was still on.

At the sound of Bree's familiar voice, Nessa fell apart.

"I just saw a wolf get murdered!" Nessa said, her voice cracking, a sob emerging. Bree looked startled.

"For real?"

"It was this sad wolf," Nessa tried to explain, but now she was crying for real, her sobs getting in the way of her words. She couldn't say the name "Omega" out loud. That would be too much. "He was so submissive and scared for himself, and somehow the big wolves—they just *knew*. They knew he was the one to go after." Saying the words out loud, the horror of that moment came rushing back to Nessa. "And they went for him. They were so...big. And their teeth! Bree, it was awful. We could only watch. These four attacking wolves, they were almost scientific about it. I felt like I was watching a serial killer. Or killers. They ganged up on him. Bree, it just was so *cruel*."

Nessa was having a hard time talking through her sobs and Bree was staring. Nessa could tell she wasn't understanding. She wasn't getting what it was like to see the submissive wolf pulled down, to know that he wasn't coming back. It was too much to take in for anyone who wasn't there, but Nessa had to try to explain.

"You're bleeding, Nessa," Bree said. "We need to get you to a hospital. Or the clinic. Something."

"And tell them what?" Nessa said. "That I was bitten a second time? What's my mom going to say? How will I explain that I went into the woods again when she very clearly told me it was off limits?"

"But you need help!" Bree said.

"Hold on," Nessa said. She took off her shoe, pulled back her sock, balled it up, and pressed it into the wound to stop the bleeding. By the time Bree had pulled up in front of Nessa's house, it had stopped flowing. Nessa wet the cleanest part of the sock with a water bottle so she could clean the wound enough to see how bad it was. Bree was holding the flashlight on her phone so that Nessa could see what she was doing. "I think it's just a puncture."

"The wolf could be rabid."

"I was treated for that already," Nessa said. "I just need to go inside and soak it. It's going to be fine. Besides, not the clinic, Bree, not now."

Nessa shivered, thinking of the last time she was there. The straps. The strange mention of Paravida. All the whispered references to strange numbers.

And that reminded her. "I almost forgot to tell you. The pack took me to Billy's house!" Nessa said. "Before we were attacked. The submissive wolf, the one who died, he led me to Billy's window."

"Do you think that Billy has something to do with why the wolves brought you in?"

"Yes, but I don't know what," Nessa said. "I don't see what the connection could be. I mean, it's not like the Larks seemed particularly excited to see the wolves. Mr. Lark went to get his *gun*."

"They saw you?"

"They saw me as a wolf," Nessa said. "I accidentally made eye contact with Mrs. Lark. She panicked. Then Mr. Lark came out with his shotgun, but we got away. Bree, if it hadn't been for me, if we hadn't been running for our lives, we might've had more time to avoid the other pack. Maybe the submissive wolf would still be alive."

"Nessa," Bree said, "you can't blame yourself. Wolves don't have long lives. They're not people."

"I know, but…" Nessa shook her head. She wasn't convinced, and she could see that Bree could tell.

"I think you need to talk to Chayton," Bree said.

"Chayton's gone," Nessa said, not bothering to hide the bitterness in her voice. "He's got his friends to take care of, remember?"

"I don't care," Bree said. "I'm going to call Selena. You're not really a wolf. None of this is your fault. You can't keep going in there. This is getting too dangerous. You could have been seriously hurt."

Nessa slept fitfully, dreaming about the wolf with the filed teeth, feeling the shock of pain and surprise when he jumped her. She woke feeling almost more tired than she'd felt going to bed. Bleary eyed, she pulled back her hair, showered, and threw on clothes.

Putting any weight on her foot was excruciating. But she couldn't let anyone see her limping, especially not anyone connected to the cross-country team. She had put a bandage on it the night before, after soaking it, wrapped it in ice, elevated the ankle, and taken a double dose of ibuprofen, but none of that had done any good.

Bree had had to go into school early for a student council meeting but texted:

How's the ankle?

Nessa texted her from the school bus:

I can barely walk.

Bree wrote:

GO. TO. THE. DOCTOR.

Nessa didn't reply. She knew if she went to the doctor he would say she couldn't run on an injury, and she knew she just had to run. Her Homecoming result alone would not qualify her for States. She was going to need one more good time. The stakes were simply too high.

As she was limping off the bus, she felt her phone buzz in her pocket. Stepping behind a tree, she answered it.

"Nessa," she heard, and it took her a half-second to recognize Chayton's voice. Lowering herself to the stone balustrade, she rolled her eyes.

"Where have you been?" she said. "Are all shamans this impossible to reach?"

"Are all high school girls this reckless? I heard about your adventure last night." Nessa realized Bree must have called Selena. "What the hell were you thinking, taking on aggressive wolves like that?"

"*They* attacked the pack," she said.

"That can't be true," Chayton said. "Wolves won't attack another wolf unless he comes into their territory or provokes them. You must have challenged them. Wolves don't look for fights that way."

"You didn't tell me—" Nessa began, but stopped mid-sentence because she realized she could finish it in so many different ways.

She didn't know there were aggressive wolves out in the woods.

She didn't know if she was supposed to be following scents when she was out, the way she felt she wanted to when she was in wolf state, or to hide from other animals.

She didn't know how any of this worked, and even though Chayton had told her to pay attention to her feelings and what was happening when she changed, she didn't know that there was anything she could identify as a trigger for her transformation except the moon.

Chayton wasn't going to let her finish anyway. "I'm out here in Wyoming, trying to get my buddy through a sweat lodge purification he desperately needs, and you're back in Michigan, flushing wolves out of their known territory, which any shapeshifter would know to respect—"

"Look," Nessa said. "I'm sorry I'm not Native and you're stuck dealing with me, but I didn't ask for this! I didn't do anything wrong. I did what you told me to. I was alone. It was dark. It was the full moon. You haven't told me anything useful. You didn't tell me we'd be snooping around people's houses, and getting shot at and then running into a rival wolf pack. It was this huge rumble, and for your information I was in the process of getting myself out of there. And the other wolves, they wouldn't let me go."

Chayton asked a question but Nessa couldn't understand it—the connection was going in and out.

"Say that again?" she said.

"You were trying to run away?"

"Of course!" Nessa said. "The wolves were attacking this

big wolf who is in charge of everything and this other wolf who was *murdered* was defending him. One of the same pack came after me, and I felt him bite my ankle."

"He came after you *from behind*?" Chayton said. "You were running *away* from him?"

"Of course," Nessa said. "I'm actually *not* stupid. I would have never tried to get anywhere near the wolf from that invading pack. Especially since he had those creepy filed teeth like that one I tried to free from the trap."

"What? What kind of teeth? You're breaking up."

"They were sharp, like they'd been filed down or something to make them sharper. And they were huge, too, these wolves."

She explained how the big gray wolf had protected her and then seemed to know the others in her pack.

"Oh, good," Chayton said, dropping the accusation in his tone. "I'm glad he's doing something right."

"You know that wolf? Is he part of the pack?"

There was silence on his side of the call that went on long enough for Nessa to start to wonder if the call had been dropped.

"You still there?" she said.

"I'm thinking," he answered. "Something bad is going on. How's your ankle?"

"Sore," Nessa said. "I'm supposed to run tomorrow. There's a meet. It's where you qualify for States."

"You absolutely cannot run on a bad ankle," Chayton said.

"I have to," Nessa said. "If I don't make States, I don't know what I'm going to do. Recruiters will be there. Colleges. I've worked so hard."

"Listen to me," Chayton said, his tone verging on nasty.

"You've got to heal. These wolves coming into your territory, being that aggressive. This is an issue. You have to be ready to fight."

Nessa remembered seeing the submissive wolf go down. "Is Billy Lark okay?" she said.

Instead of answering her question, Chayton told her to sleep with a poultice of garlic, comfrey, cabbage, and plantain on her ankle, wrapped tightly in plastic wrap. "I'll ask Selena if she has any of those around. I've got to go now."

Chayton hung up, and Nessa just stared at the phone.

CHAPTER TWENTY-NINE

essa managed to limp her way through the school day. Pretending to have a sore wrist, she went to the nurse, took the ace bandage she was dispensed, and wrapped it around her ankle where no one could see it under her jeans. It still hurt, but not as much, and with the extra support she was better able to hide the pain.

Fortunately, there was no practice that day. Coach kept them inside, where, instead of *Chariots of Fire*, they watched the first hour of *Unbroken*. Soccer had a short practice, so Cassian snuck into the screening and scooted his metal folding chair close to Nessa's. Cynthia was sitting in the row in front of them. Even though they were friends, it made Nessa feel weird to have Cynthia leaning back to laugh when the track team was on the ship to the Olympics in Germany and taking full advantage of the all-you-can-eat situation on board (in the movie). Nessa didn't know what the joke was, but it was clearly something. She didn't ask, though. Cassian might be friends with Cynthia, but Nessa still did not trust her.

This time Coach didn't see Cassian in the dark room and he got to stay until Coach turned the movie off.

"Good luck tomorrow," Cassian said, pulling her aside when the movie watching was breaking up. He walked with her slowly outside, into the dark, heading toward the parking lot.

Nessa had the feeling that he wanted to kiss her again. Somehow she didn't want him to. All she could think about was getting the ace bandage off and soaking her ankle again. How was she possibly going to run in a race the next day when she could barely walk now?

"Thanks," Nessa said. Just then, Bree beeped from across the lot. "My ride's here." She waved at Bree, then smiled at Cassian as she hobbled off. Nessa could tell by the look on his face that Cassian was surprised.

Chayton was true to his word, and sure enough, Nessa found a plastic bag of herbs for making a poultice hanging on her front door. The note with instructions was from Selena. Nessa felt highly skeptical as she soaked the herbs and then wrapped them around her foot, but they felt good—tingly and cool.

Nate, hopping around the kitchen in train pajamas he still wore even though he'd grown out of them three years ago and the pants barely covered his knees, held his nose dramatically at the smell.

The next morning, the swelling on Nessa's ankle was almost entirely gone. She rotated it while still in bed and felt nothing bad. It hurt a bit when she stood right on it, but after another double dose of ibuprofen, the pain was hardly noticeable.

Nessa tested putting her weight on her ankle as the team moved off the bus, and while the varsity girls ran a few laps to warm up, Nessa visited the medical tent and had the trainer tape her ankle. The trainer winced when he saw the bruising and the puncture marks left by the wolf's tooth. "What did that to you?" he said.

"My brother left a woodworking project out in our garage," Nessa lied. "Nails. Thank goodness I got a tetanus shot last month."

"Yeah," the trainer said, looking skeptical. If a kid hadn't come in with a sprain just then, Nessa was pretty sure the questions would have kept coming.

On the starting line, Cynthia, uncharacteristically, turned back and bumped fists with everyone on the varsity team, Nessa, then Hannah, then Erin Cominski and Nora Liles. "Do your best," Cynthia told them all, and Nessa was impressed and surprised until the horn sounded and it was time to go.

At first, her ankle felt fine. She ran at the front of the pack, neck and neck with Cynthia. She ran down a gravel road around a landfill/junkyard, and then up a hill and around an old cemetery. She was running fast. She felt strong. With about a mile to go, Nessa passed Cynthia. That's where her ankle gave out.

It twisted slightly underneath her. She kept running. She

kept up her pace, but she could feel her opposite arm swinging too much, compensating for the fact that she was favoring her other leg.

She dropped back, a few runners she'd passed now passing her. She tried not to let this get to her. She took a deep, ragged breath. It wasn't that far to the end of the race. She just had to run through the pain.

Then she rolled her ankle again. This time she stopped, cried out in pain, and crouched down over it. Within seconds, the pack she was running with was gone, and runners she hadn't even seen before were passing her.

Nessa stood.

She willed herself to move forward and she did, but her ankle hurt worse with each step. Nessa felt like she was running in slow motion, as if underwater. Runner after runner passed her by.

Nessa kept going anyway. She had no sense if she was running fast anymore. She was just running. As the course returned to the school grounds, she straggled into the chute, knowing the top runners had already finished. Embarrassingly enough, Coach Hoffman came over to comfort her. "Are you hurt?" he asked. "You're limping."

Nessa didn't say anything. She swallowed.

"Hey," he said, leaning down. "You okay?"

"What was my time?" she choked out.

"18:10," Coach said.

Nessa wiped the tears away with the back of her hand. She would have killed for that time last year, but now it felt way too slow. "I'm pretty sure that time's going to take you to States," Coach said. "It's not what you ran at Homecoming but it's still very strong, and the two numbers together will let you qualify."

CHAPTER THIRTY

The cross-country bus and the boys' soccer bus pulled into the parking lot behind Tether High at about the same time. When Nessa climbed off, carrying her pillow and sleeping bag and backpack, Bree was leaning against the hood of her car, talking to Gabe. By the time Nessa had dumped her stuff in the back seat and texted her mom that the bus was back and she was with Bree, Cassian had wandered over. "How'd you do?"

"I rolled my ankle," she said, trying to control the emotion she felt. "I ran 18:10," she told him. "How about you?"

"We won. But forget about that. I wondered about your limp. Are you sure you're okay?"

"Yeah, it's getting better," Nessa fibbed. She didn't feel like going into it. She was relieved when Cassian let the subject drop. It was getting chilly. The sun was beautiful on the horizon, and everyone was hanging around, chatting, savoring the moment.

Just as the passing cars were turning on their headlights and the trees were turning inky black against the still light-filled pale blue sky, a motorcycle turned into the Tether High parking lot. Nessa thought nothing of it at first.

But then she saw that the bike was weaving around as if the driver were scanning the crowd of kids still hanging out at their cars. The bike was headed in her direction, its lights blinding her until, at the last minute, the driver turned the bike 90 degrees and brought it to a decisive stop. Nessa saw that the rider was a man in leathers. When he took off his helmet and shook out his long hair, Nessa saw that it was Chayton.

There was something about him, about the sight of him. It was just the way he swung a leg over the wide seat of the Harley, or the spread of his strong, fine fingers as he palmed the helmet. There was something considered and deliberate in every gesture he made. Not to mention that as he stowed his helmet on the back of the bike and unzipped his jacket, you could see his sculpted abs under his thin shirt. In spite of how annoying and unreliable he was, Nessa felt something in her throat tightening just looking at him, and from points across the parking lot she heard a few different girls start to whisper. One of the boys whistled.

"Who the heck is that?" Cassian said, his voice low so only Nessa could hear. "Do you know him?"

"Unfortunately," Nessa said, "I do."

She took a few steps toward Chayton, meeting him about halfway between his bike and Bree's car, a safe distance from the others. Nessa was wary. She felt like they were representatives from opposing armies, meeting to agree on terms before battle. Every pair of eyes in the parking lot seemed to be turned their way.

"I thought you weren't running on that ankle," Chayton said.

Nessa was still in her racing tank with the bib number pinned on.

"I thought you were in Wyoming."

"I was."

For another minute, they just stared each other down until Chayton finally said, "So, you think being stubborn makes you strong—is that it?"

Nessa did think that, but the last thing she would do was admit it here, so she didn't say anything.

"You're not going to hear me, I get that, but I'm not going to dance around you either. This is serious, what's happening to you, and it's dangerous. This isn't the time for some teenage rebellion horseshit. I'm not your parent."

He turned then, and Nessa thought, *Okay, so he came down here to yell at me for running the race and now he's going off in a huff. Fine. Be crazy.* But after he straddled his bike, and slid his helmet on, he reached behind him and pulled out another. Lifting his chin in her direction, he said, "I'm going to teach you something that will offer you better protection than what you've been doing. You gonna come with me?"

And Nessa hated it, but she felt just then that he had won. Because all the lightness of the moment in the parking lot was gone, replaced by the fear. It was like getting woken up in the morning before you're ready.

Back was the fear she'd felt—smelled—facing down the

other wolf, tracing back to every other fear she'd had in her life. The white wolf who bit her, the fear that Nate would not grow up to be okay, the fear that she wouldn't get out of Tether, that she wouldn't go to college, that she wouldn't be able to run. And also the fear that she *would* escape someday, and that she'd no longer have a mom and a home.

She returned to Cassian, who looked peeved. She started to speak, then shook her head numbly because she had no idea how to explain. She looked at Bree, whose jaw had dropped, at Gabe, who looked like he didn't quite know what to do with his face. "Sorry, guys," Nessa said. "I've gotta go."

And then she walked over to Chayton's bike, threw a leg over the saddle, put on the helmet, and placed her hands gingerly on either side of his waist.

"Oh, no, sweetheart," Chayton said. "When this bike starts moving, you gotta be holding on for real." Nessa reached around to grasp him fully around the middle. Through the leather of his jacket, his muscles felt like they were made of steel. The bike peeled away from the parking lot. Nessa could feel the loose hair flowing behind her as the bike picked up speed.

"If I'm not home in an hour," Nessa shouted into the wind, hoping Chayton could hear, "my mom's going to freak out. She's going to call 9-1-1." Nessa was pretty sure this wasn't true. Vivian had more pressing things to worry about than Nessa's coming back late. Vivian trusted her daughter.

"Don't worry," Chayton said. "I'll have you home before your precious mama so much as notices that you were gone."

CHAPTER THIRTY-ONE

Riding on the back of Chayton's bike, Nessa got cold. As they passed through Tether's Main Street and then out in the direction of the old Dutch Chem plant, her teeth started to chatter and her fingers to ache. She held on tight to Chayton for warmth as much as to keep from slipping off the seat when he took the curves, and when they got to where they were going—the side of one of the smaller roads leading out of Tether—they pulled over next to a random farm field.

Chayton said nothing but found a flannel shirt in his bike's trunk box and tossed it to her. Nessa wrapped it around her shoulders, missing the winter jacket she'd left in the back of Bree's car.

"Where are we?" she asked, looking around.

"We're at the old distillery," he said, pointing. "See that?" Nessa peered into the darkness and, yes, behind some trees, she could see the dark outlines of a building. "A buddy of mine is reopening the place. He's going to make his own whiskey, which is kind of ironic."

"Why?" Nessa said.

"One of the reasons people invented whiskey was because the water was contaminated and would make you sick. Now we've got whiskey coming out of the town with the poisoned water supply."

"Not anymore," Nessa said. "Not since the Dutch Chem cleanup."

"Whatever," Chayton said, walking away from the bike, jumping a narrow ditch, then digging into the cold dirt with the heel of his boot. "Do you see what's growing here?"

Nessa didn't follow him. Keeping her arms crossed in front of her chest, she said, "Aren't those weeds? It's November."

"Wrong," said Chayton. "It's rye." He reached down with his hand and picked up a handful of something—a few small strands of what, in the dark, looked to Nessa vaguely like grass. "You know much about rye?"

"Is it what makes rye bread?"

Chayton nodded. "Rye's the kind of miracle plant that white farmers used for centuries and then forgot all about. They didn't need it after they came over here from Europe and stole so much rich land from Native Americans. At least, until it all turned to dust and blew away after a hundred years of erosion and soil degradation. The dust bowl—when white farmers began to know what it was like to be like us."

Nessa felt like she should apologize or something, but Chayton was moving too quickly.

"Now, farmers have been learning to live in better harmony with the land. They're going back to methods from their homelands, and rye is part of that. You plant it in fields where nutrients have been sucked out, and it restores the soil. It grows in the harshest conditions. It grows in the winter. It sends down deep roots so that when it's time to plant corn, those plants' roots can have a path to follow, and everything gets better established right away.

"And then, with some varieties of rye, bonus! You can harvest and make whiskey. My friend's got his own field here, but really, what's brilliant about his plan is farmers will let him grow his crop in their fields for free—it's like a favor to them."

"Wow," said Nessa, sarcastically. "This is *fascinating*."

"It is," Chayton said, ignoring her tone, picking what still looked to Nessa like simple prairie grass. He stepped back over the ditch to take Nessa's hand, press the rye grass into her palm, and close her fist around it. "For someone with a wolf issue, rye can be your best friend."

Chayton climbed back on the bike, waiting until Nessa realized she was meant to follow him. After she'd climbed on, Chayton gunned the engine, driving down the rutted dirt road past the distillery building he'd pointed out, and then to another field, where brown stalks of what looked like wheat were growing waist high. "This is what rye looks like when it's mature," Chayton said.

After climbing off the bike, he walked into the field and Nessa followed him. "You feel that?" Chayton said. Nessa wasn't sure what he meant. The dry grasses were brushing her arms and enveloping her, but instead of feeling itchy, she felt like everything around her had gone quiet, the way she felt in the band room at school, which was lined with dense foam panels meant to deaden sound. There was more, too, now that she stopped to consider it. In spite of Chayton's loaner shirt, she had still been freezing standing in the other field. Now, she was so warm, her fingers and toes ached with the return of sensation.

She nodded at Chayton. "I feel it," she said.

"Wolves and rye have a sacred relationship," Chayton explained. "You can come in here and feel things go quiet. Your feelings, your desire, your drive—everything that turns you into a wolf—it comes to a stop when you're in here. If you're stuck as a wolf, come find this place. If you need to change but can't, rye can help. Any rye will do it—young, old—but dry and tall like this is the best, just ready to be harvested. This is your sanctuary.

"That gray wolf you saw there last night was one like you, but older, more experienced. He knew what he was doing. You can bet he's managing things with rye, keeping his experience mellow and under control."

"He was a…a human?"

Chayton shrugged. "Clearly. And he's been a shape-shifter for a while, given the serious street cred he must have. The alpha's not going to sniff noses with just anybody."

"Were the aggressive wolves that attacked us people also?" Nessa asked.

"Those wolves, no, unless there are some seriously scary people walking around. If they were, chances are I'd know them already via Mike."

"Your friend at the garage?"

"Yeah, at the garage, that's right," Chayton said in a way that made Nessa suddenly guess that the garage was not really a garage, that there was something else going on there, something sinister and secret. "Those wolves with the teeth. Watch out for them. There's something not right about them."

"Are you worried?" Nessa asked.

"Yeah I'm worried," he said, like Nessa had asked a stupid question. "I've been hearing stuff from my connections in the natural world, and I knew something was going on. I didn't know the extent of it until you started talking about them last night."

"What about Billy Lark?" Nessa asked. "Why did the wolves bring me to his house?"

"I don't know," Chayton said. "Next time you transform, go back there. Sniff around a little more. A wolf can find out more through one good whiff than Uncle Sam can from the last decade of wiretapping all our phones."

"Maybe that other wolf, the one with the street cred, could," she said.

"But he wasn't picked for this," Chayton said. "You were." He removed a knife from his pocket, opened the blade, and cut a few stalks of the rye. "Take this." He passed it to Nessa. "Take it home. Put it somewhere where it will dry, and when it's ready, you can arrange it in a circle somewhere safe, when you are alone. This will allow you to transform when you need to. And most important, return to human form as well."

"You mean, not just at certain moons?"

"Yes," Chayton said, simply. "Though it will always be easier when the moon is new or full."

Nessa found herself laughing.

Chayton raised his eyebrows sardonically. "You find this funny?"

"A little," Nessa said. "I'm just laughing, thinking of the look on my friends' faces when you came to get me on your motorcycle."

"The rye is relaxing you," Chayton said. "It will do that. It's like the drumming." He shrugged and smiled. "Tell me what the wolves have been saying to you."

"What they've been *saying*?" Nessa laughed again. "I told you, I can't really understand them."

He rolled his eyes.

"Do *you* speak their language?" Nessa asked.

"Not the way you will be able to soon. Or I *assume* you will be able to, once you realize they're talking." He took a deep breath. "Wolves speak to each other all the time. They're as much in communication with one another as we are. Like us, they use both body language and vocalizations, but they also use scent."

"I knew that," Nessa said defensively.

"Don't expect to hear words," Chayton went on. "Expect to hear intention. Let the sounds, or postures, or scents that you detect pass right through the language centers of your brain and land instead in the parts of you that process emotion. Understand what a wolf is feeling, and you will know what the wolf is trying to say."

Nessa took her mind back to her night with the wolves during the new moon. "They seemed happy," she said. "The first time. We were all happy. It was just so much fun. This might sound stupid, but we were all just playing together. They were yipping and whining and stuff, and we all sang together, but no one seemed worried or scared."

"That sounds like a ceremonial celebration, a welcoming of you."

"Then the other time, they were…scared." Nessa was surprised that she'd found this word lurking in the back of her now-relaxed brain. "Before the aggressive wolves found us even," she went on. "They seemed like they had a purpose, somewhere to be."

"That's something you'll need to find out from them. You'll need to know what the wolves mean for you to do. If they're leaving tracks near you, that might mean they want to protect you from something. It might also mean they want you to follow the trail, to find something."

Nessa shook her head. "I barely feel like I can protect myself."

"Maybe that's what's holding you back," Chayton said. "Your worry that you will not survive, that's keeping you from giving your whole self over to the wolves."

"It sounds like what I do when I race—I hold back because I never know how much I'm going to need to store up for the end."

Chayton nodded toward her injured ankle. "That was really stupid, running today," he said.

"No it wasn't," Nessa said. "Running is what I do. It's my ticket out of here."

"No," Chayton said. "Wolf is what you do now. You have to understand that. And let's just hope that next time you encounter that aggressive wolf, you're not running on an injury. Wolves are amazing at recognizing when an animal is compromised. They can smell the weakness."

"You think I'm an animal that wolf was…hunting?" Nessa said.

Chayton looked her dead on. "Wolves are always hunting."

Nessa felt weak suddenly. In spite of the warmth and comfort she felt in the field of rye, she'd been standing on her ankle too long. She could feel it beginning to throb.

Chayton ended the lesson there. "That's enough for tonight," he said, leading her back in the direction of the bike. For a fleeting second, Nessa wanted to tell Chayton that sometimes she wondered if being a wolf was a kind of cheating, that it was giving her an unfair speed advantage in cross-country. But Chayton had already resolved that issue. Wolf is what she did now. She had no choice.

As she stepped out of the field, Nessa pulled Chayton's flannel shirt tighter around her body. "Can we find somewhere to go that's warm, maybe?" she said. "I'm freezing."

Chayton gave her a look of disbelief.

"I know, I know," Nessa grumbled. "I'm not exactly one-with-nature, wolf-girl material."

"You said it, not me," he commented.

But then Chayton seemed to relent. "Come on," he said, finding a blanket in the box for her to drape over her shoulders. "I'll take you home."

CHAPTER THIRTY-TWO

Over the next two nights, Nessa's life became a tunnel. States was exactly two weeks away. She just had to get there and, on the way, make it through one more transformation, which she was hoping would be light because it came on a new moon, not on the full.

But first, she had to survive yet another ride on the Rumor Express. As if her performance at Homecoming, the doping accusations, and Cassian's romantic interest had not been enough, now she'd been seen disappearing from the school parking lot on the back of a Harley, driven by a long-haired Native American man.

"How do you know Chayton?" Luc asked one day.

The question took Nessa by surprise. "He's just a friend," Nessa said.

"Oh, yeah?" Luc said, clearly skeptical. "You know his other friends?"

Now that Nessa's ankle had healed, she was running out in front with Luc most of the time at practice, though she had the feeling that if he got going in a full sprint, he'd still be able to leave her in his dust.

"Do you?" she said.

"Yeah, of course," Luc said, sounding offended and sarcastic in a way that came as a complete mystery to Nessa. "We're both First Nation. Of course we know each other."

"Oh, come on," Nessa said. "You asked me."

"Okay, fine," Luc said. "He cured my cousin's acne. He sat with him and lit some stuff on fire and started chanting, and by the end of it that guy was soaked in sweat."

"How was the acne?"

"It got a lot better, actually," Luc said. "But my dad had also gotten him to give up sugar." Luc's laugh came out as a little snort. "My dad's an engineer—kind of the last person to get into all that shaman stuff."

"What do you think? Do you think Chayton cured your cousin?"

"I have no idea," Luc said. "What do *you* think? You know Chayton better than me."

Vivian must have been more worried about the Dutch Chem study than she'd admitted because she decided to take Nate to his next appointment.

She came back flushed and happy, a smile of relief on her face. Swinging her bulky purse off her shoulder and on to the end of the kitchen counter, a gesture that had meant "Mom's home" for as long as Nessa could remember, Vivian said, "I want you to know that I had a long talk with Dr. Raab about the details of the study. There's really nothing for you to worry about."

"Did he show you the straps on the tables?" Nessa asked.

"He'd just had them removed," she said. "Ann Lark had said something about it. It really is amazing, the level of care these kids are getting. They screen their blood for any sign of the pathogens that might result from the Dutch Chem contamination, plus we know they're all on an intensive vitamin regimen, and they're being screened for every possible disease. He told me one kid showed early genetic markers for Hodgkin's, and they were able to do an intervention that would have needed to be much more invasive if they'd waited until the child was an adult."

"Genetic markers?" Nessa said. They had done a unit on the human genome project in her Bio class freshman year, and she knew what was involved with genetic analysis—it was more than just adding a solution from a dropper and seeing what happened. It was centrifuges and computers. "They're analyzing the kids' genes? Isn't that really expensive?"

Vivian pulled a tightly wrapped package of frozen sausage out of the freezer, snipping off the metal clips on the ends and dumping it into a bowl to defrost in the microwave. "They've got funding," she said. "The research they're doing, he wasn't saying it, but I think they're trying to find a cure for cancer. And did you know that for any kid in the study with a sibling born after the study began—the clinic is paying to bank that child's umbilical cord blood? That's something you have to do privately, and most people can't afford—it's thousands of dollars, and then you pay to store the blood for years on top of that."

"Did he say anything about Paravida?" Nessa asked. "Was Mrs. Lark there?"

Vivian shrugged. "He didn't mention Paravida. You might have misheard. And I didn't see Ann today. But Cassian Thomas was there with his little sister. He said to say hello. I didn't realize you were friends with him. He seemed a little surprised I didn't know more about how much you two have been seeing each other."

"Yeah," Nessa said, too busy trying to work out whether or not she should still be worried to pick up on her mom's interest in Cassian.

Vivian had never been one to pressure her kids to cop to their social lives, something that generally worked to Delphine's advantage, not Nessa's. She let the subject drop now, passing Nessa a colander of washed potatoes to chop and talking about a cat she'd helped treat at Dr. Morgan's. Nessa put the conversation about the clinic on pause. But she wasn't done asking questions.

The fact that three runners from Tether High's team—Luc, Nessa, and Cynthia—had qualified to compete at States was a big deal. Coach Hoffman would drive the three runners down the night before in his ancient Dodge minivan—they were staying in Midland, the small city not far from Detroit where the meet would be held. The student council had chartered a bus to bring other supporters down that day and they had gotten so much interest, they then chartered another, putting together a pancake supper on Sunday night to help defray the costs.

Nessa was seated between Luc and Cynthia on the dais at the fundraiser, up in front with Coach Hoffman, Principal Sarakoski, and Tether's mayor, Dan Miller, Tim's dad. Standing in line for pancakes, Nessa had been greeted by kids she knew, kids she didn't know, and adults from the town. There was a hand-painted sign that read Run Like You Mean It, and one of the town selectwomen gave a speech about how Nessa, Luc, and Cynthia should be seen as fitness inspirations for everyone living in Tether.

Cynthia leaned across Nessa to whisper to Luc, "Is this your first time being some lady's source of inspiration?"

"I thought I was yours already," Luc whispered back. Which was a remark Nessa had no idea how to interpret, though Cynthia laughed and sat back in her seat like a cat that had just swallowed a songbird.

Nessa found herself thinking that of all the great mammal predators, wasn't it strange that most of them—lions, tigers, cheetahs, panthers, leopards, cougars—were a form of giant cat, and only one, the wolf, was a relative of the dog?

But before the race that Saturday, Nessa had to confront the new moon. "I just want to be able to think about the race and not have to think about wolf stuff," Nessa complained to Bree, when they were walking down the deserted school hallways to the bathrooms.

"Are you feeling anything yet?" Bree said. She looked at her watch. "It's only three days away."

"I don't feel as much as I did before," Nessa said. "Maybe it's the rye."

Nessa had made a sachet out of the rye Chayton had cut for her, and she slept with it under her pillow. She carried another one in her backpack and a third in her pants pocket. She was feeling calmer than she had before. Her hearing was getting sharper, smells were coming in stronger, and she felt restless in the ways she had in the days leading up to the other transformations, but she didn't feel quite so out of control. "I'm just really hoping those scary wolves aren't waiting for me," Nessa said.

Nessa had been reading up on wolf aggression, learning as much as she could about why a wolf would be out on its own, challenging others, looking for fights. But still, the wolf's attacking her made no sense. Usually wolves laid down a lot of scents, letting others know they were near, giving them ample opportunity to avoid a fight.

"Do you think they were trying to take over the pack's hunting grounds?" Bree said.

"What else could it be?" Nessa said. "That's how wolves survive, right? They come into a pack, kill the alpha, and assert themselves as the new leader."

"But didn't Chayton make it sound like he had no idea what those wolves were doing?"

"Chayton doesn't know everything," Nessa said.

Bree cocked her head. "He knows a lot."

"Yeah, but he's the one saying I have to figure out what the pack is looking for. He thinks they're going to tell me. Which is crazy, right? I mean, they took me to Billy's house. Who knows why? Maybe he was throwing them scraps of food out his windows."

"Maybe Chayton wants you to ask them. Maybe that's why he's trying to tell you how to listen to them more. How to talk."

"Yeah, right," Nessa said, feeling suddenly overwhelmed at the idea of talking to a wolf, of making herself understood. It was impossible. "They're going to be all..." Nessa made a combination of barking and whimpering sounds. "And I'm going to be like, 'Farmer Bent is threatening to cut down your sacred tree of life? Oh, no, we have to stop him!'"

Bree leveled a gaze at Nessa. "That's the plot of *Avatar*."

"Right," Nessa said. "My bad."

"If Chayton thinks you can figure it out, you're going to be able to figure it out. And speaking of figuring out mysterious men," Bree raised her eyebrows, "what's going on with *Cassian*?"

"Nothing really." Nessa shrugged. "I don't know, to be honest."

"But, but—" Bree spluttered. "*Why*? He took *you* out! Two months ago, your face would have exploded just thinking about going on a date with Cassian, and now, you're all like, 'I don't know, I'm just not feeling it...' Nessa, he's like the Harvard University of boys, and he's offering you early admission."

"I think you might need some help with that metaphor."

"I think you might need some help with your priorities," Bree countered. "I'm just saying, Nessa, and I think you agree: dating Cassian is one for the bucket list. It would be like, high school, done, check. Memories made. Goals achieved. Ambitions realized. Now you can get old and have babies or go make a difference in the world and know that you have lived."

Nessa shook her head and smiled at her funny best friend. She didn't know why she wasn't feeling more for Cassian. It puzzled her. She liked him well enough when she was with him—and the memory of kissing him could still make her blush. She had had a crush on him from afar since ninth grade. It was just that when she wasn't with him, she sometimes forgot that he existed.

"Maybe I just don't like being chased," she said, hearing how arrogant that sounded. She glared at Bree, who was rolling her eyes. "By super hot high school guys *or* by super scary aggressive wolves."

CHAPTER THIRTY-THREE

The new moon was scheduled to rise at 10 a.m. on Wednesday. When Nessa woke up at 4:30 a.m., she looked out of her bedroom window and saw that Chayton was standing outside at the curb, leaning against his bike, his arms crossed in leather sleeves. Slipping into track pants and an old pair of running shoes, Nessa snuck through the bedroom hallway, opened the front door noiselessly, then tiptoed down the driveway.

"What are you doing here?" she whispered. She glanced up the street to make sure no one else was outside. "Do you realize how much trouble you're going to get me into?"

"I thought you might be ready to shift," he said. "I wanted to see if I was right."

"I was hoping to hold out until the school day was over," Nessa said, but even as she was speaking she could feel something moving up along her spine.

"You look ready," Chayton said. "Want a ride?"

Even as Nessa nodded, Chayton was already handing her the helmet. By the time they reached the trailhead, Nessa felt as anxious and ready to go as she had on the starting line of every race she'd ever competed in.

"Hold on," Chayton said, swinging his leg over his bike and moving as quickly as Nessa had ever seen him. He pulled a sheaf of more dried rye from the trunk box of the bike and, heading into the woods with Nessa behind him, arranged the grasses in a circle just off the path. He took her by the shoulders. "Look me in the eye, okay, hold on, okay?"

Nessa could feel her entire body starting to shake. "I think I'm going to throw up," she confessed.

"You're not going to throw up," Chayton said. Holding her shoulders, he guided her to step into the circle of rye. He closed his eyes and started to speak, his voice rising into a soothing rhythm. "You're going to change, Nessa. In a few moments you will allow the animal inside to express herself in the form of a beautiful white wolf. You will pass through rye, which has sustained your ancestors when they lived closer to the land, and which sustains our land now. You will return to this earth through the portal of grain, coming from the wilds of running to the grain that is the foundation of our table. Be one with the Spirits that guide our life on this earth."

Chayton had closed his eyes while delivering this statement, a wind rising to blow his long hair.

When he opened his eyes, Nessa felt he was seeing her from

far away. He let go of her shoulders, and Nessa started to run, her legs flying out from under her, the pumping motion in her arms lifting her with each extension of her body.

The wolf pack was not waiting for her today in the early dawn and when she went looking for them, they were nowhere to be found. She ran to the lake where she'd first seen them. The shoreline was deserted. She ran to the rise near Billy's house and looked down on the Larks' darkened windows. The rocky outcropping was swept clean. She thought about getting closer to the house but didn't want to go alone. Before, she'd had Omega as her friend, but now Omega was…Nessa felt her throat closing up.

Feeling lonely and useless, she turned for the trail. How was she supposed to figure out wolf communication if she couldn't even find any wolves?

She returned to the circle of dry rye stalks that Chayton had set up, stopping inside, feeling the safety of the familiar, slightly yeasty smell, the quiet the circle provided. She stood there panting, recovering from the long run, her heart rate slowing, her muscles twitching as they often did when she came to rest after a race in which she'd pushed herself to the limit of her capabilities.

She looked down—she was standing on her own two legs in her track pants and her old sneakers, trembling in the frigid morning air, her breath before her in clouds.

She stepped out of the circle, leaving the stalks where Chayton had laid them, fast-walking out to the trailhead to tell him everything that had just happened, only to find that he was gone. Spent as she was, Nessa was going to have to jog all the way home if she wanted to make it look plausible that she'd only gone out for a morning run.

Nessa called Bree to tell her what had just happened. They talked about everything Chayton had told Nessa—about how the dried rye had smoothed the transition, given her more control, about wolf communication, about cultivating the ability to transform in and out of wolf state not just at the new and full moons.

"I wish I'd been able to get down to Billy's house again," Nessa said. "I know that has to be part of this—the wolves brought me there on purpose. But there is nowhere to hide down there. Last time, I nearly got shot."

"You definitely don't want to get shot," said Bree. "You'll figure it out."

"I keep thinking I should try to warn him. Or warn his mom. But about what?"

"Sure," Bree said. "You'd call the Larks and tell them Billy is in danger, and you know this because you are that wolf they saw outside his bedroom window."

Nessa held her head in her hands. Bree was right. She couldn't warn the Larks if she didn't know what she was supposed to warn them about.

"Wait! I know!" Bree said. "I'll call and offer to babysit. We know Billy and his parents from the clinic. It won't be weird."

Nessa nodded. "Sure. You can give it a try."

As Thursday turned into Friday, Nessa had to stop thinking about wolves and Billy and Chayton. She had to focus on States. Her ankle was healed, she was running strong in practices, this was her chance, and until the full moon, she wouldn't be able to get closer to understanding the wolf mystery anyway.

Then it was Friday afternoon, and Nessa was suited up in her good luck blue hoodie, hoisting her overnight bag over her shoulder, high-fiving Nate goodbye at the front door, and climbing into Coach Hoffman's car.

Cynthia engineered it so that Nessa was sitting in the front with Coach Hoffman, listening to stories about his daughter Martha, who was now twenty-five and getting her teaching degree in Iowa, while Luc and Cynthia listened to Luc's music in the back, a pair of earbuds shared between them. Nessa was amused to see that when she turned to look at them, Luc was sleeping soundly, and Cynthia was staring out the window, a look of focused concentration on her face.

They went to bed early—Luc bunking in with Coach, and Nessa and Cynthia each plugging into their music, focusing on the race the next day.

They met up again in the hotel's breakfast room. Nessa forced down a bowl of Raisin Bran and an English muffin with peanut butter. Cynthia had brought her own food—plain yogurt, chia seeds, wheat germ.

"You guys aren't having the *waffles*?" Luc said and proceeded to go back to the plastic cups of batter and the machine five times, patting his completely flat stomach, and then stuffing one last slice of bacon in his mouth. "Breakfast of champions," he said with his mouth full, then burped.

"Wow," Coach said eventually. "I've been watching high school athletes eat for almost thirty-five years, and even I'm impressed."

At that, Cynthia stood up quickly, as if angry, pushing back her chair, and walked out of the breakfast room. "Was it something I said?" Coach Hoffman said, looking from Luc to Nessa.

"Nah, it was me," said Luc. "She's a charter member of the Society for the Prevention of Cruelty to Waffles, so I wasn't being exactly…sensitive."

It wasn't even funny, but Nessa found herself laughing. Too much. Pretty soon she was choking and Luc was saying, "Easy there, Tiger."

"I think we're all a little on edge," said Coach Hoffman. "I'll go find Cynthia. Be down in the lobby in fifteen."

Every race Nessa had competed in before today had been at a mediocre high school track, usually several decades beyond newness, but today's race was at a college track. Everything felt big, and fresh, and real.

There were parking attendants, giant banners hanging over the entrance to the field house with the Michigan Cross-Country Association logo on them, and tents set up with directions and first aid and giveaways. Nessa, Luc, and Cynthia each received a backpack, a two-pack of running socks, and samples of sports drinks, just for competing.

"*Sweet!*" Luc said, and Nessa couldn't have agreed more. Even Cynthia—who had been keeping to herself since breakfast—seemed pleased.

A crowd was forming, and Nessa realized that the stadium seats that usually stood mostly empty during high school meets were going to be filled. She'd known about the 100 spectators on two chartered buses coming down from Tether, of course, but she hadn't registered that would translate to 100 spectators from every other school across the state.

The teams were directed to a large tent behind the stadium where each school had a table, folding chairs, mats for stretching, and a hospitality basket of waters and energy bars. The tent had flaps, and heaters were set up in the corners so the runners—most racing in the slimmest of tank tops and briefs—would not get cold.

The morning passed in a blur. Nessa stretched, listened to music on her phone, jogged to the Porta-Potty units, took some selfies, and listened to a last, frenzied Coach Hoffman pep talk.

And then she and Cynthia were heading to the starting line, located inside the football stadium. As the runners took their places on the starting line, the roar was deafening. Nessa looked up into the stands to search for the enormous orange rubber hand her mom had attached to a garden stake so Nessa would be able to see them.

While scanning for it, her eyes tracked across dozens of faces she recognized from Tether. She saw her ninth-grade math teacher. She saw Bree, who had painted a stripe each of Tether High's red and gold on her cheeks and put her curly hair into a high ponytail tied with red and gold ribbons. She saw Cassian in the middle of the crowd of beautiful seniors. When he caught her eye, he waved excitedly.

Moving on, Nessa's eyes finally found the orange hand. She saw Delphine cheering, her hands cupped over her mouth like a megaphone, Nate looking cold and uncomfortable in the crowd, Vivian's face tense and drawn as if she could feel how much this race meant to Nessa. They both knew there might be college recruiters in the stands right now, and if there weren't, they certainly would be following the race's outcome. Nessa noticed her hands were balled into fists thinking about how much she wanted—no, needed—this to be a good race.

This was not what she should be thinking about, she knew. She should be engaged in positive imaging, thinking about what it felt like to run when she was running well. She followed Cynthia into position, willing herself to remember the wolves. They were always in her mind, with her the way the characters in a really good book stay with you. It wasn't hard for Nessa to conjure the feeling she'd had when she was running with them.

She closed her eyes, and for a microsecond she could smell the pine trees and damp leaves and animal odors of the woods. The roar and cheering of the crowd faded into the background, and as if she were standing in a field of rye, she forgot where she was. She forgot who she was.

Looking down at the turf, she watched her sneakers move into position, lining them up with all the other sneakers. She waited, in a strange state of relaxed readiness, for the blast of the air horn. She didn't feel that she was so much inside the moment as that she was watching someone else inhabit it.

The sound of the start broke the spell. Nessa remembered exactly where she was. But by this point she was already running, and she was already out in the front of the pack. This was bad, she knew that. But Nessa couldn't stop herself. She could not slow herself. She felt far too loose and relaxed in her stride to risk making any kind of a change.

The course wound into the woods on a wide, gravel trail, and Nessa heard her feet making crunching sounds. She heard the sound of a squirrel darting through the woods on her left. She couldn't put her finger on what was so un-race-like about these sounds, and then it occurred to her: they were the sounds you hear when you are running alone. In a race, the noises of the other runners would drown them out.

Where were the other runners? Nessa shot a look behind, and saw that the closest was several hundred meters behind her. She was running the race in reverse—getting her sprint in now. She wouldn't be able to maintain this pace. She could only hope she'd given herself enough of a lead that she'd be able to hold on when the others were making their moves.

She ran on, feeling her heart starting to burn in her chest, as if it were a mechanical engine with the ability to overheat. Even Coach Hoffman would have told her to slow down, she knew that. He would have told her not to give everything she had this early on. But Coach Hoffman was not here. Coach Hoffman had not run mile after mile all summer long, had not given himself over to running as Nessa had. Coach Hoffman did not know how much it meant to her that she give this race her all with every single step she was taking.

Instead of slowing down, Nessa pushed herself harder. She ran up a low hill, and turned left, following an arrow at a cross-roads. The trail looped around at this point, and then turned left and headed back down the hill. There was a cabin on the right, used for sap collecting—this college had an agriculture program. Nessa passed the cabin. She felt the trail leveling out. She knew that meant she was close to the end of the second mile. Could she pick up her pace even more?

She was afraid to try. The muscles in her calves were growing brittle; she felt like they were made of paper, that they might tear. But now she was past the second mile marker where the trail looped around the crossroads again. Nessa's arms were pumping, her chest was heaving. She didn't think she'd run this fast even when she was a wolf. She didn't think she'd run this fast ever. Each step took her closer to where she wanted to be, closer to who she wanted to be.

She was tired, but she had not forgotten how much she wanted to run her absolute fastest. She worried she'd be too tired for the full mile she had ahead of her, but she wasn't too tired for the next step she had to take. Then the next after that, and the next after that.

Nessa broke out of the woods as the trail reemerged on to the athletic fields, in sight of the stadium, and she was greeted by a deafening silence.

But this time, it wasn't the silence of running alone. It was the silence of a thousand people not talking. Not even breathing. She could tell that something was wrong. The crowd was aware of her—she could feel their eyes on her.

Had she gotten lost? Was the sad fact that at this one most important race of her life, she had made the most colossal mistake of her running career—making a wrong turn in the woods?

Nessa came close to stopping but she knew that the way she was running, she wouldn't be able to start up again if she turned around and tried to find her way back, so she continued forward. As she did, she felt one of her legs buckle. She nearly tripped over her own footfall. But she managed to catch herself and keep moving. And just after she caught herself there was a roar from the crowd that was at once the most surprising and the most affirming sound Nessa had ever heard.

She'd seen plenty of diagrams of sound waves over her years watching science documentaries on TV with Nate, but never before had she *felt* them. But she felt them now. Her exhausted legs absorbed the energy of the noise as if it were an electric stimulus. She felt lighter, and she was able to increase her pace once again, even though a moment before, the best she would have hoped for was not stopping.

The crowd continued to cheer, the sound pulling Nessa along. She knew that she was running on borrowed energy and it wouldn't last long. She had to cross the line. She was desperate for it, starving for it. So she sped up even more, passing the first cone into the chute, her spikes digging in for the last 50 steps.

She wasn't sure she had 50 steps in her, but again, with each one, she knew she just had at least one more, so she kept taking them. And then suddenly she was past the finish and she was still running and she knew she could stop but she didn't know how.

The sound of the crowd was still with her, making her feel that people were almost on top of her, but at the same time that she was alone. And then somehow Coach Hoffman was shouting in her face, words she didn't understand, and she had slowed down, and she actually hadn't just stopped, she'd collapsed, and he had his arms around her and she was shaking. She couldn't stop shaking and Coach was actually crying, which was weird, Nessa thought, until she realized she was crying too.

"You did it. You did it," Coach was saying and her mom and Delphine were there and jumping on top of her, hugging her. Nessa started to see the other runners coming in now, one girl, then another, and then two, and then a cluster of five. Suddenly it was a crowd, streaming across the line. And it occurred to Nessa that she had actually just run out in front and stayed there, finishing the race significantly ahead of the next-closest competitor. It was why she felt so weak. Nessa knew—suddenly—that she had won.

Won.

States.

She'd been hoping to get a good time, to get the attention of a recruiter. To beat Cynthia. To get a scholarship to cross-country summer camp.

"What—" she said to Coach. "What did I run?"

"You didn't see it?" he said. She shook her head. She looked at Vivian, who had an arm around her, holding her up.

"Nessa," Vivian said. "You ran a 14:53."

No matter how many people came over and wrapped their arms around Nessa, crinkling the silver blanket someone had wrapped around her shoulders when Nessa's teeth started to chatter, Nessa had a hard time understanding that she had done what she'd done. Her mom held both sides of her face and planted a huge kiss on each of her cheeks. Delphine seemed kind of shy to be near her, and Nate was nowhere to be seen, but Bree nearly knocked Nessa down with a bear hug. Kids from school Nessa barely knew hit her on the arm or gave her high fives. Cassian was there for an instant with a hug and a kiss that brushed her hair, and then there was a bunch of adults introducing themselves.

Someone led her over to a podium. There was brass band music playing, though she couldn't tell where it was coming from. All she was aware of was the warmth on her face. She tried to remember the race, but all she could think about was how in a few minutes it would be found out that something had not gone the way it should have.

Her 14:53 was unheard of for high school girls. In her wildest dreams she'd hoped for a 16:00, but that had been an outside hope. She'd have been happy with 16:30. Nessa looked out at the crowd. *It's been worth it*, she thought. *Everything.*

It wasn't until the car ride back—Nessa, Luc, and Cynthia rode with Coach Hoffman again—that the understanding of what she'd just done started to sink in. Cynthia had also had a strong time, finishing in the top five for the state with a 16:37, and Luc had placed third among the boys.

"Nessa," Cynthia said, shaking her head. It was like whatever resentment she'd had toward Nessa had been vaporized by the mushroom cloud of Nessa's achievement. "That was—I saw you head out in front and I thought you were going to die, and then when I heard the roar—I was still in the woods—I put it together. Wow."

"Good job," Luc said, giving her a nod that was the first reaction Nessa didn't find totally embarrassing.

"You too," she said. He smiled—one of the first times she had seen him smile—like they were in on the same joke.

She didn't exactly sleep in the car as much as she went into a deep trance, staring out into the woods. She kept feeling the footsteps, the way her mind had focused on each next step, the feeling that her chest was pushing her forward. The race had…hurt.

She was proud, too. She could feel herself smiling out the window, and she started to let her mind travel forward, thinking about how this might change things for her, wondering if she'd ever be able to do it again.

And then Nessa decided to stop thinking ahead. Coach Hoffman had told them there was going to be a welcoming celebration of all three of their amazing times back in the parking lot at Tether High. The school was setting up a sound system for music, and a few parents had volunteered to bring donuts and hot cider.

"It'll be too cold to be out there for long—it'll be dark—but for an hour or so I think we all could use some celebrating."

Nessa nodded. She agreed.

But when they pulled into the lot, it didn't look like a party. The two chartered buses were there, the banners had been hung, the tables groaned under huge platters of donuts, hot cider was set up in giant urns. But no music played on the huge speakers that were set up. Dave Uletsky, the sophomore star DJ, was standing away from the table, his arms crossed over his chest, talking quietly to Mr. Williams, the technology advisor. Kids were standing in clusters. Nessa could see that some were crying. Others had their arms around each other. Something was very wrong.

Spotting Coach Hoffman's car, Bree fast-walked to meet them, and when Nessa rolled down her window, Bree leaned in. "Something terrible has happened," she said, looking up at Coach to include him in the news. "It's Billy Lark," she went on. "He's—." Tears welled up in Bree's eyes. "Nessa, I'm so sorry, but he's dead."

CHAPTER THIRTY-FOUR

illy Lark is dead?" Nessa cried. "It can't be possible."

She sprang from the car and grabbed Bree's arm. Billy was just a little boy. Sure there had been horrible things that happened to the kids Nessa's age who were most affected by the Dutch Chem mess. But Dutch Chem was gone. Tether was safe now. Wasn't it?

"I know, it's hard to believe," Bree said, wiping at her eyes with the back of her hands in a way that let Nessa know she'd been crying already. "But it's true."

Cynthia and Luc had gotten out of the car. Cynthia hurried off to meet her family. Luc waited, gave Nessa a long look, nodded and headed off on foot into the dark. Coach was hugging his wife next to her car on the other side of the lot.

Nessa was bewildered. And she had a terrible sinking feeling. Had the wolves been warning her?

"How did it happen?" Nessa asked, snapping back. "When?"

"This afternoon," Bree replied. "He had some kind of seizure."

"A seizure," Nessa repeated. Did people die of seizures? She was thinking she understood what seizure meant. Until now it had not included death. Nessa felt tears coming, thinking of Billy's eyes rolling back in his head, his mom holding him, calling his name. Billy was just so…little and helpless.

"No one really knows exactly what happened," Bree continued, sniffing a bit. "He was gone by the time the ambulance arrived. His mom told them he'd never had anything like this happen before."

Nessa looked around. Now the somber atmosphere in the parking lot made sense. Parents were here, picking up their kids. The Larks kept to themselves, and Billy was home-schooled—but still, everyone had known who Billy was. Tether was too small a town not to have one family's tragedy belong, in some way, to everyone.

"Do you think that it has anything to do with the study?" Nessa asked Bree in a low voice. "Did Mrs. Lark say anything about fevers?"

Bree shook her head no.

"Is my mom here?" Nessa asked. "Have you seen her? Does Nate know?"

"Yeah," Bree said. "She's with Nate, on the other side of the buses."

Nessa understood that Nate could not handle the crowd

that was gathering in the parking lot, especially not with the level of emotion being expressed. Hugging made Nate's skin crawl. "She said she would wait for you there."

"Bree, something is not right," Nessa said, this time with urgency. Bree stared at the pavement and then looked up, her eyes filled with tears.

"I know."

Nessa headed past the buses where her mom was waiting with open arms. But even her mother's hug did not comfort Nessa. "It's so awful, Mom," was all she could say. "Billy was so little."

"I know," said Vivian, smelling the way she always did, like the disinfectant she used to wipe down the exam room between consultations at Dr. Morgan's, and lavender soap and coffee. "I know."

When Nessa pulled away from her mom, Vivian rubbed a hand over her own eyes like she was trying to prevent a head-ache that was coming on. "He was the same age as Nate," she said. Vivian reached into her purse for her car keys. "Come on," she said. "I'll drop you off at home. I want to bring a hot dish over to the Larks." Vivian turned to Nessa and gave her shoulder a squeeze. "You were amazing today."

Nessa nodded dumbly, said goodbye to Bree, and followed her mom. Of course this was what her mother was going to do. In Tether, when someone died, the town rallied around the family. Half of the town showed up with a meal, which they would heat up in your kitchen, serve, and clean up after. They would send their husbands or sons or daughters outside to shovel your driveway, mow your lawn, and walk your dog. People would come out to help even those families who kept mostly to themselves, like the Larks. It didn't matter.

While Nessa showered, she knew that in the kitchen her mom would be making tuna noodle casserole: boiling the pasta, opening the cans, mixing up the tuna and onion, shaking out the buttered breadcrumbs on the top.

Moments from the race kept flashing through her mind, getting mixed up with thoughts of Billy. She thought about the aggressive wolves, imagining them in the woods she'd been running through, imagining them in the fields by Billy's house.

Nessa got dressed in jeans and a clean fleece sweatshirt. The smell of tuna noodle casserole was reminding her that she'd barely eaten all day. She knew Vivian wouldn't expect any of her children to come to the Larks—she would have made two casseroles so she could leave one at home. Nevertheless, Nessa blow-dried her hair, pulled it back into a ponytail, and joined her mom in the kitchen, where she announced, "I want to go with you. I want to pay my respects to the Larks."

On the way over in the car, Nessa said what she knew her mother had to be thinking.

"Mom, remember what I told you about that day at the clinic? How Mrs. Lark had become suspicious that something about the study was making Billy sick?" Nessa said.

Vivian was silent. She turned down the Larks' road, but their driveway was full. She and Nessa had to park more than a hundred yards away.

"Then she made a fuss at the front desk and barged into the examining room, and then, after five years, we find that they were restraining the kids? Billy was getting fevers after each visit. And he didn't look well. Anybody could see that." Nessa took a deep breath. "Do you think the study has something to do with Billy's death?"

Vivian shut off the ignition and turned to Nessa. "I don't know if the health study had anything to do with it, but I promise that I am going to try to find out."

They got out of the car and walked to the Larks' front door in silence. She could tell the conversation was over. Nessa carried the casserole dish, keeping a few steps behind her mom. It was intimidating, heading toward the house. They could hear Mrs. Lark wailing from all the way down the front walk. Nessa imagined her in the living room, surrounded by women, sitting on the sofa.

But when Nessa and her mother entered, the living room looked untouched. Men and kids were standing around. There was a green corduroy couch and a recliner, but no one was sitting on either. A few of the men were holding beers. All the women were in the kitchen, which is where Nessa and Vivian headed.

Mavis Cartwright seemed to be in charge. She was generally in charge wherever she was. She ran a daycare where Ann Lark used to work as an aide, Billy coming along with her. There were about six women bustling around, an urn of coffee sending off steam from the counter, platters of cut-up vegetables on the table, and a few plates of cookies and brownies covered tightly in plastic wrap.

"Over there, dear," Mrs. Cartwright said, indicating that Nessa should put the casserole dish on top of the stove.

"Where are the Larks?" Nessa asked quietly, looking around because she hadn't seen them.

Mrs. Cartwright shook her head. "They're in Billy's room, with him still." She turned to Vivian. "Ann wouldn't let them take him to the mortuary. She wants an autopsy. She's called up Dane Sampson from hospice who is arranging to have them pick up the body. The clinic here would do some of that for free, but she would have none of it."

"So Mrs. Lark thinks Billy's death had something to do with the clinic study?" Nessa asked. She tried to make eye contact with her mom, but Vivian looked away.

Mrs. Cartwright looked back at Nessa in shock. The idea that the clinic study was not 100 percent hunky dory had never entered her mind.

"Ann Lark is not right in the head at the moment. And no one can blame her," she said tersely.

Case closed.

They all turned when they heard another wail coming from Billy's bedroom. It was so loud and strangled it didn't sound human. *Did they put Billy in his bed?* Nessa wondered. *What'll happen when the hospice workers come?*

The women had put some of the casseroles out on the table, and people were starting to fill plates. Someone brought a plate to Billy's room down the hall. Nessa watched the door open as one of Mrs. Lark's sisters stepped inside, and she remembered herself as a wolf watching Mrs. Lark herself standing in that doorway, the moment when they made eye contact and Mrs. Lark screamed.

Nessa was starving, so she took a plate of food. Some kids from school were there, and they'd taken over the den where the TV was off out of respect, but still, there was laughing and joking. She saw other people from town—Gina, the receptionist from the clinic was there with Dr. Raab's nurse, Mary. It was nice of them to come, but they looked awkward and weren't mingling with the others, even though they were Tether natives. Nessa wondered if they felt guilty. She ate her plate of food by herself in the hallway, which was filled with framed pictures of Billy as a baby, Billy holding a piece of driftwood on the shore of Lake Michigan, Billy on a swing, Billy silhouetted against a tall field of wheat with the sun almost setting behind him.

Looking at the pictures, she felt her throat closing up, and she could no longer even taste the food.

Chayton had told her the wolves had turned her into one of them for a reason. He'd told her to try to figure it out. And then the wolves had taken her here.

Something in Nessa's gut told her: it wasn't over yet. She could unravel this, she could piece together why the wolves knew so early that Billy was in trouble and why they wanted her to know as well. She had to decode the message, and she had to do it soon. Ann Lark was no fool. Nessa could not think of another mother she knew who was more attached to her kid.

She left the hall, looking for a place to throw away the food she was unable to finish. She passed the front door just as it opened, with Cassian, Sierra, and Mr. and Mrs. Thomas on the other side, entering the Lark's home.

"Nessa!" Cassian whispered, clearly happy to see her. His eyes lit up. He stepped forward to let his parents pass.

Cassian's dad leaned in and said, "Great race today," in a kind, but low, voice. Sierra just stared at her. Cassian's mom gave Nessa a sad half-smile as she carried a basket of buttered rolls into the kitchen.

"Hey state champion," Cassian said, softly, like he meant the words to be just for her. He leaned forward and kissed her on her forehead.

Nessa tried to smile. Cassian had been kind to Billy, the way he was kind to everyone. He had played soccer with him and Nate in the waiting room. Cassian treated both boys like they were star campers and he was the counselor everyone wanted attention from.

"It's so awful," she said, her eyes filling with tears.

Cassian looked her straight in the eye. "I know. I feel sick about it. Honestly," he said. "I mean, when was the last time we saw him at the clinic? Two weeks ago? It all feels unreal."

"Exactly," said Nessa. "Can you imagine how his mom feels right now?"

"I know," Cassian said. "He was their only child."

It wasn't lost on Nessa that after several years, most parents had assigned the chore of clinic to an older child like Nessa or Cassian, or a babysitter. At the least, they carpooled. But not Mrs. Lark.

"She's in Billy's bedroom," Nessa said. "Her close friends let the minister in, but she won't talk to him. They haven't even taken away the body."

"Creepy," Cassian said. "They just put out some seven-layer bars. Let's get some and go outside?"

"Okay," Nessa agreed. She certainly didn't want to stay inside anymore, looking at pictures of towheaded adorable Billy and realizing they were all that was left of his story.

Outside, Cassian's energy was all sunlight, no sadness, as he cheered her again for her victory. They moved around to the side of the house.

"Nessa, you must be reevaluating the entire story of your life right now," he said. "I mean, you're going to get recruited. Somewhere amazing. Have you thought about that?"

"Honestly, not yet. I don't really want to right now," Nessa said.

"Don't let what happened to you today get swept under the rug," Cassian urged. "Do you know why my dad came back here after college? His dad got sick. He had little brothers. No one else was around to join the law firm—no one was old enough. And my grandma told my dad it wasn't a bad life. They had the lake house, the pool; it's a good place to raise kids. But you know what?"

Nessa didn't know what. She'd never thought about Cassian's dad one way or another. He was a lawyer and did whatever it was lawyers did. She'd always assumed he'd gone to college and law school and come back because he wanted to, because back then in the 1990s, Dutch Chem and Tether were still going strong.

"He's fine. He's happy and all. But he told me that if I even think about coming back here after college, I'm going to find a locked front door. He says he won't keep me on his health plan, and he'll refuse to pay for my car insurance."

Nessa smiled wistfully. Cassian's family might not be rich, but the things he described were luxuries to her.

"My dad's not kidding," Cassian said. "Even now, with work picking up, he'd move everyone to Arizona given half a chance."

"Arizona!" Nessa said. "You mean sand and cacti and deserts?"

"You bet. My mom's sick of the mold in the basement. She wants a new house with tile floors and ceiling fans. My dad could play golf year-round. Sierra would finish school where kids are cheerful and feel like they have a future. People are just happier out there."

Cassian put a hand on her arm, let his hand wrap around to her back. "My dad loves what's happening to you, Nessa," he said. "He talked about it the whole way here."

Nessa thought, *I doubt your dad would be happy with* everything *that's happening to me.*

"You've got to keep looking ahead," Cassian went on. "The way you do when you run a race, right? You don't worry about the people you're leaving behind, do you?"

Nessa looked at Cassian, his sunny face, and wondered what he really meant. His hand on her back gave her a shiver.

"What were you thinking when you ran?" Cassian asked, drawing her closer. "What's it like to know everyone on that line's gonna try their best, and you're going to absolutely slay them anyway?"

"I don't think about it like that. It feels…" Nessa trailed. It was getting hard for her to concentrate with Cassian's face so close to hers. She could feel his breath on her cheek as he leaned back against the siding of the house and pulled her toward him. "It feels," Nessa started again, "like I never know if I'm going too fast, or not fast enough. In this race today, half the time I felt like I must have taken a wrong turn or something. I couldn't think of any other way to explain being so far out in front."

"You're amazing," Cassian said, brushing his lips on her cheek. "You don't even have any idea of how beautiful and fierce you are."

When he kissed her, Nessa felt the same way she'd felt when he'd kissed her before, like something inside her had just caught fire. He smelled amazing, like aftershave mixed with wood smoke, and the way he held her made her feel like they were figure skaters and he could make her spin into a triple jump just with a flick of his self-assured wrist.

But then she reached a hand behind her and touched the aluminum siding of the house, cool and gritty with a film of dirt blown off the cultivated fields. The grit was distracting, and the cold was like a conduit, channeling her attention around to the other side of the house, the side where she had made eye contact with Mrs. Lark through Billy's window.

Here she was kissing Cassian when Billy Lark had died right here, hours before. With his small body still lying somewhere nearby. With all of this going on, Cassian was telling her to think about her future, herself, to keep running. And now the cold had seeped through her hand up into her body. She felt like the part of her that had been enjoying kissing Cassian had gone into hiding. She pulled away.

"Are you okay?" he said.

"No," she answered. "I'm not. I'm not okay with—" She took a step back. She pointed to the space that she had just opened up between them. "—this."

"Did I say something wrong?" He looked concerned, but more than that, he looked confused. Nessa smiled wearily. All she'd wanted since the fall of ninth grade was for Cassian to be her boyfriend, and here the thing that she'd always believed most connected them was the thing she didn't like. Had he never been told no before?

"A little boy is dead," she said. "You're telling me not to think about him, but I have to." She didn't explain the aspect of this statement that involved the wolves and her missing whatever message they'd been trying to send her about Billy, but she felt there was truth in her statement regardless.

"Nessa, I didn't mean—"

"Cassian," Nessa said. "You did mean it. And that's okay. For you. But it's just not—it's just not me." As she put her feelings into words, Nessa understood how true they were. "Whatever is going on between us, I don't think I want it anymore."

"Okay," Cassian said. He held up his hands like he'd just touched something hot. "Totally get it. But I thought you were feeling it. You seemed like it."

Nessa felt her face go hot. She *had* been feeling something.

"I'm not feeling it right now," Nessa said. She tried to make it clear that she was sure. And as she made it clear, she felt increasingly that she was sure. She didn't want Cassian. "I gotta go back to my mom."

CHAPTER THIRTY-FIVE

ack inside, Nessa found Vivian in the kitchen making coffee while Cassian's mom loaded the dishwasher. A few other women Nessa recognized were clustered at the small breakfast table, talking quietly.

"They're going to come for the body a little later," Mrs. Lark's sister was saying. "Poor thing, we got her to let go finally. Hospice should be here soon."

Nessa found herself suddenly feeling light-headed, like she was going to pass out.

Vivian took one look at her daughter and stood. "You," she said to Nessa, "need to go home. After the race...did you eat?"

Nessa hadn't really. She'd tried. Vivian took one of Cassian's mother's buttered rolls from the countertop and shoved some tuna salad into it, plopped the whole thing in a napkin. "Here," she said. "Put that in your mouth." She took Nessa by the elbow. "It's been a long day," Vivian said. "There are plenty of people here taking care of Ann and Will. It's time for you to get some sleep."

Although she couldn't ignore what felt like a lead ball of sadness in her belly, Nessa was glad to head home. She changed into sweatpants and crawled under a fleece blanket on the sofa. Delphine was watching a *House Hunters International* marathon. Nessa felt tired in a way that traveled deep into her bones, but she didn't want to get into bed. Scenes of the day looped over and over in her mind—running, the happy blur of winning, the sickening return to school to find out Billy was dead, and then being so close to the sound of Ann Lark crying, knowing his body was still in the house. Vivian was right. It had been a long day. Nessa slept.

But Nessa did not sleep well. In a dream, she saw Billy again. He was looking at her as she'd seen him in the exam room at the clinic, strapped to the examination table, looking up at Dr. Raab with blank eyes. Nessa could not tell if his expression was one of trust or fear.

Then she saw Nate in her dream. He was running in the woods, being chased by the aggressive wolves. Nessa saw the pink and black skin of their mouths, the saliva dripping off their teeth, their breath raspy but determined as they loped, almost lazily, after Nate. He was running as fast as he could, and he kept looking back, his face a mask of terror. Nessa wanted to scream at him that he was going to slow himself down if he kept looking to see who was behind him. It was bad running form.

But then the wolves caught up to Nate. They began to lunge at him, snapping at his sides, knowing it wasn't about the one hit that would bring him down but the series of them. It was just a matter of time. And Nate was screaming for her, screaming, "Nessa, help me!" but it wasn't his voice, it was Ann Lark's, and she was saying, "I can't let him go. I can't. He's too young. He's just too small."

Nessa sat up with a start. It took her a moment to place herself, to sort out what was real in the dream and what was terror. To recognize the sounds she heard not as wolf growls but as the happy fervor of international house hunting successfully concluding yet again.

Delphine had been glued to the show. But she noticed Nessa's open eyes and turned to talk to her instead. "Nessa?" Delphine said, pressing Mute on the remote control. "Are you okay?"

Nessa rubbed a hand over her eyes. Her entire body ached, the adrenaline of the day long gone, leaving behind the stiffness it had been keeping at bay. She'd pushed her muscles past where they had ever gone before, and now she was paying the price in pain.

"I'm fine," she said. "Just need to take some ibuprofen or something."

Gingerly, she swung her legs over the side of the sofa while Delphine turned the volume back on, switching over to *Project Runway*. Nessa felt weak, holding on to the wall as she made it to the bathroom, and her hand was shaking as she lifted the glass of water to her mouth, depositing two ibuprofen and swallowing fast.

Ibuprofen wasn't going to cut it. She was craving something else. What was it? Some food? More sleep? As her mind unfogged, she remembered first the yeasty, fresh smell and then the association clicked.

Inside her room, she opened the sliding doors on her side of the closet. Chayton had given her stalks of rye that time he'd taken her out to the distillery on his motorcycle. She reached for the sachet she had made and hidden from her mom and sister.

Then, she hadn't known. But now...just placing a hand on the brittle sheaf was energizing and settling.

Nessa checked her phone. There was nothing from Bree.

Bree had really loved Billy, and her family hadn't gone over to the Larks'. Nessa wished Bree had been there instead of Cassian. She texted Bree:

How are you holding up?

When Bree didn't answer, Nessa wrote one more text:

I'm going to try something with the rye. I need to understand what the wolves were trying to say.

No three dots of continued conversation appeared. Maybe Bree had gone to sleep.

Gathering a small bunch of dried rye, Nessa snuck first out of her room and then the house. The Kurlands lived in the last lot on the street and it backed right up to the woods. Nessa gave the yard a wide scan and intentionally avoided the line of sight from the window of her mother's bedroom. Vivian was on the phone with Aunt Jane. Making her way to the cover of trees, Nessa registered that the sliver of a moon had risen.

Arranging the rye in a circle the way Chayton had done in

the woods, Nessa stepped inside, expecting to feel calmer and more relaxed, the way she had before.

What she was not expecting was that she would transform into a wolf. Sure, Chayton had said she would learn how to do that eventually, but Nessa had assumed that was advanced shape-shifting. But here she was nevertheless, noticing the heaviness of her paws on the earth, feeling the strength and steadiness in her back, conscious of the position of her tail.

She felt electrified, all her fatigue replaced by a desire to run. As if the inside of the circle were carpeted in hot coals and she'd just stepped on them, she jumped out and started to sprint. Before she consciously registered what she was doing, she had made it far enough that she no longer recognized the landmarks near her house. But it didn't matter—she wasn't following landmarks. She was following trails of smells.

When Nessa reached the ridgeline above Billy's house, she sat back on her haunches and howled, calling out in five different tones, which was a trick she'd picked up from one of the pack brothers. Nessa had understood instinctually that it made you seem more intimidating to wolves who might be within listening range, making it sound like you were part of a five-wolf pack. She had to find the other wolves and ask them what she was supposed to be doing, try harder to find out why they had picked her.

But they didn't call out to her, and no wolves came.

She wondered what to do next. Nessa looked down the slope toward Billy's house. There were fewer cars than before, but the Larks still had many visitors. Nessa wondered if Mrs. Lark had been coaxed away from Billy's body, if the hospice workers had come to take it away. With a rumble in her belly, she remembered the seven-layer bars and then quickly transitioned in her memory to the platter of cold cuts, particularly the roast beef. As a human, she might have chided herself for thinking about food, but wolves never pretended they were above their hunger.

Remembering how she and the submissive wolf had been picked to look inside Billy's windows, Nessa was seized by a desire to see him again—to know if Ann Lark was okay, to see if Billy's body was still there.

Headlights coming down the road caught Nessa's attention, and she saw that a white van was approaching on the long, lonely road leading to Billy's house. As it turned the corner into Billy's driveway, Nessa started to run, realizing this might be the van coming to take Billy to the hospital in Saginaw.

She approached the side of the barn and, sticking to the shadows where she and Cassian had been standing just a few hours before, she had a view of the front door.

What looked like two paramedics were knocking and were quickly allowed in. Nessa scooted around the side of the house to Billy's room, where she saw that they were already moving quickly to complete the job they'd come to do. One was unrolling the stiff rubber of a child-sized black body bag and pulling down its heavy, institutional zipper, while the other must have been arranging Billy's body in such a way that his legs and arms were organized inside the bag.

Nessa couldn't see much of anything at all, not Billy's body itself—just the shape of a foot under a blanket and a hand that slipped out of the paramedic's grasp before he tucked it into the bag.

When Billy's hand slipped, Nessa gasped. Or at least she

thought she gasped. The noise she heard herself make was a yip, and then she dropped down, watching from the shadows as Mrs. Lark turned quickly, her pretty eyes narrowed. You could tell she'd been crying and now, looking out the window, she shivered.

Nessa knew why. Mrs. Lark was remembering when she'd seen the wolf looking in her window. Nessa, the wolf.

Mrs. Lark bit her lip and wiped at her eyes. Nessa guessed that remembering the wolf hadn't so much frightened Mrs. Lark as reminded her that the last time she'd heard one, she'd had a child, and now she had none.

The paramedics unfolded a light aluminum stretcher, expanding it on the bed next to Billy and then gently sliding the body bag on top of it. Taking the ends, they lifted it and carried it away.

Poor Billy, Nessa thought for the hundredth time.

Without consciously making a decision, she started loping after the van, sticking to the shadows of the fields, hanging back about twenty or thirty feet. She figured she'd stick with it as long as the end of the road, where it would turn left to head toward Interstate 75.

But the van didn't turn left. It turned right, and started to pick up speed.

This made no sense, Nessa realized. There was nothing in the direction the van was heading in. Where were they taking Billy?

She'd thought she was running at an all-out sprint but managed to increase her pace. She did not like what was happening here, but she could not even guess what it all meant.

Wolves can run faster than humans but not as fast as cars, and Nessa grew tired. She kept going anyway, somehow convinced it was important that she stick with Billy's body. Nessa's side struck a low branch that she'd been running too fast to see. It knocked her over, and she rolled a few times before righting herself into a crouch. She stopped, trying to get her bearings, checking to make sure she wasn't injured.

The tumble turned her completely around, and by the time she spotted the van again, it was so far down the road that she knew she would never catch it. She was going to have to let it go, and she panted, feeling her chest burning, her ribs heaving, her tongue lolling out of her mouth.

Then, the van stopped and turned right again. Nessa had a sharp, bad feeling. The van was taking the turn off toward the old Dutch Chem plant. Why on earth was it headed there? It wasn't a road it was turning on to. More like a two-mile-long driveway.

So Ann Lark was right. Something about the continuing health study *was* fishy. Paravida was involved in Billy's death. Something was very wrong.

Finding new energy in her revulsion at the thought of Billy being manhandled one last time, Nessa caught up to the van while the driver was checking in at the guard booth. For years the booth had stood empty, and anyone who wanted to had been able to drive around the old Dutch Chem campus without permission. But since Paravida had bought the company out of bankruptcy court, the plant's guard booth had been rebuilt and was staffed by a uniformed security officer now. Nessa got close enough to see that the driver of the van was showing the security officer some paperwork.

Nessa peered at the guard from her distance, and the sharp feeling came on stronger as she recognized him: Pasty Pete Packer from school! What on earth…?

This must be his second job, his moonlight shift for Paravida. Recognition of his face cleared up nothing in Nessa's mind. Pete scanned the driver's paper carefully, spoke into a walkie-talkie, then pressed a button that lifted the electronic arm that had been blocking access to Paravida Road. The van's brake lights flashed a few times as the driver prepared to accelerate, and then the van was whooshing forward on the asphalt that Paravida had paid a lot of money to install at the facility. It was a strange investment in an empty building.

CHAPTER THIRTY-SIX

Paravida's chain-link fence was electrified, but it stopped several hundred feet in from the road.

This will be easy, Nessa thought, walking with her tail held high, feeling smart and unstoppable.

But then she smelled the tracks of an aggressive wolf. Uh-oh. If one of them were hanging out in this area, that was a danger.

Then she smelled another one.

And a third.

She knew she should turn back, look for the pack, get help. But she didn't. She just couldn't leave Billy Lark all alone.

Maybe she would get lucky. Maybe the hostile wolves were

hunting. Or better, digesting a recent kill. Or prowling around, going on the warpath somewhere far off. They would eventually discover that Nessa had been there. She knew her paws would secrete a scent pattern, letting the aggressive wolves know exactly who had been here. She would deal with the repercussions later.

Then she saw lights up ahead and recognized the freshly paved parking lot lit by enough fluorescents for a nighttime baseball game. She breathed a sigh of relief. Whatever manmade challenges she was going to encounter at the plant couldn't be half as terrifying as those killer wolves.

Unfortunately, she soon realized there was no way for her to get anywhere near the building. The incomplete fence at the entrance was an illusion. Here were two more fences, about six feet apart. Both were electrified and topped by double coils of barbed wire. Unlike the outermost line of fencing, these contained the full perimeter of the facility.

The more Nessa looked at it, the more it resembled a prison. Why did a pharmaceutical plant require guard towers? And all those lights?

Nessa contented herself with circling the grounds, scoping out the exits and entrances, looking for information, trying to determine where Billy's body would be headed.

The building had small high windows, and the doors were closed and, Nessa presumed, locked. The parking lot was illuminated, but mostly empty, even though spots had been lined and numbered as if a corps of workers were expected to arrive the next morning.

Given the emptiness of the lot, it wasn't hard to find the van, parked near what looked like a loading bay for trucks.

Staying in shadow as much as possible, regretting not for the first time that she was a white wolf, a fact that caused her to nearly glow in the dark, Nessa got as close to the loading dock as she could, sat down on her haunches, and waited to see if there was anything she could hear.

There was nothing. She stood and padded silently toward another spot to see if she could hear better there. She heard a sucking and swishing sound and saw that the double swinging doors had been opened, slapping against each other as the swinging motion of their opening slowed.

Who had opened them? Nessa tried to focus on the loading dock, but it was too far away for her to see much in the shadows. Then she located the smell of a cigarette. It must have just been lit because she first smelled butane from the lighter.

On top of that, there was a smell that must have just wafted out of the doors the smoker had opened. It smelled like Dr. Morgan's but also like the biology labs at school. Frog dissection. It was the smell of formaldehyde. Nessa was getting closer.

She waited, listening to the sound of the smoker closing his lips down on the cigarette—a soft smacking sound. She heard the clinking of metal instruments in a different location. That sound was fainter and came from inside. Eventually the smoker finished the cigarette and went back indoors. Now there was the sound of low voices and more clinking. Nessa was now sure they were metal instruments on metal trays. She strained to hear.

There were two voices, one dictating to the other, punctuated by the occasional "Got it" and "Um-hum."

"Development of the prefrontal cortex consistent with eleven-year-old boy. Growth plate adhesion evident."

"Got it."

"Growth detected on the anterior aspect of the occipital lobe. Diverse embarkation on the cerebellum."

"Okay."

"I'm moving on to the body's cavity," the first voice announced. "Let's open his chest."

This must be Billy's autopsy, Nessa thought.

She heard the whine of a saw as it cracked open the chest cavity, breaking Billy's ribs. And then she figured they were weighing parts of a body, because some of the names had meaning for her, like "spleen" and "large intestine." There were sounds of electronic beeps and a voice would recite a number of grams.

"Wow. This is nasty looking. The poor kid had no right kidney left. It appears to be completely degraded," the second voice said.

"We'll need to keep it for study, Harry," the older voice answered. "We were using the 7IRG to try to get the kidney to grow back. It obviously did not succeed."

Who is Harry? Who are they all? Nessa thought.

Nessa heard the plop of a wet mass hitting a metal pan. She winced.

The one time when the string of words finally became a conversation was when the two started to have a discussion about something they referred to as A23D7. Apparently, whatever that was, there was some disagreement between the doctor (Nessa assumed it was a doctor) and his assistant about how to gather this particular object. Or was it a substance? It started to sound like it was a tissue sample. It sounded like it had something to do with the brain. Nessa could not be sure.

Suddenly there was a voice coming into the room via a crackly speaker Nessa assumed was an intercom. "Team Osiris," the voice said. "We're going to need to wrap up this operation and make the delivery as scheduled. Over."

"All right, Boss," said the second person.

"All personnel, assume lockdown positions. Commencing security procedure seven. Repeat, commencing security procedure seven. Assume lockdown."

The message cut out and was replaced with an ear-piercing shrill siren.

Nessa knew what a lockdown was from school. It was not a drill.

She looked around and realized that she was in terrible danger. Coming toward Nessa, as she stood outside the fence listening to Billy's autopsy, were wolves, traveling single file in a line that stretched back as far as Nessa could see and smell. These wolves, with filed teeth and matted fur, standing taller than Nessa, were trotting fiercely as if on the warpath, ears pricked and ready for the moment when they made their move. There must have been at least thirty in all.

CHAPTER THIRTY-SEVEN

This wasn't a regular wolf pack. This was a...swarm. Where had they all come from?

Nessa looked to the left and then the right and began to panic. The facility was at her back and the hostile wolves out in front. She scanned the hills behind the plant for a possible route of escape. But there was none.

The line of wolves just kept getting closer.

She went into a pre-attack crouch, waiting for the lead wolf to lunge. She'd started to pant and she felt herself darting in one direction and then the other, the way the brothers and sister had moved during the wolf attack at the Larks'.

And then the hostile wolves trotted right past Nessa.

They weren't coming for her.

They continued on, ignoring her, and soon entered the circle of light cast by the stadium-like fixtures outside Paravida. When they did, a section of the chain-link fence slowly started to rise—it was a gate! And a human inside the facility must have controlled it. As if it were their normal routine, the wolves began to pass through the gate, heading inside.

Was this gate in the fence a giant dog door?

Were the aggressive wolves Paravida pets?

Passing through the opening in the fence, the wolves moved into the light of the parking lot. Nessa got glimpses of the parts of their bodies that best reflected light: their teeth, the silvery tips of their fur, the shine of their yellow eyes, the pink of their ears. And at least five of the group had places where their fur had recently been shorn and a line of stitches could be seen.

Once inside the facility, they jockeyed for position. It was as if each one believed itself to be the alpha.

Two of the aggressive wolves began to attack each other. This wasn't play fighting. Something must have happened in the line. These wolves were going crazy. Each was up on its hind legs, trying to get the other's throat. They separated only when there was a cracking sound that Nessa felt in her molars—a gunshot. One of the wolves was lying on the ground. The others were trotting by, distracted by the sudden smell of meat that permeated the air. They picked up their pace.

Where was the shooter?

She remembered the guard towers. And then, when she looked at the nearest one, she saw a shadowy figure behind the thick glass window and the barrel of a gun sticking out through an opening in the glass.

Nessa would have run if she had not suddenly detected another animal immediately nearby. Another wolf...the gray wolf. She could tell by his scent. Not wanting to attract the attention of the killer wolf pack, she turned her head slowly toward the scent.

The gray wolf came to stand behind Nessa, to one side, up on a rise, as if he had been there awhile. Nessa wondered, was he here for Billy too? Or had he been following the killer wolves?

This was the second time she'd seen him, and both times had been in the aggressive wolves' company. He lifted his chin and she lifted hers back.

When he started to trot off after the line of aggressive wolves and then turned to give Nessa a look, like, "What's taking you so long?" she realized he wanted her to follow him.

Into Paravida.

Nessa couldn't believe he was asking her that. But when he turned a second time and pawed the ground, gesturing like he was a bull getting ready to charge, Nessa followed.

They joined the end of the line of wolves passing through the gate. Nessa noticed that the gray wolf was amping up his submissive behaviors—ducking his head and tucking his tail so that Nessa barely recognized his demeanor. He checked to make sure she was looking, though, and that's when she realized she should follow suit. She was so scared; the submissive postures were barely faked.

Under this cover, Nessa and the gray wolf followed the line of wolves into the Paravida campus, through a covered passageway between the building with the loading dock and another like it.

They were headed for what looked like kennels. There must

have been 60 cages covered in chain-link fence, sitting inside a cavernous warehouse that was surrounded by low buildings.

The handlers were armed guards in riot gear. Nessa couldn't see their faces through the shaded visors on their helmets, but she knew they were scared by the way they were balanced forward on their toes instead of sitting back on their heels.

"C'mon, kids," one called out, trying to sound brave as he directed the wolves into their cages, one per cage. A second guard was one step ahead, throwing a haunch of meat into each empty kennel. It occurred to Nessa, watching their feeding frenzy, watching their disregard for the fallen wolf, that these weren't wolves. They were monsters.

Once inside the cages, dinner eaten, the wolves seemed more angry at one another than at the guards. They threw themselves against the doors or charged the chain-link fencing walls as if they would bite and claw their way through steel in order to murder their neighbors.

As the last of the aggressive wolves was being locked up, the gray wolf slipped behind the wall of a building where he could not be seen by the guard, and Nessa followed.

Sticking to the shadows at the edges of buildings, they made their way back to the loading dock, where the van that had been carrying Billy's body was now parked. Or at least Nessa thought it was the same van. It was white, windowless, without identifying markers. The gray wolf sat at the base of the steps leading up to the loading dock, and Nessa climbed up, understanding he meant for her to go inside while he stayed on guard.

Slipping through the swinging doors and entering a hall, she followed the lingering odor of the cigarette up a flight of stairs and into a long hallway. She heard the clinking and clattering of metal on metal clearly now—and the sound of the voice that was dictating. Her heart raced, every sense on high alert.

Holding her breath, she padded down the long hall toward the room. Would she find Billy's body? What then? Just bark at the people performing his autopsy?

The door to the room opened, and a man emerged from it, hiking up the belt on the pants of his guard uniform, whistling softly.

Nessa froze.

She hunkered down, tucked her tail, lowered her head, as if somehow he wouldn't see her. Would she appear invisible to him the way she had to the aggressive wolves?

No. She would not. This guard was not a wolf. He was a man, headed most likely to the bathroom, confronted with the sudden realization that standing on the polished floor in front of him, in the crystal clear light cast by fluorescent bulbs, was a wolf.

If Nessa hadn't been so scared of what he would do—and aware of the fact that there was a gun in the security-guard holster attached to his belt—she might have been more appreciative of the look of complete panic that crossed the guard's face. He looked like he was about to throw up.

The guard pressed a button on the walkie-talkie clipped to his shoulder, and said, "Code Lupine. Building Eight. Reinitiate lockdown." And then, as Nessa was considering this repeat command now directed at her, the guard reached for a gun, took aim at Nessa, and fired off a shot. The crack that followed was the most shrill, most mind-altering sound Nessa had ever heard.

Without looking back to see where the bullet had gone—it

hadn't hit her—Nessa ran. Down the stairs, down the first floor hall. She took a flying leap off the loading dock, the gray wolf behind her.

She prayed the guard wasn't behind them right now. She didn't dare look.

Whatever code he had initiated when he spoke into his walkie-talkie must have involved the wolf door closing. Nessa could hear it, the mechanical cranking of its descending on its chain. She and the gray wolf sprinted for it, got there just in time, slipped under, and kept moving at a hard sprint.

They were at least a mile away from the Paravida plant when he stopped. Panting heavily, they faced each other.

Nessa wished she could explain what had happened, what she'd seen.

It was awful to get shot at and not be able to process it with words.

The gray wolf must have waited for her. Who was he, anyway?

This was a little strange to think but Nessa felt flattered by his attention. Here he was, this alpha wolf who was always alone and obviously revered and almost all-powerful. He was the kind of wolf Big One would sniff noses with, as friendly equals.

When he fell into step with Nessa, she didn't know quite what to do. She kept tripping over her own paws and wasn't able to look him in the eye. Which was probably for the best, considering that, to wolves, that was a challenging gesture.

Maybe he was an old man? He certainly had the look of weariness about him, like he'd seen a lot. He took care of everyone, defending the pack without being part of it, following her to Paravida, or at least following the killer wolves. Maybe this guy could use a friend.

And so she did something she normally would have done with her siblings. She ran sideways into him and then jumped back a few feet to show him that she wasn't actually attacking him, just playing.

The wolf looked at her, warily almost, she thought. Then he did a quick crouch, lowering his front paws and head to show he wanted to play.

Yay! Nessa thought. She got the old man to show a little spark.

She ran to the gray wolf, plowing her shoulder into his head. He looked surprised, drawing back, and then with one powerful paw, he flipped her. But playfully. She could tell the difference. She wriggled free and sprang up again, as if to say, "Want a piece of me? Put up your dukes." She could play too. She was trying to be funny, exaggerating her boxer-at-the-ready pose, hoping he could tell.

And he could! He wasn't shaking his head and laughing—wolves didn't do that—but he lay down and yawned, showing her just how very unimpressed and unintimidated he was by her. He pretended he wanted to do nothing more than give his paws a thorough chewing over, but then he betrayed himself by sneaking a glance up at Nessa.

Nessa felt her tail shoot up into the air, her nose lift.

Then lone wolf stood up and trotted off, his tail high too.

Nessa followed him, thinking it was still a game, until she realized where he was taking her. Home.

When they reached the edge of the woods behind her house, he stopped moving. *He knows where I live*, Nessa thought.

Nessa touched noses with the gray wolf briefly before returning to the circle of rye. She knew the gray wolf couldn't see her transform—the Kurlands' utility shed blocked his view. But she wondered what he would make of the fact that where there had been a wolf, there was now a teenage girl.

She peered into the woods to look for him as she crossed the lawn but saw nothing. The gray wolf was gone.

He was gone, Billy Lark was dead, and Nessa was no closer to understanding any of it.

Back inside, the first thing she did was check her phone. No message from Bree. Nessa had to tell her what she had seen. Bree would know what to do.

There were so many questions. What had they done to Billy? And why? How did they manage to get his body? Where was it now? What had Paravida done to the kids in the Dutch Chem study?

Suddenly, all Nessa could do was sleep.

CHAPTER THIRTY-EIGHT

*I*f Vivian hadn't woken Nessa up the next morning, she might have slept all day.

She jerked awake in her bed and bolted upright.

"What time is it?" she asked. She could tell from where the sun was that it was late. "I've got to see Bree."

She looked at her phone. Bree had texted:

Call me when you get up and I'll come over.

"Bree can wait," Vivian replied. "There are some people here to see you."

"People?" Nessa said, though her question came out more as a groan than as a word. Nessa looked at the screen on her phone. It showed 11:17 a.m. "Who is here?" she said a little more coherently.

Nessa noticed that Delphine's bed was not only empty but also made. How had she slept through all of that?

"Recruiter kind of men," Vivian replied. "Nessa, I think you'd better get your face washed and put some clothes on. The first just showed up out of nowhere about an hour ago. I told him you were asleep, and he said he could talk to me first anyway while he waited for you to wake up. I made him some coffee and was about to come wake you when another one just arrived. They're scouts, and they're saying all these things about coaches who want to come up here—to Tether—just to take us out to dinner. They're talking about all these programs. Michigan, Stanford, Kansas. Real schools. I don't think you want to miss this."

Nessa registered several feelings. A kind of nascent joy burbling in her stomach. Surprise at her careworn mother sounding so excited. Nessa was used to her mother being strong, or calm, or dignified, or even funny. But giddy? This was new. She sat up. Images from the night before came into her mind—the blazing lights, the Paravida guard taking a shot, the gray wolf standing behind her in the night, leading her home.

Had all that *really* happened?

But then Vivian's words shook her into the present again.

"Did you say Stanford?" Nessa said, leaping up.

Last summer, not long after she'd started her training regimen, Nessa had looked up Stanford on the internet. She'd known Cynthia was going to cross-country training camp there.

She'd imagined it would be pretty lush, and still it blew her away. She paged through picture after picture of manicured lawns, blooming flowerbeds, and spacious dorm rooms with kids wearing sporty clothes. There were palm trees! People who graduated from there went on to be presidents of companies, senators, world-class athletes. They invented things and made scientific discoveries. They became surgeons and lawyers and judges and wrote books or directed movies that Nessa had actually heard of. And the cross-country team won everything. Kids from there went on to the Olympics.

"I'll take a quick shower. And be right there."

Vivian nodded, and disappeared.

Nessa had never moved so fast getting showered and dressed. Vivian had pulled a coffee cake out of the freezer and was serving it warm at the kitchen table when she came in. Nate was watching TV with the volume low, and Delphine was doing homework at the computer, looking over with an amused expression every few minutes to check out the random men in identical golf-shirt/chino/loafer outfits (a third recruiter had arrived).

After Nessa shook their hands and sat down, the men whipped out shiny folders full of brochures from colleges and printed sheets of stats about various cross-country programs. They had already given copies of everything to Vivian—Vivian had moved them to the top of the microwave where they kept the phones in chargers.

The whole thing was a bit overwhelming.

"Nessa, I'm Mike Byrum," said the recruiter with the soft brown hair brushed across his forehead, the pressed green golf shift, the gray leather folder, and the gold pen. His handshake was a work of art—just the right amount of pressure, just the perfect rhythm. "I'm especially glad to meet you. I remember sitting in Allyson Felix's kitchen when she was your age, and I worked to get her a full scholarship to the University of

Southern California. As you know, the rest is history."

Next the recruiter with curly red hair, a red golf shirt, pressed chinos, a burgundy leather folder, and a silver pen shook her hand. "Nessa," he said, "I want you to know that I'm here not just to serve the programs I represent but to help you make what is going to be the most important decision of your life. I am determined to get you into the best school—" He pointed at Nessa's throat and for a second she wondered if she'd misbuttoned her shirt or spilled something. "The best school not just for your cross-country career but for your entire future. Because that's what's at stake here."

Nessa realized she might not have looked carefully at the third recruiter until he stood. He was wearing chinos, but they were wrinkled. His shirt was not a golf shirt neatly tucked into a belted waistline but an oversize flannel shirt with pens in the breast pocket. He had gray hair, was balding, and had a vacant, somewhat surprised expression on his face, like a person who was about to confess that he'd misplaced his glasses.

"I saw you run yesterday," was all he said. "Your back left foot was dragging behind your right. It's not a huge deal." He pronounced "huge" without the "h." "But it opens you up for injury, and it's something you might want to talk to your coach about cleaning up. College-level scouts, that's something they're going to see."

Standing behind the three men, Vivian gave Nessa a significant look. This was the one Vivian was backing.

"Okay," Nessa said.

The three recruiters started to talk. They didn't have offers for her just then; they mostly wanted to get to know her, they said. They wanted to see what kind of school/experience she was looking for. What kind of program would be a best fit and then start talking to coaches.

"Trust me," said the one with red curly hair. His name was Chuck, Nessa thought. Or maybe the other one was named Chuck? "There's going to be a great deal of interest in you. A great deal."

"You're going to have your pick of program with a full ride," said the brown-haired one. He was named Mike, Nessa thought. "I'm hoping I can be here to help you."

The gray-haired recruiter put a hand on his stomach and hoisted it up and over his beltline as he reached across the table for his third slice of coffee cake. "Can you believe we all here used to run a five-minute mile?" he said. "Ugh. I read recently that athletes have more propensity for weight gain in later years. Who knows why. This is delicious, Mrs. Kurland. I'd ask for the recipe, except I don't cook."

Chuck and Mike closed their mouths deliberately. Nessa wondered if the three of them spent a lot of time in the same kitchens of the same high school athletes. They didn't look like they were struggling with weight gain. But no one pointed that out.

"What school do you represent?" Nessa asked the recruiter with the big belly and gray hair.

He burped a little bit behind his hand. "Stanford," he said.

And at that, the two well-dressed recruiters moved their chairs back slightly, as if conceding their ultimate defeat.

As they continued discussing the different schools they represented and what coaches were looking for, Nessa found it hard to focus.

As hard as she'd worked toward this moment, it was difficult to envision the actual outcome, that she, Nessa, would one day leave this house and this town and travel far away to become a college athlete.

What happens at these schools when you need to transform into a wolf?

Nessa snapped to attention when Mike leaned toward her.

"Have you thought about that at all?" he said.

"Sorry," Nessa said, realizing she must have missed the question. "Can you repeat that?"

But just then the doorbell rang again, and there was yet another man in a golf shirt and chinos. "Come on in," Vivian called out from the kitchen, like this guy was a trick-or-treater on Halloween. "You take cream in your coffee?"

The new guy stepped to the side so he could get a view of the kitchen table. He was much younger than the others. "No need for coffee for me," he said. "I'm not here to try to scout your daughter."

"You aren't?" Vivian said.

Delphine and Nate each looked up from their screens.

"I'm representing Paravida?" the new man said, sounding as if he was asking a question. "I'm on the community relations team. I'm based out of corporate? Over in the Chicago office?"

"Well, I figured you didn't work at the plant out here, because no one does, as far as anyone can tell," Vivian said crisply. Vivian, like everyone in Tether, had not yet forgiven Paravida for providing close to zero local jobs.

As if that were the biggest of their problems, Nessa thought bitterly.

The handsome man—he looked like he could be the host on the red carpet—spoke again, "Did you know we're the corporate sponsors of the cross-country team at Tether High?"

Nessa did know. She knew it because of the new uniforms they'd been given when she was a sophomore and because of the Paravida Award that Cynthia had won last year. It was—to put it bluntly—everything Nessa had ever wanted. A scholarship to the summer training academy of your choice, a GPS running watch, a new wardrobe of running clothes, including four pairs of shoes and two spikes over the course of the year.

Was this man here to talk to her about…?

Nessa couldn't utter the word. Not even in her own head.

"Nessa Kurland," he said. "I'm Joe Napier. It's my sincere pleasure to inform you that you've been selected as the next Paravida Award recipient. I don't know if you're familiar with the program, but it's something we at Paravida are very excited about and believe represents the company's true commitment to the community of Tether."

Nessa stood up. Regardless of how important the moment might be, the events of the past twenty-four hours suddenly rearranged themselves in her head. It was time for these men to go.

"Thank you Mr. Napier," she said with the biggest smile she could muster, considering that one of his Paravida coworkers had tried to shoot her with a gun less than twelve hours earlier. "I need to discuss all of this with my coach. He'll be in touch with all of you very soon, I'm sure."

She looked over at Vivian and saw that her mother was staring with her mouth a little open. Nessa gave her the hairy eyeball, and suddenly Vivian got it.

"Thank you, gentlemen," Vivian said, standing up. She started clearing coffee cups, even though the recruiters weren't done drinking. She picked up the coffee cake without even offering a slice to Joe Napier, and she cleared her throat. "Okay everyone. We are thrilled. But we've got to get Nate to his soccer game!"

This got Delphine's attention. Nate didn't play soccer on a team.

"As you can imagine, yesterday was quite a day. I think we're all tired," Vivian said, moving toward the front door. "It wasn't just Nessa's win. A little boy named Billy Lark, who was a friend of ours, died suddenly and inexplicably. The whole town is in shock. We were there until late last night."

At the mention of Billy Lark, the recruiters got quiet, stood, promised they would be in touch. It was clear they had no idea what to say or do and preferred to run for cover. Joe Napier didn't look any different. Nessa studied his face as her mother was talking. Did he know Billy's body had been inside the Paravida facility sometime around midnight the night before?

If so, he made no sign of it. He just looked hurt and confused, organizing a sheaf of papers for Nessa and Vivian to sign—personal conduct forms, forms agreeing to wear a Paravida logo at all times, forms promising they would never sue Paravida—Joe Napier called this "boring legal stuff."

As soon as he was gone, Nessa heard Delphine's voice calling, "Nessa! Get out here. We have a surprise for you!"

Nessa returned to the living room, where Delphine had just finished dividing a liter of ginger ale into the four mismatched wine glasses Vivian never used.

Delphine's pretty face was flushed. Her eyes were sparkling. Nessa saw that Vivian was leaning against the counter, her hands braced behind her, watching, her face warm with pride.

"It's pretend champagne!" Delphine said, passing glasses to

everyone, including Nate.

"To Nessa!" Delphine made Vivian and Nate say, like this was the last scene of a movie. They all took sips.

"To Stanford!" Vivian said. They all took sips again.

CHAPTER THIRTY-NINE

As soon as her family's celebration toast was over and the recruiters had been dispatched, Nessa was frantic to meet and talk with Bree. Magically, the house emptied out within minutes. Nate didn't hang out with other kids often, but there was a boy down the street whom he played Pokémon with, and he announced they had a meet-up at noon. A few minutes later, Vivian left for Sunday call at the animal hospital, dropping Delphine at a Girl Scouts meeting on the way.

Nessa texted her friend. She wasn't sure why, but as soon as Bree arrived, she dragged her into her bedroom and closed the door. She just felt like they needed the extra privacy. She hurriedly caught Bree up on what had happened the night before—the body snatch by Paravida, the eerie autopsy she had overheard, the terrifying killer wolf pack, the mysterious gray wolf, their narrow escape from the Paravida campus, even Pasty Pete. She finished with the surreal visit by the recruiters and an emissary announcing she had won the Paravida Award.

"Whoa," was all Bree could say when Nessa was done. Her eyes were saucers.

They sat there for a few minutes, silently absorbing the implications.

"Bree, I don't know what to think anymore. I feel like I don't *know* anything anymore. We all thought Paravida was this great company, that they were coming to save our town, help the kids, and now....How can there be so much evil in yet another company? What has Tether ever done to deserve this?"

"What *are* they doing to the kids in the study?" Bree said, more a statement than a question. "That's the question. We all should have suspected something when Paravida appeared, the white knight to fulfill Dutch Chem's settlement with Tether. I mean, why? What's in it for them? Some patents?" Bree shook her head. "Billy's body is the thread. That's what is going to lead us to answers. Do you know what they did with him after?"

"You mean after they shot at me? No idea," Nessa answered. "The Larks think Billy's body was going to the hospital in Saginaw for the autopsy. Mavis Cartwright and some other women were in the kitchen last night gossiping about it. Mrs. Lark didn't trust Paravida to take Billy. So I assume Paravida somehow got him to Saginaw Hospital."

Bree's eyes narrowed, like her thoughts had shifted course.

"What about the guy from Paravida who offered you the prize?" Bree asked. "Anything strange about him?"

Nessa thought about it. She shook her head. "No. He seemed professionally nice," Nessa said. "He claimed he was based in their corporate office in Chicago and told us he works in community marketing. He's probably never even *been* to Tether."

"Did he touch anything in the house? Use the bathroom? Leave anything behind?"

"He was in front of us the whole time," Nessa replied. "He left some permission papers for my mom and Coach to review and sign. Why?"

"If they're on to you, and they might be, he could have planted a listening device," Bree replied. "Where are they now?"

"You mean because I was there the day Mrs. Lark discovered that the kids in the study were being restrained?" Nessa asked. "So were you."

"No. I mean because they have your blood. From the doping test. And based on what you're telling me about the strange pack of killer wolves, I just wonder about all of that. If they can steal an eleven-year-old's body for an autopsy out from under his parents' noses, they can plant some dope in a locker." Bree stood up. "Where are those papers?"

They rushed into the kitchen. The papers were on the counter in a slick folder with the Paravida logo embossed in three raised triangles on the cover. They searched page by page and found nothing. Bree got down on her hands and knees to examine the flooring and carpet under the chairs where the four men had sat, and ran her fingers under the rim of the kitchen counter. Still nothing.

Nessa was stunned. Bree was right. What could happen if they knew she'd been bitten? And planted the dope in her locker knowing she would be required to submit to a blood test? What did they want from her now? Were they after her like Billy?

CHAPTER FORTY

few hours later, Bree and Nessa lay on their stomachs in the leaves, in a dense thicket of trees, staring at the Paravida campus down below. It was dusk. Bree was propped on her elbows, looking through some binoculars they had borrowed from Bree's aunt, who was an avid bird-watcher.

"Just observing some Emerald-Crested Boobie Thrushes," Bree had said breezily, waving the binoculars in her aunt's direction as they ran for the car. "Extra credit for Chemistry! We'll have them back by dark."

Nessa had started laughing out on the front walk.

"What does bird-watching have to do with Chemistry?" she asked. "And what's an Emerald-Crested Boobie Thrush?"

"No idea," Bree said. "I was improvising."

There was a single, long driveway into the Paravida facility. They couldn't approach from that direction or they would be seen. So they had parked the Monster on an old logging road and hiked a quarter mile to the top of a ridge from the opposite direction.

"I don't see any white van," Bree said.

"It's gone," Nessa said. "Last night it was parked right there." She pointed to the building with the loading dock. "The autopsy was being performed inside."

"Where are the wolf kennels?" Bree asked.

Nessa showed Bree the passageway. They could not see the kennels from where they were. "You can't see it, but trust me— it's awful. Like some depressing zoo from hell."

Nessa hadn't mentioned it to Bree, but she was being careful to sniff for the aggressive wolves, to make sure they wouldn't be ambushed. But their scent was faint. None had passed anywhere near their current position in at least a few days. She guessed they might already be in lockdown for the day.

"The spotlights are affixed to the five guard towers," Nessa added. "It looks like daylight when they are on."

Only two of the five guard towers appeared to be staffed— one guard in each. Neither one was Pasty Pete. Nessa supposed he had to sleep sometimes. The first guard was reading a magazine, and the second one appeared to be asleep.

"I know what!" Bree said, sitting up.

"What?" Nessa asked.

"Tim!"

"Tim who?" Nessa asked. "Tim Miller?"

"Yes. Tim Miller. Think about where Tim Miller works."

"You mean his after-school job? I have absolutely no idea," Nessa said.

"Come on," Bree said. "Yes, you do. Mr. Pre-Pre-Med? Mr. Paramedic Volunteer?"

"Oh," Nessa said. She was remembering now. "He volunteers at Saginaw Hospital!"

"Exactly," Bree said. She sounded very pleased with herself. "We can ask him about how they track bodies for autopsy. I bet he would look into it. If we asked nicely."

"Okay. That's an idea. Worth a try," Nessa agreed.

Bree was already calling. It went through to voicemail. Nada.

Just as she ended the call, Nessa saw one of the doors to the kennel building open. Four men quickly emerged, two in lab coats and two dressed in guard uniforms. Nessa grabbed the binoculars.

"Oh my god. I think they see us!" she said.

Did they pick up the cell signal from Bree's phone?

One of the lab coats was pointing toward the ridge where they were hiding. A walkie-talkie crackled and one of the guards in the towers stood up. The door in the fencing clanked to life, and began to ascend. Moments later, Nessa saw the aggressive wolves emerge from the kennel building and run toward the exit.

"We need to get out of here. *Now!*" she said. She jumped up and pulled Bree up by her hoodie. They turned and ran back the way they came. Nessa could smell the wolves getting closer just as they were safely back in the Monster.

CHAPTER FORTY-ONE

essa and Bree drove down the logging road as quickly as they could and back out on to Route 18. They passed a Paravida SUV heading toward them, but there was too much traffic on the road for them to stand out. They returned the binoculars, declined an invitation to dine with Bree's aunt, and drove to Nessa's. They tried Tim Miller again from the car, but no luck.

"Let's get to school early tomorrow and catch him before the first bell," Bree suggested, and Nessa agreed.

The next morning, when Nessa and Bree pulled into Tether

High, the parking lot was empty; none of the buses had arrived. But even so, they still had no luck finding Tim. Nessa did have to field lots of high fives and all kinds of admiration for her win on Saturday. She figured it was worth the cause.

"Who knew he was such a man of mystery?" Bree complained, when the bell for first period finally rang. "See you at lunch?"

Nessa nodded.

Nessa noticed that people were subdued and the halls were quiet as people walked to first period. Even though Billy was homeschooled, he would have been known to many kids from Little League (he'd been a terrible player but his mom brought the best post-game snacks). They'd seen him at the library and the health clinic, and his picture was always in the paper every year when he helped build the model train set up in the Town Hall lobby during the Christmas season.

Mr. Porter spoke into the intercom during morning announcements, letting it be known that he was keeping his office door open all day in case anyone wanted to speak about the events of the weekend or other related issues.

Then Principal Sarakoski got on the intercom. "In the midst of our sadness for Billy Lark, I'd still like to acknowledge the achievement of junior Nessa Kurland who came in first place on Saturday and became the State Champion in the cross-country 5K. Cynthia Sinise and Luc Restouille also turned in excellent performances. Congratulations to Nessa and the entire Tether High cross-country program."

Someone three classrooms down let out a loud whoop, which set off muted clapping and cheering. Nessa could hear it up and down the halls. She felt her cheeks turn red. She should be savoring the win, but it felt wrong, somehow, to be celebrating anything at the same time they were thinking about Billy.

Heading to math after third-period Spanish, Nessa passed Coach Hoffman. "I need to speak with you, young lady," he said. "I heard you had some visitors on Sunday. You didn't sign anything, did you?"

"Of course not," Nessa said, smiling at Coach's excitement. "I told them they had to talk to you."

"Good. And ask your mom to call me. I'm really not pleased that they descended on you so quickly. I thought they'd at least give you twenty-four hours."

After Pre-Calculus, Nessa finally caught up with Bree at lunch. And this time they were in luck.

Tim was at lunch with the other guys from cross-country. For the first time, Nessa noticed that Luc sat with them as well. He could have been included in the beautiful senior table. Cynthia at least would have wanted him there. But he chose to sit with this quiet, smart, occasional-pot-smoking cross-country crowd of runners instead.

He was staring at Nessa as she came over like he was expecting her to be headed in his direction.

"Hey," she said, putting up a hand. He raised his eyebrows. She noticed he was eating a roast beef sandwich with two hands, and there was another sandwich under that one, ready to go.

"Wow," she couldn't help observing. "Two roast beef sandwiches. That's quite a commitment to carnivorous-os-ity?" They laughed together at the way the word had got away from her.

"Yeah, sometimes turkey feels like you just put more lettuce on top of your bread."

It was weird about Luc. When Nessa stopped to think about it, they barely knew each other. They'd had maybe five conversations. But comparing the way she felt around him to the way she felt around Cassian, there was a difference. It seemed that there was always a real conversation going on. And then afterward, she always noticed there was another conversation going on underneath the first one.

Maybe that's what happens when you're on the same team as a guy, instead of crushing on him for the better part of two years. It definitely felt better.

"Tim," Bree said, getting his attention. "Nessa has a question for you."

"I do," Nessa concurred, pivoting from Luc. "I was wondering. That is, Bree and I were wondering…" Suddenly Nessa realized she had no idea how to frame the question. You couldn't exactly just come out and ask someone to look up a person's health records in a hospital. Nessa was pretty sure those should be private.

Bree must have noticed that Nessa was at a loss, because she stepped in just then. "You work at Saginaw Hospital, right?" Tim nodded, looking wary. "I would love to do something like that next year," Bree gushed. "It's so…*driven* of you."

Flattery, Nessa noted, worked wonders. And Bree was particularly good at dishing it out. Maybe this was how you get elected to student council three years running.

"I totally recommend it," Tim said. "But I don't work at the hospital. I volunteer there. Actually, technically, I have an internship."

Sid Hall put an arm over Tim's shoulder. "He takes out the garbage!" Sid shouted. "He's the garbage intern!"

Tim blushed. "Shut up, Sid," Bree said, though she was smiling as she said it. "Maybe you can come talk to us over there?" She said to Tim, gesturing to the area near the windows. "It's quieter."

"Sure," Tim said.

"I think he's actually Vice President of Garbage!" Sid shouted after them, his mouth full.

"Yeah," said Bree dismissively when they were out of Sid's earshot. "So Nessa and I were wondering if you know what happens to bodies."

"Dead bodies," Nessa clarified, and when Bree shot her a look, Nessa realized this was putting way too creepy a spin on things. Maybe she'd let Bree do the talking.

"We were actually having a little discussion," Bree said. "Because Nessa heard that Billy Lark, the poor little guy, that his mom was freaking out. She heard she wanted to send his body to the hospital for an autopsy. And we were wondering, do autopsies even happen in hospitals? Do you even need a doctor for them?"

Tim straightened up, looking pleased to be asked. Bree was brilliant, Nessa decided.

"Actually you do need a doctor," he said, nodding. "You need a doctor and a pathologist. They don't have to be on site, but they need to be in the hospital because sometimes the samples aren't going to keep in the way you would hope, and it's easier if they have access to the same computer system and protocols."

"Wow," Bree said. "That's fascinating."

Tim was warmed up to the subject now. "You were asking about Billy Lark," he said. "And I did hear that, about his mom asking for an autopsy. Saginaw has a morgue and autopsy department but also acts as the county morgue. Any time there's anything unusual about a death, our pathologists are the ones who make the determination. I can check if Billy's body was brought into the hospital if you want."

"If it was, is there any chance they would have sent Billy over to Paravida to get that done?" Bree asked this casually, like the question had just occurred to her.

Tim frowned. "Paravida?" he said. "Why would it go there? They're not connected to the hospital. I think you need to have a license or something to do autopsies. There's no way the body would have gone there."

"Can you find out?" Nessa said, then, "Ow!" That last part was because Bree had just kicked her in the shin. She could see why Bree had kicked her, too. Tim was looking suddenly suspicious.

"It's kind of a Snopes.com thing," Bree said, confiding in Tim. "Want to nip those urban legends in the bud."

"Yeah, okay," Tim said. He seemed to relax again. By this point, lunch was ending, and kids were moving off to their lockers or their next class. "I'll be in touch when I learn something," he added. Then he headed off in the direction of the science lab where he spent free periods washing out beakers.

Bree seemed to be hurrying as well. "Where are you going?" Nessa said.

"The library," Bree said. "*We* have stuff to research. Come on."

CHAPTER FORTY-TWO

The school librarian enforced a strict quiet policy, so Nessa and Bree headed to the computers in the stacks on the far side of the main reading area. There were two stations free side by side, and they grabbed them. Someone was sitting only three seats away, but she had earphones on so she couldn't eavesdrop.

"Okay," Bree said, whipping out a notebook. "Let's go over what we know so far."

"Paravida buys Dutch Chemical out of bankruptcy three years ago. They announce that the purpose of the purchase is for some patents," Nessa began. "And they will continue to fund all Dutch Chem obligations to Tether."

"Right," Bree agreed. "Why do they do that? Dutch Chem

came with lots of baggage. Which patents was Paravida after? That's a place to start."

Nessa nodded. "Agreed."

"What was that weird letters and numbers thing that the doctor said during the autopsy?" Bree asked. Earphones girl, deep into a session of World of Warcraft, groaned.

"7IRG. You know, it could be a patent," Nessa said. "Aren't patents assigned by number?"

"No idea, but we can check," Bree said. "And that name you overheard? Harry?"

"Yes, I think it was a second doctor. There was the person performing the autopsy. And someone recording the results. A woman. Then a second man spoke up. Then the first doctor called him Harry."

"Not much to go on," Bree said, chewing on the end of her pen. "Do you think that the doctor performing the autopsy was Dr. Raab?"

Nessa paused.

"I don't *think* so," Nessa answered. "I would have recognized his voice."

"Anything else?" Bree asked.

"Yes. The aggressive wolves. There is something very wrong with them. What is Paravida using them for?" Nessa asked. "Several of them had incisions too."

"Incisions? Where?" Bree asked.

"In their bellies mostly. One on its shoulder," Nessa answered. "Could it be from fights?"

"Probably," Bree agreed. "I'll research wolves and patents. You dig into Paravida's history?"

"Sounds good," Nessa answered.

Bree and Nessa powered up the computers and got to work.

The library was quiet and warm. Nessa went back to the Paravida website she'd looked at weeks before, scrolling again through the images on the home page, trying to figure out in what ways they could possibly relate to what she'd seen the night before—the wolves, the labs.

When Nessa rolled over "About the company," she selected "Board of Directors." She scrolled through professional-looking photos of men and women along with brief bios. She read a few of them, and then leaned back in her chair, blowing air out through her teeth.

Paravida had a Senator and two federal judges on their board. The Detroit Chief of Police. Convenient if you needed a sympathetic ear in Michigan law enforcement. Another person who had been provost of UC Davis. People with power. Could they make a body appear to be locked in a drawer in a hospital morgue when in fact it was being stored someplace else entirely?

The other thing that struck Nessa was how many different businesses Paravida ran. Chemicals. Steel manufacture. Medical devices. Pharmaceuticals. Nessa said, "Look at every-thing Paravida does. They're enormous. They're all over the world. They take in more money than some small countries. So why pick on Tether?"

"Because we have something no one else has?" said Bree.

Nessa continued the hunt. She decided to dig further into the Pharmaceuticals division. She found Dr. Raab, Nobel laureate. His bio linked out to the research institute he worked at in San Francisco. There was a long list of his published arti-cles. Unlike high school students, these scientists wrote in groups of four or five. She scanned several pages of articles and names. Suddenly she saw something that made her heart rate shoot up. She hurriedly clicked a few more links.

"Bingo!" Nessa whispered.

"What?" Bree said, looking over her shoulder.

"All these papers, the ones authored by Dr. Raab? There are always coauthors. Every single one is written by at least three or four scientists. From 1998 to 2001, Dr. Raab co-wrote seven papers with a guy named Dr. Fong. *Harry* Fong. And he's an expert in chemical enhancement. It's when cells recover when exposed to something called chemical scrubbing. There's this weird thing that happens where tissues damaged by exposure to chemicals don't just heal, but improve. It has to do with stem cell regeneration. Like, right here, a guy burned in an acid spill—the pictures are gross—his nose was pretty much gone, but then doctors grafted skin from his shoulder to cover it, and the shoulder skin *turned into a nose*. Which I don't need to tell you shoulder skin is not supposed to be able to do, right?"

"That's creepy," said Bree.

"Guess who Dr. Harry Fong worked for?"

"He didn't work for the Institute?"

"No," Nessa said, pausing dramatically. "He worked for Dutch Chem."

"No way," Bree breathed.

"Yes, way," Nessa said.

"So there's something about our damaged cells, the cells of people like Billy Lark, that make them into stem cells?" Bree wondered.

"Yeah, something like that," Nessa said.

They sat there taking it in. Then Bree spoke. "That idea of

the nose. Growing on its own. Is that what they're doing?"

"It's scary to think about this," Nessa said. "Not just about Billy. But for Tether. I mean, without Paravida, Tether would have disappeared. Everyone would have had to move away."

"I know," Bree said.

The bell rang for next period.

"I've figured out this much. 7IRG isn't a patent. Patent numbers are at least seven digits long with no letters," Bree announced as they shouldered their backpacks.

"Okay. We'll have to finish later," Nessa said.

That night there was a candlelight vigil for Billy in the Veteran's Memorial Park in the center of town. The marble monument told the story of Tether—a town that had barely been more than a farming settlement when it sent fifteen men to fight in World War I, then 80 to World War II. Dutch Chem came into existence in the early 1950s, tripling Tether's population.

When Nessa arrived at the vigil, she saw a crowd had formed. Some of the same people she'd seen at Billy's house, but many more kids from school were there. People held candles, and the music teacher from the Lutheran church was singing a hymn and strumming a guitar. A lot of the older people were singing along.

Nessa saw Mr. and Mrs. Lark up at the front. Mrs. Lark was wearing a parka that was too large for her—her shoulders were lost inside it, and the sleeves completely covered her hands. Mr. Lark had an arm around her, but they stood slightly apart.

The minister stood up next and explained that Billy's funeral would be held the next day and kept private. Today was a chance for townspeople to express their grief. He read a passage from the Bible, and then there was another song.

When Nessa got closer to the front, some of Billy's cousins stood up to read poems. The minister stepped down from the gazebo to stand with the Larks. Nessa heard murmurings between them and stepped closer.

"It's a beautiful thing," the minister said, "to see how much love there was for your boy. A lot of people in Tether are sharing your sense of loss today."

Nessa didn't want to look like she was staring, so she mostly looked down at her candle. But when Mrs. Lark answered, she stole a glance at her.

"Can they bring him back?" Mrs. Lark said, her face twisted in pain and anger. Mr. Lark pulled his wife closer to comfort her.

"Now, Ann…" the minister began.

"No," she said. "My child was stolen from me. And now he won't have a chance to grow up."

The minister didn't say anything for a minute, and Mrs. Lark choked out a sob. "I knew," she said. "I knew from when he was a baby that he was special. Fragile. I was always so careful with him…" She started crying for real again. Nessa realized talking to Mrs. Lark directly was out of the question. Not now, anyway.

Nessa turned back around, seeing that the crowd had grown in just the fifteen minutes since she'd arrived. She saw a lot of kids from school, a lot of the teachers. As the crowd surged forward, she could hear the echoes of Mrs. Lark's crying in her head. She had to get out. She felt claustrophobic and jumpy.

Wolfy, in fact. Nessa felt the way she had when her body was preparing to transform.

Even though it wasn't even close to the next change of moon.

Pushing through the crowd, Nessa bumped into Luc.

"Nessa," he said. "You're here?"

It was weird the way he made it into a question. Why wouldn't she be? "My little brother was the same age as Billy," she said. "They are both in the clinic study. We knew Billy from that."

"Oh, I'm sorry," he said.

"Why are *you* here?" Nessa asked, leaning in. Because it was strange, wasn't it, that Luc would have anything to do with Billy? He'd just moved to Tether. Billy was homeschooled. How could they have connected?

Luc hung his head and his eyes seemed to look inward and far away. Suddenly Nessa realized how rude her question sounded.

"That's not really what I meant," she said. "I just figured since you were new to Tether…" Her voice trailed off.

"No, it's okay," Luc said. "I don't really know why I'm here either. It's just…very sad. That this kid died."

Nessa wanted—inexplicably—to tell him about Paravida and the strange ambulance trip to the old Dutch Chem plant the previous night. But she stayed silent. "I know," was all she said.

"So I heard you won the Paravida Award," he said. "Congratulations."

"Thanks," Nessa said. "It's kind of…I don't know."

"A little too much all at once?"

"Yeah," she said. She smiled in relief. She knew Luc understood. She knew she couldn't go around saying what she really thought of Paravida. At least not yet.

"Hey," Luc said, seeming to change the subject. "Want to hear something weird?"

Nessa looked at the crowd. There were even more people

gathered. There must have been at least 200. "Sure," she said.

Nessa followed Luc to his truck, which was still parked in the lot behind school.

"Come up here," he said, helping pull her up into the open bed of the truck. Two folding chairs stood empty. He pointed to one. "That's for you." They both sat down.

"It's like we're watching fireworks," she said.

He nodded, "But we're not watching. We're listening." He closed his eyes. "Do this. What do you hear?"

Nessa at first heard singing. The people at the vigil had started another hymn. She remembered how during the Dutch Chem lawsuits, Tether's downtown had turned into one long, continuous protest rally, with environmental activists and left-ists bused in from all over the country. Most of the people who actually lived in Tether thought they were nuts. But still, Nessa could remember how the streets had been filled with their singing, especially at nighttime when they would switch from the songs about their demands to songs about peace and nature.

"Not the music," Luc said. "Listen to what's coming from the woods."

It was hard *not* to listen to the music, but Nessa tried anyway. She heard wind in the pine trees behind the soccer field. She heard rustling in the leaves. Squirrels? She heard…

"Sorry if this seems like some crazy become-one-with-nature crap," Luc said. "There seriously is something to hear."

And then Nessa did hear the sound he meant. Or at least, she thought she heard it. It must have been coming from very far away—the outer limits of her range. It was so far she could hardly believe Luc could hear it too.

She heard the pack. They were singing songs of their own.

Big One was leading. Sister was chiming in. Every time they dropped the line, Mama would pick it up.

It occurred to Nessa that their pack had been small to begin with, and with the loss of the submissive wolf, it was getting smaller still. Maybe she was thinking of this just now because she was hearing so much sadness in their voices. They sounded just as sad as the humans, actually.

"You hearing what I'm hearing?" Luc asked her, and she hesitated. The wolves were pretty far away. She was surprised Luc could hear them. If she admitted she could, would Luc be like, "What wolves? I'm listening to the wind chimes hanging in front of True Value"? (Nessa could hear those too.) But then Luc made it easy for her. "The wolves?"

Nessa opened her eyes in a flash. She suddenly felt uncomfortable. She couldn't say why, only that she felt that Luc knew more about her than she'd thought he did. She stood. "Sorry," she said. "But I gotta go." And without waiting for him to say "okay" or "bye" or anything, she took off, jogging back to the center of town

CHAPTER FORTY-THREE

Tim Miller was waiting for Nessa and Bree at their lockers the next morning, holding a piece of paper up in the air like it was money and he was waving it to make a bet in the middle of a big fight.

"I've got your information," he said, and then lowered his voice. "I'd never looked that stuff up in the hospital system before, but one of the residents gave me his password so I could enter a medication request in a patient's chart, and I was able to get into the system."

"Wow," said Bree, and for once Nessa didn't think she was exaggerating just to make Tim feel good. Nessa was impressed as well.

Tim spoke in a low voice. "It's actually pretty fascinating, how they track bodies," he said. "There's something called a chain of custody—all these documents where one person signs off on the body and notes the time they took charge of it. Sometimes you hire a private company to move a body around; sometimes it's done by the medical examiner's office. In either case, there's never a time when you don't know exactly where a body is and who has it."

"Can I see?" said Nessa, holding out her hand for the printout.

Tim passed it to her, and as she read it, he leaned over her shoulder, using a finger to show her the entries in what turned out to be a log of movements, tracking the body from the Lark home to the hospital. It recorded the precise time when the ambulance crossed the Tether town line and then every subsequent town between Tether and Saginaw.

"So according to this," Nessa said, "the body entered the hospital's system at 11:34 p.m."

"That's right," Tim confirmed.

"And it never went anywhere else?"

"No, it never did."

"What if they changed it?" Nessa said.

"That's impossible. They couldn't. See this code?" Tim pointed to a tiny series of numbers to the right of the entry. "This appears when there's information in the system that only could have been added by someone with a hospital authorization key."

"What's that mean?" Bree said.

"It's basically a shortcut. The hospital double-checks all that info, and it's available publicly and doesn't need to be notarized or attested to by a hospital employee in legal investigations."

"Couldn't one of those people have changed it? Couldn't someone have stolen the key?"

"I don't think so," Tim said. He was shaking his head vehemently. "You'd have to have a really strong connection. You'd need someone like a judge or a Senator to make that change."

Bree gave Nessa a significant look. They thanked Tim, pocketed the printout, and headed off for their first class.

"Maybe it wasn't Billy you heard them autopsying at Paravida," Bree said when he was gone.

"I think it *was*," Nessa said. "Did you notice what Tim just said about fiddling with the chain of custody? That you'd need someone with the power of a judge or a Senator to do it? Well, the Paravida board has both, and the Chief of Police of Detroit for good measure. It's on their website."

"Whoa," Bree said. She stopped.

"What are we going to do next?" Nessa said.

"We're going to break into the clinic and look for Billy's records," said Bree. She squared her shoulders and stuck her chin out.

"Are you serious?" Nessa said.

"Yes," said Bree. "If Billy had those special scrubbed cells, my guess is that they were using him to test some new therapies. And it backfired. The autopsy would then become essential to help tell them what went wrong. Even if you have judges and Senators on your board of directors, I'm sure you don't ask them to help out covering up an illegal autopsy. Unless you have a really good reason."

"You think we can break in?" Nessa said.

"Can we? I already infiltrated their system once!"

Nessa drew a total blank.

"With Cassian, remember?" Bree prompted. "I totally hacked the appointment calendar back in September. This spy stuff comes very naturally to me." She half-closed her eyes and raised her eyebrows as if she were modestly deflecting an enormous amount of praise.

"Oh, brother," Nessa groaned, and then she realized Bree wouldn't have suggested the break-in if she hadn't already been obsessing over how to make it happen. "Okay. What's the plan?"

CHAPTER FORTY-FOUR

H ere's what we're going to do," Bree explained over Oreos at Nessa's kitchen table. "Since the clinic closes at eight o'clock, we'll get there just before eight, like 7:50. I'll run in and tell Gina at the desk that I have to pee. She knows us, so it won't seem weird."

"And then you'll stay in the bathroom until after they close?"

"No, that won't work. Gina and Mary will remember me. You'll be the one in the bathroom."

"I thought I was waiting in the car."

"You'll be waiting by the back door."

"Of the clinic?"

"Right!"

"What about security cameras?" Nessa said, separating the two halves of her Oreo.

"I've thought of that. Halloween masks," Bree said.

"Seriously?" Nessa said. "You think that'll work?"

"Remember my plan to get the most popular guy in school to fall for you? That plan worked."

"For a while," Nessa said.

"For a while? What do you mean, 'for a while'? Cassian is crazy about you. The whole soccer team is talking about it."

Nessa shrugged. "I told Cassian I wasn't interested anymore, and I'm not."

"What!? When did this happen?" Bree demanded.

"At the Larks' that night when my mom and I brought the tuna casserole over," Nessa replied. "The Thomases were there."

"You break up with the hottest guy in the entire town of Tether, and you didn't tell your bestie?" Bree practically shrieked. "What's wrong with you?"

"Well, there were a few other things going on," Nessa said.

"Yeah, well, you still need to keep your priorities straight," Bree deadpanned. When she saw the stricken look on Nessa's face, she rolled her eyes. "Just KIDDING."

"Let's get back to the plan," Nessa said. She put both halves of the Oreo in her mouth, prepared to listen.

"*After* I go to the bathroom," Bree said. "I'm going to go to the water cooler and get a drink. While I'm drinking, I'll stand at the bulletin board. As soon as I verify no one's looking, I'll take two steps to the back door, pop it open for you, and then make sure that I am seen leaving the way I came in."

"It sounds so simple," Nessa said.

Bree held up another Oreo as if offering it up for a toast. "The best plans always are."

Breaking into the clinic was easier than Nessa had thought it would be. Or maybe it was just that Bree was more skilled as a criminal mastermind than her sunny attitude would suggest.

First, Bree dropped Nessa off behind the clinic. Nessa was careful to avoid anyone's line of sight from the windows as she made her way to the back door. She heard the Monster drive around to the front of the clinic and then its engine went quiet. She stayed close to the building and slipped on an old princess mask of Delphine's.

After about five minutes, the back door opened. Nessa caught the handle before it closed. Once inside the hallway, she saw just the back of Bree's shoe as she turned the corner by the desk on her way out the door.

For a minute, Nessa stood still, listening to the sound of her own breath, feeling a chill on her skin, registering the smell of disinfectant. She was a few steps away from the alcove where she'd had her blood taken when she'd been accused of doping.

Now, she wondered not for the first time if her blood had been shipped off to Paravida, just like Billy's. But even if it had, what did they want it for? Were they doing the same thing to the wolves that they had been doing to Billy?

Slipping into the bathroom quickly, Nessa closed the door behind her and encountered an unanticipated wrinkle in the plan. The windowless room was pitch dark, the only light coming from a gap at the bottom of the door. Nessa felt her way across the room, holding on to the changing table like it was the railing of a balcony.

And then she waited. She flipped open her phone and checked the time. It was already 7:58. She would wait until 8:10 before leaving the room. Bree had watched the parking lot empty the night before and knew that all of the workers left within minutes of the official closing.

The time dragged. 8:01. 8:04. Finally, 8:09. Nessa counted to 60 slowly in her head, then opened the bathroom door.

The door let out a groan and Nessa froze, but then she saw that the hallway was lit only by the red Exit sign at one end. Nessa poked her head into the staff kitchen and the various offices on her way down to the empty reception area. She tried the door to a storage closet. It was open. She tried the door to the suite of offices where the Dutch Chem study was administered. Locked.

Nessa moved to the back, listening at the door for the return of Bree's car. When she heard it—Bree cautiously parked at the edge of the lot, near the woods—Nessa waited for a light knock on the door, and then she opened it.

"Oh my god, I can't believe we're in!" Bree half-squealed, half-whispered through her Freddy mask.

"Are you sure everyone's gone?" Nessa asked.

"Absolutely," Bree said. "I heard Mary leaving while I was in the bathroom. There were three other cars in the lot, and they're all gone."

"Okay," said Nessa. She told Bree about the doors to the clinic study rooms being locked. "Now what do we do?"

"Let's start with Mary's desk," Bree said. "Maybe she keeps keys?"

"Wait," Nessa said, putting a hand on Bree's arm. She paused at the mini-greenhouse where Mary grew cheery succulents. "I feel bad, going through Mary's stuff. I mean, she's kind of like our friend. She's always super-nice to Nate."

"It's one of two possibilities," said Bree. "She's in on it. Or she'll be glad if we figure out she's mixed up in something that's bad for kids."

"You're right," Nessa agreed. She plowed ahead.

Bree sat down in Mary's chair while Nessa held Bree's phone with the flashlight app over her head. In her drawer, they found the usual office stuff—a stapler, rubber bands, pens, gum, Post-its. There was a little makeup kit and a hairbrush. There were a couple of pictures of Mary with her family. They used to live in Tether, Vivian had told Nessa—they lived in Saginaw now. Her grandmother had a nice smile, and there was no grandfather. There didn't seem to be anything else, so Bree shoved the metal drawer closed. And it caught on something.

"Huh," was all she said. She slid the drawer open and closed it more slowly this time. It caught again.

"Just a second," she said. This time she pulled the drawer out all the way and set it carefully on the floor. She reached her arm in as far as she could and burst into a big smile.

"Keys," was all she said.

Seconds later, Nessa and Bree were sitting at a desk in the main examination room of the kids' clinic study, or the North Central Michigan Long-Term Pediatric Inclusion Study, as it was formally known.

"Let's start with the computer," Bree suggested.

She hit a key, and a blinking cursor asked for her username.

"Crap," she whispered. "Any ideas?"

"Sure," Nessa replied. "How about TRAAB, for Thomas

Raab?"

"Worth a try," Bree said as she typed. "Holy crap, Batgirl," Bree said as another screen appeared. "You're hot."

Except that this time, it requested the password.

"Could it be written down somewhere?" Nessa asked. She scanned the desktop. There was a prescription pad and two pens. A blank pad. A plasticized sheet with lists of phone extensions and their owners.

"It's a known fact that people are idiots about their passwords, even Nobel laureates," Bree announced.

She typed in "123456" and hit Enter.

The small dialog box shook violently and rejected it.

Next she tried "Paravida."

Another rejection.

"Try 'stem cell,'" Nessa suggested.

Bree typed, and as soon as she hit the Enter key, all of the lights in the clinic came on, and a special red security light that Nessa had never noticed began to flash on and off. There was a loud horn sound, and a mechanical voice announced, "PLEASE LEAVE THE PREMISES AT ONCE. THIS IS A GOVERNMENT-APPROVED LEVEL FOUR SECURITY SITE. PLEASE LEAVE THE PREMISES AT ONCE."

Bree and Nessa looked at each other. Nessa could hear the faintest sound of a police siren in the distance. "We've got to get out of here. NOW!" Nessa cried.

Bree pulled open the filing cabinet under the desk and grabbed a couple of folders hanging there. Nessa was already halfway out the back door.

CHAPTER FORTY-FIVE

Nessa easily sprinted the short distance out the back door of the clinic to Bree's car. For once, Bree kept pace. They leapt into their seats, pulled off their masks, Bree started the engine, and pulled out so quickly she laid down some rubber on the new tarmac. Instead of turning on to Willow Street, she scooted cross-lots into the back parking area of Tether Credit Union and then a small strip mall. She instinctively drove in the direction opposite the rapidly approaching police siren. When she saw a car ambling down Center Street, she signaled and turned to follow it. As they drove past the Tether town square, they could see the flashing lights of the police car as it pulled into the clinic a quarter of a mile away.

They drove straight to Nessa's without a word. Another police cruiser passed them, siren wailing, headed to where they had come from. When they parked in front of Nessa's yard a few minutes later, their bubble of tension and fear suddenly burst, and they both started to laugh. Hysterically.

"Oh my god, that was close," Bree finally managed to wheeze.

"You're not kidding," Nessa said.

"The computer must have been connected to a security system. Three wrong passwords, and it activates an alarm system," Bree said. She sounded amazed.

"Have you ever heard of the police responding so quickly before?" Nessa added. "They were there in less than three minutes."

"That's what I guess you get with Level Four security," Bree said. Which started them laughing all over again.

The front porch light went on and Vivian stuck her head out. "You girls coming in? Where've you been?"

"Okay. We've got to get control of ourselves," Nessa said.

"Can you take the files? My mom sometimes looks in my room," Bree said.

Nessa looked at the seat next to her. Vivian was coming down the walk, so she quickly shoved them into her backpack.

"If you find anything good, text me. Otherwise, let's throw them out. I'll figure out where," Bree said.

Nessa hopped out of the car, headed up the front walk, and gave her surprised mom a peck on the cheek—"Hi Mom!"—before heading inside. Bree gave Vivian a cheerful wave, and without waiting put the Monster in drive.

"Teenagers," Vivian muttered. She shook her head and watched the Monster turn around and head in the direction of

Bree's house. "Always up to something."

Nessa grabbed an apple from the bowl in the kitchen and headed to her room. She would have to wait until everyone was asleep to look at the files. And Delphine was a night owl. Nessa looked at the clock, pulled out her novel for English, and started to read. It was something called *Jane Eyre*, and the time flew. Before she knew it, Delphine was showered, changed, and under the covers. The rest of the house was already still. When she heard Delphine's breathing change and slow down, she put her book aside, and went out to the living room with her backpack.

The first folder had no label. It contained, oddly, a bunch of clippings about the Dutch Chem lawsuit, dating back ten years, and the Paravida takeover. They were from sources like the *Wall Street Journal* and not the local Michigan papers.

Next was a folder filled with information about how to care for succulents. Mary's personal life in a nutshell, apparently.

A file marked "Personnel" contained tax forms, and there was another about the clinic's employee benefits.

Then things got more interesting.

The next file folder was simply marked "Mary Clovis." It contained Mary's retirement account statements. What was strange to Nessa was that she was pretty sure that it was for a personal, not corporate, retirement account. She paged through them carefully. They dated back almost thirteen years. The sums invested steadily grew with each paycheck, until seven years ago, when she started to withdraw, sometimes in large amounts. Mary once had $145,744 worth of stocks and bonds. Today the account was worth less than $38,000.

Nessa looked at the heading at the top of the most recent statement, and Mary's employer was listed as "Rock Creek

Investment Partners/Paravida."

Mary works for Paravida? she thought.

It wasn't totally strange, she supposed. Mary seemed to be Dr. Raab's right hand. She did not work in the regular part of the clinic as far as Nessa knew. And Paravida funded the study. So it made sense. But what had happened to all the money? As far as she knew, Mary had no kids and her parents were both deceased.

Nessa continued to page back into Mary's contribution history. Then she came to a line that made her startle. It was Mary's 401K contribution from 2007. It read: "Rock Creek Investment Partners/Dutch Chemical."

Now this is officially weird, Nessa thought. *Mary worked for Dutch Chem* and *Paravida?*

Nessa pawed through the rest of the file. There were some pictures of Mary when she was younger, with two women who looked similar and could have been her cousins. And then there was a picture of Mary, smiling and tan, with a handsome blond man. He had his arm around her. There was a lake behind them.

Nessa pulled out her phone and texted Bree.

No clinic study data. ☹ But some strange financial information on Mary. Plus a few photos.

Nessa saw that Bree was answering.

Good. Bring it in tomorrow and we'll discuss.

Gn.

Nessa replaced the folders in her backpack, returned to bed, and went to sleep.

CHAPTER FORTY-SIX

The next morning, Bree and Nessa parked at the far end of the lot at school so Bree could take pictures of the clippings and Mary's financial statements without being seen. She took close-ups of the photos as well.

"I'll send these to an anonymous email account and then delete them from my phone," Bree said. "They'll be there if we need them."

"Where should we toss the originals?" Nessa said. "We have to be careful. These link us to the break-in."

"We can ask Selena to shred them for us," Bree said. "She can take us into the office on Saturday when no one is around."

"Sounds good," Nessa agreed. "I'll hide them in one of the

bins in our garage in the meantime."

Nessa was concerned about her next transformation. As the moon got fuller and fuller, she could feel herself changing in ways she still wasn't used to. On Wednesday, she heard a rustling as she passed the main office at school and smelled something strong and Christmas-like—a peppermint candy being unwrapped? She started craving hamburgers again. And her energy increased. Without cross-country practices after school, Nessa started running on her own. That afternoon, she ran a 10K. On Thursday, she ran a half marathon.

Luc must have been doing the same thing because she often saw him out running when she was. She'd recognize his tall, thin form silhouetted on the opposite side of the lake she was circling, or spot him coming back down one of the lonely roads stretching out of town while she headed out on it.

On Thursday, she met up with him on a road still inside of Tether, near her house. They fell into step with each other naturally, as if they were still at practice. But that was all that felt natural between them.

When Luc said, casually, "Did you hear Cynthia got a free ride to run for Ann Arbor?" Nessa suddenly felt ready to bite his head off.

"Oh, really?" she said, trying to sound indifferent. She was thinking many things—all of which made her angry and none of which made her particularly proud: (1) The very mention of Cynthia's name reminded her that she still didn't know if Cynthia had planted the androstenedione or if it was part of a Paravida conspiracy in which she had been the target, which terrified her. (2) A scholarship to the University of Michigan was huge. It was hard not to feel jealous. (3) Why was Luc telling her about Cynthia? Were they together now?

She heard herself saying, "Why do you know this? Are you seeing her now?" before she realized how very much she would regret asking that question aloud. She felt her face going red. She missed a step and almost tripped.

Please, please, she begged the gods of awkward social moments. *Let that have sounded like I am an interested friend.*

"I'm telling you because Cynthia was on our team and you know her and…are you okay?"

"I'm fine," she said, but it came out too fast. She knew it sounded like she wasn't fine. To change the subject, Nessa asked Luc more about Chayton. Had he seen him?

And now Luc was the one who seemed bothered. "What makes you think *I'd* know where he is?" he said. "Do you think there's some kind of Native American tracking app the tribal council gives out?"

"I didn't mean that," Nessa said. "You said you knew him. I just thought—"

"I know what you thought," Luc said.

Nessa felt her chest heaving with anger. Righteous anger. "I am so sick," she spat out, "of being told I don't understand things that no one is even bothering to explain."

She imagined taking off without a word of goodbye. She couldn't wait until the next turnoff, when she could leave Luc in her dust. Luc was being so unfair! Maybe he would realize it as he gazed at her quickly disappearing form on the horizon.

The only problem was they were running on a road that ran north out of town, straight and flat like it had been drawn with a ruler. No turnoffs unless you counted creepy dirt roads that looked passable only by off-road vehicles. Nessa was forced to stay by Luc's side.

Tether really was in the middle of nowhere, Nessa thought, angry now not just at Luc but at the town. At the world. Maybe Luc would have liked the town better if he'd moved to Tether when Vivian was growing up here, when the town was the center of things and people came in from farms to shop at the now-closed stores and see movies at the now-closed theater.

"It's too bad you had to move here," Nessa spat out. "It must have been better in the UP, where at least it's *supposed* to feel like the sticks."

To her surprise, Luc laughed. "That has to be the stupidest thing anyone has ever said about the UP," he said. "Nothing in the UP feels like it's supposed to be the way it is."

"Don't laugh at me!" Nessa found herself shouting. "I am not saying things that are stupid. I am saying things that are true! You'd have to be crazy to want to move to Tether." She had stopped running and was standing in the road. Luc stopped too, a few steps away from her, facing her. "And just to be clear, I'm not trying to get in touch with Chayton because I need my acne cleared up or something," she went on. "I really need to talk to him. And I was just asking you. Okay?"

"Jeez," Luc said. "Okay. I'm sorry."

"You *should* be sorry," Nessa grumbled. She kicked at a piece of gravel on the side of the road, then looked up at Luc, half wondering if he'd just take off and leave her to run on her own. But Luc was still standing there, his hands on his bony hips. He lifted one toe after another, stretching the tops of his feet in a gesture Nessa recognized from practice.

"You don't even have acne," he said.

Nessa was too mad for this...compliment?...joke? to

register. But what Luc said next did: "I know you're worried about your brother."

"What?" Nessa said, defensive.

"Your brother," he said. "I know you're worried. Because of Billy."

"I'm not worried about my brother," she snapped. "I'm not worried about anything."

"Sure," Luc said, like he didn't believe her and didn't care if she knew he didn't.

"Why would I need to? Nate's not sick like Billy was."

"Yeah, okay, I get that. Sorry." Luc was looking at her strangely. She would think later that this was the most expressive he'd ever been.

"I guess I better head back into town," Nessa said, suddenly feeling like it was weird that she and Luc had had a fight when they weren't even really friends.

"Okay," said Luc and they started running together again, back the way they'd come.

CHAPTER FORTY-SEVEN

Thinking about the fight later, Nessa wondered how much of it had to do with the full moon. She was starting to notice a pattern of being highly emotional before transformation. It was like getting her period, but times 50.

At school, Nessa packed Chayton's rye sachet into her backpack and filled her jeans pockets with other ones she'd clumsily stapled together using fabric from an old bandana. She had to keep the transformation at bay until nighttime, but she didn't know if she could. Vivian was working late. Nessa was supposed to take care of Nate after school.

Bree would have taken care of Nate in Nessa's place except she had a student council meeting.

By lunchtime at school, Nessa was in sensory overload. Her wrists and hips and shoulders ached. Her eyes looked normal in the mirror but felt swollen to the point of closing. Her palms itched. She had a patch of fur on her right thigh, which fortunately no one could see. She kept touching her face in the cafeteria, hoping to feel if there was fur before anyone else could see. None appeared, thankfully.

And then she had to take the school bus home instead of her usual ride in the Monster. Every bump and rev of the engine felt like it was going to shock the wolf right out of her. Breathing deeply, Nessa managed to keep it together, adding 2+2, 4+4, 8+8 all the way into the thousands, the way Nate used to do when he couldn't sleep at night.

Nessa burst into the empty house. Vivian was working, Delphine was babysitting, and Nate's bus had not arrived yet. It was easier to keep the transformation at bay when there were people around. Now, the only thing that seemed to help was putting things in alphabetical order, another Nate trick for calming down.

The only problem was that Nate had much of the house already organized alphabetically. The shelf of books in the living room, the lotions and medications in the bathroom cabinets, even the tea bags in the box of assorted tea flavors in the kitchen. Nessa decided to do what Vivian did for Nate—she opened up the newspaper and started clipping articles for Nate to organize. Only Nessa was the one doing the organizing now.

As she placed PLANS FOR NEW KROGER IN MIDLAND on top of BAY CITY ATTORNEY BOUND FOR TRIAL, she kept cutting through the Paravida logo that appeared on the top of every page. How had it never seemed weird to her before that Paravida paid for the newspaper to be printed and delivered free to every house in Tether? Nessa had not thought much about that fact until now. Why—in addition to subsidizing most of the sports teams and the concerts on the town green in the summer, the Policeman's Benevolent Society, the Volunteer Fire Department, the Ambulance Corps, the health clinic, a senior center/daycare annexed to the retirement home on the edge of town—was Paravida sponsoring the only local source of information in the town? Was this why there were no stories about the wolf attacks? It was something Paravida wanted to keep quiet?

Finally, Nessa heard the roar and squeal of Nate's bus arriving and stopping at the corner, then the front door opening to signal his arrival. With trembling hands, Nessa fixed a peanut butter sandwich for him and sat down at the kitchen table to help him with math homework, Chayton's sachet pressed up against her face like she was icing a black eye. She knew that the second she let herself run—even if she just ran down the hall to her room—she'd be running as a wolf. Just thinking about running made her feel in danger of transforming. She dug her fingernails into her palm to keep thoughts like that at bay. And drew blood. Her fingernails had become sharp as claws.

By the time an hour passed, the November sky was darkening and Nessa was all too aware that she wouldn't make it through dinner and Vivian's return home. So when Delphine biked back from her babysitting job, Nessa explained that even though Delphine wasn't usually left in charge of Nate, she was going to have to be this time because Nessa had an emergency homework project and just *had* to go over to Bree's.

Nessa knew she sounded like she was lying. And that

Delphine could tell. Nessa touched her face for the thousandth time. Was there fur?

"I have homework," Delphine said. "And laundry. Nate's your job."

"I'll do the laundry when I get back," Nessa promised. "And Nate is already set up with a train movie. You don't have to do a thing."

"Okay," Delphine said, guardedly.

"He'll be so absorbed it'll be like he wasn't even here," Nessa promised. "Maybe come out in about an hour and remind Nate to pause it to pee?"

Delphine laughed.

Later, Nessa would wonder which she regretted more, leaving Nate or joking about it with Delphine.

At the moment it all felt worth it for the sense of ease that occurred as Nessa stepped into the rye circle she'd left set up in the woods. She felt the sweet rush of relief as if all the atoms and molecules in her body were finally able to relax from the strain of maintaining their human form. Even her emotions quieted in wolf form. She felt the way she did at practice after a long day—no matter what else was happening, all she had to do now was run.

Without thinking too much about where she was going—Nessa never had to think too much about direction when she was in wolf form—she headed east, following a scent. It wasn't food, and it wasn't the wolf pack, but it was something she wanted.

When she came to a ridgeline in the woods where the trees

broke away and the air currents shifted because of the break in the land and the tree cover, Nessa smelled Paravida and realized she was close. She stopped suddenly, and she heard herself whine as though she'd been hit.

Wolves do not try to overcome fear. Wolves do not have the mantra "We have nothing to fear but fear itself" stamped into their consciousness.

Fear for a wolf is a wise emotion. Fear protects you. Fear must be respected and obeyed. And Nessa felt afraid. But she continued forward anyway.

Crouching outside the chain-link fence, it kept her quiet while what looked like a small patrol of the Paravida wolves appeared on the ridgeline behind her. She noticed that this group had reddish fur marking their scruffs. Why were they different from the others?

She had smelled them even before she heard the piercing whistle calling them back to their prison. She waited until the last wolf had passed by before falling into the line, keeping her eyes down and her tail tucked as the gray wolf had shown her.

This time, Nessa followed the aggressive wolves almost all the way to their kennels. She needed to understand Paravida. Maybe there was information she could understand only in wolf form?

She dipped out of the line and into the shadows just as the last wolf was being ushered into its chain-link box. She slipped around the side of the building, heading toward the next structure about forty feet away.

On her way, she saw something that gave her pause. It was a field—a quarter acre, plowed, unfenced, planted with rye grass grown just under two feet tall. It was tall enough that she could see it was meant to be there. The grass was alive and green, even in the crisp November weather, and Nessa felt it tugging her. It would be so easy to disappear into it, and to rest.

But what was it doing here? Rye was not for wolves, was it? Only werewolves were sustained by this ancient grain. Question #2,439 for Chayton.

Not that she would ever get ahold of him again!

Nessa forced herself to turn away from the rye and back to her search.

She trotted up to a series of low windows along the building's far wall. Jumping up on a windowsill to peer inside, Nessa saw that it was some kind of a laboratory. She wasn't sure if it was the building where Billy's autopsy took place.

She recognized some of the equipment—large microscopes, a centrifuge, an assortment of Bunsen burners, a series of what looked like hot plates, a ductless fume hood. There were long bench-like counters running down the middle of the room and labeled shelves holding racks of test tubes, a row of refrigerators alongside one wall. What was different from other labs Nessa knew was the chain-link cage in the corner. Wait, no, actually there were two of them. One had a few blankets in the corner.

And then Nessa's ears pricked at attention. The blankets stood and shook themselves as a door opened on the opposite side of the room. Those weren't blankets. They were pups. Wolf pups.

Nessa hopped down from the window as a man wearing a white lab coat entered the room. She did not want to be seen.

She moved to the next set of windows around the corner of the building. This time, she hopped up on her back paws and peered into what was clearly an operating room. It was large, with a tile floor that had a drain in the center, and a stainless steel operating table was positioned under an enormous fluorescent light. It was flanked by carts holding monitors and trays of surgical instruments.

Six men and women in green scrubs surrounded the operating table. They all wore goggles, surgical masks, and gloves. Their bodies nearly obscured the table, but it looked like they were moving in and out with tools and suction—it was surgery.

Nessa could hear the beep of a heart monitor. It was steady but very rapid, which was odd. Who were they operating on? The doctor in charge looked up at the ceiling and said, "Mid-lateral incision complete." He had tiny magnifying lenses attached to his glasses, and she couldn't see much else beneath his surgical cap and face mask.

One of the assistants stepped to the side, and Nessa saw, beneath the blue hospital sheet, that whoever this doctor was operating on had a tail.

A wolf tail.

The heart rate monitor seemed to speed up. The head surgeon and a nurse in charge of the station looked at the pulsing green line.

"Okay, we've got to hurry," the surgeon stated calmly, turning back toward his subject. "Number 22 scalpel."

Another assisting nurse handed the surgeon a long, thin blade. The surgeon's back was to Nessa so she could not see what was happening. He seemed to be cutting.

"Beautiful!" he said quietly. All six people working leaned in. Nessa noticed several exchanged wide-eyed looks of amazement.

"Is the sterile transplant receptacle ready?"

Nessa realized at that instant that she knew the voice. As if the doctor read her thoughts, he turned, looking for the container. Nessa could see enough of his face to confirm her worst fears.

It was Dr. Raab.

"Check, doctor," an orderly replied. He maneuvered a cart next to Dr. Raab. It contained a small metal cooler filled with dry ice. The orderly cut open a sealed pouch marked STERILE and pulled out a square glass jar filled with liquid.

"Okay, extraction nearly complete," the surgeon said.

Nessa heard the beeps signifying that the wolf's heart rate had jumped again. It continued to quicken until it was one long beep.

"Doctor, the subject has flat lined," the nurse in charge of the heart monitor stated quietly. "His heart has stopped."

"We're almost there," the surgeon answered. "Number 12 scalpel, please. Just a few more seconds."

What was he doing? Why weren't they trying to save the wolf and restart his heart?! The surgeon exchanged the long scalpel he had been using for a small, curved blade. Nessa felt a combination of horror and panic. But she could not take her eyes off what she was watching.

"Okay. Receptacle!" the surgeon snapped.

The orderly held the small sanitary glass container forward on a metal tray.

One woman looking on gasped, sounding amazed. "Oh my god!"

"Flat line now for twenty-five seconds," the nurse overseeing the heart monitor stated.

The surgeon turned just then, and the orderly stepped

aside. It was just for a moment that Nessa got a glimpse of what he was doing, but it was enough for the image to be seared in her brain.

A human ear was growing inside of the wolf's stomach cavity.

A full-sized adult human ear.

And with a final cutting motion, Dr. Raab detached the ear, lifting it up for everyone to see.

"Congratulations, doctor," one of those attending the procedure said.

"History being made," another person chimed in. Her eyes shone with tears.

The heart rate machine continued to flat line. There were more important things than the wolf's life on everyone's mind.

Carefully placing the human ear in the liquid in the sterile container, Dr. Raab looked at the orderly and said, "We need to get this to Detroit, stat."

"Of course, Dr. Raab," the young man replied reverentially.

Before the surgeon could look up at the window to see what made the sound outside, Nessa was gone.

CHAPTER FORTY-EIGHT

essa turned and ran without thinking.

Without thinking she ran toward the wolf gate.

Without thinking why no one was shooting or why no one was closing the gate, she ran through it.

She ran until the smells of the Paravida plant were well behind her, and then she ran some more for good measure, her mind racing even faster than her body all the while, whirling in circles of thought.

Paravida was breeding these wolves for…organ harvesting? If they could grow an ear, what else could they grow? A liver? A human heart? Dr. Raab said they needed to get the ear to Detroit? Was someone there waiting for it?

As she ran, a whine escaped Nessa's throat. The wolf puppies! Nessa wanted not to have to think about what she'd seen. She wanted to get back to her family. She was supposed to be taking care of Nate. She was supposed to be preparing for a winter training season. She was supposed to be scheduling meetings with recruiters. She was supposed to be a high school junior, not a junior wolf.

She found help where she wasn't looking for it: the gray wolf.

He was waiting for her in the woods behind her house, as if he'd been looking for her all the time she'd been out at Paravida. Seeing him, all the adrenaline that had carried her on the run home leaked straight out of Nessa's body.

Nessa collapsed under the weight of the pain she had just witnessed, compulsively chewing on and licking her front left paw.

The gray wolf lay down next to her, his body pressed up against hers like they were littermates.

She leaned against him, grateful for his warm presence.

She finally understood why she had been chosen by the wolves. She had been chosen to stop this. Even if she had no idea how. Even if all she wanted to do was run away from what she'd seen.

At least now she knew: the Paravida wolves were so large and aggressive because they were being altered somehow for their true purpose, as factories for human replacement parts. They had to be. She wondered if the other wolves she had seen with incisions were growing organs too. What kind of drug or gene therapy caused pointed teeth? Where did the Dutch Chem study kids fit in?

Nessa needed to think. She needed her family. She needed

to take a long bath. She needed to call Bree. She didn't know what she was going to do, but she was going to do something. First, however, she needed to go inside. When she stood, the gray wolf rose as well. As she walked back to her house, he let her go, remaining standing. She had the feeling that he would be out there the rest of the night, watching over her and waiting for her to return.

CHAPTER FORTY-NINE

hether the doorbell at the Kurland house had rung or not while Nessa was still enclosed within the Paravida campus, Nessa would never learn. Nate never said, and Delphine was listening to music on headphones in her room and missed it.

In fact, Delphine didn't realize anyone was there until she got up in search of a snack. She was surprised to see Nate standing at the front door, and even more surprised to see that he was talking to an adult.

"Nate?" she said. "Who is that?"

"My friend," Nate said.

This didn't narrow things down much for Delphine. Nate tended to call everyone his friend or his buddy. Delphine peered more closely at the woman's tidy blue top and khakis and assumed she was a door-to-door missionary.

"Thanks, but we're all set for religion," she said, using the line Vivian had taught the kids to say.

"Oh, no, I'm not here for that," said the woman, who was starting to look familiar to Delphine. "I work at the clinic Nate goes to. I was just explaining to him that he had an appointment today."

"He did?" Delphine said. "My sister takes him to those. She's good about remembering."

The woman smiled brightly. "Of course," she said. "I know Nessa. And Bree." Looking at Nate as if this were an inside joke. "You come in at the same time as Sierra Thomas usually. You all turn our waiting room into a soccer stadium."

"I scored twenty goals on October 20," said Nate. "On September 22—I scored twenty-nine. Too many."

"No, that's impressive," the woman said. She held out her hand to Delphine like they were both adults. Delphine was already in her pajamas and was far from an adult, but she shook hands anyway.

"I called your mom," the woman said. "I asked if I could swing by to pick up Nate since he missed his appointment, and Dr. Raab's only in town one more day, so we're all booked up."

"My mom said to?" Delphine asked. She knew her mom would've called Delphine to let her know.

Except Delphine wasn't even supposed to be taking care of Nate. Nessa was. And Nessa wasn't here. Maybe Vivian had called Nessa?

"Come on, Nate, let's go," the woman said, holding the front door open.

Nate looked back at Delphine as if to say, *Do I have permission?*

Delphine hated to have to decide. Nessa and Vivian always seemed so on top of Nate's appointments and schedules. But Nate was treating this woman like she was a family friend. "Want me to go with you?" she said.

The woman interrupted. "No, sorry, that's impossible. You see, your mom signed the transportation form for Nate but not for you. I can't legally transport you anywhere."

And that sounded so official, Delphine began to believe that this woman had communicated with her mom and that bringing kids into the clinic on the days their parents forgot to bring them was part of her job.

But the second the woman took Nate, Delphine sensed that she had made the wrong decision. She called Vivian's phone, and when it went to voicemail, she called Nessa's. Strangely, she heard it ringing from inside Nessa's backpack, which Nessa had left by the door. *Funny*, Delphine thought, *Nessa never leaves her phone at home when she goes out.* And also funny—what kind of study session was Nessa going to where she didn't bring her school things?

Nessa rushed back into the house while Delphine was calling Dr. Morgan's, knowing she'd be able to reach her mom that way for sure.

"Nessa," Delphine said, hanging up the phone mid-ring because Nessa would know what to do. "This lady came and took Nate, and she sounded like she had mom's permission—or at least I thought so."

"Who took Nate?" Nessa said. "Who was it?"

"A woman," Delphine said. "She said her name was Mary."

CHAPTER FIFTY

Nessa's fingers shook as she was entering the clinic's number. "Get my phone," she said to Delphine. "It's in my backpack. Call mom. Wait! No. Call Bree!"

Nessa felt like her brain had been turned into a computer. A rational, precise thinking machine. Dr. Morgan's number went to voicemail. But Delphine had gotten through to Bree on Nessa's phone. She handed it over.

Nessa ducked into her bedroom so Delphine wouldn't hear her.

"Nate's gone!" Nessa said. "Mary Clovis from the clinic came and took him. While I was out. Delphine was covering for me."

Nessa could tell from Bree's gasp that Bree knew how bad

this was.

"Do you think she took Nate to Paravida?" Bree said.

Nessa felt her insides twist violently.

"Yes," she said.

"We have to go get him. I'll pick you up in five minutes," said Bree.

"No," Nessa said. She shook her head, trying to clear her mind. There was something she had to tell Bree. Something was wrong with the picture in her mind of the two of them in the Monster. Was it that she just couldn't stand the idea of riding in the passenger seat and feeling so powerless?

No, that wasn't the problem. It was something else. And then Nessa's mind—sorting the options quickly, methodically—finally landed on the problem with involving the Monster and Bree at the wheel.

She lowered her voice. "I need to go get him alone. I need to go as a wolf." As much as they had talked about it, having Nessa say it this way, as if it were something she could control...this was new. "I know how to get in there. I just did. I'll tell you later."

"Nessa, oh my god, let me help you, okay?" Bree said. "Let me call the police or something. And don't trust Mary, please."

But Nessa barely heard Bree's warning. She couldn't focus anymore. They'd already been on the phone too long. Nessa's mind was speeding ahead, into the woods, the rye, the speed at which she'd run to get to Paravida.

If only she had stayed there, she might have seen Nate arrive. *If* he was even there. She hoped he wasn't. But she had no other idea of where to look.

The transformation back to wolf form, the run through the woods, it was a complete blur. All Nessa could feel was her heart in her chest. It was aching from exertion, but she felt like it was aching for Nate, for fear. She knew this was her fault. She should never have left him with Delphine, who didn't understand the clinic study, and who didn't know any of this.

As she approached the facility, she knew she had to stop thinking in this way. She needed her brain to be working on the problem at hand, which was finding Nate. She'd know just from standing outside if he was there. If he was speaking, she'd hear him.

But Nate tended to shut down when he was scared. What if he wasn't talking?

Nessa thought about the exam tables she'd seen at the clinic, the ones with the thick leather straps. If that's what they were using on the kids in public, what would they be doing here, behind twelve feet of chain-link fence?

Nessa stood in the shadows at the edge of the facility. She heard the noises of the woods behind her, the chipmunks and the mice running in their burrows underground, the earthworms pushing the soil, the birds digging for bits and seeds in the brittle leaves. She heard the noises of the facility itself as well, the hum of several competing ventilation systems, a crackle of a walkie-talkie being turned on and off, footsteps passing slowly down what she figured was a long hall as they didn't pause for a turn or slow down for a door.

Far off, there was the sound of a small engine, like someone turning on a blender, and she heard a chuckle followed by a cough, which was closer than she was anticipating. She looked up and registered the guard tower. Up there? Instinctively,

Nessa took a step back, deeper into the shadow.

Nessa contemplated the fact of the twelve-foot fence.

How was she going to get back in? The aggressive wolves were already in for the night. She wished the gray wolf were with her. Mostly she wanted his company, the steady feeling she had when he was at her side. But also, he seemed to know so much about the wolves and Paravida. He might have known a different way in.

Just then, Nessa heard a piercing whistle that cut through the muted sound tapestry around her. It felt like a laser carving a burn line through her brain tissue.

Why a whistle? The pack of aggressive wolves was already inside.

But no, she could smell wolf. Were there others?

And the wolves inside the facility were definitely reacting to something. Nessa began to hear increased movement from inside the kennels. Some whined or paced, while others must have been throwing themselves against the doors of their cages—Nessa heard the rattling of chain link and the muted thump of furred bodies hitting the cement floors.

The smell rose up behind her, mixing with breezes circulating through the trees—less of the cages and chemicals used to clean them and more balsam fir and loamy soil.

Nessa fixed on the brightly lit tile and stainless steel buildings. She reminded herself that her brother might be in there. He might be strapped to another exam table. She didn't know what Paravida wanted from Nate—from Billy—but she could now imagine.

Maybe Mary had him in there. Maybe Mary was the only thing standing between Nate and whatever had happened to

Billy. Either way, Nessa was going to go in there and rescue him.

Amazingly, the gate was open. Without thinking why, Nessa passed through. Just as she did, she felt movement behind her. She remembered what it was like when the wolves were biting at her hindquarters, how she would have to fight them, turning on one, then quickly twisting around to protect her exposed side from the other.

But it was the gray wolf! When wolves looked each other in the eye, it was a challenge, but the gray wolf was looking at Nessa as if to say, "I know why you're here. I know how serious this is. I am going to help you."

Nessa returned his gaze and felt the way she felt when she passed off a baton during a relay in track. They were connected.

And then she heard something. It was small, but she recognized it. It was Nate. He said, "Buddy," not like he was talking to someone but like he was muttering the word to himself, for comfort.

She had a sense of where the sound had come from and she took off toward the sound, keeping to the shadows behind buildings. This time she was in the lead and the gray wolf followed.

Nate was here.

CHAPTER FIFTY-ONE

Something must have been making Nate nervous, because he started to mumble "Buddy" over and over again under his breath. Nessa heard a bright light sound, like a glass being set down on a counter.

"I don't want that," Nate said. Were they making him drink something?

By this point, she'd managed to identify which building Nate was in. It was two down from the wolf kennels, a squat tower of white brick. The windows were small and located high up. Nessa could not peer in. She heard whirring, like the sound of a drill.

"Why is *he* here?" Nate asked.

Why is who *here?* She silently begged her brother to say.

Please, please don't let it be Dr. Raab.

Circling the building, still keeping to the shadows cast by a bank of giant compressors, Nessa realized there was only one way to get inside to Nate. The door.

Giving the gray wolf a nod as if to say, "I'll be right back," she followed the path back to the wolf house. Locked inside their kennels now, the wolves registered her presence in the olfactory landscape. They began to bay and shake the fencing.

Nessa was glad of the distraction. She saw that the guards who were watching them began to yell. Weren't they going to notice that the wolves were reacting to something?

She heard a gun go off, and then a wolf cry out in pain. The barking stopped. The guards laughed, but they did not turn to see what the wolves had been barking at.

They are idiots, Nessa decided.

She hoped the guards wouldn't turn around now. There was no cover she could possibly use to hide—just the open rye field. Nessa could smell its comforting, homey smell as she broke into it. Inside, she felt safe and protected, looking to her left at the rows of kennels lit up until they nearly glowed, the animals inside frozen as if time had stopped and she were moving through a diorama version of the Paravida grounds, the guards doll figurines, the wolves in their cages constructions of plush and wire.

She broke out on the other side of the field and motion returned, the dogs and men moving as if they were music box ballerinas wound up again. Except they weren't ballerinas— they were slathering murderous wolves and humans in riot gear who would shoot a barking wolf rather than turn to see what he was barking at. Nessa was tripping over her now-human legs, the momentum of her run breaking down as the wolf speed nearly knocked her head over heels, her arms waving spastically, her breath ragged in her own ears, her heart racing. She ran for the shadows desperately, as one might swim to the surface after diving into deep water.

Letting herself catch her breath, she returned to a trotting pace, feeling unnerved and vulnerable as a human, her feet heavy on the ground as if she'd just removed skates. She had to be careful, she knew—this was no time to get sloppy—but the sound of Nate protesting spurred her forward. What was happening to him in there?

As she rounded the corner to the building door, she saw the gray wolf waiting for her, just where she'd left him. She felt a leap of gratitude in her chest.

The gray wolf was large and regal, his coat glossy, his shoulders strong, his back straight, his snout proud and high. She took one second to crouch in front of him, to put a hand on his chest and rub the fur there. "Thank you," she whispered, something she'd been wanting to tell him but had never had the words. "If you see someone coming, you'll let me know, right?" The wolf did not speak, but she could tell from his eyes he would stay.

Then Nessa was off, opening the door to the facility (grateful it wasn't locked), propping it open with a glove she found in the pocket of her jacket, and then following the sound of scratchy classical music up a flight of stairs.

They were playing the soundtrack of *Fantasia*. They had reached the part called "The Sorcerer's Apprentice." This song had driven Nate into a fit of anxiety when he was little. It was the sight of Mickey and the brooms that wouldn't stop dividing and dancing that made Nate want to rip his hair out. Aunt Jane had once set it up for Nate to watch during Thanksgiving dinner, and the only way to stop Nate from screaming had been for the Kurlands to leave her house and drive four hours home.

Running to one of the rooms on the first floor, Nessa did not stop to make a plan. All she knew was she had to stop the music before Nate succumbed…to what, she didn't even want to know. She had no trouble telling where the sound was coming from. She pushed open the third door on the right, stepped into an operating room like the ones she'd seen in the wolf house, saw Nate restrained by the straps of an exam chair, muttering "buddy, buddy, buddy" under his breath. She saw the boom box on the counter, only a few feet from his head and slapped her hand on its surface so that the music came to a stop.

In the quiet that followed, she took in the rest of the scene, her gaze moving from Nate's wild eyes to a body of some sort, laid out on a table. Nessa could not tell who—or what—it was because it was covered entirely with a blue cloth, but she guessed it was another wolf, like the one Dr. Raab had been "operating" on earlier.

Nessa's mind felt sluggish, but in reality it took less than a second for her to process the fact that the only other figures in the room were Mary Clovis and Pasty Pete. They were standing across the room as if they'd started to run.

"Oh," said Pete, seeing Nessa, his eyes wide with surprise.

Mary's soft face was unreadable. And then she broke into a smile. "Nessa Kurland," she said. Then, to Nate. "It's only your sister. I thought—"

"What are you doing to my brother?"

"Your brother?" Mary said. "I've been prepping him for his next appointment with Dr. Raab. Given what happened to Billy Lark, we thought it a wise precaution."

"And you thought kidnapping a child was the best way to do that?" Nessa snapped. "I wonder why."

Nessa looked back at Nate. *What had Mary been telling him?* What had he already witnessed in this place? If it had been anyone else, they would have been able to communicate with a significant look or a raised eyebrow. But of course Nate didn't have the skills to give Nessa that kind of information, or to even know that the expression on her face meant that she was looking for it.

Forgetting that he was restrained, Nate tried to lift a hand when he saw his sister. "Help me, Ness," he whimpered. "Buddy."

As she rushed to Nate's side to unbuckle the straps on his wrists and ankles, Nessa allowed her eyes to dart toward the other operating table, covered with medical sheets.

She turned to Mary, the anger boiling over.

"What are you doing with the wolves? And my brother? What sort of sick experiments are you running here?" Nessa knew her voice was rising. She sounded out of control. "You strapped him down? You played music you know he hates...on purpose? You are torturing him! What are you trying to do?"

Nessa didn't know exactly what she'd expected Mary to say in reply, but a sigh and a shrug was not it. She looked only vaguely guilty. "I know, I know," she said. "It's hard to understand the study sometimes. Dr. Raab is a renowned scientist. He won a Nobel Prize, although we're supposed to keep that quiet if we can."

"I don't care if he won the Super Bowl," Nessa said. "Come on, Nate, let's get you out of here." She put a hand on her brother's shoulder to let him know it was time to leave. Nate slid off the exam chair and they began walking toward the door. She wished she could take the wolf too, but he would be too heavy to carry.

"You're just going to let her go?" Pete demanded of Mary.

Nessa looked daggers at Pete.

"You can't stop me. People know I came here. You can't keep Nate, or me, against our will. You'll become an accessory to felony kidnapping of two minors."

Nessa's certainty was shattered when Mary touched a button under the counter she was leaning against, and Nessa heard the mechanical click and thunk that indicated the door to the room was being locked. Nessa confirmed this, rattling the handle after it would not move.

Nessa reached into her pocket for her phone.

Mary shook her head regretfully. "I'm so sorry, sweetheart," she said. "Your phone's not going to work in here. Paravida keeps a blocker on in the research rooms."

"You can't do this," Nessa said. She could hear panic in her voice. She reminded herself to take a breath. She couldn't lose control of herself.

"I'm going to have to," Mary said. She glanced at Nessa. "Orders from the top. You see, Billy was really valuable to the study. Our only way to continue the work that we were doing is to continue it with Nate. Which is actually a kind of beautiful opportunity—one of Dr. Raab's experiments with stem cell transfer might allow him to put some of Billy's material into Nate's body. He'll be able to test on both boys' genetic material at the same time, using Nate's body as a petri dish for Billy's stem cells. Not only will Nate be our new Patient Zero—this could cure his autism."

Mary walked over to a table and picked up a loaded syringe. She turned back to face Nate and Nessa.

"Don't you see the beauty in it? We are using these stem

cells to grow human organs in the wolves. We are creating life here—from stem cells, from nothing. The wild wolves? They are just one of the creations. And Nate will be the first human we...*improve*. The possibilities are limitless."

Nessa wasn't following. Was Mary Clovis truly nuts? Nessa had the urge to cover Nate's ears with her hands. She didn't want him to hear this.

"You are disgusting, you know that?" she said. "Both of you. And you won't get away with this."

"Is that so, Nessa?" Mary said, maintaining the tone of a concerned adult even as she turned to a computer terminal, and with a few keystrokes called up a video. "Are you going to do *this*?" she asked, pressing play. Pete gave a cackling laugh, knowing what was coming.

From the grainy quality of the video filling the screen, Nessa guessed it was filmed by a security camera. With a sinking heart, she recognized what part of the Paravida campus it showed—the patch of rye grass. A wolf entered from the right side of the screen, sprinting for the field. Nessa knew that it was her. Ten minutes earlier.

As horrified as she was, it was fascinating to watch her own transformation. There she was, running two steps as a wolf, then three, then a blurring fourth as her body shifted, her head emerging as if from a covering of fur, her hands pushing forward as if emerging from fur sleeves. Her tail disappeared in the single motion of rising from all fours; her elbows seemed to pull her body erect, as if the force of the running were causing her to rise.

Mary paused the video. "You're something of a creation too, aren't you, Nessa Kurland? An astounding skill that I would never have believed if I hadn't seen it with my own eyes.

Given Dr. Raab's research with wolves, I think he will be very interested to include you in his study."

"I don't think so," Nessa said. "I've seen his so-called research. It looks more like torture and animal abuse to me."

"You can't think of them as living creatures. Those are the rules of pure science. You have to think of them as nothing but a collection of cells," Mary started to intone, trying to sound wise.

"Or monsters!" Pete jumped in. "When they were puppies, they were cute, but now they give me the creeps. You lose your overtime pay if you kill one, though."

"There's something wrong with those wolves," Nessa said. "You've tampered with them. They're too aggressive to survive. They don't cooperate. They shouldn't be like that."

Mary shrugged. "I wouldn't be so sure, young lady. The world's an aggressive place. We're just keeping up with it and trying to build something more perfect and that helps others."

"But you're helping them? Paravida. Whoever they are. You grew up here, Mary. You're from Tether. Like us."

"Yes," Mary said. "But what does that even mean anymore? Dutch Chem used this town. Paravida, the white knight that came to Tether's rescue? No. The only reason Paravida set up shop here was access to a whole generation of kids carrying a fascinating range of mutations. What doesn't kill you only makes you stronger. The stupid town of Tether was so desperate for any kind of stable employment, they handed over their schools, their health records, and their kids. This place is worthless. It's a pit. Something I've learned from Dr. Raab. Hope is a drug. Your brain…it thrives on it. Too much, and the rest of the world starts to look gray and depleted. Too little? You start to die inside. People know this. *You* know this. Anyone who is smart is getting out before Tether becomes a town that time forgot. Someplace FEMA has to come in and shut down."

"I don't know that," said Nessa, realizing that just a few months before she might have agreed with Mary. "Have some pride in what you are and where you come from."

"Pride is for the rich," Mary said. "And I am not rich. I am not particularly lucky either."

"Is that why all your retirement accounts are drained?"

Mary jerked when Nessa said those words. She looked genuinely surprised for a moment, giving Nessa a chance to take a step closer to the window. Nessa had had a thought.

"What happened to your money anyway?" Nessa asked, stalling for time.

"So you were the person who broke into the Paravida rooms at the clinic. Naughty girl. I told you, I'm not lucky. In fact, I have a problem with luck."

What was she talking about? Nessa was starting to sense how crazy Mary Clovis really was. Her goofy-smiled sidekick seemed not to notice.

Mary recognized Nessa's confusion.

"Gambling, sweetheart," she said. "I have what's known as a little gambling...problem."

"So on top of being mean, vicious, and missing a conscience, you're an addict too?" said Nessa, disguising another step toward the window by leaning against the counter. She could see Nate looking at her. *Please don't say anything*, she begged him silently.

"How long has *that* been going on?" Nessa said, trying to sound nonthreatening. She hoisted herself up onto the counter.

"You don't know what it's like to live in a place where you

have no hope. You're a kid still. At your age, all you have is hope. Walking through Tether High, you can smell it. No one knows yet that they will end up in a dead-end job, that there's nothing for them in this town. The ones who think they'll get out? They might. But most of them don't have the talent or the guts or just the extra cash to get started somewhere else."

Nessa slid a hand along the counter behind her. Mary kept talking. "That's how I got started. I wanted to be a teacher. I was out with my girlfriends one night, and I made a hundred dollars on a ten-dollar roulette bet. Hope waved its hand at me. This was how I could pay for grad school. And for a while I was doing pretty well. But then I started to fall just a little bit behind."

Nessa rested her hand on the neck of a microscope like it was a dog sidling up next to her.

"The next bet was the one that I could always count on to pull me out of the hole," Mary went on. "A job at Dutch Chem. For a long time I kept things under control. But then…I didn't. Dr. Raab found out. We made an exchange. I help him implement his research, and he helps me with my debts. I'm finally building my career. This is pioneering work, and he's asked for very little."

"Kidnapping?" Nessa said. "Torturing and helping to kill children? That's very little?"

"This was my idea," Mary confessed, pointing to Nate. "Dr. Raab doesn't know. But after Billy died, I knew that he'd be mad at me. He's paranoid about people in this town finding out what's happening before he has his precious results." Mary gave a short little laugh.

"And what about you?" Nessa asked Pete, sidling closer to the microscope.

"We're getting married," Pete said happily, and put an arm

around Mary's shoulders. "We're getting married in the spring when this is all over, and Dr. Raab gives Mary her final payout. Then we're never coming back to this awful place!"

Nessa tightened her hand around the neck of the microscope and, hoping this would work, she swung her arm up and over her head and lobbed the microscope through the window. She didn't wait for the sound of a crash before she took a second microscope and did the same thing, aiming slightly to the left.

The windows were high up on the wall, rectangular, meant to let in light but not be seen through from out or in. She could only hope the microscope hurtling through the window was enough of a call for help that the gray wolf would be able to figure out something to do to save them.

It was a long shot, she knew.

Pete's reaction was swift. One second, he was staring up at the broken window in disbelief, and the next he had Nessa by the wrist and was dragging her to a corner of the lab. He was stronger than he looked and strapped her and her brother into chairs like the one Nate had been sitting in.

"What did you have to go and do that for?" Pete yelled, leaning his face in close to hers. "I didn't want to have to scare your little brother like that." Nate's eyes were closed, and his face was scrunched up, like he used to do when he was younger and heard balloons popping.

"There are people on their way here right now," Nessa yelled, more to Mary than to Pete. "This is your last chance to turn back. Let us go, and I am sure you can plea-bargain about the work in the study."

"Oh, I'm not worried," Mary said. "Dr. Raab and the people that run this place have connections. I'm sure you and Nate will be held here at his disposal. Everyone can be bought, Vivian Kurland most of all." At this, Mary Clovis let out a mean and bitter laugh. "I've been in Tether long enough to learn that much at least. Maybe the doctor can invent another doping scare— one that this time will show up in your blood?" Mary said.

"So that was you?" Nessa said. But what did Mary mean with that comment about her mother? Vivian was one of the most honest people she knew.

"You thought it was Cynthia Sinise, didn't you?" Pete said. "I saw her in the locker room, and I told Mary about how she was gloating over you. Mary hoped you'd be so dumb to think someone on your own team would plant steroids. We had a good laugh over that one, didn't we, sweetheart?"

Nessa flushed. She *had* thought that. She felt a second of shame.

"Teenagers," Mary spat out. "You all think you'll live forever. You think you can figure it all out. You can't. Life will chew you up and spit you out. And in your case, the clock will be running on an accelerated timeline. Taking steroids can be quite dangerous, you know. Perhaps you'll end up having some kind of reaction to the dangerous medications you're taking. Something requiring that you spend a great deal of time in a hospital. Where of course Dr. Raab will have the kind of unfettered access to you he was so desperate to get from the clinic study kids. He'll fry your brain like bacon and you won't be able to tell your mom apart from the big stuffed teddy bear I'm sure all your friends from school will send to cheer you up.

"Meanwhile, once I deliver the two of you—especially you with your special talent—I'm going to be spending the rest of my life on some beach in the Cayman Islands, relaxing in the shade of Paravida's giant payout."

Mary's lengthy speech masked the low rumble of growling.

Or maybe it was one of those sounds only Nessa could hear. But as Mary went on and on, Nessa noticed there was more of it. A lot of growling, actually. Coming from just outside the window.

It was the gray wolf. He was growling. And then he was barking. He was sounding outraged and desperate, and Nessa started to worry. She needed him to be calm and smart and strategic. This was not the time for an emotional response.

But there he was, crying in a way that was not just sad but made him sound like he'd been pushed to the very edge of understanding. He sounded like a wolf unhinged.

"What the—?" Mary said. She ran to the computer monitor and toggled back and forth among the grainy video feed coming in from the security cameras. Craning her neck, Nessa could see what Mary saw, and she watched what was happening with just about the same level of horror and amazement as Mary and Pete did.

Just outside the window, the gray wolf was pacing and barking like a maniac. He ran in circles like a puppy being teased with a bone, and then he stopped, and then he barked some more.

What is he doing? Nessa wondered. He looked like he didn't even have a plan. He was going to get caught. He had to stay hidden. Didn't he?

Then the gray wolf took off. Nessa didn't know where he was going, only that he was no longer in the video image. Not a minute too soon, either, Nessa realized, as she counted one, two, three, four of the guards in riot gear running into the kennels. The guards had come looking for the source of the barking and known somehow that it was coming from just beneath the lab window. Perhaps they had seen the wolf on the same video display Mary, Pete, Nessa, and Nate were watching now?

But where had the gray wolf gone?

Mary must have been wondering the same thing. She toggled between different screens. Nessa could not see what she could, but from the way Mary kept hitting the keys, Nessa was pretty sure she hadn't found the wolf, until suddenly Mary's whole body froze.

Without taking her eyes off the monitor, she yelled: "Walkie-talkie!" and Pete rushed one to her. She spoke into it in a voice that had lost all trace of control, speaking so quickly she had to repeat herself to be understood.

"There's someone at the kennels," Mary said, her voice rising in panic. "It looks like he's tampering with something. Oh, my god, how did that guy get in? He's opening the gate. Get someone over there!"

Nessa didn't understand what was happening any better than Mary did. But with her wolf hearing she could detect what Mary and Pete could not. She heard latches sliding open, the creak of gates, the brush of paws, and the faint clicking of toenails on the cement flooring inside the kennels.

"Why aren't they ripping him to shreds?" Mary said. "He's *inside the kennels with them.*" Then she shouted, "Hard lockdown!" into the walkie-talkie. But she must not have pressed the correct button right away.

The person at dispatch said, "Come again?"

But by now, the wolves had made their way over to the security guards.

Because they know, Nessa thought. *They know which are the humans who have tortured them and which is the human who set them free.*

Suddenly Nessa heard the wolves beneath the lab window, growling and snarling. A shot was fired, but then she heard human screams and one wolf whine. Had they overwhelmed the guards? Nessa knew that, counting the second group, there were at least forty wolves in the kennel. Maybe more. There were ten, maybe twelve guards max. The guards were armed, but she didn't think that would matter after one or two wolves were shot down.

She heard a clattering as if a wolf had jumped onto a box of some kind. And then the gray wolf was poking his snout into the opening in the broken window. He withdrew, then she saw his whole body launching through. The wolf landed on the countertop and then dropped gracefully to the floor.

Nate turned to Nessa. "There's a wolf here," he said, his voice hushed.

"I know," Nessa said. "But he's not going to hurt us. He's friendly."

Then there was another snout in the window. Another wolf soundlessly hitting the counter, then the floor. Another behind that one. And then a fourth.

"Are they friendly too?" Nate asked, the question phrased in a monotone though Nessa could hear the hope in it.

"Um...not so much," Nessa said.

The wolves were not coming for Nate or Nessa.

They were headed for Pasty Pete Packer and Mary Clovis. First they circled their two prey and began a high-pitched yapping. Nessa recognized the sound. A pack made these sounds together to confuse and terrify their victims. Pete had a hand up in front of his face, frozen, as if he could possibly protect himself. He could not, and he could not save his fiancée either.

Who knew how many times Mary or Pete had been in the room during Dr. Raab's experiments? Who knew what wolf torture they had witnessed or abetted? What had they done to these wolves or members of their pack?

They both screamed as the wolves brought them to the floor.

"Close your eyes, Nate," Nessa commanded her brother in a stern voice. "Now! Do not look." She closed her own eyes as well. But she could hear. Bones snapping. Ligaments tearing, cartilage shredded by filed teeth. Mary screaming. Pete begging and shouting to stop, finally just him gasping for breath.

And then more wolves began to pour in through the broken window, hitting the counter, hitting the floor, until there were six of them skulking toward her and Nate and the gray wolf. Then there were eight. And then ten.

The wolves attacking Pete and Mary paused to look up at the other wolves, blood dripping from their teeth, their muzzles stained red. Then they went back to their meal.

The gray wolf squared off in front of Nessa and Nate. Nessa marveled at how calm she felt. Why wasn't she panicking? She felt like she'd just inhaled extra-oxygenated air. She felt the way she did running through the patch of rye. As if the entire course of time had come to a standstill, and it was just Nessa alone, moving in the radiating glow of the overhead lights. She felt the quiet she had only experienced when she was running her fastest and not feeling anything but the lightness and the way the rhythm of her footsteps had aligned to the rhythm of her heart.

I have this, she believed. Even if she were strapped down, immobilized, and human…supremely vulnerable, facing a pack of ten outsized, bred-for-aggression wolves.

CHAPTER FIFTY-TWO

There was a moment when everything went absolutely still.

Nessa didn't know what had happened, only that the restraints on her wrists and ankles had loosened so much she could slip her paws out easily. *Oh,* she realized, looking down at them. *That's what happened.*

She had transformed thoughtlessly, without the moon, without rye. Now she was standing in front of the chair designed to restrain a human, but from which, in wolf form, she'd easily escaped. She was ready to protect Nate.

The aggressive wolves jumped back, momentarily confused. They moved away from Nessa and Nate, into the rest of the room.

"Nessie?" Nate said. He wasn't going to show his emotion

on his face. Not even now. But she could see the confusion deep in his eyes, and more than that, she could see that he felt abandoned. Here it had been the two of them in the room full of wolves and now it was just him.

"Nessa, you turned into a wolf."

Nessa didn't know how else to reassure him than to treat him as she would a puppy. Hopping up onto his seat, sidling in next to him, she pushed up against his face with her own, and then she began licking him, first his cheek and then behind his ear where she knew he was ticklish. Then, as he was distracted by laughing, she ripped one restraint free with her teeth. She nosed at the other, and he took the hint, using his free hand to loosen it. She hopped down. She batted Nate's right hand with the side of her face. She put a paw on his shoe. He understood and bent down to unstrap his own ankles using the buckles.

And not a moment too soon. The room had devolved into chaos. They needed to get out of there. The wolves were knocking instruments and glass vials off counters, fighting with one another on the surface of tables. They left long gashes in the soft wallboard with their claws. There were a dozen wolves in the room and each one was bent on destroying as much of what was there as they could. One wolf was systematically chewing on the keypad next to the door, gnawing and twisting his head this way and that like it was a bone with a little bit of gristle left to dislodge.

Another wolf had climbed on top of the table where the shrouded figure lay. She watched that wolf rip the sheet loose. It was Billy Lark's body, stiff and blue, a roughly sewn incision traveling from belly to neck, each place where the needle had punctured the skin marked by a small circle of black, crusted blood.

"No!" she barked out and Nessa saw the gray wolf jump up on the table. He was standing over Billy's body, his head forward, his back perfectly straight, his long legs braced for impact. He was barking ferociously at any wolf who approached. He was protecting the body.

Nessa might have joined him, but just then some of the wolves had started to approach Nate. She took a step back toward them and glanced up at the gray wolf who was defending Billy from a large aggressive wolf. It had locked its teeth into Gray's shoulder, and he was down.

With every ounce of resolve she could muster, Nessa growled and snapped at the wolves who were approaching Nate. Her bark was strong. The nearest wolf rolled back on its haunches. It joined another wolf ripping through surgical gowns that were spilling out of an overturned hamper.

But another was approaching. And another. Nessa planted her paws, puffed out her chest, and let out a bark that carried every ounce of the human word "NO" she had in her. The bark was like no other sound she had ever been able to make in human or wolf form before. It was deep and resonant, full of everything she knew as a human and an animal.

She wasn't going to back down. She knew that. She communicated that. She was here until the death.

Her confusion and sadness about what had happened in her town were wrapped up inside her bark, but also all the joy she'd known growing up here so close to the woods, the farms, the sky. She barked again and realized as the second wolf backed away that she was strong the way her mother was strong, the way trees that can bend but not crack in fierce winds are strong.

Behind her, Nate had opened a cabinet and was ripping

the caps off bottles. Nessa instantly regretted every disparaging comment she'd ever made about his obsession with his chemistry set. He was using chemical compounds as weapons now, dousing approaching wolves with hydrochloric acid like he was in a water fight, sending them whining and screaming into the corners of the room.

And just then there was a flash of light near the door. The body of the wolf chewing on the keypad went stiff as sparks flew from the wall and then the wolf collapsed to the floor. He'd electrocuted himself but he'd also killed the lights, the ventilation, and the security system. The electronic mechanism of the door let go and the doors swung open.

It took the aggressive wolves a moment to notice the now-open door, but when they did there was a collective howling like they were soldiers who had just successfully breached the walls of a besieged city. They flew from the room, streaming into the hallways even as new wolves continued to leap through the broken window, heading straight through the open door as well.

And then they were gone, leaving nothing but the echoes of destruction behind.

Nessa took the corner of Nate's tee shirt in her teeth and pulled. Carefully smelling for hydrochloric acid, she led him through the wreckage of the room to the table where Gray was lying next to Billy's body.

She nudged the gray wolf and, as he rolled over in response, Nessa smelled the blood. Then she saw it. It was fresh still, flowing, pooling under his front shoulder, where she'd seen him get bitten.

She let out a whine. She couldn't help it. She needed to transform back into human state where she'd have hands and could open cabinets and find bandages.

She butted Nate with her head, showed him what she wanted by nosing open a cabinet. He got the idea and quickly found bandages. He was inexpert, but he'd seen enough of the animals Vivian treated in the garage at home to know the basics, pressing the bandage into the wound, wrapping the shoulder, taping the wrap.

Nessa knew Nate was not strong enough to lift the gray wolf, who likely weighed more than he did, so Nessa gave the wolf another nudge to get him up and walking. He looked almost comatose, his eyes flitting in one direction and then the next without moving his head, which he was too exhausted to lift. It was hard to imagine him walking, not in the state he was in, but she didn't want to think about what would happen to him if he stayed.

Eventually, he stood. He took a few halting steps, yelped in pain, and stopped. Then he took a few steps more. He kept looking back at Billy's body, but Nessa stood between him and it to let him know he had to move forward.

Once outside, they saw that the Paravida guard towers were deserted. Lights were flashing, a siren was wailing, guards were running and jumping into Paravida vehicles. Wolves were everywhere, fighting with each other, fighting over garbage they'd found, trotting in small groups as though on patrol. One was lifting its leg to pee on the corner of a building. Another was digging a hole in a landscaped bed.

Nessa heard the mechanical gate begin to open. Someone

must have decided that the campus would feel a lot safer if the wolves were let out. She still didn't understand how the Paravida people had managed to get the wolves to cooperate before, coming at the whistle, heading straight to their kennel. Maybe the guards who knew how to use the whistle were all dead?

Leading Nate, encouraging the gray wolf to follow her, she moved toward the opening in the fence that the aggressive wolves were now streaming through. The gray wolf was moving slowly. They reached the gate just as it was closing up and got through it just in time.

Then Nessa heard a noise she would have recognized anywhere. An engine idling. But not just any engine. It was an engine whose idle sounded like it was going to choke out at any moment. The Monster.

Nate must have heard it too, because he started to move toward it, navigating the thick underbrush in the woods.

Nessa turned to the gray wolf. She didn't know how to say, "Stay here," so she just looked at him intently, concentrating on the words as much as she could. Then she ran with Nate, breaking a trail for him to follow, then letting him go alone—she sat back in the shadows when they saw the outline of Bree's car.

Nate ran for it. Bree was standing by the driver's side door, opening the back seat for him, holding him by the shoulders when he reached her, checking to make sure he was okay. Bree cupped her hands at the sides of her eyes, blocking the light coming from her car, scanning the woods, Nessa was sure, for her. Nessa moved forward, into the light, standing where Bree could see her and know that she was okay. Bree waved. Nessa lifted her chin.

Then she moved back into the shadows. Nate would have

to explain to Bree that Nessa was returning to care for the gray wolf. She was thinking she could get him home, to the garage, that Vivian would treat him, that she would know what to do.

But when she returned to the spot where she'd left him, the gray wolf was gone.

CHAPTER FIFTY-THREE

They met up back at Nessa's house. It didn't take long for Nessa and Bree to explain to Nessa's mom (most of) what had happened. Vivian called the sheriff almost as soon as they'd finished talking. They had left out some crucial details, including Nessa's shape-shifting, and dwelled on their investigation of the clinic study following Billy's death. Still, the story was horrifying. Thankfully, Vivian believed them. Nate's silence—he was so traumatized he'd stopped speaking or even answering direct questions—perhaps did more to convince her than any of the grisly details Nessa and Bree had provided.

The next morning, the sheriff, who happened to be a distant cousin of Vivian's, used their statements to acquire a warrant, and they all drove out to Paravida to investigate.

"You just need to see it," Nessa had promised. "You have to see the lab and these wolves."

She had imagined they'd find Dr. Raab in the remnants of his lab. And even if he wasn't on the premises, the kennels, the wolf building, the lab where she and Nate had been held—it would all be there.

But when the sheriff pulled up at the main Paravida gate and requested Dr. Raab, they were sent to the main administration building and met by a man in a suit who introduced himself as Dan Green, Director of Paravida Public Relations. Bringing them into a conference room, he explained that Dr. Raab had resigned from the clinic study for family reasons the previous week. It was a long commute from California, Mr. Green said, laughing. Then he assured the adults that Dr. Raab's resignation had nothing to do with Billy Lark's unfortunate death. The Dutch Chem study would go on, of course. Paravida took its obligations to the community seriously. They had found a great medical researcher in Detroit who would be taking over. Dr. Priscilla Lewandoski. Look her up!

He then crossed his legs, leaned back in his seat, and listened patiently, without emotion, as Sheriff Williams related the story of Nate's being abducted and what Nessa had seen. He looked sympathetic but in no way concerned, and when Sheriff Williams had finished, the PR director *smiled* and began speaking.

"We were aware, of course, of the break-in last night, but as you know we are very much a community member in Tether, and we had been hoping to contact the youth empowerment office and resolve this without involving the police." He looked directly at Nessa at that point. "Especially since it's Nessa Kurland, our town's running superstar, not to mention current winner of the Paravida Award. We'd hate to besmirch her image in any way and jeopardize her chances of securing a scholarship to college next year."

Nessa looked at her mother's face. At the sheriff's. They both looked confused, waiting for the evidence to call this man's bluff.

"If it's all the same with you," Sheriff Williams said. "I'd like to look around."

"Of course," Mr. Green said. "I'll take you myself." He spoke into his walkie-talkie, and a younger employee came rushing in with a ring of keys. Mr. Green ("call me Dan") ushered them out and into a golf cart to travel between the buildings.

"As you may have read on the Paravida website," he intoned over the low hum of the cart's engine, "Paravida has a strict policy of not using animals in research, in either our pharmaceutical or cosmetics divisions." He cracked an arrogant smile. "And we certainly don't use human animals, though I'm not sure we even bother to specify that policy in our public communications materials." He looked directly at Nessa when he said this and chuckled like this was a pretty good joke.

"Over there," Nessa said, pointing to the turn he would need to make to get to the wolf building.

"Here?" he said courteously. Nessa couldn't quite reconcile his calm face with the fact that they were about to come upon rows and rows of wolf kennels and a building dedicated to labs and surgical theaters where experiments were being conducted. One of the huge doors of the building stood open, and when they were able to see inside, the space was totally and completely empty.

"Wait, what?" Nessa heard herself say. "Stop the cart." She got out and ran out on to the warehouse floor. There had to be something, a trace, that indicated what had been here only twenty-four hours ago.

"They cleaned it up!" she said, running back to her mother. "This was where they kept at least forty wolves. Really vicious ones. Genetically altered, I think."

Dan Green shrugged. "I'm sorry but we've just decided to make this an overflow warehouse for items we manufacture in Asia. It's being renovated now."

"Can we see the lab where my son and daughter were held?" Vivian asked sweetly.

"The lab where the break-in took place?" Green smoothly replied. "Of course."

The lab where Mary Clovis and her boyfriend Pasty Pete had met their end was immaculate and looked for all the world like one of the exam rooms at the clinic. Nessa spun in circles, trying to take it all in. Even the windows had been repaired.

"How did you do this so fast? Change everything, clean up the human and animal remains?" Nessa asked.

"This was originally created as a first aid room when we thought we might move certain production operations here to Tether," Dan Green said, ignoring Nessa's direct questions. "But we don't envision more than about fifteen employees on site so this should be sufficient," Dan told them. "It should be complete around the first of the year."

Just then the sheriff got a call on his phone. "That was Saginaw Hospital," he told Vivian in a low voice. "They say Billy Lark's body has been in their care since Saturday night.

The chain of custody was simple and completely clear."

Dan Green was all smug smiles at the news as he led them back out into the lab's entry hall. The adults were almost out the door when something caught Nessa's eye. She walked over.

"Wait!" she said. The three adults spun around. She pointed. "What's this?"

The sheriff came over, pulled out a clean white handkerchief, and wiped it up. It was a small glob of blood-matted fur where the floor met the wall.

For the first time Dan Green looked uneasy.

"Huh," was all the sheriff said. He looked at Dan Green. "Looks like some kind of animal fur to me. You won't mind if I send this out to be tested, would you?"

Dan Green smiled. "Absolutely not. Please go right ahead. One of our guard dogs was bitten by a coyote a couple of weeks ago. I believe they cleaned the animal's wounds in here."

"I just don't understand," Vivian said later, after the sheriff had dropped them back at home. "I know you aren't lying, but what we saw today…it was nothing like what you described. Are you *sure* you were where you thought you were?"

Nessa just shook her head. She had stopped insisting because she knew she sounded crazy. She was starting to *feel* crazy.

The last loose end that Paravida managed to sew up was Mary Clovis and Pasty Pete Packer. It was announced in the *Tether Journal* the following Friday that the two of them had eloped to the Bahamas. The paper even had a picture of the couple, sunburnt and toasting each other, with a beach and a sunset in the distance. The marriage announcement included the news that Mary had accepted a position at another Paravida research facility in California, and the new couple planned to relocate immediately after the honeymoon.

As Bree said acidly, "That's a mighty piece of Photoshop retouching. Paravida truly excels at cleanup."

For the next few weeks, Nessa was angry. Angry that Paravida had gotten away with it. Angry that the gray wolf was gone. Angry at Chayton because he hadn't been there to help. Angry that Luc seemed to have moved back to the UP, or at least that was the rumor—he wasn't in school. And hadn't bothered to say goodbye. She was even angry at Cassian for starting to date her ninth-grade cross-country teammate Hannah Gilroy.

She got over it by running.

Even if it was ten degrees on the thermometer, colder when you accounted for wind, Nessa ran. Even though indoor track wouldn't start until after the holidays, Nessa ran. When the full moon rose or the new moon was due, Nessa transformed into a wolf and then ran. Transforming was getting easier every time.

Nessa always scoured the woods for any sign of the gray wolf. After she'd safely stowed Nate with Bree after their escape from Paravida, she had returned to the spot where she'd left him behind. Nessa had followed his trail that night for miles before finally giving up on it when she lost it at a stream.

"How come no one talks about how werewolves have to freeze their butts off?" Nessa complained to Bree one day. "Trust me, all that fur does not do much."

Nessa watched Nate guardedly, trying to assess the extent of any damage he had suffered. When would he start speaking again?

The answer was that it took him a week. And when he did,

it was to say to Vivian, "Nessa is a wolf."

Nessa held her breath, but Vivian assumed it was just Nate's way of processing the trauma. Nessa almost wished Vivian believed him. It was bad enough to have Vivian thinking Nessa was crazy.

"Have you tried Chayton?" Bree said in that worried tone she'd been using to ask Nessa how she was doing in the horrible month between Thanksgiving and Christmas.

Nessa just shook her head. She was so used to him being unavailable, she hadn't even bothered to call Chayton.

Bree was the one who finally did call. And this time, Chayton came right away.

He showed up at Nessa's house when she was taking care of Nate after school. She met him out front, standing on the dead grass, freezing without a coat on, noticing that Chayton's hair was crusty with road salt—he must have driven straight to her from whatever sweat lodge or vision quest he'd been leading. She took one look at him—felt him looking at her—and started to cry.

He opened his arms and held her as she got tears all over his leather jacket. "I don't understand," she said, feeling there was finally someone strong enough to be able to take on this news. "The gray wolf is probably dead. And nothing's resolved. Paravida got away with everything."

For a while Chayton just let her cry. Then he said, "For what it's worth, I'm not all that worried about Paravida."

Nessa looked up. "You're not?"

"The Paravidas of the world are going to come and go. But what Paravida has done... Those new mutant wolves that aren't being fed anymore. They were raised in captivity and did not know how to hunt, which is why they would always return to the place of their torture and mutilation. If they manage to survive in the wild, they could breed with other wolves. That's the danger."

"But my brother Nate—" Nessa said. "I still don't know exactly what they were going to do to him, except that it involved stem cells and growing organs, and it killed Billy Lark. There's some seriously terrifying stuff going on down there."

Chayton raised up a hand. "Leave it alone," he said. "Stay with the wolves."

She told him about how she'd protected Nate, how powerful she had felt.

Chayton was nodding like, yes, finally she was getting it. "You're only going to get more powerful from here on in," he said.

She felt absurdly proud.

She told him about the gray wolf, his injury. "I'm really worried about him," Nessa said. "What if he doesn't come back? What if he's—" She didn't want to say the word. "What if he's gone?"

Chayton looked at her sideways as if he were reading something into her meaning that she could not see herself.

"What?" Nessa said, laughing. Then, outraged but still laughing: "Wha-at!!? He's a wolf."

"Fine," said Chayton. But he was laughing at Nessa, and Nessa was blushing and the whole thing was totally embarrassing but also made Nessa feel light and hopeful—a feeling she hadn't even got near since the horrible night in the Paravida lab.

"You really think he'll be back?" she said.

"I think he'll be back," Chayton said. "I think he probably just needed to heal."

But as Christmas approached, Nessa could not ignore that it had been more than a month and the gray wolf still had not returned. Here Nessa was, out in the woods, crunching through the hard-packed snow, running to stay warm. The moon was full and it was a welcome relief to feel her legs stretching into wolf form, to be alone with the crisp cold air. In the days after the Paravida break-in she'd seen signs of the aggressive wolves, but now they must have dispersed, heading north, or west toward the lakeshore through the thickly wooded state forest lands.

Chayton had said this was because she was going out every night. "They're afraid of you now," he said. "You know your own strength now so they're smelling it and wisely staying out of your patch of woods."

"Wow," Nessa said. "You're making me sound really tough."

"You are," he said. And again she'd felt herself blush. Hard.

But now, in the woods, she could smell something new… or not new…something she hadn't smelled in a long time. But safe. It was…one of the brothers. The pack! Had they returned? And then she smelled the other brother. The annoying little brothers who taught her how to play. And Sister. They were heading in her direction, so she let out a howl to alert them to her presence. She hoped they would remember her.

They did. They burst into the clearing where she was waiting and immediately brought their goofy energy into a full-on wrestling session in which everyone was rolling on the ground and making funny yipping sounds.

And then she sensed another presence in the clearing and saw three wolves standing together. Mama. And the alpha, Big

One, the white wolf who had caused her to transform. Between them was a third wolf.

Gray!

Seeing all three of the wolves together, she knew what must have happened that night after the Paravida break-in. The gray wolf had walked through the water. Or swam. Or floated. Maybe he had washed up on the shore where the wolf pack was hiding from the aggressive wolves. Maybe he had intentionally gone to the place where he knew the pack to be. They must have let him recuperate with them, bringing him food and letting him rest while they patrolled and hunted.

And now they were all back. The pack had returned, bringing Gray with them. As they walked toward her, Nessa noticed that Gray was limping on the fore leg that had been injured the night they broke into Paravida together.

But it didn't matter. He was alive. Chayton had been right.

Maybe he was right about everything? Maybe Paravida *didn't* matter?

Maybe only people mattered. The land mattered. Wolves mattered.

Sniffing noses, butting shoulders, running circles around the bare trees, Nessa thought, this matters.

Nessa felt her whole body flooded with joy.

Paravida might persist, but Nessa was not alone.

CHAPTER FIFTY-FOUR

The next morning was a Monday, the last day of school before Christmas break. Bree gave Nessa a ride to school. "It was just so amazing," Nessa was saying, feeling a little silly for gushing. "I mean. He's alive. And the pack is back. That's such good news. I can't wait to tell Chayton. Maybe this means something, you know? Like, maybe we'll be able to—"

"Nessa," Bree interrupted. "I think—"

"I know, I know," Nessa said. "We need to be careful. We need help. We can't just run into Paravida this time. We have to document what we're seeing."

"No, that's not it," Bree said. "There's something I have to tell you before we get to school." She was pulling into a parking spot, and before she could finish her sentence, a kid from student council was knocking on her window. He was talking before Bree could open the door. There was some emergency going down with the Secret Santa candy cane deliveries.

While Bree explained that the hardware stores sometimes sold candy canes, and they should call there and go to the grocery store, Nessa climbed out of the Monster's passenger side and heard what sounded like a bark.

She shook her head, smiling to herself. It had been a cough she'd heard. Not *everything* was about wolves. Then, on second thought, she realized it was a laugh.

A laugh she recognized.

She stepped around the Monster's prodigious back end, and there, two rows of cars away, was Luc. He must have just parked his truck in the back corner spot and was now looking at Cassian's car, which was pulling in to a spot on the other side of the row. Cassian got out on the driver's side, and then Hannah emerged from the passenger's. Cassian walked around to meet Hannah on her side of the car and took her hand, walking into school.

Bree was now at Nessa's side. "That's what I was trying to tell you about," Bree said.

But Nessa had known they were an item for weeks, and she wasn't staring at Cassian. She was staring at Luc.

Luc was back.

"Are you okay?" Bree whispered. "I know it's hard to see Cassian with someone else, even if you, you know," she almost choked on how unbelievable this was to say, "you broke up with him?"

"No," Nessa said, not even aware of the words coming out

of her mouth. "I'm fine. Look. Luc. He's back." She wasn't even trying to hide the fact that she was staring at him.

Slowly, like he was swinging on a pendulum, Luc turned to look at Nessa. Their eyes met. A slow smile spread across his face. He didn't let go of her eyes. She didn't want him to.

She took a few steps toward him. A few more. "You came back," she said.

"I did."

Her heart skipped a beat when she heard him speak. Had Luc always made her feel this weak in the knees? Had there ever been a time where she didn't think the straight lines of his shoulders were…perfect? She was breathing shallowly and her head felt light on her shoulders.

"You were gone a long time," she said.

"I was back in the UP with my mom," he said. "A cousin of mine was building a house and they needed some help…" His voice trailed off.

He took a step toward her, and she could smell him—soap and something woodsy and popcorn. She looked up into his eyes. He raised his eyebrows.

And then he stepped even closer to her. He leaned over to speak directly into her ear. He tried to say something but couldn't. He had to clear the frog out of his throat first. He tried again. "Thanks for making me. Come back."

The words were like electricity shot straight into Nessa's spine. She knew she would remember them forever.

"You're welcome," she said. She could hear that she was playing it cool, like the words they'd just spoken to each other hadn't come as a surprise. But they had. They were huge. Her heart was racing. Her breath trembling.

Luc was Gray.

"We have a lot of work to do in Tether," he said.

Nessa shivered. Luc opened his jacket and folded her inside.

She looked out over his shoulder beyond the school parking lot, to the football fields and the track, the tennis courts, and the woods ringing the school, the woods that stretched beyond her house, beyond pretty much everyone's house in Tether. The woods where the wolves had returned to maintain the balance that was due to all.

Nessa looked back to where Bree was waiting next to the Monster. She was watching Nessa and Luc, then suddenly got very busy sorting through her backpack.

"Yes," Nessa said, turning back toward Luc, feeling his warm breath sweet on her neck, drinking him in. "We do."

The End

Acknowledgments

Weregirl is an unique book. It was originally conceived of by the team at Chooseco, a small publishing company that was founded to relaunch the *Choose Your Own Adventure* series over a decade ago. Once the idea of the book was hatched, five members of Chooseco staff held a retreat at a house in the Eastern Townships of rural Quebec and began to plot a book about a girl who is bitten by a wolf on a nighttime run and starts to transform.

Did she live in urban Brooklyn or the country's rural middle? Was she from a big family or an only child? How did she react to the shape-shifting? Who helped her? Who did she love? Who were her enemies?

This improvised Chooseco "writer's room," hashed out the broad three-act structure of *Weregirl*, including all the main characters and their backgrounds. They then invited me to join "the room," and to write the actual novel they had plotted, helping to weave the details and different plotlines of that story together into an organic whole. I was in close contact with the team as I wrote, discussing ideas almost every day. For the record, Chayton is my sole creation.

Brilliant and wonderful thanks go to everyone who partic-ipated: Shannon Gilligan, Publisher, whose creative vision for Chooseco's new teen venture has been a long time coming; Melissa Bounty, Associate Publisher and editor extraordinaire, who has been with Chooseco since she was twenty-one years old (a long time); and the other members of the fantastic Chooseco "writer's room" team: Liz Windover, Lizzi Adelman, and Mieka Carey.

Additional sincere thanks go to: cross-country coach Veronica Welsh and high school runners Jacob Kahn and Kelsey Kahn for their assistance with cross-country research; Rick Kahn, Max Kahn, and Eliza Kahn for their patience and forbearance as I disappeared from their lives, buried in my manuscript. Lucy, Yoyo, Archie, Tatum, Oscar, Oprah, and Billie for companionship and inspiration. The NYRR Brooklyn Half Marathon 2011-2016 for teaching me to love running.

This final book was also greatly aided by the exceptional work of copy editor Beth Morel and proofreader Josie Masterson-Glen. *Weregirl*'s breathtaking cover was created by Dot Greene and its beautiful pages, including the chapter headings and moon phases, were designed and laid out by Stacey Boyd. Early readers Exie Manahan, Bonnie Calhoun, Lucy O'Brien, Beth Stern, and Sarah Bounty provided useful feedback. Joy Worland of the Kellogg-Hubbard Library helped organize a group of YA readers who told us everything they liked to read about.

Thanks are also due to Michael Bell, in memory, without whom this book would not have happened.

-C.D. Bell

A Note on Fonts

The text of this book is Minion Pro, a typeface designed in the 1990s by Robert Slimbach and inspired by the typefaces developed in the late Renaissance era.

Weregirl's title font is True North, designed by Cindy Kinash and Charles Gibbons. Cindy creates fonts and designs from Vancouver, and Charles is the chief designer for the U.S. Copyright office. The other font used on the cover of this book is Ruskin, which was created by Michael Harvey and Andrs Benedek as a commission for signs for the Dean Gallery in Edinburgh.

Every chapter begins with the fanciful letters of Jellyka Castle's Queen, designed by Jellyka Nereven aka Jessica, who has been designing fonts for the past fifteen years, since she was 13 years old.

Jean Bourbon

About the Author

When she's not hanging out with her two children and husband in Brooklyn, NY, you can find Cathleen Davitt Bell writing in a decrepit RV clinging to the side of a hill in upstate New York, trying to teach herself to watercolor, or inventing her own recipes. She received her undergraduate degree from Barnard College and her MFA in Creative Writing from Columbia University, and is the author of the novels *Slipping, Little Blog on the Prairie, I Remember You*, and a co-author of *The Amanda Project*.